Beneath the skilled touch of his hands and mouth, barriers were dissolving. Sensuality long buried was coming to the surface with a vengeance. It was a new form of power Alexis could not help but revel in.

Power had always attracted her far more than pleasure, with which she had scant familiarity. She had grown up contemplating the power in her father, watching her brother having it bestowed upon him through no merit of his own, witnessing its lack in so many of the women around her. It was something she wanted very much.

James offe power. When she took him into h strength, a determina

But she wo could possibly guess.

Books by Maura Seger

EYE OF THE STORM
ECHO OF THUNDER

HARLEQUIN TEMPTATION
69–UNDERCOVER

These books may be available at your local bookseller.

Don't miss any of our special offers. Write to us at the following address for information on our newest releases.

Worldwide Library Reader Service
P.O. Box 52040, Phoenix, AZ 85072-2040
Canadian address: P.O. Box 2800, Postal Station A,
5170 Yonge St., Willowdale, Ont. M2N 6J3

ECHO OF THUNDER

MAURA SEGER

W🌐RLDWIDE

TORONTO · NEW YORK · LONDON · PARIS
AMSTERDAM · STOCKHOLM · HAMBURG
ATHENS · MILAN · TOKYO · SYDNEY

First published September 1985

ISBN 0-373-97015-3

Printed in Canada

Out of this nettle, danger, we pluck this flower, safety.
—Shakespeare, *Henry IV*, Part I

Part One: 1946-1951

Chapter One

THE LUXURIOUS APARTMENT HOUSES of Beekman Place stood like sentinels against a night sky frosted with the remnants of a late-winter snowstorm. To the east, a garbage scow moved slowly down the channel between Manhattan and Welfare Island. To the west, bumper-to-bumper traffic inched along Forty-ninth Street, most of it headed across town toward the theater district, where curtains would be rising in less than an hour.

Standing in the shadow of a service door near the main entrance to One Beekman Place, James Callahan checked his watch. It was getting on toward eight o'clock. If his information was correct, the woman he had come to meet should be arriving at any moment.

The air off the river was chill. He shivered slightly and turned up the collar of his topcoat, all the while surveying his surroundings with the alert eyes of a man not yet accustomed to the relative safety of peacetime.

Six months before, he had been a Marine major stationed in Manila waiting to be shipped out to Okinawa and from there into the invasion of Japan. After almost four years of fighting, the luck that had kept him alive till then had seemed strained to the breaking point. Though he had never dwelled on the question of his own mortality, he hadn't really counted on coming out of the war alive. But he had, and now the future was his, provided he was smart enough and fast enough to seize it.

The woman he waited for might hold the key to that.

Patience had never been his strong point. Glancing at his watch again, he wondered what was keeping her. According to his informant, a secretary at the United Broadcasting Company, Alexis Brockton was noted for her punctuality. The party she was attending had been due to start at seven-thirty. What might have been a smile drew his mouth taut as he considered that perhaps the lady wanted to make an entrance, or was simply being fashionably late.

Whichever, he didn't appreciate standing out in the cold waiting for her. Not that there was anything to stop him from strolling inside the elegant apartment house with the next group of gaily chattering men and women, slipping past the doorman, and making his way to the penthouse where the party he intended to crash was taking place. But he preferred not to be put to the bother of doing so if his quarry wasn't going to show up.

A blunt-nosed cab of prewar vintage pulled to a stop at the curb in front of the apartment house. The doorman hurried to open the passenger door. From beneath the rim of his hat, James surveyed the woman who stepped out.

She was tall and slender, with a willowy grace evident even from a distance. Her upper body was concealed by a mink jacket whose wide collar framed the pale oval of her face. A small mink cap perched at an angle on top of her head. Silver-blond hair fell to her shoulders, curling under at the ends in a classic pageboy. The flounced skirt of a pearl-gray cocktail dress covered her from the waist to mid-calves.

James frowned as he noted its length. He knew from the careful research he had done that she had visited Paris recently. Perhaps the dress was some French designer's idea of a joke. It was a shame she chose to hide her legs; from what little he could see, they would be worth revealing. On the other hand, the long skirt drew attention to her slender ankles, which weren't hard to look at, either. His gaze moved on to her slim feet, clad in high-heeled pumps that matched the crocodile clutch purse she carried, before traveling back up the full length of her.

The description he'd been given of Alexis Brockton had been good, but it hadn't quite prepared him for the impact of her beauty. Tossing aside the cigarette he had been smoking, he followed her with a quick, determined step.

She had entered the marble vestibule and stood waiting while the doorman announced her arrival. As the elderly gentleman got up to resemble a Ruritanian general and turned aside to speak into the house phone, James strolled past. He smiled politely at Alexis and continued on his way around the corner of the lobby toward the bank of elevators.

So far so good. Counting silently to ten, he waited until he was reasonably certain she had finished the little ritual at the door, then pushed the button to summon an elevator. As she joined him to wait for its arrival, they exchanged a polite nod and he removed his hat.

Up close, she was even lovelier than he had thought. He knew her age to be twenty-four, which was consistent with the unlined smoothness of her skin. Her high-boned cheeks were slightly flushed. Her eyes, beneath slanting brows, appeared to be a silvery gray, with a luster not unlike the pearl opalescence of her dress. Her lips, perfectly shaped, with a tantalizing hint of fullness, were a soft shade of rose.

Those lovely lips moved and a quiet, slightly smoky voice asked, "Do we know each other?"

Surprised, James met her cool gaze. "I beg your pardon?"

"Do we know each other? The way you were looking at me, I thought perhaps we did." The aloofness of her tone, combined with the slightest hint of deviltry in her eyes, made it clear she knew perfectly well they had never met. Piqued by her unexpected challenge, James declared, "No, but we're going to."

Alexis stared at him for a moment, as though she couldn't quite believe he had said that. When she laughed, the sound was soft and faintly husky, reminding him of a spring wind blowing through sapling branches. It was also remarkably good-natured.

"Let me guess," she said when she had caught her breath, "you're going to the Dunleaveys' party."

He shrugged lightly. "Isn't everyone?"

"No...but it will probably seem that way." The elevator arrived; they got on and she asked, "Have you known them long?"

"Uh...not exactly. I'm really a friend of a friend. That sort of thing."

Alexis nodded and stepped back to let him press the button for the penthouse floor. "These get-togethers are always like that. Somebody invites somebody else, who brings along a date who has a friend, and so on until finally nobody knows who anybody else is."

"But you've come on your own," he pointed out, unbuttoning his coat.

"Well...Liz did call up to invite me, so I thought I ought to stop by. You know how it is. One doesn't like to seem...uninterested."

"Are you?" he asked as they stepped off at the top floor. They walked down the carpeted hallway in the direction of the rooms from which the sound of music and laughter could be heard. "Uninterested, I mean?"

"No, of course not. Just busy. There's so much to do, what with the war ending and all."

"Yes..." he drawled gently, "that did change things a bit."

Alexis shot him a speculative glance. She had been studying him discreetly since they stepped into the elevator together, but now she allowed herself a look as direct as the going-over he had given her.

With his hat off, she could see the thick head of slightly shaggy black hair, a lock of which fell over his broad forehead. She judged him to be in his mid-thirties, with all those years showing plainly on his craggy features. They looked as though they had been formed by a master sculptor working with hammer and chisel on the hardest stone. Light blue eyes were deeply set beneath thick brows. Broad cheekbones hinted at a Slavic ancestor amid the black Irish that otherwise appeared to have been his forebears. His nose was strong and assertive, with a hump near the center that suggested it had been broken at least once. The squareness of his jaw warned that he was undoubtedly stubborn, an impression further supported by the hard, firm line of his mouth.

He was quite tall, several inches over six feet, which struck Alexis as a pleasant height for a man. At five feet eight without heels, she had done her share of slouching through dates. Strange that she should think of that in connection with this man, she mused as she handed a white-jacketed servant her mink. Leaving the little cap in place, she absently smoothed her hair while continuing to observe the man at her side.

He had removed his topcoat, revealing a double-breasted suit of gray worsted, a white button-down shirt and a maroon silk tie. All very proper, but still unable to conceal the latent strength of his large, powerfully built body or the barely contained sense of purpose so great as to appear almost dangerous.

Dangerous? Alexis turned the word over in her mind speculatively. In such eminently civilized surroundings, it seemed absurd to feel threatened by this man, yet she could not deny that she did, any more than she could avoid the fact that she found the sensation oddly exciting.

Perhaps it had something to do with the proprietary light in his eyes as they lingered over the bare expanse of her throat and arms revealed by the off-the-shoulder cocktail dress.

"By the way," he said smoothly, lifting his gaze to hers, "I'm James Callahan."

"Alexis Brockton," she responded automatically, accepting the hand he held out. Through her thin, wrist-length glove, she felt the warmth of his skin and a firm, not unpleasant pressure that lasted a scant instant longer than it should have before he released her.

"Let's wade into this," he suggested, tipping his head toward the crowded living room, "and I'll see if I can find us a couple of drinks."

Alexis agreed readily enough. She hadn't come to the party to meet anyone in particular, and though she knew many of the people there, she felt no urge to abandon James Callahan. On the contrary, rather to her surprise, she wanted to get to know him better.

As his hand touched her elbow lightly, guiding her through the crowd, she reflected that he was not at all her usual sort of man. Her upbringing amid the bastions of New York and Connecticut society had predisposed her to favor the genteel sons of powerful men like her father. They were polite, amusing and appropriately diffident. Which meant that they had nothing whatsoever in common with James Callahan.

"What will you have?" he asked when they reached the bar set up at the far end of the spacious living room. A young man hired for the evening to keep the liquid refreshments flowing waited attentively while she scanned the array of bottles before him. Since she customarily drank little, she was used to settling for one of the milder aperitifs. But this time she wanted something a little different.

"I think I'll try a Sea Breeze. I hear they've become quite the rage."

The young man nodded and looked to James. "And you, sir?"

"Scotch-and-water, easy on the Scotch."

With their drinks in hand, they moved away from the bar, finding a relatively quiet corner of the room beside the terrace garden, which overlooked the gleaming black ribbon of the river. From the white grand piano in a corner, the notes of prewar Tommy Dorsey tunes reached them. Fashionably dressed men and women circulated with little napkins holding canapés balanced on top of their drinks. Everyone was smiling, and the occasional bursts of raucous laughter drew only benign glances.

"How is that?" James asked as Alexis tasted the mixture of gin and citrus juice.

"Not bad. Care for a sip?"

He smiled and shook his head. "No, thanks. If there's one thing my father taught me, it's don't mix your drinks."

"Good advice. Too bad more people don't follow it." Surveying the boisterous crowd, she smiled faintly. "Ever since the war ended, there seems to have been one long party going on. Eventually we'll have to settle down and get serious."

James saw no reason to mention that some people were already very serious. It wouldn't do to air his contempt for those who had taken victory as the signal that the prewar world they remembered so nostalgically was about to return. That world in which a tiny minority had monopolized wealth and power was gone forever. He, for one, did not mourn it.

Rather than say any of this, he murmured, "You can't blame people for wanting to celebrate."

Alexis shot him a glance of unexpected resolve. "I'm not sure there is anything to celebrate. You see, I just returned from Europe and saw for myself how bad the situation still is over there. So much is needed—food, medicine, clothing—almost anything you can think of. I'm sure it's the same in the Pacific. Instead of thinking only of the war being over, people should be considering what kind of peace we're going to have."

Though she spoke quietly, it was impossible to mistake the conviction behind her words, or the intelligence that shaped them. James took a sip of his drink as he then surveyed her carefully. There was more to Alexis Brockton than he had thought. She had brains as well as beauty. Moreover, she wasn't afraid to speak her mind in a way that other young women of her social class would have considered inappropriate.

As she well knew. Watching her, he became aware that he was also being scrutinized. Discreetly, of course. He had already sensed that she was not given to revealing much of what went on behind those clear gray eyes. But nonetheless she was curious, and perhaps a little wary, of his reaction to her.

Leaning back against the banquette, he smiled. "You're a refreshing change, Alexis Brockton. I'm tired of women who have nothing to say for themselves."

Despite herself, a warm flush stained her cheeks. The lazy glance traveling over her from her slim ankles to the gleaming top of her head, where the little cap perched, spoke of his approval, and more. Meeting his eyes, she felt a shock of recognition at the desire she saw there—desire that matched her own.

It was too much too fast. She had no experience dealing with such a man. His absolute self-confidence unbalanced her, as did the latent sense of strength and virility lurking directly below the surface of the deceptively proper suit stretched over his powerful shoulders, broad chest and long, hard legs.

For an instant, she was tempted to extricate herself politely from the situation and walk away. But that thought faded almost as quickly as it arose. Not only would it have been completely out of character for her to retreat, but she suspected James Callahan would not have allowed it.

Instead, by way of a compromise, she gave him a bright, superficial smile. "That's nice to hear, but I'm tired of talking. How about telling me about yourself?"

His gaze slid from her, and he fingered the crystal tumbler that held his drink. "There isn't much to tell...."

"Oh, there must be. Since you know the Dunleaveys, or at least a friend of theirs, it's surprising that we haven't met before." She spoke airily, as though unaware of any reason for a young, healthy male to have been out of circulation for several years.

James smiled wryly. He was willing enough to play along, up to a point. "As a matter of fact, I've done quite a lot of traveling recently."

"Really? Where to?"

"Oh, all the top glamour spots. Guadalcanal, New Britain, Manila..."

Some of the color faded from her damask-smooth skin at the realization that he had actually seen combat. Quietly, she asked, "Which were you, Army or Navy?"

James shot her a pained look. "Neither. I was a Marine."

"I should have guessed."

It was his turn to be amused. "How?"

She considered that for a moment before she said, "Because I understand the Marines don't go in for a lot of ceremony. They prefer to just charge ahead and get the job done."

"Are you saying I'm impetuous?"

"No, on the contrary.... I suspect you're a very deliberate man. However, you're not particularly concerned with propriety."

"But I've been working so hard at being proper. Bought the right kind of suit and everything."

"Not quite everything." Leaning a fraction closer to him, she whispered, "Let me give you a little tip. Proper people don't crash parties."

"Crash? Me? Miss Brockton, you wound me to the quick."

She laughed softly and with unmistakable satisfaction informed him, "This isn't the Dunleaveys' apartment. They live at Sutton Place, not Beekman. Our hosts for this little get-together are the Carlisles."

Mentally cursing his failure to get more than the number of the apartment where the party was being held, James struggled to regain his equanimity. "Then why did you ask me in the elevator if I had known the Dunleaveys long?"

"To find out if my guess about you was right. You see, I noticed how you slipped past the doorman. That was very clever, by the way, and I was curious as to why you'd done it. After all, there are a lot of quite wealthy people here. I thought perhaps you were either a cop...or a crook."

"And which have you decided?"

"I think you're somewhere in between. Not a policeman—you're too...unruly for that. But not a crook, either." Flashing him a smile, she added, "Or at least I hope you aren't."

"You realize that proper people don't have conversations like this. You wouldn't by any chance, also be an impostor?"

Though he was merely teasing, knowing perfectly well who she was, James was startled by her reaction. Alexis's smile faded as she said, "I suppose I am. But never mind, I still know my way around. Was there someone in particular you came to meet?"

Yes, James thought, *you*. For some unknown reason, that was bothering him. He felt vaguely guilty about his plan to make use of her, but he was still convinced that he had no choice. Setting his drink down, he ignored her question and said, "Since we seem to have just agreed that neither of us belongs here, what do you say we leave?"

Alexis hesitated. She reminded herself that she didn't know this man, and that her first impression of him as being dangerous had only strengthened as they talked. Yet she also couldn't forget that he was more attractive—fascinating, even—than any other man she could think of. Surely it couldn't do any harm to spend a little while longer with him?

"All right," she agreed, and they stood up together. "Just give me a minute to let Liz know I dropped by."

"That's Liz *Carlisle*?" he asked with a grin.

"The one, the only. I'll introduce you."

Their hostess was a slender, dark-haired woman of about forty, with the meticulously preserved beauty made possible only by large applications of money and attention. Elegantly dressed in an ankle-length brocade sheath, she wore diamonds at her ears, throat and wrists. Her taut skin was lightly tanned, and she exuded the scent of a rare and extremely expensive perfume.

"Alexis!" she exclaimed as the younger woman appeared before her. "Darling, you *did* come after all. How nice! You know you simply cannot spend all your time in that dreary office. You absolutely *must* get out more."

All the while she was speaking, her bright black eyes were wandering over James, missing nothing. Without giving Alexis a chance to reply, she went on, "And who *is* this? Surely we haven't met. I promise I'd remember."

James took the hand she offered and did not make the error of shaking it. Instead, when Alexis had performed the introductions, he inclined his head graciously and smiled. "It's a pleasure to meet you, Mrs. Carlisle. You have a lovely home."

"Aren't you sweet to say so. But this is just a little place to hang our hats when we're in the city. *So* tiresome to be stuck out in the country all the time, don't you think?"

"Liz and Charles raise horses in Connecticut," Alexis explained softly.

"Please, darling," their hostess entreated, "don't include me in that. I personally cannot abide the smelly beasts. But they make Charlie happy, so…" Shrugging resignedly, she beamed James a smile that said, of course *he* understood.

They chatted a few moments longer before politely making room for the other guests wanting to have a word with their ebullient hostess. On their way to the door, Alexis murmured, "Don't let Liz fool you. She's as sharp as they come and probably wields more power here in New York than many politicians or businessmen."

"How so?" James asked, taking her jacket from the butler and holding it open for her to slip into. The fur was very soft against his fingers, the silk lining cool and smooth. He suspected its owner would feel the same.

"She sits on the boards of half a dozen major charities," Alexis explained, "plus a quiverful of hospitals, not to mention the Metropolitan Opera *and* the Metropolitan Museum of Art."

"Impressive," he agreed as they strolled out toward the elevator. Fastening the buttons of his top coat with one hand while holding his hat in the other, he asked, "Do you go in for any of that stuff?"

"I did, at one time...."

"But no longer?"

"No, I—" She broke off, looking straight ahead at the beaten bronze elevator doors instead of at him. Quietly, she said, "Only a very few women can make satisfying careers for themselves doing charity work. For myself, I wanted something a little more...prosaic."

"As in *down-to-earth*?"

She flashed him a quick smile of appreciation as the elevator arrived. "Exactly. I work for United Broadcasting now."

Not a flicker of reaction showed in his light blue eyes. With no more than polite curiosity, he asked, "What do you do there?"

A faint grimace curved her mouth. "I'm in charge of special projects."

Stepping out in the lobby, he remarked, "That sounds like the sort of position that can mean a great deal or nothing in particular."

"Right now it's the latter," she admitted. "But I intend to change that."

"How?" he asked. They were standing in front of the building, with the doorman waiting to see if they wanted a cab.

She took a deep breath, glad of the fresh air that cleared her head. "It's a little hard to explain."

"Then how about doing it while I see you home?"

"All right, but let's walk. It's too nice a night to be cooped up in a cab." Besides, she wanted more time with him, and a quick taxi ride wouldn't provide that. "I live on Central Park South."

That was about ten blocks north and half a dozen or so west. "Are you sure you want to walk it?" James asked, concerned about how well she would manage in high heels. His wallet might be thin, but it could still stand the strain of cab fare, if only barely.

"I'll be fine," she assured him, taking his arm before he could protest further. They started across town. The traffic had eased up quite a bit, though there was still a steady flow along the avenues. At the corner of Forty-ninth and Lexington, they passed the Shelton Hotel, where a group of young Air Corps officers were just departing. The men were pleasantly inebriated, enough so that they whistled and tipped their hats as Alexis passed. She smiled tolerantly, knowing that James's very large presence at her side prevented the young men from trying to get any friendlier.

"I guess they're still blowing off steam," she commented softly.

"Probably just got mustered out," James speculated. "I was lucky to make it back so quickly."

"When did you come home?"

"Early December."

"I was in England then."

"For any particular reason?" he asked, careful to keep his tone no more than politely courteous.

"There was someone I needed to meet, a scientist."

James tensed slightly and hoped she wouldn't notice. He managed a small laugh. "Why would a beautiful woman want to spend her time with a scientist?"

Deliberately ignoring the compliment, Alexis said, "Because he knows a great deal about something I'm trying to learn about, namely, how to transmit pictures over the air waves."

"Television? I've been reading about that lately." It was a safe comment; there had been articles in several mass circulation magazines.

"It's going to be very big. I just wish I could convince certain other people of that."

"You mean at United Broadcasting?"

"That's right. All they care about there is radio."

"Well, you have to admit broadcasting *is* radio. It's hard to imagine there could be anything beyond that."

"There will be," she said firmly, "and I'm going to be part of it. That's my special project."

James couldn't help but admire her determination and her foresight. He, too, was convinced that television was going to be one of the most powerful influences shaping the postwar world. But he was also well aware that many other people believed it would never be anything more than a novelty.

"It must be very difficult to transmit clear pictures to receivers in homes scattered all around a city or town," he ventured as they crossed Fifth Avenue and turned north.

"That's putting it mildly. I can't pretend to understand all that's involved, but I do know that enormous strides are being made. The trick is to get the right people working for you."

"Like this scientist?"

She nodded. "Professor Wilcox is one of the most brilliant theoreticians in radar. He's made major advances in improving the clarity of images that have to travel over a great distance to reach viewers."

"Sounds like a good guy to know...if you're interested in that sort of thing."

"I am, and the rest of the world will be, too...eventually." She glanced up at him, hoping for some indication that he understood. He seemed to, although he showed no more interest in the subject than she was used to encountering. It was a source of great frustration to her that the revolution she was convinced was coming in communications appeared inconsequential to almost everybody else. Certainly no one at UBC was interested in it, particularly not her father, who, as president of the network, still made all the major decisions, or her brother Graham, who was being groomed to take his place eventually.

"Will this Professor Wilcox help you?" James asked as they paused for a red light. The elegant stores along Fifth Avenue were closed, but their windows displayed an array of luxurious objects stunning in their variety and quantity, particularly to anyone who had recently been in any of the war-ravaged cities of Europe or Asia.

"I think so. He's arriving in the States early next week. If I can come up with an attractive enough offer for him, he might take it."

"I suppose he wants a lot of money," James suggested carefully. He resisted the impulse to hold his breath while waiting for her to say what it would take to convince Wilcox.

"No, he really isn't all that interested in money, unfortunately. What he wants is autonomy, the freedom to pursue his research as he sees fit. I don't have the power to promise him that."

But James did. As a partner in his own small, struggling business, it was about all he had. Fighting against a surge of excitement, he said, "He'd have to be a fool to turn you down. United Broadcasting is one of the biggest and most profitable companies in the country."

"I'm afraid that doesn't impress him. He likes smaller operations."

Better and better. Hoping that his voice revealed none of his elation, James asked, "Perhaps he'll decide he really likes the States and wants to stay here. You did say he's coming next week?"

Alexis nodded, wondering absently how they had gotten into such an involved discussion of her work. "On Monday. He's taking the Pan Am clipper in."

That was all James needed to know. Adroitly, he turned the conversation to other matters and soon had Alexis telling him about the fashion show she had gone to in Paris. "Christian Dior seems determined to change the way women dress," she explained.

"Why? They look fine already."

"But everyone's tired of skimping on cloth and making do. We're all ready for something different. Dior's introducing what he calls the New Look."

"Is that dress you have on part of it?" he asked neutrally.

This time his lack of expression didn't fool her. She laughed softly. "It's one of the first. My mother was one of his early clients, so he was kind enough to make it up for me on my recent trip." The mention of her mother was, as always, a test of her own composure. She was pleased when she was once again able to carry it off matter-of-factly.

James winced inwardly at the thought of what she had undoubtedly paid for such kindness. "It's very becoming," he insisted gallantly, and not without some justification. He suspected she would look beautiful in anything, and most beautiful in nothing. Reining in his errant thoughts, he added, "But it's a shame to hide your legs."

"I think the idea is that what can't be seen tends to be more alluring."

"Maybe to a French designer, but not necessarily to a healthy American male."

And James Callahan was certainly that, Alexis mused. Healthy, strong, intelligent and, above all, extremely attractive. If she didn't watch herself, he could turn out to be a major distraction. That was something she could not afford. To have any chance at all of getting support for television at UBC, she had to devote all her time and attention to it. Which was really a shame, because she would have liked to get to know James better. He was the first man who had stirred her interest on more than the mildest level.

When they reached the entrance to the Gainsborough Studios, where she lived, Alexis turned to him. Resolve mingled with regret when she said, "I'm sorry that I can't ask you up, but it is late."

James stared at her for a long moment before he nodded. Let her think that they would not meet again. Soon enough she would find out that she was wrong.

And when she did, she would be spitting mad.

A smile tugged at his mouth as he considered that. She was so cool and collected, her patrician loveliness untouched by the grubby world. He could admire that even as it stirred him to mild resentment. Giving in to the temptation to at least dent her aura of aloofness, he bent his tall head and dropped a feather-light kiss on her upturned lips.

The touch was so gentle and fleeting that she would have thought she had imagined it were it not for the sudden rush of sensation that curled through her. Taken by surprise, she responded more fully than she might otherwise have done.

James hesitated. He had meant to kiss her lightly and walk away, but that was proving to be more difficult than he had expected. He was tempted to find out exactly how far she would let him go. But he was also wise enough to know that if he spent the night with her, he would not be able to walk away free and clear the next morning.

Many times before, he had been faced with tough choices; often they had made the difference between life and death. Now he was fighting for something every bit as precious—his dreams.

Summoning all his considerable will, he stepped back. A slight smile touched his mouth as he ignored her startled look and murmured, ''Good-bye, Alexis.''

Chapter Two

"I DON'T UNDERSTAND," Alexis said slowly. "Professor Wilcox couldn't have simply disappeared."

"No one is suggesting that," her secretary assured her. "He definitely arrived on the clipper four days ago. Somewhere between the airport and his hotel, he..."

"Evaporated?" Alexis offered dryly. She shook her head. "I had an appointment with him at 10:00 A.M. the day after his arrival. The idea was to give him a chance to rest up after the flight. But when I showed up at the hotel, there was no record of his ever registering. What if he's sick or had an accident and is wandering around somewhere?"

"I think the police would have found him by now," Margaret Goodman pointed out soothingly. She was a middle-aged woman who had been Alexis's secretary for almost a year, ever since Charles Brockton finally accepted his daughter's determination to get a job and agreed to allow her to join the network. Margaret's unflappable presence and slightly maternal air were often invaluable. "There are no reports of anyone matching his description turning up in the hospitals or flophouses," she went on, "or being picked up for vagrancy."

Alexis thought about that for a moment, then nodded decisively. "We've waited long enough. Give Apex Detectives a call and tell them to find out whatever they can about his movements after the clipper landed."

Margaret nodded and went back to her desk outside the small, sparsely furnished office, leaving Alexis to gaze out the window at the rain-washed city. The dismal weather suited her mood. All her instincts were telling her that something was very wrong. When she had spoken with the head of the detective agency earlier in the day to alert him that she might need his services, she had stressed her optimism that Professor Wilcox could be found promptly. Now she wasn't so certain.

Shaking her head impatiently, she reminded herself that the cloak-and-dagger days of the war were over. People simply did not disappear in the middle of one of the world's largest cities. Yet the scientist seemed to have done exactly that, and until he could be found, all her plans for introducing television at UBC had to be put on hold.

The remainder of the day passed with excruciating slowness. She endured a late-afternoon meeting with her father, her brother and the heads of the various UBC divisions, during which the talk concentrated on how to achieve the most rapid expansion possible of their radio-broadcasting facilities.

"We've got a tremendous opportunity here," Graham declared, his jaded tone making it clear that he considered what he was saying to be self-evident and therefore beyond dispute. "With the war over, manufacturers will soon be hip-deep in goods to sell to a populace that's had nothing to spend its money on in years. It's going to be an all-out scramble to see who can move the most merchandise the fastest, and the best way to do that is by advertising on radio."

Alexis looked at her slightly older brother and stifled a sigh. Graham was leaning back in his chair, the jacket of his Savile Row suit undone with studied negligence, one perfectly shod foot propped on the knee of his precisely creased trousers. His meticulously trimmed blond hair shone even in the murky light from the overhead fixtures designed to mimic gas lamps from the previous century. Features as aristocratic as Alexis's own were set in a perpetual expression of disdain. At twenty-five, with a wartime career in the Pentagon's public relations department behind him, he was unrelentingly pompous, full of his own importance, and absolutely intolerant of any opinions that even mildly diverged from his own. In short, he was everything his father thought proper in a young man of his position.

From his seat at the head of the ornately carved conference table, Charles Brockton inclined his bullet-shaped head in agreement. He was a beefy man, with an ex-fight promotor's body going inexorably to fat. Not even the best efforts of his tailor could disguise that, or impart to him the air of upper-crust gentility he had longed for all his life.

It was the tragedy of that life—or perhaps more correctly, the irony—that having amassed greater wealth and power than most of the country's elite would ever possess, he still strove desperately to enter a charmed circle which would never grant him admittance.

His children, however, were a different matter. They had been groomed from birth to be part of the elite. It was his firm intention to see them both fulfill their predestined roles.

"All our research indicates that the future for radio is as good as we choose to make it," he announced stentoriously. "We have the privilege to be part of the most technologically advanced system of communications in the history of the world. Nothing will ever surpass us."

Smiling frostily, he elaborated, "When I say 'us,' I naturally mean UBC. We are going to stay out in the forefront of this industry." As he spoke, he glanced around the table. His gaze, settling on each executive in turn, prompted energetic head nodding, as though invisible strings were being pulled.

Only two participants withheld their agreement: Graham, because it would mean abandoning his pose of irreducible boredom, and Alexis, because of her genuine conviction that her father was wrong. She had tried numerous times, without success, to convince him that radio would soon be overtaken and eclipsed by television, and she was not about to pretend a belief she did not share.

Catching his daughter's eye, Charles Brockton frowned. "I know this isn't what you want to hear, Alexis. But we have to be realistic." He paused long enough to pop another violet pastille into his mouth, the kind that made his breath smell like dead flowers, then concluded, "Television will never be anything more than a scientific oddity."

"Our major competitors don't think so," she said quietly. "Let's not forget that NBC broadcast pictures of the Lincoln's Birthday ceremony from Washington to New York just a few weeks ago. CBS isn't far behind, and ABC won't wait forever. If we don't get moving soon, we're going to be shut out of a completely new era."

She had made the same argument so many times before that the words sounded stale even to her. Certainly they had no effect on the men gathered around the table, except to bore them. Graham put his hand to his mouth to hide an exaggerated yawn. "Let the other networks get involved in this nonsense if they want to," he said indolently. "The more distracted they are, the more frustrated their advertisers will become. They'll be flocking to us in droves."

Biting back the urge to tell him what she thought of that pipe dream, Alexis stood up. So far as she was concerned, the meeting was over. Certainly she was not going to accomplish anything by remaining, and besides, she was rapidly developing a pounding headache. There was ice in her voice when she said, "If you'll excuse me..."

The men stood as she did, but there was nothing more than the most *pro forma* courtesy in their action. The unwillingness of any one of them to meet her eyes told her that.

A dark feeling of frustration dogged her as she went back to her cramped quarters. Unlike Graham's antique-furnished accomodations next to her father's palatial office suite, she made do with little more than a cubicle on a floor far removed from the executive wing. Ruefully she thought that if she had been banished to the outer fringes before, her isolation would only increase now. Without Wilcox she had even less hope of making them see that she was right.

Margaret was gone by the time she got back, but the secretary had left a note to the effect that Apex was on the job and hoped to have results for her within a few days.

Alexis hoped so, too. She went home to her apartment that evening so concerned about the missing English scientist that she almost lacked the energy to think about James Callahan. Almost, but not quite. He had haunted her thoughts throughout the week since their meeting. She had only to close her eyes to see the image of him walking away from her into the darkness of that late winter night.

So preoccupied was she that she barely picked at the dinner her housekeeper had left for her. Since insisting on moving out of her father's Connecticut mansion, she had put together a pleasant life for herself, which she usually had no difficulty enjoying. Though her salary from UBC was so modest as to border on nonexistent, the trust fund from her late mother's estate more than made up for it. Amanda Brockton's last gesture of defiance had been to give Alexis what her father least wanted her to have—independence.

In a city jammed with returning veterans and their wives, all searching desperately for housing, she was lucky enough to be able to afford a large apartment in one of Manhattan's most desirable buildings. Moreover, she could live alone, something her intrinsically private nature delighted in.

Or at least it had. Lately she had been wondering if perhaps she wasn't too much alone. Her father made no secret of the fact that he disapproved of what she was doing. He had given her a job at the network only after she threatened to work elsewhere if he did not.

Ever since, she suspected, he was merely waiting for her to fail so that she would concede her mistake and do what he had wanted all along, marry someone of his choosing and have children to satisfy his dynastic ambitions. Certainly Graham showed no sign of doing so; he enjoyed his own special brand of amusements far too much ever to give them up.

If Alexis had been willing to turn herself into an elegant brood mare, she could have had her father's approval and perhaps even his love, for whatever they were worth. But that was an option she had rejected long ago. For better or worse, she had to lead her life as she believed best.

Which brought her back to the subject of James Callahan. Her half-formed hopes that he might call had been left unfulfilled. Too bad, she thought as she prepared for bed. None of the men she had known had managed to spark her curiosity to such a degree or make her feel so challenged as a woman. Yet she was also instinctively wary of him. Her wisest course seemed to be to forget him as quickly as possible.

That was easier said than done. The next few days were hectic; she was struggling to assemble a report that would convince her father to continue funding for the television project even if Wilcox failed to turn up. That task forced her to concentrate on business during the day, but it could not keep her thoughts from James at night.

More than once she woke from a deep sleep, knowing that she had been dreaming of him and wondering if she was fated to be haunted forever by a man who had no place in her world.

By the time the detective from Apex arrived early the following week to give his report, she was grateful for anything that would keep her attention where it belonged. Barely had Margaret ushered him into her office than Alexis said, ''Have you made any progress in finding the professor?''

The trench-coated gentleman nodded. He had declined to take a seat and stood with his feet planted slightly apart as he drew a small notebook from an inside pocket. Alexis had to hide a smile at his apparently sincere imitation of Sam Spade. But her amusement faded when he said, ''Professor Wilcox is living in a trailer out on Long Island. The trailer and the land it's sitting on are owned by an outfit called the Independent Broadcasting System.''

''The Independent Broadcasting System. . .'' Alexis repeated slowly. ''What is that? More to the point, *who* is it?''

The detective consulted his notebook again. ''IBS is a partnership registered in the State of New York in January of this year. Its stated purpose is to—quote—develop and broadcast programs of information and entertainment through the medium of television—unquote. There are two principles, a James Callahan and an Anthony Gargano.''

Alexis barely heard the name of the second man. She had stopped breathing at the mention of James and did not resume so until her burning lungs demanded release. Yet when she spoke, her voice was utterly devoid of expression. ''Did you say Callahan?''

"That's right, ma'am. Callahan and Gargano. Looks to me like a small-scale operation." Dourly, the detective added, "Maybe they're holding Wilcox for ransom."

"I doubt it. He's worth more than his weight in gold to them."

"Ma'am...?" The detective looked understandably perplexed. "If they snatched the guy, it's really a police matter."

"I'm afraid it isn't that simple." She was silent for a moment, taking a deep breath while she forced herself to consider the options. At length, she managed a cool smile. "Thank you, detective. Apex has done an excellent job, as usual. Just have the bill sent to my office."

The man nodded and closed his notebook with a snap. Whatever was going on, it had just ceased to be any of his business.

When he had left, Alexis sat back in her chair and struggled to come to terms with the fact that the man she had been mooning over for a week was a snake in the grass who had pulled a fast one on her. Good, healthy anger burned out whatever hurt she might have felt. He obviously thought she was a fool; it was past time to show him otherwise.

Scanning the report the detective had left, she noted that Independent Broadcasting was located on the north shore of Long Island, about fifty miles from New York. With luck, she could be there in a couple of hours.

"I'm going out, Margaret," she told her secretary as she picked up her gloves and bag and left the office.

"Planning on coming back today?" the older woman asked.

"I'm not sure." She glanced over her shoulder. "If you don't see me by tomorrow, send out the posse."

Leaving Margaret to make whatever she would of that, she hurried downstairs and around the corner to the garage where she kept her car. The attendant brought it out eagerly, with tires screeching.

"Some buggy, Miss Brockton," he said as he handed her the keys to the Packard convertible. "Had it long?"

"Just a few weeks."

He shook his head admiringly. "Sure beats driving a Jeep."

"It's...uh...not quite as indestructible."

"Ah, don't worry about that," the attendant assured her kindly. "You'll do just fine in it."

Alexis sighed and slid behind the wheel. Moments later she was heading east toward the Queensborough Bridge and the road to Long Island. A soft breeze blowing out of the south made her glad the roof was down. Brilliant sunshine warmed her skin as she reflected that getting out of the city, for whatever reason, was definitely a good idea on so beautiful a day. Still she did not let the pleasant weather dull the sharp edge to her outrage. Aware of the temptation to loiter along the way, she pressed the accelerator down and let the powerful car quickly eat up the miles between her and her quarry.

Traffic was moderate, so she was soon through the more built-up area of northern Queens, where construction of postwar housing was getting under way in response to the overwhelming demand. Farther east, beyond the limits of the city, the scene was far more placid. The potato fields of Long Island rolled by serenely, interspersed occasionally by a cow or horse pasture.

As the day grew warmer, Alexis pulled over to the side of the road and removed the jacket of her two-piece suit. She had put her hair up in a neat chignon that morning, but the breeze had freed numerous silver-blond strands. She released the rest impatiently. As busy as she was deciding what she would say to

James Callahan, she was in no mood to worry about her appearance.

Several choice comments swirled through her mind, all guaranteed to make him wither, but she rejected them in favor of a strictly businesslike approach. If she had learned anything during her months at UBC, it was never to show emotion before an adversary.

By the time she found the turnoff leading to Independent Broadcasting's headquarters, she had schooled her features to blankness. But her expressionless mask cracked slightly when she finally reached the end of the pitted road and saw what confronted her.

Three dilapidated trailers were parked around a corrugated tin shed. From the base of the shed rose a rickety transmission tower that looked as though it dated from the earliest days of radio. Several sea gulls perched on the wobbly lattice work. Half a dozen cows nibbled contentedly at the grass nearby, while from behind a paddock fence at the far end of the field, several sloe-eyed mares watched absently.

Alexis shook her head dazedly. Perhaps the Apex Detective Agency was mistaken after all. Surely no one involved with such a shoestring operation could possibly have gotten the better of her?

Approaching the nearest trailer, her heels sinking into the dirt, she swatted a fly away and tried not to think how foolish she was going to feel if it turned out that she had come on a wild-goose chase.

Those thoughts increased when the trailer door opened and a woman stepped out. She was in her late twenties and wore a simple cotton sundress that left her tanned arms bare. Her chestnut hair was swept back in a ponytail that emphasized the heart-shaped purity of her face. Resting one hand on the fertile swell of her stomach, she shielded her eyes from the sun as she called, "Hi. Is there something I can do for you?"

"I'm not sure," Alexis admitted, coming closer. "I may be in the wrong place."

"That's very possible out here." The woman laughed good-naturedly. She stepped down the small flight of stairs from the trailer, going slowly in deference to her pregnancy, and said, "You're welcome to come in and rest. Maybe we can figure out where you were going."

A little boy of about five or six had followed the woman outside. He peered at Alexis from behind her skirts.

"I'm Maggie Gargano," the woman said, offering her hand. She placed the other on the boy's shoulder gently. "And this is Matthew."

"I'm pleased to meet you," Alexis murmured. With the woman's name had come the realization that she was in the right place after all. "It looks as though my sense of direction is better than I thought. I'm Alexis Brockton and..."

"Oh yes, of course," Maggie said hastily. "James thought you might drop by."

"H-he did...?"

"Uh-huh. He wasn't sure exactly when, but he did say it would probably be soon." Smiling encouragingly, she added, "I've just made a pitcher of fresh lemonade. Perhaps you'd care for some. James is in the lab with Professor Wilcox. They're liable to be a while yet."

"I can imagine," Alexis murmured as she accepted her hostess's suggestion and followed her into the trailer. The little boy tagged along, observing her from a safe distance.

Inside, the trailer was remarkably neat and orderly. The front was given over to a compact kitchen and eating area that sat four. A partition toward the back was folded open. Behind it Alexis glimpsed a double bed covered with a cheerful paisley spread that matched the curtains fluttering at the windows.

"It's not much," Maggie said without apology, "but with the housing shortage so severe, we're lucky to have it."

Alexis thought for an instant about her own spacious apartment and stifled a surge of guilt. Forcing herself to remember why she had come, she said, "Does one of the other trailers belong to James?"

"That's right." Maggie smiled at the little boy gently. "He and Matthew share that one over there." She gestured out the window at the adjacent trailer. "And Professor Wilcox has the third. Although," she added with a chuckle, "the good doctor doesn't spend much time anywhere except in the lab. It's hard to get him out even for meals."

Alexis was still trying to digest the information about James and the little boy. Surprised, she said, "Then Matthew isn't your son?"

"No, though he's certainly my friend. It's great that he and his father are finally having a chance to get acquainted."

So James had a child. Looking at the little boy more closely, Alexis could see the resemblance. He had his father's clear blue eyes, beneath slanting brows, and his chin was the same stubborn shape. But his hair was golden brown and his mouth more finely drawn.

Even as she wondered about the child's mother, Alexis smiled at him reassuringly. "It's nice to meet you, Matthew," she said softly. "Do you like living here?"

He nodded but did not speak. She had to be content with a shy smile that barely touched his eyes before fading.

"How about some cookies with that lemonade?" Maggie asked him. She set them on the table in front of him and made sure his glass was full before turning back to Alexis.

"I suppose you're awfully steamed up," she said quietly.

Alexis didn't even try to deny it. "I'm madder than hell."

"Aren't supposed to say 'hell,'" Matthew chimed in.

The two women exchanged a startled look. Ruefully, Maggie said, "You're right, angel. But grown-ups forget every once in a while."

"Not you," he insisted loyally.

"I'm afraid so; you've just never heard me at my worst. Lord only knows what sort of mother I'll be." She patted her stomach sympathetically. "Poor little thing. No wonder he kicks up such a storm."

"When are you due?" Alexis asked, startling herself, since she had never before taken any interest in the details of pregnancy.

"Not until June," Maggie said, "but there have been certain signs..." She cast a quick glance at Matthew, obviously anxious not to worry him. "The doctor says everything's fine, but Anthony—that's my husband—is still walking around on eggshells. In fact he ought to be down here any minute for his half-hourly check."

Barely had she spoken than the trailer door opened and a tall well-built man strode in. He was dressed in worn khaki pants and a sweat-streaked shirt unbuttoned to the waist. His black hair clung to his head, while his swarthy skin glowed from his exertions.

With a pleasant nod to Alexis, he bent and kissed his wife gently. "Hi, sweetheart, how are you feeling?"

"About the same as I was thirty minutes ago," she murmured without rancor. "At least now Matthew and I have some company. This is Alexis Brockton."

"I thought as much," the man said as he offered his hand. "I'm Anthony Gargano."

"One of the two founding partners of Independent Broadcasting," Alexis added.

He grinned and ruffled Matthew's hair. "That's right. The other founding partner is still in the lab with the latest member of our staff."

Despite her best resolve, Alexis's temper flared anew. "Are you telling me you've formally hired Professor Wilcox?"

Anthony shrugged lightly. "I don't know what else you'd call it. He's living here, Maggie feeds him, and he's on the payroll. So I guess he's part of the team."

"He was supposed to go to work for UBC," she pointed out tightly.

"I guess he changed his mind." Anthony studied her for a moment before he said gently, "Why don't you come along and talk with James about it? I know he feels badly that he left you in the lurch."

"How scrupulous," Alexis muttered as she rose. Thanking Maggie for her hospitality, she followed Anthony out of the trailer. The walk to the tin shed that housed the lab gave her a chance to gather her thoughts and ask a few questions of the tall man at her side.

"Have you known James long?" she began.

"Several years. We were in the Marines together."

"Does that mean you trust him?"

Anthony shot her an assessing glance. "Only with my life, or those of my wife and child. Why do you ask?"

Before such an unrestrained declaration of faith, Alexis was taken aback. Defensively, she said, "I only met him a few days ago, but I wouldn't trust him as far as I could throw him."

"Because of the stunt he pulled with Wilcox? If it's any consolation, that was really out of character for James. Normally he'd cut his throat before trying to take advantage of someone."

"Why did he make an exception in my case?" Alexis asked grimly.

Anthony stared at her with an unreadable expression in his ebony eyes. "As I said, maybe you'd better talk with him about it."

"I intend to," she muttered as he opened the door to the shed and they stepped inside. Alexis had to blink several times before her eyes began to adjust to the dim light. When they did, she looked around slowly.

Unlike Maggie and Anthony's trailer, the interior of the lab was a jumble of machinery, benches, wires, worktables and boxes. Hardly a square inch of surface was uncovered and the floor was barely visible. In the midst of it all, crouched over a table, was Professor Wilcox. The scientist's bald head gleamed in the pale light as he trained a camera on the still life arranged before him and spoke into a microphone.

"Everything's fine over here, James. How does it look at your end?"

"Not too bad," a familiar voice responded from behind a wall at the other side of the room. "I can clearly make out the shape of the vase, but the flowers are a little blurred."

"Excellent," Professor Wilcox exclaimed. "We're making progress."

Anthony leaned closer to Alexis and murmured, "Yesterday the vase looked like a bread box and the flowers could have been a swarm of very large moths."

Alexis did not return his smile. Instead, she asked, "How powerful is your transmitter?"

"Fifty thousand watts."

About standard for a radio station. But what the partnership of Callahan and Gargano was planning to use it for was quite a different matter. "Do you expect to get licensed?" Alexis inquired coolly.

"Would we be wasting our time around here if we didn't?"

She looked him directly in the eye. "I don't know, Mr. Gargano. Right now I'm trying to figure out why two apparently sane men with families to support are involving themselves in an experiment that many very well-informed members of the broadcasting community believe is doomed to failure and which could therefore cost them every penny they've got."

"Maybe we just don't know any better," a deep voice suggested.

Turning swiftly, Alexis found herself on eye level with a very broad, bare chest covered by a thick pelt of curling black hair. James had left the other room and come to stand directly behind her. He was smiling sardonically, apparently amused by her sudden distraction.

"Excuse the informality," he said, "but it gets a little hot back there."

"I can imagine," Alexis muttered, inwardly cursing the low heels she had chosen to wear that day, as they put her in such a disconcerting position. Pride forced her to meet his teasing gaze as she said, "I won't comment on the appropriateness of your being somewhere very hot, Mr. Callahan. We need to talk."

His smile broadened and he shot her a look of unfettered amusement. She was every bit as lovely as he remembered, and as angry as he had expected. What he had not anticipated, however, was the surge of pleasure he felt at seeing her again. Hoping it didn't show, he said, "If you insist."

"I do, and you know perfectly well why." As he took her arm to guide her out of the lab, she added, "What's the matter? Are you afraid no one else should hear what I have to say?"

"Hush," James ordered peremptorily, "you'll disturb Professor Wilcox."

Pulling her arm free, Alexis glared at him. Torn between her desire to let him know exactly what she thought of his behavior and her innate reluctance to create a scene, she contented herself with muttering, "The idea of your kidnapping that poor, innocent man. You should be ashamed of..."

"Oh, Miss Brockton," Professor Wilcox interrupted, the fog of his absorption at last penetrated by her presence, "how nice to see you. I do want to thank you, my dear."

Staring at the bespectacled, middle-aged scientist, Alexis murmured, "What for, Professor Wilcox?"

"Why, for suggesting to James that I might feel more at home with Independent Broadcasting than with your company. You were absolutely right." Gazing happily around the cluttered lab, he added, "This is really much more my cup of tea."

"You told him it was *my* suggestion?" Alexis demanded in an aside to James. "How could you do such a thing?"

"I just wanted him to know you had his best interests at heart." Gazing down at her challengingly, he added, "You do, don't you?"

"Of course, but this is ridiculous. He could have had everything he wanted at UBC."

"What's that, my dear?" Professor Wilcox inquired benignly, glancing up from the camera he was manipulating.

"I...was just saying that we would really have liked an opportunity to make you happy at UBC."

"Oh, James told me that. But why go to all that trouble when the perfect place already existed?" Before she could respond, the scientist went on excitedly, "James, I think I've got that problem with the flowers licked. Would you mind taking another look?''

"Not at all, professor." Taking hold of Alexis's arm again, he steered her toward the room in the back. "And I'm sure Miss Brockton would like to see the progress we've been making. Wouldn't you, Miss Brockton?''

The look he shot her suggested very strongly that it would not be wise to refuse, if only for the sake of her dignity. He was perfectly capable of bodily removing her. "Delighted," she bit out through clenched teeth. A highly amused Anthony stood aside as they passed, his mouth set in a wry smile.

"There it is," James said, gesturing toward the small television receiver set on a bare wooden table. The screen was very small, not more than eight inches in diagonal. The casing had been removed to expose the bulky glass picture tube and cumbersome wiring. A cable linked the set to the camera in the next room. As Alexis watched, interested despite herself, the image of a vase with flowers in it appeared on the tiny screen.

"That is fairly clear," she admitted grudgingly.

James scrutinized the black-and-white image. "It's as good as it's possible to get with present-day equipment. As I'm sure you know, several manufacturers are working hard to produce larger sets with better picture quality."

Alexis did not underestimate the importance of that. For television to be accepted, the public had to be willing to watch it for hours at a stretch. No one would willingly stare at a grainy, fuzzy image for more than a few minutes.

"I hope they succeed," she said quietly. "Otherwise, none of this will ever amount to anything."

"They'll make it." With what she had already come to think of as his usual self-confidence, James added, "The real problem will be providing sufficient programming. That's where outfits like Independent Broadcasting come in.''

''Do you actually believe you can compete with the networks?'' she asked, not bothering to hide her skepticism.

James nodded firmly. ''This is going to be a gigantic industry, far larger than radio. There will be room for plenty of companies, at least in the beginning.''

''If you're truly convinced of that, why aren't you willing to compete fairly?''

His shoulders stiffened as he eyed her carefully. ''You're referring to Wilcox?''

''Exactly. Why did you go to such lengths to get him away from me?''

''Because I had no alternative,'' James said somberly.

''There's always an alternative.''

''Not when the odds are so lopsided. I had to do something to even them up.'' Looking intently at the coolly beautiful woman before him, he strove to make her understand. ''Try to see it from my point of view. Anthony and I came back from the war with just two things, a damn good idea and barely enough cash to get us started. To stay alive in this business, we've got to scramble, just like we did in more battles than I care to remember.''

''But we're not at war anymore,'' Alexis protested. ''You can't go around acting as though we are.'' Silently, she added, *And I don't like being cast in the role of the enemy.*

''Some things don't change with peacetime,'' James contended. ''We're still fighting for position and resources, still trying to put together a winning strategy.''

''And that's what you intend to do, isn't it? Win, no matter what?''

He shook his head firmly. "I don't want victory at any cost. On the contrary, all I want is the good life I fought for and saw too many men die for. Most of all, I want to be able to take proper care of my son."

Alexis sensed that he was telling her the truth as he saw it. He really did not consider himself a particularly ruthless man, only a pragmatic one. Yet he had done something she regarded as unethical; even worse, he had made her feel used.

They had ceased talking and were staring at each other. Off to the side, the gray image of the vase and flowers continued to flutter on the small screen. Neither took any further notice of it.

Alexis had stopped resisting the desire to really look at him. She let herself drink in the sight of skin the color of aged whiskey, stretched tautly over a body that was a startlingly graceful composition of bone, muscle and sinew. None of the ungainliness of youth was in evidence, nor was the creeping erosion of age. He was poised at the moment in his life when potential was becoming reality.

That fascinated Alexis, especially since she felt herself to be in the throes of a similar process, though admittedly not so far along. Instinctively, she wanted to learn more about him and at the same time to give some small release to the emotions he set off within her.

Without pausing to think, she lifted her hand and touched him lightly, tracing a long, white scar that ran from his left shoulder, across his chest, to the top of his flat abdomen.

James sucked his breath in urgently. Her touch, feather-soft as it was, sent a shock of pleasure through him. His hand closed over hers, holding it against him.

"W-where did you get that…?" Alexis asked hesitantly. His response was highly gratifying, even as she wondered what could possibly have possessed her to touch him.

"In a fight somewhere," he murmured absently, drawing her closer.

For a moment, she acquiesced, letting him savor the yielding warmth of her. Only when she felt his surging hunger did she recover herself sufficiently to pull away. A little huskily, she murmured, "This isn't right. I came here to discuss business, not for any…personal reasons. But even if that weren't the case—" her eyes met his accusingly "—what about Matthew's mother, your…wife?"

James's mouth hardened into a grim line. Any mention of Charlotte was distasteful, but beyond that, he found the suddenly aching need of his body an embarrassment. It made a mockery of his accustomed self-control. "My wife is dead," he said coldly. "She was killed in an accident several months ago." Alexis made the appropriately sympathetic response, which he ignored. "That's why I was rotated home so quickly. We'd been divorced for several years and she had custody of Matthew. With her gone, there was no one to care for him."

He didn't add that the accident that killed his former wife had happened because she had been drunk while driving. Only a miracle had saved the driver of the car she had swerved into. Nor did he see any reason to explain that she had never been a fit mother to Matthew, and that had she lived, he would have been fighting her for custody of their child.

It was enough simply to be reminded of Charlotte. All his old suspicion and resentment of women surged to the surface. Alexis saw the change happening in him, and though she did not understand its cause, she realized that he was closing himself off from her, shutting down any avenues of communication that might have existed between them.

Before that happened, she made one last effort to get through to him. Very softly, she said, "James, will you tell Wilcox that I really wanted him to go with UBC and let him make up his own mind?"

His hand tightened on hers. She could see the struggle going on in him, the temptation to do what she asked warring with the determination to hold on to his sole advantage. Slowly, he shook his head. "I can't. The man is genuinely happy here, but even if he weren't, I'd do my damnedest to keep him. He's simply too important to us."

Alexis nodded slowly with regret she could not mask. He had set the terms, but they would both have to live with the consequences. Stepping away from him, she said quietly, "You've made a mistake, James. But it will be a while before you realize that."

Chapter Three

PRIDE DEMANDED that Alexis retaliate for James's preempting of Wilcox. That and the instinctive knowledge that if she let him get away with it, she would lose both his interest and his respect. Before the month was out, she had the satisfaction of topping his bid for precious broadcasting equipment and forcing him to find another supplier who charged more. James recognized the action for what it was—the biblical eye-for-an-eye—and accepted it as such.

He found himself thinking about Alexis a great deal more than he would have liked. That spring and summer were very busy; he and Anthony struggled to get IBS on its feet, but in the quiet of balmy nights, when the only sounds were the hum of insects and Matthew's quiet breathing, there was time to remember the gilt of silver-blond hair and the flash of pewter eyes. Then his body stirred restlessly and his heart ached with a feeling he did not want to identify.

For Alexis, the months were equally hectic. She recovered from the loss of Wilcox sufficiently to assure that UBC's television project would continue, however grudgingly. Her days were spent in meetings with technicians, performers, advertisers—all people she hoped to convince that television was the coming thing. They listened to her patiently, if only because of who she was and how she looked, but only a few were swayed. In the rare hours she allowed herself away from work, she dated several old boyfriends, young men who knew better than to presume she had more than the most passing interest in them.

In July, she took a week off and spent it at her father's Connecticut estate. They saw little of each other, since she rose early each morning to ride and did not return before Charles Brockton had left for the office. She played tennis, swam, went dancing at the country clubs on the Sound, and was grateful when the week was over and she got back to work.

The Federal Communications Commission, the government agency that controlled access to the airwaves, announced that it would issue licenses for television broadcasting. All other concerns fell by the wayside as those astute enough to understand the potential worth of the licenses concentrated on assuring that they would not lose out.

Alexis prepared for her appearance before the Commission with great care. She knew that because of UBC's late start, she was at a disadvantage in dealing with the other networks. But she also had far greater resources than many of the independents who would be among those vying for the licenses. Given even a small amount of luck, she should come out all right.

Had she been willing to trust to that luck, she might have relaxed. Instead, she put in long nights at the office, refining the documentation she would present to support UBC's petition for licenses. The day before she was scheduled to leave for Washington, she worked until after midnight and was glad that she had no train to catch the next morning. Instead, she treated herself to an afternoon flight from LaGuardia airfield.

The capital was hot and muggy as she had expected. Her white linen jacket and coordinated black skirt were soon badly creased. The ruffled blouse stuck to her skin and her calfskin pumps pinched her slender feet. Her small suitcase seemed loaded with rocks. Checking into her hotel, she could think of nothing except a cool bath and a chance to rest awhile.

Until she turned away from the reception desk and saw the man standing at the far side of the lobby. Her first thought was that James was almost as attractive when he was formally dressed as when he wore nothing more than frayed khakis and sweat. His thick black hair was neatly trimmed and his square jaw had been recently shaved. Despite the heat, he had not unbuttoned the double-breasted jacket of his linen suit. His tie was still properly knotted at the neck of his starched white shirt, and his trousers maintained a razor-sharp crease. Even his shoes shone brilliantly.

More aware than ever of her dishevelment, Alexis smothered a sigh. She should have anticipated running into him. It was to be expected that he would come to Washington for the licensing hearings, especially since his partner, Anthony Gargano, must be busy helping his wife with their first child.

In another moment he would see her and she would have lost the opportunity to take the initiative. Before that could happen, Alexis abruptly made up her mind. She strolled across the carpeted lobby and smiled gracefully. "I thought I noticed you standing here. How have you been, James?"

His surprise vanished almost instantly, replaced by a wariness she couldn't help but enjoy. It was a testament to her own skill and determination that she had made him cautious of her. "Not bad," he said slowly. "How about you?"

"Busy, of course, but I'm sure you can say the same. I suppose you're here to meet with the FCC?"

"That's the plan." He was silent for a moment before he added, "We're here for the same reason, then?"

Alexis shrugged lightly. "UBC's winning approval to begin television transmission is really just a formality, but I thought I should show up anyway." As she spoke, she watched him carefully to see if he believed she was as confident as she claimed.

If he didn't, he gave no sign of it. Instead, he said, "Since you have no reason to be worried about the outcome of your own petition, perhaps you'd like to help distract someone who's a little more concerned."

"Would that be yourself?" she asked, ignoring the sudden fluttering in her stomach. His suggestion that he would not be adverse to her company won her grudging admiration. Clearly, he was not a man who ran away from a challenge.

"Who else?" he asked lightly. "Anthony is so wrapped up in Maggie and little Teresa that he's barely aware of what's going on down here."

Forgetting for the moment the tensions flowing between them, Alexis smiled warmly. "So they had their baby. Did everything work out all right?"

"Maggie says so, and she ought to know, since she used to be a nurse." Quietly, he added, "It happened a couple of days after your visit. In the middle of the night, of course." A soft laugh escaped him. "Anthony was always so cool under fire, but he came pretty close to panicking when he realized the baby was actually on the way two months early. Fortunately, both she and Maggie came through fine."

The warm affection in his voice made Alexis's throat tighten. She realized how much he cared for his friends and caught herself wondering what it would feel like to be included among them. Searching for a safe topic, she asked, "How's Matthew?"

James's smile broadened. "He's great. I can't believe how fast he's growing." He was silent for a moment, his mind on his son, before recalling himself to the present. Quietly, he asked, "Are you staying here at the hotel?"

She nodded and gestured ruefully at her crumpled suit. "I just got in a few minutes ago and I'm afraid I'm a bit of a mess."

"I wouldn't say that," James murmured. Amusement crinkled around his eyes as he added, "But perhaps you'd like to change and rest up for a while before we have dinner. There's a little seafood place by the river I think you'll like."

His calm presumption that she would fall in with his plans rankled Alexis, but she sensed he was deliberately teasing her and refused to play along. Instead, she said, "It's a good thing we're business associates; otherwise I'd be tempted to think that you don't know how to ask for a date."

"Oh, I know how, all right," James murmured, smirking. "Sometime I'll show you."

Alexis pointedly ignored that. She left him a few minutes later, having agreed to be ready at seven o'clock. Upstairs, in her room, she showered and changed, all the while telling herself that there was no possible harm in going out with him. He was merely someone with whom she happened to share certain business interests. If she could remember that, she'd be fine.

When she had pinned her hair up in a soft chignon and zipped herself into a dress of pale yellow batiste with short sleeves and a full skirt, she sat down to wait for him. Barely had she settled into a chair than a desk clerk called to let her know that James was in the lobby. She found him standing beside a large potted palm, smoking a cigarette that he put out when he saw her get off the elevator. "Feeling better?" he asked as they walked outside together.

"At least a little more human. It's no wonder Congress wants to adjourn soon. How did they ever pick Washington as the capital, anyway?"

Chatting about the vagaries of politics and weather, they strolled along the broad avenue, past the reflecting pools and on toward the sluggish gray swathe of the Potomac. Alexis glanced around curiously, wondering where they might be headed.

"There's the place," James said, gesturing toward what looked for all the world like an old paddle-wheel steamer moored alongside a rickety wooden dock. "It's run by a friend of mine," he explained as they stepped on board. "We were in the service together. When he got back, he started this up."

"I suppose a lot of ex-servicemen are going into business for themselves," Alexis speculated, noting that the interior of the paddleboat was cheerfully decorated and scrupulously clean. It was also crowded with diners, despite the early hour.

James had called ahead, so they were seated quickly. A waitress dressed like a dance-hall girl from the previous century handed them menus and took their drink orders.

When she was gone, James said quietly, "I'm glad you managed to convince your father to get involved in television after all. If that business with Wilcox had really derailed you, I would have felt bad."

Alexis raised her eyebrows skeptically. "Would you?" Implicit in the question was a reminder that if he truly regretted what he had done, he would have taken the opportunity to repair the damage.

The words came out more sharply than she had intended. James looked at her steadily for a moment before he asked, "You don't think much of me, do you?"

Surprised by his bluntness, she hedged. "That's not true...exactly." His silence encouraged her to go on. "You're obviously very hardworking and determined. You're not afraid to tackle a challenge, and I have the impression that you're a good father. Those are all very admirable qualities.''

"Thanks,'' James muttered dryly. "Maybe you could get me into the Boy Scouts.''

"Oh, I don't know if I'd go that far,'' Alexis teased. More seriously, she added, ''To be frank about it, I think I was a little envious of the way you took Wilcox away from me. While I certainly don't approve of your methods, I admire your decisiveness.''

James looked at her as though he doubted that she meant what she said.

"Really,'' Alexis insisted. "Part of my problem at UBC has been learning to stand up for myself.''

"It's not unusual for women to have difficulty with that,'' he pointed out, accepting finally that she was being sincere.

They broke off for a moment to glance at the menus and give their orders to the waitress, then resumed their discussion.

"That's because we're brought up to rely on charm to get us what we want.'' Alexis laughed ruefully. "Charm gets me absolutely nowhere at UBC.''

"I'm surprised to hear that,'' James admitted. "I'd think being the boss's daughter and all, you'd be able to do pretty much whatever you wanted.''

"'Fraid not. If my father had his way, I'd be busy finding a suitable husband and settling down to raise children.''

He frowned slightly as he opened a package of saltine crackers and offered her one. "Do you have something against marriage?''

Alexis was saved from having to answer immediately by the arrival of the waitress bearing two huge shrimp cocktails. Several minutes passed before his attentive silence again made her feel compelled to respond.

"Marriage is fine in theory...and I'm not saying I'd never want to give it a try. But I'd like to enjoy my freedom for a while."

"You realize you're bucking a national trend," James pointed out lightly. "Women all over the country are rushing to get married and start families. We're already starting to hear about a postwar baby boom."

"I can understand how they feel," Alexis admitted. "After the terrible destruction of the past few years, it's only natural to want to seize some kind of security. But there's so much I'd like to do that I won't be able to accomplish if I get married."

"Why not?" James asked.

"Let me put it this way: If you had a wife, would you want her spending twelve hours a day at the office or would you expect her to be home waiting with your slippers and your dinner?"

"The latter, I suppose, but surely there's satisfaction in creating a good home? Maggie certainly seems happy, even though she's given up nursing for at least a few years."

Alexis thought back to the woman she had met three months before. Though she had spoken with her only briefly, she had to admit that Maggie Gargano had appeared very content. But perhaps that was because she had a husband who obviously loved her and whom she loved in return. "I suppose it's different when you really care about someone....." she said thoughtfully.

"It does seem that way," James agreed.

Struck by his choice of words, she wondered if he had not had that sort of relationship with his late wife. Since they had gotten divorced, whatever love might have existed at the beginning apparently had not lasted.

Unable to bring herself to ask him so personal a question, Alexis changed the subject. She soon had him talking about the progress at Independent Broadcasting, where Wilcox had perfected the camera he'd been working on.

"He's managed to reduce the weight," James explained, "so it's much easier to handle. We can even mount it on top of a small truck to travel directly to the scene of a news event."

"UBC is planning to do the same. My guess is that news and sports will be the best bet for television, at least in the beginning."

"Sports?" James repeated thoughtfully. "Anthony and I have been talking about that. He's got a brother, Dominick, who just got a contract to play in the minor leagues. Dom is convinced that baseball should be televised."

"It already has been, back in '39. NBC had broadcast a game between Columbia and Princeton."

James sat back in his chair and looked at her admiringly. "You are either a fanatical baseball fan or you've learned even more about television than I thought. Which is it?"

Alexis smiled engagingly. "Couldn't it be both?"

"Somehow, I can't see you really interested in those kinds of diamonds. But you do strike me as the sort of person who wouldn't go into something without learning everything possible about it."

"I did do my research pretty thoroughly," she acknowledged.

"Hmmm...I wonder just how much you've figured out...."

Their eyes met across the table. Softly, Alexis said, "Enough, I think. For example, I'm convinced that the FCC's current willingness to award licenses fairly easily won't continue. Sooner or later, there's going to have to be a crackdown or we'll have complete chaos on the airwaves."

"That's exactly the conclusion I've come to," James told her. "Which is why I'm determined to get what I came here for."

Alexis thought about what he had said off and on through the rest of dinner and on the walk back to her hotel. In the lobby, she thanked him politely for the meal and they parted with a handshake, as befitted business associates. Lying awake that night, she tried to concentrate on what she would say to the Commission the following day, but instead she found herself thinking about how easy it had been to talk with James.

Their previous encounters had made her all too aware of his fierce determination and confidence bordering on arrogance. Now she was far more conscious of other aspects of his personality, including a willingness to accord her respect as an intelligent, responsible adult rather than merely viewing her as a pretty woman. Not many men in her experience were capable of that.

She concluded that James had depths to him she had only begun to suspect, and she fell asleep at last, hoping that his bid for a license would succeed, if only so that their paths might cross again.

Back in New York, with UBC's license in hand, Alexis immersed herself once again in work. Her schedule was more hectic than ever, as plans were made to begin trial broadcasts almost immediately. Margaret took to hovering over her like a mother hen, insisting that she wasn't eating properly and was working herself into an early grave. Alexis couldn't bring herself to explain that hard work was all that assured her ability to sleep at night. Even so, her dreams were haunted by a dark-haired man with vivid blue eyes.

She saw James again, briefly, later that summer at the introduction of RCA's new television sets. As he had predicted, picture quality had been greatly improved. The estimate that more than a hundred thousand sets would be sold the following year didn't seem too exaggerated.

Which meant that the scramble for programs to broadcast was really under way. NBC was already on the air with a weekly variety show, newsreels and a roundup of sports events. The Dumont network weighed in with a romantic drama and Westerns. UBC joined the fray in October, when Alexis supervised production of an interview show that featured popular personalities talking about themselves with a genial host. It was broadcast from a surplus radio studio on the other side of town from UBC's headquarters. After the initial start-up, the major problem confronting participants was the winter wind that whistled through the cracks in the walls.

Her frantic work schedule left her little time for social engagements, but she did date occasionally. On New Year's Eve she was at a party at the Waldorf-Astoria, a celebration also attended by Liz Carlisle, who asked what had ever happened to the ''delicious man'' she had brought to her place.

Alexis wondered the same. She could only presume that James was as busy as she herself. Independent Broadcasting came on the air a few weeks after UBC, but declined to compete for viewers in the evening when the still-tiny audience could choose among several programs. Instead, IBS broadcast during the day, interspersing talented but unknown comedians and singers with a lineup of cooking and sewing instruction shows for the legions of war brides striving to be good homemakers, plus a regular feature on child care hosted by Maggie and starring a delightful baby Teresa. When industry observers finished raising their eyebrows, they admitted that perhaps IBS had stumbled onto something.

Alexis ruefully agreed, though she knew the strategic coup had not been an accident. After some slight hesitation, she gave in to her impulse and wrote James a brief note congratulating him on his ingenuity. Two days after she dropped it in the mail, he called.

"If what I hear is anything to go by," James said, "you've been working round the clock. I've been doing the same and I'm more than ready for a break, so how about dinner and a movie?"

Alexis's slim hand tightened around the receiver. "Is this the demonstration you promised?"

He laughed and surprised her by remembering. "You mean when I said that when the time was right, I'd show you that I knew how to ask? Yes, I guess this is it. So what do you say?"

Several possibilities sprang to mind, including a plea that she was simply too busy, which would have been the truth. But she really had no desire to refuse. Instead of her interest in him lessening, it had only increased. Perhaps getting to know him better would dull the luster of his uniqueness and enable her to view him as simply one more man worthy of no more than passing notice.

Or so she told herself as she left the office a little earlier than usual and went home to prepare for their date. Stalwartly ignoring the small voice that warned her that James was unlikely ever to be simply one more man, she showered and changed. The navy-blue wool dress she selected came from Dior's spring collection. Its snug, buttoned bodice was set off by a voluminous pleated skirt worn over a stiff petticoat. The skirt resembled a fully opened flower, from which her upper body gracefully emerged. With it she wore square-toed pumps, a wide-brimmed hat and the ubiquitous white gloves.

The doorman rang to announce James's arrival at precisely 7:00 P.M. Alexis asked that he come up, then hurriedly fastened the snap on a short string of pearls and went to open the door.

"Come in; you're right on time."

As he stepped into the apartment, James glanced around. The entry hall led directly to a large living room with floor-to-ceiling windows. Black and white tile floors and plain white walls were the setting for the art-deco furnishings Alexis's mother had purchased during the 1920s and which had been relegated to a warehouse after her death until their rescue by her daughter. Alexis knew they were now considered hopelessly old-fashioned, but she unabashedly enjoyed the sensuous shapes and almost barbaric colors, finding in them a release from the generally cool and aloof pose she presented to the world.

James knew only that the apartment spoke of taste and means beyond his ability to match. That made him uncomfortable, and wasting no time, he suggested they leave. "The movie starts at nine, so we ought to be going."

"Fine," Alexis said, relinquishing her intention of offering him a drink. She excused herself briefly to get her purse from the bedroom, then rejoined him. James had parked his vintage 1940 Hudson in front of the apartment building. Alexis got in; he closed the door for her, then went around to the driver's seat. They pulled away into traffic before either spoke.

"Lindy's okay for dinner?" James asked without taking his eyes from the road.

"Fine. It's one of my favorite spots." That happened to be the truth, even though she'd only been there once or twice, but she didn't expect him to believe her.

He didn't. Raising an eyebrow, he said, "I'd have figured you for somewhere fancier."

"That doesn't mean I can't enjoy good plain food." Her mild response hid a spurt of annoyance. If he really thought she was a spoiled little rich girl, why had he bothered to ask her out? Moreover, if he thought she wouldn't like Lindy's, why had he suggested it?

Their truce was in danger of becoming a sometime thing, when James suddenly grinned. "So I figured wrong. What do I know, anyway? You're not exactly the kind of woman I usually date."

"Let me guess; you like redheads."

He shot her a startled look. "How did you know that?"

Alexis laughed and settled back more comfortably in her seat. "I could claim to have a crystal ball, but in fact it was just a lucky shot." She wasn't about to reveal the source of her deduction—namely, that redheads were associated with passion—a quality she suspected James was fully equipped to appreciate.

"If it makes any difference to you," he said wryly, "I'm developing a taste for blondes."

She shook her head in mock chagrin. "It would have been far more effective to say one blonde in particular."

"Would you have believed me?"

The sudden seriousness underlying his question took her aback. It suggested a depth of feeling on his part that she didn't feel ready to confront. Instead, she glanced out the car window as they headed south on Fifth Avenue.

The secretaries and salesclerks had gone home, catching their nickel rides on the subway to Bensonhurst and Sunnyside. In daylight, the city tended to look harried and grim. The buoyancy of the early postwar days had been lost as the realization set in that far from settling all the world's problems, the war had hatched a new and even more ominous set. It was only at night, when darkness cast a gracious cloak over reality, that glamour and exuberance returned.

Alexis turned back to him slowly. "I don't know. There's a great deal about you that I don't understand."

"I can say the same about you," he pointed out quietly. "When I look at you, I get a glimpse of a way of life totally removed from anything I've ever known."

"You make me sound as though I'm from a different planet," she protested.

"You might as well be. Our backgrounds couldn't be more at odds."

"Then why are we—" She broke off, abruptly aware of what she had been about to say.

So was James. With a grin, he finished the question for her. "So attracted to each other?" When she tried to object, he went on firmly. "Don't bother denying it. We both know it's true. You were right when you said the way I handled the Wilcox matter was a mistake. From a practical viewpoint, I still don't think I had any choice. But there are other considerations, which is why we're out together tonight."

"It sounds as though you have all the answers," Alexis grumbled, though she couldn't really manage to be annoyed at him. Whether she wanted to admit it or not, he was right.

"I've got a few, enough to know that whatever's going on between us is too strong to fight. Seems to me the smartest thing we could do is get to know each other better and see where it goes."

"Perhaps it won't go anywhere," Alexis suggested with just a touch of hauteur. She wasn't about to make anything easy for him.

"Maybe not," he agreed. "We've got a lot of obstacles to overcome."

"That's certainly true," she said with a hint of asperity. "For instance, you tend to take a great deal for granted."

"As a matter of fact, I never presume anything. That's how I stayed alive in the war, and that's how I get ahead in business."

"We're not talking about war *or* business," Alexis reminded him as he pulled into a parking lot near the restaurant.

James helped her out of the car and tossed the keys to the attendant. "I know we're not," he said, looking directly at her. "But you've got to admit there are similarities."

With a rueful shake of her head, she took the arm he gallantly offered. "Don't think for a moment that I am going to comment on that."

"Chicken."

"Cluck-cluck."

An older couple walking past them did a double take that made both James and Alexis laugh. They exchanged a grin as they strolled into the restaurant.

Lindy's had been immortalized in the stories of Damon Runyon, who called the place Mindy's and filled it with a collection of oddball characters who spoke in rhyming patois and had hearts of gold. Real patrons weren't quite like that, but the mystique clung, drawing wide-eyed tourists in to mingle with the regulars.

Alexis and James fit into neither category; they were simply New Yorkers looking for a decent meal, something Lindy's could more than provide. The pastrami was superb, the cole slaw excellent, the cherry Cokes rhapsody and the cheesecake sublime.

"I'm not going to be able to eat for a week," Alexis groaned as she swallowed the last bite of a pickle before turning her attention to dessert.

"You do have a healthy appetite," James acknowledged, secretly relieved that she was enjoying the meal. He had picked Lindy's because he wanted to know right off the bat if she was as unpretentious as she acted. It seemed unlikely, given her background, but Alexis had managed to surprise him yet again.

"Speak for yourself," she groused good-naturedly. "At least I didn't eat *two* pastrami sandwiches."

"I'll eat anything I don't have to cook for myself."

"It must be tough to manage in the trailer."

"Oh, we got rid of those. Once IBS started bringing in some money, Anthony and I found a couple of houses not too far from the station."

Alexis reflected wryly on how easy he made that sound, as though there were no desperate housing shortage, with people lining up for the privilege of living in converted garages and Quonset huts. Somehow, she wasn't surprised. James struck her as a man who knew exactly how to get what he wanted, and his partner was much the same.

"How are Maggie and Anthony? And the baby, Teresa, isn't it?"

"That's right. They're all fine. Tessa's got several teeth and gets into everything. She's adorable."

Alexis laughed at the thought of the baby keeping them all on their toes. "What about Matthew? Is he still growing so fast?"

"Faster," James assured her. "He's in first grade and seems to like it a lot, but he's happiest when he's helping to look after Tessa."

"So he doesn't feel jealous of her?"

"No…we were a little worried about that in the beginning, because he's so close to Maggie, but he seems to have appointed himself her big brother."

"It sounds as though Tessa's a lucky little girl."

"I suppose, considering what can happen to kids if they get born into the wrong kind of family."

"What do you mean by wrong kind?" she asked.

"Poor, too crowded, unconcerned…"

"Being a conscientious parent doesn't require a lot of money. All it takes is love."

"I suppose that's true," James admitted. "God knows, my folks never had two dimes to rub together, but they brought me up to believe that anything was possible so long as I worked hard enough."

"Are they still alive?"

"No, Da died in an accident on the docks in '27. Ma caught pneumonia a year later and followed him. I was sixteen then and started running pretty wild. A priest in our parish steered me into the Marines. I've always been grateful for that."

"Despite all the action you saw in the war?"

"Somebody had to do it. Anyway, that's enough about me. Let's talk about you."

Alexis's cool gray eyes slid away from him. "I was born and raised in Connecticut, went to Bryn Mawr, and served on several charity committees before going to work for UBC."

The summation of a quarter century of life into a handful of words disconcerted him. He was left to wonder if she was always so unrevealing of her past or if she simply refused to reveal it to him. Whichever might be the case, he was still driven to know more.

"Is Graham your only brother?"

"You don't think he's enough?"

"Hmmm...I see your point. What about your mother? I haven't heard her mentioned."

A shutter dropped over Alexis's gaze. "My mother is dead. She has been for a very long time."

"I'm sorry," he began automatically.

She ignored him, glancing down at the thin watch fastened around her wrist. "If we're going to make the movie, we really should be on our way."

He acquiesced reluctantly. They walked the few blocks to the Capital theater, where Frank Sinatra was playing in *It Happened in Brooklyn*. The movie had gotten mixed reviews, though Bosley Crowther of the *Times* had said Sinatra's performance had casual charm.

James liked it well enough, if only because it didn't intrude on his private ruminations. Sitting in the darkness beside Alexis, listening to her soft laughter and breathing in the delicate fragrance of her perfume, he thought about the world she came from and how different it was from everything he had known.

Once, he would not even have allowed himself to desire her, believing her to be completely unattainable. Slowly, over the year they had know each other, he had come to feel very differently.

James smiled grimly in the darkness. The No Trespassing signs that popped up as soon as he tried to get beyond her polite facade were both tantalizing and irritating. They served to increase his determination even as they reminded him that he would accomplish nothing through hasty or impetuous action.

To overcome her natural wariness, he would have to convince her to trust him. That would be simpler to achieve if he could be sure such trust was justified.

Chapter Four

AFTER THAT EVENING AT LINDY'S, Alexis continued to see James occasionally. They shared perhaps a dozen dinners, usually caught on the fly at the end of a hectic day. Their encounters were always pleasant and undemanding. James understood without needing to be told that Alexis was far more comfortable with situations that required little of her emotionally. That was fine with him, since he felt the same way.

When she was free on the weekends, which was rare, since either business or social obligations kept her occupied, she joined father and son on their excursions. Matthew loved Coney Island and the Bronx Zoo. Wherever they went, he brought home something for Tessa, even though she was still too young to always appreciate his choices.

In the spring of '47, the country took a break from talk of the Marshall Plan to feed Europe and the creation of Israel to concentrate on what most everyone agreed was far more important anyway, the new baseball season.

"Nobody can hit off Ralph Branca," Matthew exclaimed, almost bouncing up and down on the back seat of the Hudson. It was a clear, sun-washed day at Ebbet's field, and he was there to see his honorary uncle, Dominick Gargano, play his first game as a Dodger. For a seven-year-old, life could not get better. "He's the best pitcher the league's got. Right, Dad?"

"Absolutely," James agreed, with a lopsided grin for Alexis. "But the Dodgers don't have to worry about pitching anymore to win. Not now that they've got Dom."

Matthew nodded in vigorous agreement, then looked around eagerly as they walked through the gate on the center-field side and up the steep ramp. It was dark in there and the sudden glare of sunlight upon emerging at the other end made everyone blink. Opening his eyes, the little boy saw the emerald-green diamond far below and smiled beatifically.

Alexis watched him fondly. The child who had hidden behind Maggie's skirts the day they met now had long arms and legs that looked too big for him, like a puppy's paws. In features and outlook, he resembled his father, except that Matthew had an innocence James had long since outgrown.

"Hi, there," Maggie called when she spotted them. As they slipped into their seats, she gave Alexis a quick hug and smiled at James. "We're glad you could make it. Dom said he wanted all the help he could get."

"He won't need it," James said as he greeted Joseph and Maria Gargano, Anthony's parents and Maggie's in-laws. "The smartest thing Branch Rickey has done was bringing him up from the farm team."

"Smarter than bringing Jackie Robinson out of the Negro League?" Matthew asked teasingly.

"Well, maybe not quite that smart," James admitted, "but it's still right up there."

"What did I tell you, Pa?" Anthony asked as he nudged his father in the ribs. "Dom's gonna to be a star."

"I hope so," the elder Gargano murmured, "God knows, he's wanted this long enough."

"I think we're all more nervous than Dom could possibly be," Maggie confided with a grin. She put a hand over her swelling belly and sighed. "With all the excitement, this little guy is kicking up a riot."

"Maybe he wants to join the game," Alexis suggested as she beamed a smile at Tessa. Barely past her first birthday, the little girl was already a charmer. She turned huge hazel eyes on Alexis and smiled back winsomely.

"Anthony better keep a shotgun handy when she grows up," Alexis murmured to Maggie, who grinned and shook her head.

"He won't have to bother. Matthew has already made it clear he gets to approve anyone who wants to—as he puts it—play with Tessa."

Alexis laughed and turned her attention to the field where the organist was about to go into the national anthem. The audience rose for it, then settled back down for the start of the game.

As the teams ran out on the field, there were boos for the Phillies and cheers for the Dodgers, though Dom's entry with the second string got only cursory notice. At least from most of the crowd. From his family and friends he got a standing ovation. He stood proudly in his uniform, his head thrown back, dark hair gleaming in the sunlight when he doffed his cap and grinned in their direction. At twenty-six, he was at the peak of his mental and physical powers, and ready to prove it.

"Show 'em how it's done," Anthony yelled. Shaking his head, he added, "Who would have ever thought I'd be coming here to see my kid brother play? The whole time we were growing up, he kept saying he wanted to be in the majors, but I never really took him seriously."

"I guess now we've got to," Maggie said, her voice reflecting her pride in her brother-in-law. She propped Tessa up on her lap so that the little girl could see more clearly as the first pitch was thrown.

The Dodgers were in fine form, confirming rumors that they already had their eye on the Series. Still, the Phillies were formidable opponents and nothing was guaranteed.

Jackie Robinson had an excellent day, coming to bat three times with a double, two runs batted in and a homer in the bottom of the fifth. Not exceptional for him, but still a crowd pleaser. As the innings rolled by and the long rays of the sun slanted westward, the little group there to see Dom began to glance anxiously at the clock.

"He'll get on, won't he, Dad?" Matthew asked. "Even though they're winning, they still need him. Right?"

"Maybe they don't want to risk his getting hurt," James suggested gently. "They could be saving him for a closer game."

Matthew was not to be consoled. He had come to see Dom play and would be satisfied by nothing less. Alexis ruffled his hair and drew him close, offering what comfort she could, but he remained long-faced and glum. Tessa quickly caught his disappointment and whimpered plaintively.

By the top of the eighth inning, the score was Dodgers 7, Phillies 4. When the opposing team was retired in quick succession without a hit, the crowd cheered. Their confidence must have spread to the dugout, for halfway through the bottom of the eighth, Dom was sent in as a relief hitter.

"Please Lord, don't let him miss," Maria Gargano murmured as she fingered the rosary beads, which had suddenly appeared in her hands, and watched her son step up in front of the catcher. He adjusted his cap, knocked the dirt from his cleats with the tip of his bat, and took his stance.

Robin Roberts was on the mound for the Phillies. With a well-deserved reputation as a tough pitcher, he was an intimidating sight for any rookie, but Dom showed no sign of running scared. He let the first pitch go by, took a swing at the second but narrowly missed, and on the third sent the ball soaring toward right field, over the forty-four-foot-high fence, and into Bedford Avenue, where fans who couldn't afford tickets waited on the chance of just such an occurrence.

The crowd roared its approval as Dom trotted around the bases. The umpire had already circled his arms to signal a home run, so he could afford to take it a little slow, his head back and his white teeth gleaming as he savored the moment.

Alexis became aware that she was on her feet, shouting, and sat down again, somewhat bemused. Despite Matthew's best efforts to explain baseball to her, she still didn't really understand all the rules, but that didn't prevent her from recognizing what had just happened. A rookie player on his first time at bat had hit the ball out of the Dodgers' Stadium and into Brooklyn history.

"That's my boy!" Joseph Gargano yelled, hugging his wife. To no one in particular, he explained, "That's my son down there!"

The people around them grinned and called congratulations. Back on the field, Dom's teammates were patting him on the rump. Before he returned to the dugout, he turned again and looked up into the stands, throwing his folks a thumbs-up signal.

The game concluded a short time later, with the Phillies failing to add another run. A victory celebration at the elder Garganos' Brooklyn home followed, with Dom arriving, shortly after it got under way, to a hero's welcome. Alexis hadn't met him before but quickly took to the clear-eyed young man with the appealing combination of confidence and humility. He was a great deal like his brother Anthony, but rather more open and outgoing. Inevitably, the talk drifted to a com-

bination of baseball and television, with Dom holding forth his
conviction that the new medium was perfect for sports.

"Some network or independent station is going to make a
big breakthrough by providing regular coverage of games,"
he said as he sat on the overstuffed couch, drinking a beer. He
glanced at James and his brother. "I keep hoping it will be you
guys."

"So do I," Anthony agreed, "but we can't afford that kind
of coverage right now. Maybe in a few years." Looking toward Alexis, he added good-naturedly, "Unless UBC beats us
to it."

"That's always a possibility," she assured him matter-of-
factly. "But if Dom's right—and I think he may be—there will
be enough interest in sports to keep all of us busy."

Maggie popped her head in from the kitchen to announce
that dinner was ready, and everyone trooped in to eat. The
Garganos were particularly pleased to see that Alexis did full
justice to the traditionally Italian meal and encouraged her to
tell them stories about her trip to Europe shortly after the war,
which had included a stopover in Rome.

She was pleasantly tired by the time the party ended. As always, James insisted on seeing her home. Matthew was just as
happy to drive back to Long Island with Anthony and Maggie, especially since that meant he could spend more time with
Tessa.

Leaving the Hudson under the watchful eye of the doorman, James escorted her upstairs. He waited while she found
her keys, then took them from her and unlocked the apartment door.

Alexis looked up at him sleepily as she dropped the keys back
into her purse. "All that fresh air and wonderful food have
knocked me out."

He smiled gently, thinking that she did look rather like a little girl who had played too hard. The silvery blond hair was in disarray and her cheeks were slightly flushed. Translucent lids drooped over gray eyes that had the sheen of fine old silver. His hand found its way under her chin, lifting her head so that he could see her more clearly.

She blinked once, twice, but made no effort to pull away. Instead, she stood very still, absorbing the effect of his touch. Since that first evening when they met, James had kissed her several times, but always very lightly, as though in no more than friendship.

That had oddly piqued her curiosity. By withholding his passion, he had set himself apart from all the overeager, fumbling young men she had brushed off so easily in the past. His restraint was a challenge she could not resist.

Her fingers curled around the hand that held her chin. He let her draw it away as she stepped within the circle of his arms.

''James…''

''Hmmm…''

''How long have we known each other now?''

''Let's see…. It was a little more than a year ago that I crashed the Carlisles' party.''

''I seem to remember that you kissed me that night.''

''Did I?''

She glanced at him chidingly from beneath her thick lashes. ''You know perfectly well you did.''

''And I have since.''

''That was different.''

''Really? How so?''

''It wasn't…friendly.''

His mouth curled at the corners. ''No, I suppose it wasn't. After all, if you remember, we weren't friends then.''

"And now we are?"

He nodded slowly. "I certainly hope so."

Alexis fought down a wave of chagrin. It was all very well and good to be friends, but she was beginning to realize that she wanted more from James. Had, in fact, for quite a while.

"James..."

"Hmmm..."

"Perhaps I should kiss you this time."

He swallowed against the rising excitement that tightened his throat and nodded. "By all means, feel free."

Oddly enough, she did. Free to stretch the boundaries of her self-restraint, to dip a toe in what were, for her, the uncharted waters of emotional involvement, all the while telling herself that passion was a normal part of life and it was only natural to want to give in to it. She and James seemed to understand each other so well; both had their priorities straight and their lives worked out. Surely she would be safe with him.

Or so she thought, until the warm firmness of his mouth against hers reminded her that safety was always a relative thing and that sometimes the greatest dangers came from within oneself.

A soft gasp of pleasure broke from Alexis as she felt the gentleness drop away from him, replaced by a hunger that matched her own. Standing in the dimly lit corridor, the only sounds muted by thick walls and plush carpeting, they strove together urgently. His hands slid down to grasp her waist, the thumbs stroking delicately back and forth over the flat plane of her abdomen. James shifted slightly, bringing her between his thighs, making her vividly aware of the effect she was having on him.

"Alexis...if we go on like this, you'll have to invite me in."

The gentle double entendre, uttered with exactly the right touch of tender humor, reassured her that the situation was not completely out of hand. Which was just as well, since it was proceeding so much more rapidly than she had anticipated.

"I'm not sure I'm ready for that yet," she told him honestly, searching his face for any sign of annoyance or impatience. When there was none, she relaxed slightly. "I'm sorry for giving you the wrong impression just now."

He stepped back and ran a hand through the thick ebony hair that had become mussed. "That's all right," he said soothingly. "It took me by surprise as well." That much was true; though he had been anticipating just such an occurrence, he hadn't expected it to happen after a prosaic day spent with family and friends. Teasingly, he added, "If this is the effect baseball has on you, we'll have to go to more games."

"I wouldn't mind," she told him softly. "I like being with Matthew and the Garganos." When he pretended to be wounded, she hastily corrected herself. "And with you, too, of course."

"I guess that will do," James said lightly, "for the moment." He dropped a quick kiss on the tip of her nose, laughed at her startled look, then added, "I'll be in touch."

Alexis nodded, glad that he was making no effort to rush her. Had he done so, she would have pulled back instantly. As it was, she found herself looking forward eagerly to seeing him again.

But in the meantime, there were problems at work that demanded her attention and kept her from thinking about James too much.

"I'll admit there's more to this television business than I thought at first," Graham said one afternoon as they were leaving a meeting of the UBC executive board. "In fact, it looks as though there might actually be a future for it." Pressing the button for the elevator, he looked at her meaningfully. "You've done a terrific job, but it's unfair to expect you to carry the burden alone."

Alexis shot him a noncommittal glance. She had been prepared for exactly this contingency for some time. During the many meetings called to discuss the swift and dramatic changes overtaking their industry, she had occasionally spied a baffled look in their father's eyes. Slowly she realized that he was growing old and that the present was becoming too much for him.

Graham clearly believed himself more than ready to step into the breach, to take over from his father and from Alexis as well. That she was determined to prevent, not by opposing it outright in a confrontation she could not hope to win but by out maneuvering her brother at his own game, as only another Brockton could do.

Smoothly, she said, "I agree completely, Graham. The more help I can get on this, the better."

Taken aback by her cordial response, he nodded warily. "Oh...well, good. Perhaps we should get together and discuss a division of responsibilities."

She laughed lightly. "Surely we don't need anything as formal as that? After all, we are brother and sister, all part of the same team. Aren't we?"

"Of course...but..."

"Television is in such a state of creative flux right now, I think it would be a terrible mistake to try to restrain it by imposing a rigid management structure. Everybody should simply be doing everything they possibly can to make it work."

"Sure, but..."

"Otherwise, we'll need a lot more money."

Graham winced as though she had struck a nerve, as in fact she had. Nothing was dearer to him than the bottom line of the annual profit and loss statement; anything that detracted from it met with instant suspicion. "Why do you say that?"

"It's simple. Once people are told they're responsible for so much and no more, they tend to limit their activities to those areas. So more people have to be hired to take up the slack. The additions to the payroll want to look very busy in order to justify their existence, so they run around having meetings, writing memos, that sort of thing. All of which takes time and cuts into the amount of work that actually gets done, so more people have to be hired, who have meetings, write memos, and so on." She paused for breath, then concluded, "I'm afraid it's a vicious circle."

He nodded ponderously. "I see what you mean..."

Alexis was willing to bet that he did. Graham's department at UBC ran pretty much as she described. Or perhaps stumbled along was a better description. Still, it made money, if only because radio continued to draw the bulk of advertising dollars. A situation she intended to change very soon.

After their discussion by the elevator, several weeks passed, during which Graham was seemingly content to let her continue to run the TV division her own way without interference. He was busy with the crusade to root out Communists who were alleged to be infiltrating the inner sanctums of government and industry, and he showed no inclination to give her activities more than passing attention, although he did drop by occasionally at the ramshackle studios on the West Side to see what was going on.

There was a great deal to see. Alexis had convinced several leading radio personalities to try their hand at the new medium. Some of the comedians who had become national stars on radio were shy of making the change, but they found it hard to resist the lure of reviving the old vaudeville routines that relied so much on the audience being able to see the performer. Similarly, several of the nation's top crooners, whose mellow voices could be heard in homes across the country, liked the idea of being seen as they sang, rather than merely heard.

At first it was a lark for them to come across town to the bedraggled studios and strut their stuff in front of the cameras. They brought their friends with them to watch the flickering gray images on the television sets, and a party atmosphere often prevailed. Alexis didn't mind, so long as she got what she wanted. Besides, all the activity kept her from wondering too much about why James had yet to call.

In addition to its popular interview show, UBC launched a variety hour of singing, comedy routines and dancing. Several of the most successful dramatic series were transferred to the small screen. When none of the popular newscasters would agree to give up their secure radio audiences in favor of television's riskier appeal, Alexis hired a young reporter from the city desk of the *New York Times* to run the news department and appear on camera.

Winston Harcourt proved a stroke of genius. He was tall and slender, with aristocratic features and dark hair going prematurely silver. His reassuringly calm manner projected perfectly through the camera lens and right into the homes of his viewers. For fifteen minutes each evening, he told them what was going on in the world. Sometimes, he even had newsreel footage of his stories. At the end of each broadcast, he signed off with the words "Good night, America, and God bless," which Alexis had thought up for him.

Winston also had one other very significant skill; he made the perfect decoy. With him as her escort, Alexis could attend social events without raising eyebrows. On the contrary, no one who met him failed to be impressed with his urbane charm and genuine intelligence. Even Charles Brockton liked him.

"You're doing a fine job, Harcourt," he told the newsman one summer evening over dinner at the Brocktons' Connecticut estate. Winston was part of a house party spending the weekend there, but it was tacitly understood that he was Alexis's guest.

"You tell the public what it needs to know without a lot of extras thrown in," the network president continued. "Too much information just confuses them, not to mention boring the hell out of the sponsors."

Winston and Alexis exchanged a quick look, his rueful, hers wryly patient. "Thank you, sir," he said cautiously, "but I have to admit that I'm rather concerned about the small amount of time given to news. We're living in such a turbulent era, it seems to me that people need to know far more about what's going on in the world if they're to make intelligent decisions."

"Decisions about what?" Graham chimed in from across the broad expanse of the mahogany dinner table positioned beneath a gleaming crystal chandelier that had once hung in the château of Versailles. Unbuttoning his dinner jacket, he leaned back in his chair and twirled the stem of his wineglass. "All the public cares about is security. Why do you think they're all flocking to the suburbs to live in slapped-together houses, have three-point-four children or whatever it is now, and play bridge every Friday night?"

"These are the same people who went through the horrors of the Depression and the War," Alexis pointed out. "Is it so strange that they should want to feel safe?"

"That's the whole point," her father snorted. "They're like rats that have just climbed out of the water onto a boat, and they're scared to death of anything that may rock it. Look at the way they've pounced on the Communists."

Alexis didn't want to get into that particular subject; she and her father had already argued about the fairness of purging anyone who was suspected of even flirting with leftist ideology.

"If the public can become concerned about the possibility of Communists infiltrating government and industry," Winston said cautiously, "then perhaps we can also interest them in other issues."

"There is no other issue," Graham said flatly. "Nothing else strikes so directly at the bedrock of American life."

Recognizing the phrase from a recent speech by a member of the House Committee on Un-American Activities, Alexis frowned. The Communist scare sweeping over the country worried her. It showed signs of developing into a witch-hunt.

"Your father and brother seem to be big fans of the Red baiters," Winston said the following day when they were driving back to town together.

"They'll support anything that protects their interests. If the great mass of ordinary people can be made to believe that Communists are the gravest danger facing the world, they won't be paying much attention to what the capitalists are doing, so people like my father and brother will be free to operate without inconvenient scrutiny."

If Winston was surprised by this rather cynical summation, he gave no sign of it. Instead, he was silent for a while, seemingly content to sit back and enjoy her smooth handling of the convertible as it tooled along the turnpike. The warm draft of wind sent her hair streaming out behind her and flushed her cheeks. He watched her unobtrusively out of the corner of his eye, enjoying her beauty.

"I hope you had a good time this weekend," Alexis said as she became aware of the silence stretching out between them. The visit with her family had predictably made her tense, but that was no excuse for ignoring Winston.

"The estate is lovely," he said with a smile.

The corners of her mouth turned up. "That's a very diplomatic comment. It's all right to admit that my father and brother annoy you; they do the same to me."

"Is that why you generally keep your distance from them?"

"Yes," she admitted. "I can only take them in small doses, and even then it's difficult."

"Yet you work with them."

"Not directly. My father has no interest in television and Graham is involved in other things, so I'm left fairly independent."

"For the moment," Winston said. "But what if that changes?"

Alexis's hands tightened on the wheel. He had raised the very point she least wanted to consider. All the progress she was making at work might be destroyed if it came down to a head-to-head clash with her on one side and her father and brother on the other. Much as she have liked to think otherwise, she suspected she would lose.

"I'll have to cross that bridge when and if I come to it," she said as lightly as she could manage. "There are far more immediate problems to worry about."

He smiled gently. "Such as a certain news commentator who keeps arguing for more airtime?"

"You're not a problem," she told him sincerely.

"I hope not."

The husky softness of his voice sent a stab of resentment through her. James's continued silence had become first bewildering, then painful. She wished with all her strength that the feelings he had aroused in her could have been directed toward Winston instead.

Determined not to think about the man who had left her feeling frustrated and aching, she redoubled her efforts to make UBC television a success. Her days passed in a blur of activity as she came up with ideas for several more programs, found the right performers and convinced them to take a chance on the new medium, cajoled sponsors, fended off Graham's protests about her rapidly increasing production budget, and assured her father that everything was not getting out of hand.

Inevitably, the late nights finally caught up with her. Standing in the wings during a broadcast of the interview show, she suffered a dizzy spell and went reluctantly to a doctor. His prescription was simple: several days of rest, preferably far from the office.

Ignoring the litter of travel folders that immediately appeared on her desk, Alexis decided the most she could afford to take off was a long weekend, which she preferred to spend at the beach house on Long Island she had purchased several years before.

The house stood on a bluff overlooking an expanse of white sand, surrounded by scrub pines and salt grass. Its clapboard siding was weathered to a soft blue-gray, which all but blended with the sea and the sky. Walking up the flagstone path to the door, Alexis breathed deeply and felt a sense of peace drift into her with the tangy air.

The interior was rustic without being stark. Weathered beams and plank floors lent a mellow glow to the scattering of overstuffed couches and chairs. Braided rugs and calico curtains provided a note of warmth. Pleasantly beaten-up tables and cupboards advertised the fact that no special care needed to be taken. It was a place to relax, curl up in front of the stone fireplace and ignore the rest of the world.

Within an hour of arriving, Alexis was prepared to do exactly that. She had changed into a pair of toreador pants and a softly tailored blouse held in place by a wide belt. Her bare feet were slipped into sandals and she had pulled her hair back into a ponytail. With her face free of makeup, she turned it to the sun as she left the house and strolled toward the beach.

Cool, damp sand trickled between her toes. A soft breeze grasped playfully at tendrils of hair, pulling them loose from the rubber band. Watching sandpipers skitter back and forth at the waterline, Alexis climbed up on a rock and smiled. Already she felt more relaxed than she had in a very long time.

Until she happened to turn her head and see the man coming down the beach toward her.

At first she thought her imagination must be playing tricks on her. She was overly tired, the sun was in her eyes; she'd had almost nothing to eat that day. It wasn't so surprising that she should conjure up the image that had haunted her dreams for far too long.

But the image kept approaching, growing clearer with every step, and she was finally forced to admit that it was real.

Standing up, she wiped her damp palms on her slacks and stepped quickly off the rock. Too quickly; for an instant she lost her balance and began to slip.

James quickened his pace, reaching her in time to keep her from falling. Lifting her off the rock, he set her down but made no effort to release her.

"Looks like I got here just in time," he murmured, his voice deep and unexpectedly gentle.

Alexis stared up at him warily. "I thought I was imagining things when I first saw you."

His clear blue eyes shone with interest. "Does that mean you haven't forgotten about me?"

"Oh, I practically have," she assured him breezily. "After all, it's been quite a while."

"I'm sorry about that. I really had meant to call long before this."

Her silence told him she doubted that very much, and in fact, she was right to do so. Initially, he had intended to let her simmer for a few days, hoping that would dissolve whatever remaining hesitation she felt. But events had gotten away from him, with the result that weeks had gone by before he was able to get in touch.

"Matthew's been in the hospital," he explained quietly. "His appendix almost burst and there were complications."

"Oh, no," Alexis exclaimed, completely forgetting her annoyance. "Is he all right now?"

"Yes, thanks to penicillin, but he had a rough time of it. If Maggie hadn't realized what the problem was, it might have been too late." As he spoke, he shook his head wearily, still unable to get over how close he had come to losing his son. More than anything else that had ever happened to him, that had brought home to him the precariousness of all his plans and redoubled his determination to make them succeed.

"Perhaps I could go to see him," Alexis suggested softly.

"He'd like that," James assured her.

They stared at each other for a moment before she asked, "How did you manage to find me here?"

He smiled faintly. "It wasn't easy. Your secretary is very protective. I had to explain about Matthew before she'd tell me where you were."

Alexis nodded, unsurprised. Margaret was highly discreet, but she also had a soft spot a mile wide for all children and those few men she regarded as worthy of Alexis's interest.

"Are you staying here long?" James asked as they walked together along the beach. The sun was slanting westward and the air had turned slightly colder.

"Until Monday."

"On your own?"

She shot him a surprised glance, wondering if she had imagined the tautness in his voice. "I need some rest."

"Does that mean you're not in the mood for company?"

"Why...no...but aren't you busy?"

He shook his head. "Matthew will be asleep by now; if you don't mind, I'd appreciate your coming over to see him tomorrow. In the meantime, how about having dinner together?"

She thought about that, trying to remember how hurt she had been by his silence. Even knowing there had been a good reason for it, she was still frightened to discover how vulnerable she was with him.

Yet she had never been one to give in to fear. "All right," she said softly, "but since I brought so much food with me anyway, why don't we just eat at my place?"

James wasted no time agreeing. Together they walked down to the beach. About halfway to the cottage, his hand reached out for hers.

Chapter Five

JAMES LEANED BACK against the foot of the couch and savored a rare sense of contentment. He was sitting on the rug in front of the fireplace and its cheerful blaze. Through the nearby window, he could see the moonlight pouring over the water like liquid silver. At his side was a snifter of brandy, the finishing touch to a simple but superb meal of grilled steak, baked potatoes and salad.

Alexis had surprised him yet again. He hadn't expected so beautiful and elegant a woman to be able to fend for herself in a kitchen, any more than he had thought she would have such a warm sense of humor or such great strength of character.

"I suppose you know you're perfect," he murmured, turning his head to look at her as she sat next to him on the rug. Firelight gleamed on the silver-blond hair that fell to her shoulders. Her skin was faintly flushed. The thick fringe of her lashes hid her eyes, but he could tell from her voice that she was gently amused.

"Of course I do. What else should I be?"

"Nothing. I like you just the way you are."

She took a sip of her brandy and put the snifter down again before she said, "Have you ever thought how odd it is that we've become friends?"

"No, can't say I have. Fate has a way of making things work out."

She looked up, meeting his eyes. "Is that what's involved here, fate?"

"I'm beginning to think so."

When had he moved nearer to her, Alexis wondered absently. Or was it she who had moved? His mouth was very close. She stared at it, noting the firm lips and the glimpse of white, even teeth.

Huskily, she murmured, "You have a dimple in your chin."

"I have another one, too."

"W-where...?"

The corners of his mouth turned upward. "Wouldn't you rather find it for yourself?"

A wave of warmth moved through Alexis. The muscles of her upper thighs suddenly felt tight. "Do you think I'm going to?" she asked.

He raised a hand, tangling his fingers in her hair. Cupping the back of her head, he gently held her still. "I'm beginning to hope so."

The touch of his mouth on hers was feather-light at first, so soft that she might have imagined it, except that her imagination could never have conjured up its effect.

Translucent lids fluttered shut over silver-gray eyes as a floodtide of sensation seeped through her. She breathed in sharply, savoring the fragrance of clean wool, sun-warmed skin and strong, virile man. Against the sound of her own heartbeat, her doubts were faint and muted.

The surface of her skin was vividly alive, bathed from the inside by the fire of her own need, mingling with the heat of the large, male body so close to hers. A soft sound broke from her, half sob, half sigh.

James pulled back, fractionally. He was not surprised to find her looking at him warily. "James..." she said slowly, "are you sure you know what we're doing?"

His mouth touched hers again, tasting, savoring, tempting. Huskily, he murmured, "I've been hungry for you for a long time. I don't want to wait any longer."

Neither did she. She wanted this man; beyond reason, beyond even common sense. She had wanted him from the beginning. Even when she had told herself they could be satisfied to be no more than friends, she had really been waiting for the flow of time, and inevitability, to bring them together.

Fate, he had said. She preferred to think of it more as a matter of mutual recognition. They belonged with each other; the time for pretending otherwise was over.

Her fingers trembled only slightly as they reached for the buttons of his shirt.

James knew himself to be a good lover; he had the skill and took the care to bring a woman to the peak of fulfillment before succumbing to it himself. So he was not concerned about his need for Alexis; it was the intensity of that need that startled him and ultimately overcame all other considerations.

Her body was remarkably beautiful, delicately made and pale in the firelight. As they removed each other's clothes, his eyes feasted on her so hotly that she flushed. It was then that he began to suspect her own relative inexperience.

"Aren't you used to being looked at?" he asked softly as he ran his hands up along her rib cage to cup the undersides of her breasts.

"N-no...not like this."

James wasn't really surprised. She was so refined, so cool and fastidious that sex must strike her as a rather messy activity. He would enjoy showing her differently.

Beneath the skilled touch of his hands and mouth, barriers were dissolving. Sensuality long buried was coming to the surface with a vengeance—a new form of power Alexis could not help but revel in.

Power had always attracted her far more than pleasure, with which she had scant familiarity. She had grown up contemplating the power in her father, watching her brother having it bestowed upon him through no merit of his own, witnessing its lack in so many of the women around her. It was something she wanted very much.

James offered power. When she took him into herself, she would take his strength as well as the confidence and determination that fueled him.

But she would also give...more than she could possibly guess.

All sense of being whole and inviolate within herself faded. Not easily, but in jerking fits and starts as she wavered between panic and fascination. She was skittish as a wild filly, yet mesmerized by the gentle caress of his voice and the firm control of his body.

He was beautiful, she realized dazedly, not in any way she had been taught to think of beauty but in a raw, primitive sense that awakened new perceptions. Her hands and eyes ran over the cleanly articulated muscles, the long, hard limbs and warm, smooth skin. Dark hair rough in texture clung to his chest, spreading from just below his collarbone and down in a tapering line along his flat abdomen to his groin. His sex fascinated her. The arching protuberance should have been ugly but somehow wasn't. One of her slender fingers reached out, stroking him experimentally.

He gasped softly but did not pull away. Easing her down on the carpet in front of the fire, he murmured, "Take me into your hand, sweetheart."

She obeyed and his response was immediate. "Fascinating," she whispered against his mouth. "Does this happen often?"

"Not as much as when I was eighteen," he admitted with a laugh, "but I suspect that may change."

"You mean I'm causing you to regress?" Her gray eyes gleamed with pleasure at the thought. She wanted to affect him as deeply as he affected her.

"You're certainly causing something," he gasped as her hand tightened around him, moving gently back and forth along the length of his shaft. "Something tells me you're going to be very good at this."

"You did say I was perfect."

"True…" He moved over her slightly, trapping her hand between them. "But I wouldn't mind seeing you a little mussed."

"That's going to take work."

"I'm very industrious."

"Mmmm…so you are…. That feels so good."

"How about this?"

"Even better…. Are you sure it's legal…?"

"Probably not, but I won't tell if you won't."

"M-mum's the word."

So it was, for quite some time. The only sounds were the sighs and moans of lovemaking intermingled with the crackling of the fire.

James took his time with her. Never had he known so unbridled a sharing of intimacy. Always before, something inside him had held back, or been held back, by the unwillingness to expose too much of himself.

This time he had no choice. Alexis took all of him, leaving him no room for evasion or pretense. The experience shook him to the core, yet he could not resist repeating it. They made love on the rug before the fire, then again in the double bed under the eaves. By dancing flames, by starlight, in the soft wakening of dawn, she was everything to him and he to her.

By the time morning came, each knew they had passed over a line beyond which there was no return. For better or for worse, they were lovers.

Alexis found that she enjoyed her new relationship with James in many unanticipated ways. The lovemaking was wonderful, but so was the affection and camaraderie. She liked coming home from the office to fix dinner for him on the nights when Matthew stayed with Maggie and Anthony. Her housekeeper could have easily prepared the meals, but she preferred to do it herself. The domesticity made a pleasant contrast to her business life and reassured her that professional success did not detract from her femininity.

Maggie and Anthony treated her like an old friend. Their second child, Joseph, Jr., had been born the week the Dodgers lost the World Series to the rival Yankees. Dominick found consolation in being a godparent, sharing the honor with a friend from the war days, Sheila Fletcher, who came east from her home in Chicago for the christening.

About a week later, Alexis and James shared a quiet dinner with Maggie and Anthony at their Long Island home. Over lasagna, salad and crisp, warm bread, talk turned to the recent past and the war that had marked them all.

"I was a perfectly happy sergeant," Anthony said, "until this guy here—" his head slanted toward James "—insisted on trying to turn me into an officer."

"I didn't just try," James protested. "I succeeded. Hell, you even won a medal."

"Don't remind me. The only good thing about that was the dress Maggie wore to the presentation ceremony. Remember?"

"If I said I did, you'd get mad."

"Yeah, I guess so." Anthony laughed reminiscingly. "But that was some evening. All those speeches, and Delia keeping us in stitches..."

"Who's Delia?" Alexis asked, only to break off when she realized that Maggie had just kicked her husband under the table.

"No one," he said quickly. "Just a friend of...uh...ours."

James was paying studious attention to his lasagna. Anthony had developed a sudden fascination with a crack in the wall next to the dinner table. Matthew was busy amusing Tessa. Baby Joseph was asleep in his bassinet. That left Maggie to murmur diplomatically, "It was all such a long time ago, or at least it seems that way. So much has changed since we came home."

Alexis was far too polite to pursue the topic under such circumstances; she willingly let Maggie draw her into a discussion of the fashions that were sweeping the country. Dior's New Look had been seized on by clothing manufacturers who recognized a godsend when they saw it. Through a propaganda barrage in women's magazines and elsewhere, they had promoted the idea that no one with an ounce of refinement would be caught in anything but the newest styles.

Refilling everyone's plate, Maggie said, "When I got out of the hospital, my entire pre-pregnancy wardrobe was out-of-date. I didn't have a thing to wear. Not," she added with a twinkle in her eye, "if I was going to be in step with the rest of the country."

"There was nothing wrong with those other clothes," Anthony insisted. "They looked great on you." Across the table, they shared a private smile. "But then, anything does."

"You can see why I married this guy," Maggie teased. "He's so good for my ego."

"Hey," her husband protested, "I thought it was because I was so romantic."

"Romantic?" Maggie repeated in mock dismay. "Nobody who proposes to a woman when she's wearing bloody surgery greens is romantic."

Alexis laughed at that, but she did not mistake the gentle tolerance in her friends' eyes. Maggie and Anthony shared a love that was as vast as it was enviable.

"They were really meant for each other, weren't they?" Alexis asked a while later as she and James strolled the short distance to his house.

He agreed. "I can't imagine one without the other."

Was that a note of wistfulness in his voice, she wondered. It was hard to believe that he had any interest in marriage, given his experience with his first wife. Even as she recognized a niggling sense of regret in that, she told herself it was undoubtedly for the best. Her career had to come first, especially since it was proving to be even more difficult than she had expected. There were all sorts of problems to deal with, not the least of which was the rapid fear of Communism beginning to affect every aspect of the nation's life.

The House Committee on Un-American Activities had opened hearings into alleged Communist infiltration in the movie business, and the effects had spilled over into the broadcasting industry. It seemed as though any opportunist who could afford a letterhead was suddenly transformed into a superpatriot.

The America Committee was a prime example of this. Originally run out of a warehouse in New York by an ex-clothing salesman and a lawyer who had previously specialized in ambulance chasing, it quickly achieved a reputation for no-holds-barred Red baiting.

Through a newsletter, which was mailed free to top executives nationwide, the Committee spelled out how various businesses were being used as dupes by Moscow. So rousing were its tirades that checks poured in, presumably from good citizens anxious to fight subversion and, not incidentally, to avoid seeing their names on the next list of fellow travelers.

With firm financial backing secured, the Committee moved to expand its services. An ambitious project was begun to assure that the employees of all major organizations were free of leftist taint.

"I think you'd better look at this," Margaret said when she brought the letter to Alexis. Her normally composed features were rigid with distaste. She waited while the younger woman quickly scanned the neatly typed paragraphs.

Alexis's eyes were dark when she looked up. "They can't be serious?"

"I'm afraid they are," her secretary said softly. "I've heard that similar letters have been received by all divisions of UBC, as well as the other networks."

"They want us to supply background information on all our employees," Alexis read disbelievingly. "Education, travel, political affiliations, magazine subscriptions. . .*magazine subscriptions*?"

"Those are the areas they look at when they investigate someone for Communist sympathies."

"Well, they aren't investigating anything here," Alexis insisted. She let the letter drop with disgust. "I'll just ignore it."

Margaret was silent for a moment before she said hesitantly, "I'm not sure you can. From what I've heard, the other divisions of UBC have been told to cooperate."

"By whom?"

"Mr. Graham."

Alexis's mouth tightened. She couldn't claim to be surprised by this news, but it nonetheless distressed her. "I suppose I'll have to think about how best to handle this," she said reluctantly. "There has to be a better way than just giving in."

Margaret nodded, though her eyes showed no real hope that an alternative could be found. She left the office quietly, shutting the door behind her.

Alexis read the letter again and stared out the window for a while, trying to come up with a plan that would protect her staff from both the Committee and her brother. She briefly considered going to her father but put that possibility aside when she realized that the senior Brockton was no doubt in full sympathy with his son's actions.

Which left her where? To provide the information was unthinkable, yet to refuse to do so would invite interference in her division so great as to threaten everything she had achieved.

Later that evening she was still pondering what to do as she prepared dinner for James. A Billie Holliday record was playing in the background; the steaks were under the broiler, and she was breaking up the lettuce for a salad while he mixed drinks.

Handing her a martini, James dropped a kiss on the nape of her neck and asked, "Tough day?"

She smiled faintly. "How did you guess?"

He touched a light finger to the corner of her mouth. "There's a tiny pulse beating here. That happens when you're tense."

The extent of his knowledge about her made her uncomfortable. "It was nothing," she insisted, turning away from him. "How was your day?"

"About the usual. Three major crises, several minor ones, a two-hour lunch that should have been a fifteen-minute phone call. Typical."

He didn't seem to mind. In fact, he appeared to be in very good humor. So much so that over the steak and salad, she finally asked him what was uppermost on her mind.

"Have you ever heard of the America Committee?"

James put down his fork. "Of them and from them. They sent a questionnaire about our employees."

"I got it, too. My first instinct was to ignore it."

"But you aren't going to?"

"No," she admitted reluctantly. "Graham has instructed all the other divisions to cooperate with the Committee, so I'm going to have to find some way around that."

"Why don't you do what I did?" he asked.

"What's that?"

"Lie."

Alexis's eyes widened. She pushed back in her chair and stared at him. "What are you talking about?"

"It's simple. They sent a questionnaire asking for all sorts of information about employees, right?" Without taking her eyes from him, she nodded. "They're looking for Communist affiliations," he went on, "no matter how remote or far-fetched. Right?"

"Yes...but what has that got to do with lying?"

"So I just filled it in with any old crap. Fact is, it was kind of fun."

"I don't understand. . ."

"I made it all up. With the employees' cooperation, of course." He grinned broadly. "We had a hell of a time last week, sitting around after work, dreaming up answers to their questions. They want to know about education, so we told them that one guy had never gotten farther than P.S. 58 and another had been a Rhodes scholar. Then, on political affiliations, we made half the staff Democratic and the other half Republican. We drew straws to pick who was which. But it was the part about magazine subscriptions where we really had fun. Ever hear of the *Barbershop Quartet Monthly* or the *Hat Collector's Newsletter*?"

"N-no. . ."

"I've got guys working for me who apparently read those faithfully."

"So it was all a big joke to you," Alexis said. "I don't see it that way. This is serious business."

James shrugged unconcernedly. "Only if we let it be. This 'Red menace' will fade away after a while. It's just a phase we're going through."

"You can't take it so lightly," Alexis insisted. "Don't you realize that people's lives are being destroyed because they've been labeled Communists?"

"I'm sorry about that," James said quietly, "but people suffer for all sorts of reasons, most of them stupid."

"But there's a principle involved," Alexis protested. "The right to privacy and protection under the Constitution. How can you just cooperate with them?"

"I didn't cooperate. I beat them at their own game."

"Are you sure? They'll find out you lied and come after you with a vengeance."

"Maybe," he acknowledged, "but witch-hunters tend to take themselves very seriously. They'd never suspect that someone would make a joke out of them. By the time they do, chances are this craziness will have run its course."

She was silent then, partly because she could think of nothing to say, but also because she was having a hard time coming to terms with his concept of morality. Or perhaps *expediency* was a better term.

While she had to admire the way he had turned a crisis into a pratfall, she couldn't banish the uneasy feeling that something about his tactics was wrong.

"James," she murmured later that night as they lay in bed together after making love, "about those questionnaires. Did you consider refusing to fill them out?"

"No," he said, without opening his eyes. "That would have been tantamount to cutting IBS's collective throat."

"But even to give the appearance of going along with the Committee encourages them to continue their attacks."

He sighed and turned over to face her. "What do you want me to say, Alexis? That I should have thrown away everything I'm working for because of some noble ideal?"

"You make it sound foolish, but someone has to stand up to them."

"Why? They'll go away after a while on their own."

"Like the Nazis did, or the Fascists?"

His blue eyes flashed impatiently in the darkness. "You're blowing this all out of proportion. Get a little perspective on the issue and you'll understand what's happening."

"The issue," she bit out, "is the same one plenty of men like you died for: freedom."

"Don't wave the flag at me," James snapped. "I shed my share of blood for it while good old boys like your brother were sitting pretty behind some stateside desk. Now I want something better, and I'll be damned if I'll let some bunch of Communist-hunting fruitcakes take it away from me."

The implacability of his tone stung her. He spoke as coldly as though they were adversaries sitting at opposite sides of a meeting table instead of lovers lying together in the aftermath of intimacy.

Her silence was a response in itself. After several strained moments, James propped himself up on an elbow and gazed down at her regretfully. "I'm sorry, Alexis. I shouldn't have spoken to you like that."

"No," she murmured, "you shouldn't have."

"It's just that...I don't like what I did any more than you do. It wasn't an easy decision to make. I only did it because I couldn't stand to see everything I've worked for threatened by something so crazy."

Alexis thought about the slighting reference Graham had made to people struggling to find some measure of safety, and how she had reminded him what those same people had suffered through economic collapse and worldwide bloodshed. She had thought herself better than him because she could empathize with others from far less privileged backgrounds. But now she wondered if that was true.

In the abstract, it was fine to say that survivors of the Depression and World War II naturally wanted to find some measure of security for themselves and their children. But when it came to accepting the behavior that led to individuals close to her, she had a problem.

"I understand why you did it," she said slowly. "I'd hate to lose everything I've worked for, too."

"Then, do the same thing," he suggested as he drew her closer, his long fingers gently stroking her hair.

"I can't.... For one thing, UBC is simply too visible. We can't get away with the tactics a smaller outfit can use. Besides, I have a feeling that Graham knew I'd get my back up over this and he'll be watching very carefully to see how I react."

James frowned in the darkness, wishing there was something he could do to help her with her brother. Short of dropping him off a cliff, nothing occurred to him. "Perhaps you can stall them...."

"Maybe...I'll certainly have to try." She snuggled closer, drawing strength from the nearness of his body, and drifted to sleep wondering when life had become so complicated.

"I SUPPOSE YOU'RE ALL WONDERING why I called you here today," Alexis said with a wan smile.

The assembled staff of the television division chuckled weakly. They were all gathered in a conference room behind the sound stage, everyone from the youngest gofer to the most senior director. Only the on-camera talent was absent. Since they all had separate contracts with UBC, Alexis took the view that they were not, strictly speaking, employees and therefore not included in the Committee's request.

Propped up on the edge of the table cluttered with empty cardboard containers of coffee and crumpled sandwich bags, she said softly, "I'm afraid I have some bad news. As some of you may have heard, the America Committee is requesting information on the backgrounds of our employees."

A stir ran through the two dozen or so people. Several appeared deliberately unconcerned, but the rest looked worried. "I'm going to be frank with you," Alexis went on, "I don't want to provide the information. I think it's an invasion of privacy and nobody's business anyway. But company policy is to cooperate.''

She paused for a moment, letting these words sink in, before she continued. ''So copies of the Committee questionnaire will be handed out. I'd like you to look it over carefully, and then I'll be scheduling appointments to discuss your responses with each of you.''

''What's there to discuss?'' a bland-faced sound engineer asked. ''If a guy's got nothing to hide, there's no problem.''

''It's not that simple,'' Alexis corrected quietly. ''I'm not going to turn this into a political discussion, but I will say that from what I've seen of the Committee's investigations so far, they aren't conducted with any degree of care. Instead, they seem characterized by innuendo and other smear tactics. I don't want any of my staff to fall victim to that.''

The engineer shrugged dismissively, accepting his copy and left. Several others did the same. But the rest remained, anxious to be reassured. ''We'll do the best we can,'' Alexis promised, wishing that she could say more. Her inability to control the situation distressed her greatly. She still wished she could simply have thrown away the questionnaire, but her meeting with Graham had made it clear that would be extremely foolhardy.

''No one can be exempt from company policy,'' he had explained ponderously. ''It would set a very poor example if a Brockton were given special privileges not available to the other division executives. I'm sure you agree with that.''

Alexis refused to be maneuvered into agreeing with him about anything. Instead, she said, ''The policy is wrong. It denies people due process.''

Her brother had smiled tolerantly. "We're not talking about any sort of legal proceeding. All the Committee wants to know is what sort of people are in sensitive positions, including in the communications industry. It's simply a survey."

"Are you saying that no one will be fired or otherwise suffer because of the answers he gives?" she asked, making no effort to hide her disbelief.

"I'm saying that we all have a responsibility to protect our country from the Communist menace. We've been very naive up to this point, and that has to end."

"There has to be room for different opinions," she protested even as the futility of her position sank in on her. Graham wore his self-righteousness like a shield; there was no piercing it. She would simply have to do the best she could to protect her staff and her principles.

At first, that seemed to be easier than she had feared. The interviews with the employees went very well. Since she had taken the trouble to speak with each alone, and since they already knew and trusted her, those who had any concerns about their pasts were willing to air them frankly. Often a small omission, a minor rewording, a shift of emphasis, was enough to place the individual above suspicion.

Alexis began to feel some measure of confidence in her ability to handle the situation without resorting to James's tactics, which in any case would not have worked for her. But that confidence abruptly disappeared when she came face-to-face with a problem she could not solve.

It began simply enough late on Friday evening, about a week after the questionnaire had arrived, when Margaret stuck her head in her office door and asked to speak to her for a few minutes.

"I thought you'd already left," Alexis said, smiling. She was pleasantly tired, more relaxed than she had been in a while, and she was in the mood for some company.

The older woman sat down gingerly on the edge of a chair across from the desk. Her hands were folded in her lap, the fingers plucking at her blue serge skirt. "It's about the... Committee."

"That's going better than I'd expected. We should wrap it up within the next few days."

"I-I hope so.... The questionnaire is very complicated."

"Not really," Alexis said slowly. Tension was beginning to creep back over her as she got a hint of what might be on Margaret's mind. "We haven't done yours yet, have we?"

"No...and that's what I wanted to talk with you about." Her head shook slightly on the thin stem of her neck. "I'm afraid I may have a problem."

Alexis took a deep breath and leaned back in her chair. Gently, she said, "Perhaps you'd better tell me about it."

"It was all so long ago," Margaret said faintly. "I was only nineteen, trying to find work to help my family. My father and brothers had lost their jobs in the Depression; we'd had to give up our home; it was getting hard just to put food on the table."

Her face tightened as she remembered the anguish of those days, but she went on grimly. "I went to a meeting with a friend of mine. It was held in the union hall. There was a speaker from Citizens for a Fairer America. He talked about how unjust it was that a few people lived in luxury while so many others had trouble feeding their children. What he said made sense, so I joined the group and did some work for them: handing out pamphlets, helping to organize rallies, that sort of thing."

"Surely there was nothing wrong with that..." Alexis ventured.

"I didn't think so at the time," Margaret agreed. With a touch of defiance, she added, "I still don't. But accusations have been made lately that Citizens for a Fairer America was a Communist front group. Some people who belonged have been subpoenaed to testify before the House Committee on Un-American Activities."

A wave of apprehension washed over Alexis. She now understood, all too well, the source of Margaret's fear. It was one thing to leave out small details of one's life to avoid suspicion; it was quite another to deny membership in an organization coming under intense scrutiny. Yet to admit it would be to risk the wrath of the witch-hunters.

"We'll have to come up with a way around this," she said slowly.

"Can we?" Margaret asked, her pale lips barely moving.

"I don't know," Alexis admitted, "but I certainly will try my best." Her eyes flashed angrily. "This is exactly the sort of situation I was concerned about when I told Graham I didn't want to cooperate. People being punished for exercising their freedom of speech and assembly is revolting."

"M-maybe the solution is simply for me to resign," Margaret suggested hesitantly.

"Is that really what you want to do?"

The older woman shook her head. "This is the best job I've ever had, and I'd hate to lose it. But the alternative—" She broke off, her mouth tightly compressed as she fought against tears.

Alexis stepped out from behind the desk and put an arm around her gently. Even as she struggled with her own apprehension, she tried to reassure Margaret. "Don't worry. We'll find a way out. I promise."

At length the older woman seemed somewhat comforted. She left, still shaken and afraid, but at least with a glimmer of hope that the situation might not be beyond redemption.

Alexis wasn't so sure. Despite her promise, she seriously doubted her ability to protect Margaret. All she was certain of was that she would do everything possible. Several days later she filled out the questionnaire without making any mention of the secretary's involvement with Citizens for a Fairer America. That was hardly an ideal solution, but no alternative seemed possible.

At first, it looked as though she might get away with it. The Committee sent out a routine letter acknowledging receipt of the information and then there was silence. Alexis was beginning to relax when she was abruptly summoned to her father's office.

Her visits to the executive floor were generally confined to the main conference room; it had been months since she had last been in Charles Brockton's private domain. As always, the sheer size and luxuriousness of his quarters put her off stride.

She glanced around at the brocade-covered walls, the polished wood floors covered by Oriental carpets, the high ceilings with lavish plaster medallions. A fortune in antiques was crammed into a space larger than many people's houses. Most of the pieces were eighteenth-century British and lookd as though they had once belonged to a prosperous country squire; others were ornate artifacts from the reigns of Louis XV and XVI. Looking at the garish displays of marble and gilt, Alexis thought it possible to understand the origins of the French Revolution simply by seeing what wealth had once been squandered on.

Her attention was drawn back to more immediate problems by the sight of Graham positioned beside her father's massive desk. He was standing while Charles Brockton sat, a ponderous figure in a leather wing chair so large that it seemed to engulf him.

"I didn't realize you would be here," she said to her brother as she smiled coolly in her father's direction.

"I asked him to attend," Charles Brockton said before his son could reply. The coldness of the look he fastened on Alexis made it clear she had done something to provoke his displeasure. "Sit down," he ordered without further explanation.

Reconciled to his arbitrariness, she did as he said, but not without a glimmer of distaste. Even if her father lacked all parental feeling for her, he should at least accord her the courtesy due a hardworking professional whose division was showing an ever-expanding profit for UBC.

Before she could be tempted to mention any of that, Graham said, "There's a matter that needs to be straightened out, Alexis. In all sincerity, I hope we can do it quickly."

An alarm bell went off in Alexis's mind. Graham speaking of sincerity made her instinctively apprehensive. Cautiously, she asked, "What's this about?"

His answer was to pick up a sheaf of papers on his father's desk and regard them somberly, as though he were a judge examining a particularly indicting piece of evidence.

"I'm referring to the report you prepared for the America Committee. There's a very significant omission, one so serious that I can't understand how you could have let it happen."

The sinking feeling that gripped her left no doubt about what he was referring to. Rather than allow herself to be played with like a mouse trapped by a cat, she decided to take the offensive. "You know that I objected to filling out that questionnaire in the first place, but I did so because it was company policy. As far as I'm concerned, it's over and done with. I have far more important matters to occupy my time and attention."

"Nothing is more important than the safety of this country," her father snapped. Resting his hands flat on his desk, he pushed himself to his feet and glared at her. "You lied about Margaret Goodman, either that or you let her pull the wool over your eyes. That woman was a member of Citizens for a Fairer America, nothing but a front for the Kremlin. For all we know, she's still working for them."

"Do you hear what you're saying?" Alexis demanded, caution vanishing before the white heat of her anger. "Margaret has been with UBC for eighteen years. She's as loyal an employee as anyone could hope for. The idea that she could possibly do anything to harm us, much less her country, is ludicrous."

Graham smiled sadly and shook his head. "I'm afraid you're too innocent, Alexis, and too trusting. The Communists depend on nondescript, seemingly honest people to undermine our institutions. And they depend on dupes like you to let them get away with it."

His voice stiffened on the last words, making it clear that the gloves were off. That was fine with Alexis. The thoroughbred's temper she generally managed to keep so carefully restrained was bursting free.

"Of all the hypocritical, self-serving things to say! You don't give a damn about this country, and you don't care any more about this company than how much money it puts in your pocket. You're willing to destroy a decent, honorable woman who's never done you any harm simply to get at me."

"You're taking this far too personally," Graham insisted patronizingly. "I am simply questioning your ability to manage a division of this network when you can't get the truth from one employee.''

"That's it in a nutshell," Charles Brockton agreed. His smoothly barbered cheeks glowed with righteous displeasure as he contemplated the disappointment that was his daughter. "I trusted you, Alexis. Against my better judgment, I took you into the company and let you indulge your interest in television.''

"Indulge?"

"Despite the fact that it took vital funds away from the other divisions," he went on, ignoring her. "I kept telling myself that it didn't matter that you were a woman; you were also a Brockton and you would be up to the job." His voice dropped several octaves. "Sadly, I was wrong.''

Alexis's hands gripped the arms of her chair as she stared from him to her brother. The eyes of both were hooded and expressionless. Slowly, she stood. "Does that mean you're firing me?''

A flicker of something—surprise at her directness; perhaps even a shred of admiration—darted across her father's face before it instantly went blank again. "Of course not. You've simply been trying to handle too much responsibility. Henceforth, Graham will head the television division and you will report to him.''

Near to choking on the mere thought of that, Alexis murmured, "What about Margaret?''

"Her employment had already been terminated," Graham interjected smoothly. "What happens to her now is not our concern.''

A sick feeling of helplessness gripped Alexis. In the face of such carefully engineered injustice, she was powerless. Yet she still had to at least try to set things right. "You have no right to do that. It's shameful."

Her brother shrugged dismissively. "Your views on the subject are already quite clear; they don't need repeating. Just remember that as an employee of UBC, you will be expected to conform to all corporate policy *to the letter*."

Alexis had no difficulty interpreting that: He would be watching her like a hawk, and the moment she did anything that he could find a reason to disapprove of, he would have her head.

A glance at her father left no doubt that he approved of what Graham was saying. She swallowed tightly against the bitterness of abandonment and betrayal spreading over her and held her back rigidly straight as she walked away.

Chapter Six

ALEXIS DID NOT WANT to be alone that night. She knew that she would go over the conversation with her father and brother again and again, the hurt growing every time she thought of it. Instead, she needed bright lights, music and the comfort of other people. None of which was hard to find in a city that never slept. She knew of several parties she could attend, where her last-minute presence would be warmly welcomed. But only one in particular appealed to her.

Stopping by her apartment long enough to change into a beaded silver evening gown cut to lovingly hug her curves, she took a cab uptown to Harlem. The stretch of Lenox Avenue in front of the Plantation Club—heir to the renowned Cotton Club—was crowded with wide-eyed tourists and carefully blasé regulars, all come to hear some of the best jazz outside of New Orleans and to watch the floor show.

Making her way through the press of people waiting to get inside, she murmured a name to the maitre d'. His smile flashed brightly against the darkness of his skin. With the slightest movement of his hand, he turned her over to an assistant, who escorted her through the maze of tables toward a party already in progress.

James saw her first and stood up. "Alexis...I didn't realize you planned to join us." He had told her about the party but hadn't expected her to attend.

"That's not much of a greeting." Beaming a smile at the other occupants of the table, she slipped into a chair James automatically held out for her. "I just felt like a little company and I remembered you'd all be up here tonight."

"It's great you could make it," Anthony said. He raised a hand and beckoned a waiter, requesting another champagne glass.

"That's a lovely dress," Maggie added. Her eyes were slightly puzzled, but her smile was warm.

When her glass was filled, Alexis raised it in a toast. "Here's to IBS's first anniversary on the air. May there be many more."

They all drank to that, though James only sipped. He put his glass down and leaned closer to her. "It's very nice of you to say, but there are some other people at UBC who might not appreciate the sentiment." He glanced around the room, trying to see if there was anyone on hand likely to report her presence to her father or brother.

"So what?" Alexis asked. She was feeling pleasantly reckless, willing to forget her problems and concentrate on having a good time. Taking another sip of champagne, she shrugged. "Who cares what a couple of hypocrites think?"

Anthony and Maggie exchanged a worried look but said nothing. James stared at her for a moment, his blue eyes narrowing, then reached over and touched her hand. "What's wrong, honey?"

He was normally so sparing in his use of endearments that she had to swallow suddenly against the tightness in her throat. "Nothing. We're here to celebrate, right? So let's do it."

James would have liked to pursue the subject, but not in front of Anthony and Maggie. Though he didn't doubt that his friends would understand, he didn't want to do anything to spoil their fun.

For several hours they enjoyed the excellent jazz and the steady flow of champagne. Maggie drank little, since she was nursing, but she still managed to match Anthony's high spirits.

Alexis was glad they were both having a good time, but she was also relieved when the evening at last came to an end and she left with James. Matthew was staying with Tessa and Joe, Jr., in Brooklyn with the elder Garganos, so they were free to go to her apartment.

Once there, James wasted no time getting to the heart of the matter. He rejected her suggestion of a brandy and said, "Tell me what's going on, Alexis. Something very serious has obviously happened."

Her mouth twisted in what might have been a smile but wasn't. "I got my blinkers ripped off, that's all."

He stared at her for a moment before muttering an imprecation under his breath. "It's Graham, isn't it?"

"Got it on one. Dear, sweet brother set me up to take a fall."

"The America Committee?"

She pretended to widen her eyes in awe. "Are you always so smart, or have I just been incredibly dumb?" Her voice broke and she looked away quickly.

James crossed the room in a couple of strides to take her by the shoulders. "Alexis...whatever's gone wrong, tell me. We'll face it together."

How she wished they could. Since realizing the full extent of her brother's betrayal and her father's complicity, she had felt utterly alone and lost. Even though she had given up years ago the hope of being loved by her family, to know how little they really thought of her hurt deeply.

Her head dropped as she said, "I got caught trying to protect an employee by omitting sensitive information about her from the questionnaire. Although I can't be absolutely sure, I suspect that Graham knew all along what would happen and used it to get control of the television division away from me.''

''And has he?''

''As of this afternoon, I officially report to him.''

James's mouth tightened. He cupped the back of her head and gently urged it against his shoulder. Holding her close, he said, ''Dammit, I wish there was something I could do.''

With her face buried in his chest, she managed a weak grin. ''Maybe you could discover I was adopted. Right now, being a Brockton doesn't feel so great.''

''We can't choose our families,'' he reminded her softly. With an arm around her waist, he guided her over to the couch and sat down beside her. It was cool in the room; he reached for the afghan lying folded on an ottoman and spread it over her.

''That's nice,'' Alexis murmured as she closed her eyes. A tremulous sense of comfort was beginning to spread over her. Cradled in James's arms, reassured by his strength and care, the pain she had been feeling since that afternoon eased a little.

But not entirely. She still had to face the reality of what had happened. With Graham in control of what had been her division, she didn't see how it would be possible for her to stay on. Much as she hated to give him what he undoubtedly wanted, she saw no alternative but to leave.

''It's really a shame,'' she murmured tiredly.

''What's that?'' James asked.

''I suppose I'll have to look for a new job.''

His arms tightened around her as his body stiffened. ''You mean you're leaving UBC?''

''I don't have any choice. Graham isn't about to share control with anyone. If I try to stay, he'll make my life miserable.'' Though she didn't underestimate the difficulties of finding a new position for herself, she was reasonably sure that she would be successful. All three of UBC's rival networks were now avidly involved in television, as were several independent broadcasting groups such as IBS. With her solid credentials and reputation for getting things done, she stood a good chance of being hired without too great a delay.

But that wouldn't be the same as owning part of the business. Being simply an employee would require quite an adjustment. Unless... Sitting up slightly, she cast a cautious look at James. "Didn't you tell me a few months ago that IBS is looking for investors?"

"Yes, of course; we need all the money we can get to expand. But what has that got to do with—" He broke off, eyeing her warily. "Alexis, if you're thinking what I think you are, it's not a good idea."

"Why not?"

"Because I don't believe that people who are as close to each other as we are should try to work together."

"You and Anthony are close."

"That's entirely different, as you well know. I'm really sorry about what's happened and I'll do anything I can to help, but let's not jump from one problem to another even more severe."

Stung by his failure to appreciate what she thought would be the perfect solution, she withdrew from him, sitting up straighter and wrapping the afghan around herself. "You're really convinced that our working together would be a mistake?"

"Yes, I am." He ran a hand through his thick black hair impatiently. "We're very much alike in certain ways. Both of us like to be in control. With Anthony, it's easy to avoid stepping on each other's toes. He runs the technical side and I take care of the creative. But that's where you'd want to be involved, isn't it?''

"That's what I've always done at UBC," she said tautly. "And I happen to be very good at it. IBS does all right in the daytime, when you don't have any real competition, but you still can't cut it against the networks at night. I could change that."

"How?" he demanded, his lean cheeks flushing slightly at the mention of his difficulty in getting the all-important evening audience that advertisers wanted so much. It was a sore point with him, so much so that he reacted far more harshly than he should have. "By bringing in more cigar-chomping comedians with dusty vaudeville acts or two-bit musicians who barely know which side of a French horn to blow through? No, thanks."

Alexis's gray eyes, normally so cool, glittered dangerously. She took great pride in the programs she had created for UBC and would not let anyone disparage them with impunity. Her chin rose a notch as she glared down her nose at him. "I smell sour grapes."

James stared at her as though he thought he had heard wrong. Did she really think he was being petty? Slowly, the big hand resting on his knee clenched. "You've had a very upsetting day..."

"Not so upsetting that it's rendered me incapable of understanding what you mean. You think my shows are trash and you don't want to work with me." A pulse beat in the corner of her mouth. She was too tired for patience, too disillusioned for hope. "All right; if that's the way you feel, there's nothing I can do about it. Nothing I *would* do. You'd better leave."

"Alexis...let's talk about this. I spoke too harshly, but I only want to protect what we have."

Her eyes met his challengingly. "Just what is it we have, James? You spend a couple of nights a week here. I feed you and sleep with you. Outside these four walls, we don't see each other except when Matthew is staying over at Maggie and Anthony's, or somewhere like that. If we pass each other on the street, we barely nod."

"Because we're competitors! If our personal relationship became known, you'd be hurt by it."

"I've already been hurt! By being forced out of UBC. The reason for keeping us a secret is gone. We don't have to do it anymore."

"And that's fine. I've gotten sick and tired of it anyway. But that doesn't mean we should work together."

"So you want everything to go on as it has been, with the only difference being that we'll be able to be seen together?"

"That's a big difference," he insisted, wondering why she didn't realize it. Couldn't she be happy about the break they had gotten thanks to Graham's stupidity? "There will be a lot less pressure on us."

"Maybe it was the pressure that was keeping us together," she said woodenly.

"What the hell does that mean?"

Alexis looked at him sadly, as much surprised by her words as he was. "I'm not sure, exactly. But I do know that something's wrong between us. We've been lovers for almost a year, yet we never talk about the future, never make any plans together. And now, when we finally get the chance to do that, to really share our lives, you don't want to."

He stared at her as though he were about to deny the fairness of her charge, but he did not. Instead, a shield seemed to drop into place between them, and she sensed his withdrawal as though it were her own.

"I'm sorry you feel that way," he said tonelessly. "You've never given any indication that you were unhappy before."

"I didn't think about it," she admitted, unable to completely suppress a twinge of sympathy for him. The need to give comfort was so instinctive that it was all but impossible to shut off. But she had taken her stand, and she meant to stick to it. Shivering slightly, she went on. "I just kept going from day to day, absorbing myself in work and telling myself that I didn't want anything more than I already had. What happened today forced me to realize how I had been deluding myself. I do want more. I *need* more."

"And it seems that I can't give it to you," he said slowly, resignation creeping into his eyes. He cared deeply for her, in his own way, but he also resented the sudden challenge she presented. He felt that her failure to know herself better had somehow been a failure in her responsibility to him.

There was really nothing more to say. James left shortly thereafter. Alexis remained on the couch for a long time, thinking about what had happened. Her provoking of the confrontation bewildered her. What had made her decide that this was the time to have it out with him?

Only slowly did the answer come, and brought with it tears. In the soft gray light before dawn, she cried for the child who had never known the love of parents or brother, who had tried every way she knew to earn it, including shaping herself into a form she thought they would approve.

But it hadn't been enough. They had seen her strength and ability not as a tribute to them but as a threat. And they had acted as one to break her.

The hunger for love, approval, security, had boiled out of her that night. She had turned to James, hoping he would be able to provide it all. And instead, she had found what she should have expected to encounter; he was burdened by his own fears and disappointments that prevented him from truly committing himself to another person.

In the aftermath of two such profound upheavals in her life within a single day, a welcome numbness settled over her. Later the raw pain of loss would have to be coped with, but for the moment she could think only of finding some safe place in which to lick her wounds.

Stalwartly, she told herself that she was fully capable of facing the world on her own, needing no one to help her. But Winston Harcourt had a different idea. Barely had she arrived at the office the next day—quite a bit later than usual because of her sleepless night and the effort needed to appear more or less normal—than he slouched in with a quiet smile and a cup of coffee, as though he had been waiting for her.

"I thought you might be able to use this."

She nodded and took it gratefully. The hot, sweet liquid revived her somewhat and made her feel at least a little better able to cope with what lay ahead. "I suppose they'll send someone up from the typing pool to replace Margaret," she murmured.

Winston perched his lanky frame on the corner of her desk and took a sip of his own coffee before replying. "I've got some contacts that might be able to help her find a new job."

Alexis shot him a grateful look. "Good. I'll be calling her this morning with some suggestions of my own. Thank God there are still some people willing to fight this insanity."

"Margaret should be all right," Winston assured her. "I'm far more concerned about you. Got any plans?"

Despite herself, she smiled. "What makes you think I won't be staying?"

"Not a chance," he said flatly. "Brother Graham is going to be left with his hands full, which is exactly what he deserves.

I figure it won't take him more than a month or two to start running this network into the ground. When that happens, I don't plan to be around.''

Alexis's tapered eyebrows rose in surprise. ''You're quitting?''

''My contract's up for renewal in three weeks. I've already told my agent not to accept any offer from UBC.''

''It won't be hard to find an alternative. You're the best in the business.''

''Thanks to you. I haven't forgotten who gave me my first shot at this.''

She shrugged lightly. ''It's the future I've got to be thinking about, not the past. I'd better get on the phone to some of my own contacts and see about lining up a new job.''

Winston hesitated for a moment. His warm hazel eyes looked at her candidly, missing nothing of the pallor beneath the artfully applied makeup or of the strength in the slender body covered by the elegant wool suit. Quietly, he said, ''I've got a suggestion that might help. Neither of us buys the idea that television news will never be anything more than a fifteen-minute recital of the headlines with a few pictures thrown in, right?''

She nodded slowly, wondering what he was leading up to.

''You've run the news department ever since creating it, functioning essentially as a news director. Isn't that so?'' he went on.

''I suppose, but I've also done lots of other programming.''

''That's why you're perfect for what I have in mind. You could sell the executives of another network on the idea of expanding news coverage by using proven programming techniques. You could bring in more personalities, more action, more of everything that the advertisers want. But at the same time, I trust you not to sacrifice journalistic credibility.''

Alexis frowned thoughtfully. ''You mean...we'd offer ourselves as a team to another network? To do an expanded news show unlike anything that's currently on the air?''

''That's it.'' Excitedly, he said, ''Some very smart people think a great deal will be happening in the next few years, at home and abroad. If that turns out to be right, we're going to be involved, whether we want to be or not. There will be a greater than ever demand for news, and television should be able to supply it.''

''I suppose...but, Winston, are you certain you want to link your fortunes to mine? We both know how hard it is for a woman to get a management job in this or any other industry. Plus there is the fact that I'm a Brockton; my father and brother have made a lot of enemies. I may find myself being tarred with guilt by association.''

''That won't happen,'' he insisted confidently. ''Everyone in the business knows how hard you've worked and how much you've accomplished in the past few years. All they're going to think is that your family deserves to lose you.'' He grinned boyishly, the very picture of eagerness. ''So what do you say?''

Despite herself, Alexis laughed. Being with Winston always made her feel good. He was a calm, reassuring presence in her life, never pressing her to give more of herself than she could but always making it clear that he had the highest regard for her. He was also the only man of her acquaintance who she could truly say had shown wholehearted approval of her career. James had generally avoided mentioning it, supposedly because they were business competitors. But in the aftermath of his refusal to work with her, Alexis had to wonder how much he had resented her success.

Determined not to let thoughts of him intrude, she deliberately gave Winston a dazzling smile. ''I realize it's early yet, but what do you say we discuss this over lunch? I know the quaintest little bistro on the East Side.''

A flirtatious Alexis was irresistible, not that Winston would even have thought of refusing. He had bided his time patiently, waiting for an opportunity to turn their professional relationship into a personal one. With her departure from UBC—and the significant omission of any mention of her going to IBS—he thought he might finally have his opportunity.

James thought so, too. He had been aware of Winston's true interest in Alexis and had chafed at the other man escorting her to social occasions. But he had never before felt the full weight of jealousy until he learned that she and the newscaster were in negotiation with CBS for a package deal that would have them working together even more closely than before.

Several weeks had passed since the evening at the Plantation Club and the confrontation in her apartment. He had picked up the phone a dozen times to call her, but he had always put it down again, not knowing what to say.

He told himself that he would forget about her. She was only a woman, after all, and he had long ago vowed to never again let one of them get her hooks into him. As Alexis herself had said, their relationship had been casual.

Except that he could remember nothing casual about the fervency of their lovemaking, which had grown even more intense and satisfying over time. Nor could he casually dismiss the many evenings when he had relaxed in her company, warmed as much by her intelligence and humor as by her beauty.

And then there was Matthew to consider. His son was eight years old, an age when feelings were particularly vulnerable. Though he showed his less than most children, it was clear that Alexis's sudden diappearance from his life had left the little boy baffled. James had tried to explain it to him, but he knew he had failed. How could he have hoped to do otherwise when he couldn't explain it to himself?

The plain fact of the matter was that he missed her. Her absence was a gnawing ache at the center of his being. Each morning he woke knowing that he had dreamed of her and hoping that this would be the day his loneliness would begin to ease. It never was. As day followed day, his need for her grew until it finally began to block out all other considerations, even injured pride and self-preservation.

And with the acknowledgement of that need came jealousy.

He had never known it before, at least not in such a stark, unrelenting form. Growing up in Hell's Kitchen, he had wished for the things that other, more fortunate people had, but he was always almost arrogantly confident of his ability to get them for himself. In the war, he had occasionally envied those who stayed safe behind the lines, but the envy was always tempered with contempt.

Only now did he know the fierce, gut-wrenching sense of possessiveness and the need to protect what he considered exclusively his own.

The irony of his situation did not escape him; he had had the opportunity to bind Alexis to him and had thrown it away. He had, to all intents and purposes, presented her to Winston Harcourt on a silver platter.

In his calmer moments, he had to admire the other man's strategy. Harcourt had waited patiently, never pressuring Alexis, seemingly content to be the understanding friend and colleague. Which didn't mean his feelings weren't perfectly sincere. He seemed genuinely to want what was best for her. That was fine with James, except that he was damned if he'd let another man provide it.

At the end of the fourth week of their separation, as spring was settling over the city, James decided that it was time to show Harcourt the error of his ways. He dusted off his confidence, mustered his courage, and went looking for Alexis.

She was not easy to find. With the CBS negotiations at a particularly sensitive stage, she had prudently withdrawn from view. At first, he feared she might have gone off with Harcourt, and had difficulty controlling his rage at the mere thought of that. He had Margaret to thank for his relief at discovering that she had gone out to the beach house again.

After tracking down the secretary at her new job with an independent radio station, he finally coaxed her into revealing Alexis's whereabouts. Margaret was intensely protective of her former employer because of Alexis's attempts to shield her and her all-out effort to find her work. She wasn't about to do anything to harm her.

"We just had a little misunderstanding," James had insisted. "You know how stubborn Alexis can be. Unfortunately, I'm the same way. The whole thing got blown completely out of proportion."

"Well...I suppose it would be all right," Margaret ventured. Despite everything she had been through, she was an unrepentant romantic in love with happy endings.

Once he knew her whereabouts, James wasted no time. He left the station and drove out to the beach house. Finding that Alexis had gone out, he let himself in through a back door. Seated in the living room where they had made love for the first time, he relived those memories as he waited for her to return.

She did so shortly after dark. He hadn't bothered to turn on a light, and the discovery of a large, shadowy figure seated on her couch brought a strangled scream from her.

James was instantly on his feet, reaching out to her. "Hey, I'm sorry; I didn't mean to scare you."

"Well, you did!" she gasped, her hand slowly coming away from her throat. She stepped back from the door shakily and stared at him. "What are you doing here?"

Hardly the affectionate greeting he had been hoping for, but then, he had only himself to blame for that. "I wanted to talk with you," he said gently. "Somewhere we wouldn't be disturbed."

With the easing of her initial fright, Alexis began to really take in the fact of his presence. He looked thinner than she remembered, the lines of his face more harshly drawn. The last month had apparently been no easier on him than on her; she could only hope the reason was the same.

"I've missed you," he said, as though reading her thoughts. "Nothing's been good lately."

She knew exactly how that felt. Though negotiations with CBS were proceeding toward what promised to be a successful conclusion, life had taken on a curious flatness. She found it impossible to get enthused about either her prospects for an exciting new job or her relationship with Winston.

A twinge of guilt stabbed through her at the thought of Winston. He wanted more than she could give; that was becoming increasingly evident with each passing day. She almost wished that he would run out of patience with her, as James would inevitably have done by now.

Instead, Winston was a paragon of reason and tolerance. He deserved someone far better than herself, and at the earliest possible opportunity she intended to find such a person.

But first she had to cope with herself. . .and with James.

"W-what did you want to talk with me about?" she asked as she stepped carefully around him and went to stand in front of the fireplace. The ashes in it were cold, but it wasn't difficult for her to remember how bright the flames had once been.

James shoved his hands in the pockets of his slacks and followed her. He stood awkwardly, consumed by the thought that what he said in the next few minutes would determine his chance of happiness for years to come, perhaps forever.

"I've reconsidered about your buying into IBS," he said slowly. "I think it's a good idea after all. But more than that, I think. . .we should get married."

Alexis looked at him blankly, as though he had suddenly taken to speaking Greek. She had understood the first part of what he said, and knew a moment's flutter of hope at it. But then. . . "M-married. . .?"

"That's right. Plenty of people do it. We could be very happy."

"You told me you never wanted to get married again."

"I never said that in so many words," he protested, wondering frantically if he had.

"You certainly gave the impression that your ex-wife had soured you forever on marriage."

She sat down hastily on the couch where he joined her. They kept the width of a cushion between them. James managed a wry grin, though he was feeling anything but amused. Being so close to her stirred needs he had kept rigidly suppressed for weeks now. He shifted uncomfortably on the couch. "Don't you believe a man can change?"

"I suppose. . .but frankly, it seems almost too good to be true."

"Does that mean you like the idea?" he asked quickly.

"I...don't know.... It's very serious." The possibility of marriage to him thrilled her, but it also made her very wary. She did not have to be told that they would both be taking a risk.

"All good things in life are serious," James insisted, moving a little closer to her. His blue eyes were tender, and he looked very confident. "But we have a much better chance at happiness together than most people. After all, we know each other very well and we share a great many interests."

That was true, yet it was also an oversimplification. She knew him as a lover, not as a husband. Their shared interests were mainly professional; he had already voiced his doubts about their ability to work together.

And yet...to reject what he offered would be to reject a very special part of herself, the part she was only beginning to come to terms with.

"Do you really think," she began tentatively, "that we could make it together?"

"Yes, I do." The distance between them lessened farther. He put his arm around her shoulders and, despite the slight stiffness of her body, drew her closer. "Trust me, Alexis. When I hurt you, I hurt myself doubly. That's a lesson I've learned for all time. We belong together."

She wanted so badly to believe him. Her need for comfort and security was becoming unbearable. His seductive voice, the warmth of his breath on her cheek, the nearness of his hard body, all combined to drown out her doubts. Only one thought remained clear in her mind: With him she would have strength and safety.

Tilting her head back, she met the urgent demand of his mouth with her own and let that be her answer.

Chapter Seven

ALEXIS AND JAMES WERE MARRIED on Friday, May 7, 1948.
The weather was fair and slightly cool, with temperatures
hovering around fifty degrees. The ceremony took place at the
Church of Transfiguration in Murray Hill. Dubbed "the little church around the corner" in recognition of its nineteenth-
century role as a sanctuary for those society disdained, it was
the scene of more weddings than any other church in the city.

Marriages were performed there with a minimum of fuss;
the obliging clergy asked few questions and delivered no ad-
monitions. Since James had been automatically excommun-
icated from the Catholic Church when he divorced his first
wife, there was no difficulty about a difference of faith. That
was fortunte, since combining their disparate lives involved
enough problems as it was.

To begin with, there was the question of where to live. "My
apartment is big enough for all of us," Alexis pointed out as
she and James lay in bed together on an upper floor of the Plaza
Hotel, where they were spending their weekend honeymoon.

It was shortly before dawn; the last of the chairs had been
put up on the tables at the Copacabana and Twenty-one, the
cleaning women had gone home from the office buildings in
midtown, the milk trucks had not yet begun to make their
deliveries.

The city paused to catch its collective breath. Only a few
muted sounds penetrated the thick walls of the room with floor-
to-ceiling windows overlooking Central Park: the distant clank

of metal garbage cans being emptied into a truck, the far-off whistle of a tugboat, the discreet whisper of the elevator at the far end of the plushly carpeted hall.

James propped himself up on an elbow and regarded her with a faint smile. In the aftermath of their lovemaking, her gray eyes were uncharacteristically heavy-lidded and her mouth pouted softly. He liked her to look that way; it made her seem more manageable. "We have to give some thought to Matthew. He's already had enough to cope with. Taking him away from Maggie and Tessa might be too much."

"I realize they mean a great deal to him, but he seems happy about our marriage."

He nodded, pleased by his son's acceptance of Alexis, but also somewhat surprised that he had shown no concern about what effect the change in his father's life might have on his own—almost as though he were carefully avoiding thinking about that. Slowly, James said, "I don't think it would be good for him to leave the only real home he's ever known."

Alexis smothered a sigh. She had promised herself that she would not cause problems between James and his son. She wanted what was best for them both, but also for herself. "Children that age are very adaptable," she pointed out reasonably. "I went away to boarding school when I was eight and it didn't hurt me any."

James lay back and stared up at the ceiling. This was not the time to get into a discussion of her childhood, not when she must still be hurting from her father and brother's refusal to attend the wedding. Charles and Graham Brockton had made no secret of their disdain, which James privately suspected was fueled by fury at their inability to control Alexis. He'd been just as glad to do without them but resented the unhappiness they had caused her. She needed to know that her new family was far more considerate.

"Let's give it some more thought," he suggested. "Since we'll be moving IBS's headquarters to Manhattan, it might make sense to keep the apartment here. But I'm not crazy about the idea of bringing a child up in the city, so holding on to the house might also be a good idea."

Alexis chafed a little at that, even as she admitted that it would be smart not to try to make any more major decisions before she'd had a chance to adjust to her new roles as business partner in IBS, wife to James and mother to Matthew.

She was confident about the first and eager to get started. The second troubled her a little, but she was fairly certain everything would fall into place; after all, they were hardly naive kids with their heads in the clouds. As for the third, honesty forced her to admit that she knew nothing at all about mothering and was scared of doing something wrong.

"Maybe I should talk to Maggie," she said, thinking out loud. "She's run off her feet by Tessa and little Joseph, but still has time to help with Matthew." Ruefully, she added, "I really have no idea how she does it."

"Lots of women manage," James pointed out reassuringly. "Besides, once we have kids of our own—" He broke off at Alexis's startled look. "You have considered that, haven't you?"

"Well, no, not actually. You never mentioned anything about it and I just presumed that..."

"That what?"

She sat up slightly, holding the covers to her breasts. "That we'd go on as before."

"We were having an affair then; this is different."

The flat assertion that marriage automatically conferred an entirely new set of expectations disturbed her, especially since he had never thought to ask her opinion.

"Not everything has changed," she ventured carefully. "For one thing, I'll still be working."

He smiled soothingly. "IBS won't always be a small-scale operation, honey. The day will come when you'll be able to give up your job and..."

"Give it up? I'm just getting started."

The smile faded, replaced by the beginnings of a frown. "Let's be reasonable, Alexis. Most women your age have already had several children. You can't wait much longer."

"Twenty-seven is hardly over-the-hill," she pointed out caustically.

"It is almost, as far as childbearing is concerned. Maggie had a rough enough time because she waited that long. You don't want to make it even more difficult on yourself, do you?"

His offhanded presumption that he knew more about so intimately female a matter than she did irked Alexis. A sharp retort sprang to mind, only to whither as she recalled that the doctor she had consulted about birth control when she and James became lovers had said much the same thing. Even as the white-haired gynecologist had grudgingly fitted her for a diaphragm, he had made it clear that she would be better off both married and pregnant.

"Of course I don't want to set myself up for any problems," she admitted, "but I'm not sure that I..." She broke off, unable to voice what was in her mind. Even to suggest that she might not want children went so deeply against the accepted norm as to be unthinkable. Instead, she sought safer ground: "I'm not sure I'd be a good mother."

James shook his head indulgently and nestled her closer against him. "Don't be silly. All good women make good mothers."

A slight smile curved her mouth. "Is that what I am, a good woman?"

"I would hardly have married you otherwise."

She supposed that was meant as a compliment, but it didn't come across that way. Instead, it suggested that he was unlikely to have much patience with her doubts.

"You seem to have it all figured out," she murmured against his chest. Their bodies were entwined beneath the covers; she could feel the warm length of his penis brushing her belly.

He turned slightly, drawing her beneath him. "I'm old enough to know what I want." In the darkness, his smile was a white slash. "And how to get it."

Alexis remembered that in the weeks to come, as the full meaning of his words began to sink in. She quickly discovered that working with James was nothing at all like working with her father and brother. On the one hand, he was far more honorable and forthright. On the other, he had his own ideas about how things should be done and expected them to be carried out.

"We need more information about the type of people buying television sets," he insisted one afternoon as they sat in the new offices on Madison Avenue. The large infusion of cash made possible by marriage to Alexis was already transforming IBS from a shoestring operation into a business with the polished sheen of success. James tried not to resent that, telling himself she had only speeded up a process that would have happened eventually anyway, but he still tended to be more protective of his authority than he might otherwise have been.

"The day is already passed when programs could be thrown together without adequate research. By the end of this year,

there'll be almost two hundred thousand sets out there.''
Leaning back in his chair, he went on, ''That's close to a million potential viewers. We've got to know who those people are before we can figure out what they want to watch.''

''We can't base our decisions on pseudoscientific mumbo jumbo,'' Alexis protested from the other side of his wide desk, ''and we can't twiddle our thumbs while the networks are putting new shows on the air almost every day. We have to take a few risks.''

Glancing down at the neatly typed sheet of paper in front of him, James said, ''You're talking about more than a few. According to this, you want to launch a dozen new programs by the middle of next year.''

''That's right, and I want to begin right away with blanket coverage of the presidential election, including continual broadcast of returns throughout election night.''

''Truman is sure to lose; all the polls say so.''

''Polls have been wrong before. Remember back in '36, when the *Literary Digest* did a straw poll and predicted that Alf Landon would beat FDR handily?''

''Methods have improved a lot since then,'' James pointed out.

''Maybe so, but I still think Truman has a few surprises up his sleeve. Election night could be a lot more interesting than most people think.''

''Perhaps. . .but what about this item here, convention coverage? No one wants to watch a bunch of politicians sitting around smoking cigars.''

''No, but I'd bet they'd like to hear some of the speeches and see the actual balloting. That's history in the making.''

''History bores most people. They like action, excitement, fantasy.''

Alexis took a deep breath, determined not to show her annoyance. "If you would glance down the rest of my list, you'll see shows that provide all those elements."

He did so, only to raise his eyes abruptly. "What's this about Delia Follett?"

"She's the new actress Paramount is making such a fuss about."

"I know who she is; what I want to know is why you want to build a television show around her."

"Because she's a natural comedienne and the studio is trying to turn her into just another sexpot starlet. I've spoken with her manager, and he says she'd welcome a chance to prove that she's got talent."

"So how come one of the networks hasn't grabbed her?"

"Maybe they're too busy doing research and studying statistics." When he failed to rise to the bait, Alexis shook her head impatiently and stood up. She walked to the tall windows overlooking Madison Avenue, staring out unseeingly until a vague memory surfaced. Turning back to him, she asked, "Didn't Anthony mention someone named Delia you knew when you were in Australia?"

James glanced off into the middle distance. "It's not that uncommon a name."

"No...but if it is the same person, maybe you're the one who should talk with her, instead of me."

"I don't think that would be a good idea."

Memory gave way to the stirring of suspicion. "It is the same person, isn't it?"

A low sigh escaped him. "Yes."

"How did you happen to know her?"

"She was in the USO when I was stationed in Brisbane."

"And you...became friendly?"

"If you're asking me whether or not we had an affair, the answer is yes. Now, is there anything else you want to know?"

Stung by his bluntness, she took refuge in dignity. "You could have just said so right away, instead of making me ask. After all, it's not as though we were married then or even knew each other."

James's large hands clenched on the burled leather top of his desk. "And of course you're far too sensible to be jealous of something that happened before I met you?"

In fact, she was rather put out by the thought of him with the voluptuous redhead, but she wasn't about to admit that. It seemed so petty; the stereotypical response of the insecure woman.

Cooly, she said, "If you don't mind, I'd like to stick to the subject at hand, namely the new shows."

James stared at her for a long moment before he abruptly pushed the list across the desk toward her. "Do whatever you want; just don't go over the budget or forget that any decisions you make can be revoked if the research indicates you're wrong."

Before she could respond, he pulled a file out of the stack on a corner of the desk and immersed himself in it.

Alexis pivoted on one heel and strode out of his office, shutting the door behind her with dangerous softness. James did not raise his head again until he was sure she was gone. Then he grinned ruefully.

So much for trying to provoke her. The cool, imperturbable facade she showed to the world gave way only when they were in bed together, and even then only with difficulty. That was part of her fascination for him: the fire beneath the ice, the challenge of stripping away her self-possession until she yielded completely.

Sometimes, in the calm light of morning, he felt a niggling sense of shame at his refusal to let her keep anything of herself from him. But each time she faced him composedly over the breakfast table, with every silver-blond hair in place and all traces of the night's passion eradicated, his resolve hardened.

He simply could not afford to let her win the subtle battle going on between them. She already had too many weapons on her side: birth, breeding, beauty, wealth. With very little effort, he could be in awe of her. Instead, he preferred to keep his pride and manhood intact by reminding her with remorseless frequency that beneath all the polish and glitter she was a woman like any other.

But was she? Giving up the effort to read whatever was in the file, he reached for the morning paper and took a desultory glance at the page one headlines. Stalin was threatening to blockade Berlin. If he did so, the city would have to be supplied completely by air. More headaches for Harry Truman, who had more than enough already.

Shaking his head, he tossed the paper aside. The war wasn't over three years and already it looked as though there might be another on the way. Crazy world. Somehow, it had seemed saner back when all he had to worry about was getting shot or blown to bits.

Then at least he'd known what he wanted: to stay alive and to win, preferably both. Now it wasn't so simple. Silently, he considered his priorities: He wanted to be a good father to Matthew and any other children he might have. He wanted IBS to succeed and make him a lot of money. And he wanted a good marriage.

Why was that last? Certainly it wasn't the least in importance. On the contrary, he was determined not to repeat the mistakes of his first marriage. Perhaps too determined. Alexis was nothing at all like Charlotte; with the benefit of hindsight, he could now see that his first wife should have married a man who would have expected nothing more from her than a clean house, a decent dinner and a warm body in bed.

That hadn't satisfied him, not by a long shot. He had wanted far more. The fire beneath the ice. The challenge of a mind as keen as his own and a will as strong. Alexis.

He shouldn't have told her about Delia, or at least not so bluntly. She was bound to be upset, even though she didn't show it. Which was exactly the problem. He wanted her to be as possessive of him as he was of her; he wanted to know that he really mattered to her and wasn't simply a means to an end.

Damn women, he thought mildly as he rose and stretched, his body hard and taut beneath the perfectly tailored suit. Tie a man in knots if he let them. He wasn't about to. Not when the alternatives were so much more enjoyable.

ALEXIS WAS ALSO LEARNING about alternatives. Rather than give in to her anger and insecurity over James, she channeled both into her work, pushing harder than ever to take IBS in front of the networks. While he went off on a nationwide tour to line up affiliate stations and Anthony kept the day-to-day flow of business running smoothly, she concentrated on the new shows.

Coverage of the political conventions in July went well. Both were held in Philadelphia, chosen because it stood midway on the coaxial cable linking Washington, D.C., and New York. Winston Harcourt laughed about that. "It's only the beginning," he advised when he called Alexis from there. Whatever anger he had felt at her sudden marriage seemed to have faded; they were friends once again. "Before we're done, we'll see entire conventions designed around television."

"I'll be glad if we can get a few people up to the booth for interviews," she said. "Is there much action at CBS?"

"Quite a bit; it's amazing how many politicians want to get on television. Even with this damn heat, they're happy to sit under the lights and sweat for as long as we'll let them."

"How does the election look to you?" Alexis asked.

"Truman's sunk. I like the guy, but he doesn't have a chance. It'll be Dewey all the way."

"I'm betting against that." Quietly, she told him about her plans for IBS's election night coverage, knowing her confidence would be respected.

"That would be a fabulous idea if the race turned out to be close, but in this case, I hope you've got some backup planned."

Alexis did, though she was loathe to use it. A grade-B movie starring Ronald Reagan would have little impact against the shows scheduled by the networks. IBS could take a real drubbing, unless Mr. Truman pulled off a stunner.

The sultry heat of Philadelphia in July gave way to the sodden humidity of New York in August. People crawled out on fire escapes to sleep; department stores did a booming business in fans, men came to work in short-sleeved white shirts; and movie theaters that could advertise they were 'air-cooled' sold out for every show.

James came home from his trip with only three stations signed to carry IBS programs. They had hoped for more, but competition from the networks and continuing doubts about the future of television worked against them. He was tired and had little to say. They spent weekends at the house on Long Island with Matthew. Maggie was still looking after him most of the time, along with Tessa and baby Joe.

She seemed happy enough with the situation, but sometimes Alexis wondered if that was really the case. Over Labor Day, a neighbor's child fell from a swing and split his chin. Maggie cared for him with such skill that the doctor who arrived on the scene complimented her and asked her if she'd thought about going back to nursing. She said no, but with a wistful look in her eyes.

Alexis and James' six-month anniversary came and went. They were both too busy to take much notice of it. Between long hours at the office and commuting between the apartment and house, often on different schedules, they saw little of each other. When they were together, they made love hungrily, even voraciously, as a substitute for other forms of communication.

The leaves in Central Park turned to crimson and orange. Overcoats came out of storage. The breath of carriage horses lined up near the Plaza misted the air. Maggie had grown pumpkins that the children carved into jack-o'-lanterns. Or at least Matthew did, while Tessa urged him on with wide eyes and little Joseph tried to take his first tottering steps.

Delia Follett signed to do a half-hour weekly comedy program on IBS. Alexis didn't ask how James had convinced her to agree, and he didn't volunteer the information. The show would be done in Hollywood, and in a break with the networks, it would be filmed instead of live. Alexis was convinced that by removing the hectic, often nearly hysteric element of live television—in which actors had to race breathlessly from set to set while struggling to remember their lines and avoid tripping over props—quality would be improved.

The premier of ''Our Gal, Sal'' indicated she was right. Delia's character, a scatterbrained nightclub singer always falling in and out of trouble, quickly captured the nation's heart. Introduced right before election day, she proved infinitely more popular than Harry Truman seemed to have any hope of being.

"It's not too late to change the lineup," James advised as they were rising early to vote before going to work. "We could still go with the movie instead."

Alexis finished brushing her teeth and shook her head. "Dewey hasn't run a very inspiring campaign. Anything could happen."

"You'll be off the air by 10:00 P.M."

"Then I can join you, Maggie and Anthony at Sardi's after the show." They were going to see Lynn Fontaine and Alfred Lunt's latest play while she spent the evening in the broadcast booth. Alexis was sorry to miss it, but she thought what she planned to do was more worthwhile.

Still, by curtain time she was having second thoughts. Truman had taken an early lead, but that was no surprise, since the Democratic-controlled cities reported first. Perhaps more significant was the fact that the bulldog edition of Chicago's *Tribune* had hit the streets with a headline blaring Dewey's victory. The radio commentators were accurately reporting the returns that kept Truman out in front, but pollster George Gallup was on the air repeatedly explaining why that wasn't to be taken seriously.

At 10:30 P.M. Maggie, Anthony and James emerged from the theater and crossed Forty-seventh Street to a bar. It was the second intermission of what had proved to be an excellent show, and they were in a good mood, talking about what they had just seen as they waited for their drinks to arrive. A radio was on behind the bar, but the drone of meaningless numbers being read by the commentator was barely perceptible.

"Is it all over yet?" James asked as he paid the bartender.

The man grinned and shook his head. "Doesn't look that way. Old Harry's pulled a fast one."

James excused himself and headed for the phone. He got through to Alexis on the fifth ring. In the background, he could hear harried shouts and the frantic clatter of wire-service machines. As he listened, three bells went off urgently, signaling a breaking story.

"What the hell's going on?" he yelled into the phone.

"Truman's leading in Ohio," Alexis shouted back. "It looks as though he's got Wisconsin, Iowa and Colorado. We could use some help down here."

"We're on the way!" Hanging up, he went in hurried search of Maggie and Anthony. They could see the rest of the show some other time; right now there was history to help make.

"Thank God, you got here," Alexis said fervently when they had piled up the stairs to the broadcast studio that just then looked more like a three-ring circus. "Truman's lead has gone over a million and there's no end in sight."

"Where's it coming from?" Maggie asked bemusedly.

"Nobody's sure," Alexis said as she accepted a stream of wire-service tape thrust at her by a harried assistant. "Seems to be broad-based; urban, rural, male, female, young, old. They all like Harry."

"Are we the only television station with full coverage?" James demanded.

"We are," she confirmed, "and the phones have been coming off the hooks with calls from people telling us how much they appreciate it."

James nodded decisively. He tossed his jacket onto a chair and began rolling up his sleeves. "Then let's keep them happy. Anthony, you get over to Republican headquarters at the Roosevelt and try to corner Dewey. While you're at it, get on to anyone we can trust in Missouri and find out where the hell Truman is and when he'll be available for comment. Maggie, you take charge of keeping the vote tabulated. We want to be able to tell the audience where it's coming from and what it means. I'll be on the phone to Democratic leaders around the country for statements to be read on the air. Alexis, you..."

"Yesss..." she murmured dryly, challenging him to forget whose idea this had all been in the first place.

He grinned and dropped a quick kiss on her mouth. "You just keep on doing exactly what you've been doing. And if you need anything, yell. It's going to be a long night."

Very long, but also exhilirating. Not until almost noon the next day did Thomas E. Dewey, former governor of New York, concede defeat to Harry Truman, former haberdasher. IBS remained on the air all that time. James and Alexis both took turns in front of the camera when the newscaster's voice gave out. Maggie kept an endless stream of sandwiches and coffee flowing along with the vote totals. Anthony produced brilliant footage of the mood at Republican headquarters giving way first to disbelief and then to despair.

And all the while the phones continued to ring as viewers called in to say they liked what they saw. Liked it a lot.

More people watched IBS that night than watched all the networks combined. And many continued to watch after the excitement of the election died away and Harry Truman began his second term. Enough to triple advertising revenues, draw in more affiliate stations, and assure IBS's financial success, at least for the moment.

"I can hardly believe it," James said when he totalled up the figures and saw the profit they were making. "If we go on like this, we'll gross over a million dollars in 1949 alone."

"That's still small potatoes compared to the networks," Anthony pointed out. "The name of the game is programming. If we've got the shows people want, we should be able to sell them to more stations."

"I agree. We do that, and nothing will be able to stop us."

He was wrong. But before that could be discovered, more personal issues demanded attention. Riding high on IBS's success, James began pressing Alexis once again to become pregnant.

She resisted vehemently. "I'm not ready. There's too much going on at work for me to want to leave."

"That's what you said last year when we got married. How much longer do you intend to wait?"

"I don't know.... Until it feels right."

"Which may be never."

Although he spoke mildly, Alexis did not mistake the steel in his voice. She finished hanging her suit away in the closet and turned to him. He was stretched out on the bed, still wearing the shirt and slacks he had put on that morning. In deference to the spread, he had removed his shoes. His arms were folded behind his head. The relaxed pose did not fool her. She could feel the coiled strength in him clear across the room.

"Never is a long time," she pointed out quietly as she reached for her silk robe and wrapped it around herself. Although she had a full slip on over her bra, panties, garter belt and stockings, she felt the need for further covering. His clear blue eyes had been wandering over her with distracting appreciation, giving her a very good idea of where the discussion would end if she let it.

She had given in like that too often, foregoing any real airing of their problems. That couldn't go on forever. Sitting on the edge of the bed, she said, "I understand that you want more children, James, but we've only been married a year and so much has happened during that time. I just feel that we need more of a chance to get to know each other on our own…along with Matthew, of course.''

Beneath lowered lids, he regarded her steadily. ''We hardly see anything of Matthew.''

''That isn't true. We spend every weekend with him and you frequently drive out to see him during the week.''

''That's the whole point. I'm tired of being a visitor in my son's life; I want to be his full-time father. Moreover, I want him to have a mother of his own, not someone who's just taken him in out of the kindness of her heart.''

Alexis started to reply, then thought better of it. He did have a point. Maggie had been wonderful about caring for Matthew, but she wasn't the little boy's mother and she did have two children of her own. ''Perhaps…'' she ventured slowly, ''we should move out to the Island so we could be with him every day.''

''With our schedules, we'd be home after he goes to bed and be gone again at the crack of dawn. It's not so bad if one parent is doing that, but I can't see it with both.'' He shook his head firmly. ''No, so long as you're determined to keep on working, I think the best solution is to bring Matthew into the city to live with us. He's nine years old now, old enough to handle the separation from Maggie and Tessa.''

Skipping over his reference to her continuing to work, Alexis said, ''I think you're right. When I was his age, I loved the city and wanted to spend every possible moment here.''

''It's not as though there weren't good schools….''

''On the contrary; I'll start making inquiries right away.''

''His grades are good, there shouldn't be any problem. But what about after school?''

Alexis frowned; she hadn't thought of that. "The house-keeper will be here."

"So he'll be coming home to some strange woman he doesn't know."

"He'll get to know her. She's very nice. Besides, there are after-school activities. It's time for him to learn social dancing, piano, that sort of thing."

James shot her a disgusted look. "He likes baseball and hockey, *that* sort of thing."

"A little polish won't hurt him."

"Or his father?"

"I didn't say that. You're always putting words in my mouth."

She stood up, determined to put some distance between them, only to be stopped when James's hand lashed out, the fingers curling around her wrist. "Running away won't solve anything. We've put this off long enough."

"I am simply uninterested in getting into a ridiculous argument."

As she tried again to stand up, the collar of her robe slipped, revealing the swell of her breasts above the lacy bra. James's gaze drifted downward. His hold on her tightened. "You're right. Why fight when we can..."

"I'm not in the mood." That was a lie; much as she hated to admit it, being close to him had set off all the usual longings. After almost a year of marriage, she would have thought some degree of indifference would have set in. But on the contrary, she wanted him more than ever.

James smiled lazily. He sat up and with his free hand touched her breasts beneath the thin fabric. Instantly, her nipples hardened. "It appears you're mistaken," he murmured as he bent forward.

Alexis tried to evade him, but failed. His mouth found hers unerringly, his hand tangling in her hair to hold her still. Resentment flared through her, of his strength, his skill, his sureness that she would not be able to resist. Most of all, of his knowledge of her and his willingness to make use of it for his own ends.

"I don't want to," she insisted raggedly when he at last raised his head.

He laughed softly. "You will."

Alexis raised a hand, intent on pushing him away, only to have it captured and held firmly in his. Between clenched teeth, she muttered, "Go to hell."

His smile widened. "I have another destination in mind."

"It's not fair..."

"Neither is life."

"I'm not protected."

"I can count as well as you can; this isn't the right time of the month for you to get pregnant."

"Famous last words."

His eyes were very dark above her as he lowered her to the bed, trapping her body under his. Already the stiffness of anger was giving way to something far more insistent. What followed would, she knew, be infinitely pleasurable and satisfying, if only physically. But it would not wipe out her resentment of the ease with which he expected to manipulate her.

Or her determination not to let him get away with it.

Chapter Eight

MATTHEW MADE THE TRANSITION to city life with apparent ease. Alexis and James both went out of their way to get home earlier, and most weekends were spent at the house on the Island. They enrolled him at the Trinity School, where he did well. At nine, he already showed the promise of his father's height and size, and was a welcome addition to the soccer team. Tessa, initially dismayed by his departure, was consoled when she was allowed to see him play in several games.

On a weekend when Anthony and Maggie came into New York, the two couples went to see *South Pacific*, which was just beginning its run on Broadway. They agreed that the rave reviews were deserved, though James got a little tired of hearing Alexis sing "I'm Gonna Wash That Man Right Out Of My Hair" every morning in the shower for weeks afterward.

The Dodgers made it to the Series again, but still they couldn't beat the Yankees. It was a bitter defeat for Dom, who injured his knee in the last game while trying to slide home. He recovered but had to face the fact that his baseball career wouldn't last forever.

At dinner parties on the fashionable East Side, talk centered on China, where Mao Tse-tung had recently taken power; on the atomic explosion detected in Russia, which might or might not mean that the Soviets had the Bomb; and on Alger Hiss's second trial, which got under way shortly before Thanksgiving. The first had resulted in a hung jury and complaints from Congressman Richard Nixon that legal technicalities had been used to avoid a conviction of treason against the Harvard lawyer and aide to FDR.

The decade that had seen both war and peace was ending in confusion, and fear.

Alexis tried not to think about any of that as she prepared for the holidays. IBS was doing well; Matthew seemed happy; her marriage to James was, if not tranquil, at least cordial. They continued to have their differences at work, where he was forever cautioning against her more imaginative schemes, but at home things were better. He had stopped pressing her to become pregnant, though she knew he hoped she would agree to do so. Her twenty-eighth birthday arrived, reminding her of a clock ticking away inexorably somewhere in the background of her life. She found herself considering the possiblity of motherhood with less than her usual disfavor, but on her terms, not his.

Thoughts of family were very much on her mind as the Christmas tree went up in Rockefeller Center and decorations appeared in the store windows. The holidays had never been a particularly warm or happy time in the Brockton household, but they served to remind her that more than eighteen months had passed since she had had any contact with her father and brother.

Not that she didn't keep abreast of what was going on at UBC. She knew that Graham had taken over the TV division and was having trouble keeping it going. Several affiliates had left UBC for the other networks and a couple had come over to IBS. Two comedians and a singer Alexis had recruited had since departed, fed up with Graham's arbitrary management. The news division was in disarray; no sports broadcasts were planned, even though they were becoming increasingly popular on the other stations; and the budget for new equipment had been cut to almost zero.

None of that surprised her, but it still hurt to see the erosion of what she had worked so hard to build. She wondered why her father didn't step in and put a stop to it. Though Charles Brockton had viewed television with curt disdain, he had always been a consummate businessman who put profit above all else. There were rumors that the heart condition that had plagued him for a decade was worsening steadily. He spent his days shuffling papers in his antique-filled office, rarely venturing out to inspect the empire tottering beneath him.

Alexis debated long and hard before deciding to go see him. She told no one what she intended, not even James, who would surely have disapproved. Late on a Friday afternoon, the week before Christmas, when she was certain that the UBC offices would be all but empty, she ventured into the building for the first time since her angry departure the year before.

It was a relief to get inside, away from the leaden sky threatening snow and the hurrying crowds intent upon obligatory good cheer. The marble vestibule had the hushed atmosphere of a cathedral. Her heels tapped out a staccato beat as she walked to the elevators, waited for the bronze doors to slide open, then stepped inside.

As the paneled and gilded box swept her upward, Alexis unfastened the mink coat that had been James's gift on her birthday. It had replaced the several other furs she had bought over the years for herself and which were now kept diplomatically in the back of her closet. Beneath the mink, she wore a neatly tailored navy wool suit and organdy white blouse. The brief walk from the curb where the taxi had deposited her to the door of the building had not dulled the shine of her admittedly impractical shoes or placed any unsightly splotches on her slender legs clad in pale silk stockings. The neat cloche hat with a slight veil was still perfectly in place, as was the coil of silver-blond hair at the nape of her neck.

She had deliberately refrained from making any special effort with her appearance, but was gratified nonetheless to know that she looked every inch the lady. If her father thought their estrangement had diminished her in any way, he was due for a surprise.

In fact, the surprise turned out to be hers, and it was not pleasant. Having found the reception area on the executive floor deserted, as expected, she made her way to her father's office, past the empty desk of his secretary, and knocked lightly on the mahogany door. At his muffled "Come in," she did so, only to stand blinking for several moments in the dim light.

Heavy curtains were drawn over the windows. A single lamp was lit, casting most of the large room into shadows. The heat was turned up, adding to the stultifying atmosphere. In the ornamental fireplace, an electric log glowed in a mocking effort at cheeriness.

The motionless air carried a melange of odors: the acrid smell of the patent iron tonic her father had swallowed daily for years, the cloying scent of the violet pastilles intended to mask it, the fetidness of an old body in which the juices of life were turning inexorably to corruption.

A stooped figure sat at the massive desk. It did not stir as Alexis entered.

"Father...it's me..."

No answer. She stepped farther into the room, closing the door behind her. The heat was rapidly becoming oppressive, but she hesitated to take off her coat before she was certain of her welcome. "Father...?"

"Wondered when you'd show up," a voice rasped from the shadows.

She paused, her hand still on the doorknob. When her father lapsed into the careless syntax of his youth, he was either very tired or very angry, or both. Hesitantly, she said, "I...wanted to talk with you..."

Something that might have been a laugh distorted the air between them. "Thought you might. Come closer; let me get a look at you."

She did as he said, stopping about five feet from the edge of the desk. His shape became clearer; thin white hair defining the top of it, shoulders still broad but hunched, a once barrel chest that seemed to have caved in, yellowed hands with prominent veins emerging from cuffs that looked too big.

"New coat?" he wheezed. Typically, he focused on the badge of privilege and affluence.

"It was a birthday present," she confirmed and then, in a gesture of defiance, added, "from James."

"I know his name. Callahan; Irish, ex-Marine. Knew plenty like him back when I was just starting out."

Alexis doubted that, but she was not disposed to argue the point. Instead, she said simply, "He's my husband."

"So it seems." A harsh sound, somewhere between a laugh and cough, broke from him. "You've made your bed."

"You left me no choice."

"Because I sided with Graham over that questionnaire business?" At her brief nod he shrugged. "Had to. He's my son...and heir."

At least he was making no pretense of having acted out of some deep moral conviction that the country was in danger. His motives went no further than self-interest.

"You never considered any alternative to Graham, did you?" she asked, hating the bitterness that crept into her voice but unable to hide it completely.

"Yourself, for instance?" He leaned forward, casting his face into the light. His eyes were narrowed to little more than slits surrounded by gray puffiness; his jowls hung pendulously and his neck looked shrunken; the collar of his shirt as oversized as the cuffs. He wheezed again, then went into a spasm of coughing that did not end until he had pressed a white linen handkerchief folded into a square against his thin mouth and expectorated into it.

"Funny thing about children," he said at length, when he had regained his breath. "Both of you look like your mother, and I used to think you were both like her all the way through. But you've got a broad streak of me inside, girl, whether you want to admit it or not."

"I've come to terms with that," Alexis said softly. "It's just too bad the same can't be said for you."

He spread his lips in what could pass for a smile and gestured her impatiently into a chair. "Long as you're here, you might as well sit down. And take that damn coat off. I've seen all I need to of it."

Alexis did as he said but she did not make the mistake of relaxing. She sat upright in the chair opposite the desk, her back straight and her gloved hands folded neatly in her lap. Silence stretched out between them for several minutes as each regarded the other steadily. At length, she said, "You're ill."

He nodded as though her bluntness satisfied him. "That why you're here, 'cause you expect me to die soon?"

"I hadn't gotten that far in my thinking," she said composedly. "It was curiosity more than anything else that made me want to come." Not completely true, but it would do for the moment. She was only beginning to recognize her motives for being there.

Her father grimaced and reached for the carved cigar box on top of the desk. His spotted hand shook slightly as he flipped it open and selected one of his favorite Havanas. "You always were a cool one. How does Callahan handle you?"

"He manages," she said dryly. "It's you we're talking about. Have you seen a doctor recently?"

"Seen a gaggle of 'em. All say the same thing. Stop working, smoking, drinking, chasing women. Then what the hell use is there being alive?"

Despite herself, Alexis smiled. "I see what you mean. But surely you could compromise? After all, Graham is supposed to be running things now."

"Is running things," he corrected sharply. His voice dropped on a note of weariness as he added, "For better or worse."

"From what I've heard, it's worse."

"You want to believe that, don't you? Proves you were right."

"Was that ever in doubt?"

A long sigh escaped him as he fell back in his chair, making no effort to light the cigar he kept clasped between his fingers. "Damn shame you were born female. Never quite forgave your mother for that."

"There was a great deal you never forgave her for."

"Is *that* what you're here to talk about?"

"In a way. . ." She paused for a moment, collecting herself. "I've been thinking about her a lot lately, I guess because I'm also thinking about having a child of my own."

Her father whistled softly, the first time she had heard him do that in years. A memory flitted over the landscape of her mind: spring afternoons at the Connecticut house and an Irish setter who had come in response to that sound.

''You called Bridie like that,'' she said softly.

''You remember her? Couldn't have been more than five when she had to be put down.''

''Four-and-a-half, and there's a great deal I remember.''

''Hmmm…yes, seems like there is. So you're thinking about having a baby. There was a time women didn't think about it at all; it just happened to them. But be that as it may, Callahan must be really getting to you.''

''He's a good man.''

''That why you want to do it?''

''Not entirely…I want something of myself to go on into the future.''

He nodded slowly. ''Immortality…that's always the draw. It doesn't work, though. Having children is like throwing dice, there's no telling how they'll add up.'' When she didn't comment, he went on. ''Look at you and Graham. You got the brains and the backbone; he was left to run catch-up. That's not easy for a man.''

Her eyebrow rose very slightly, enough to provoke another wheezing laugh. ''See what you mean,'' her father admitted. ''He thinks I don't know about those bars he goes to downtown.'' Resignedly, he added, ''What the hell, it takes all kinds.''

''At least he's discreet.''

''He damn well better be. Besides, there's nothing to say he won't get married some day and have kids. Plenty of men like him have done the same. With the money and power he stands to inherit, he's a damn good catch.''

Alexis resisted the impulse to point out that she wouldn't wish marriage to Graham on any woman. Realistically, she knew plenty would jump at it with their eyes wide open.

"He may be able to provide you with grandchildren," she said evenly, "though I wouldn't bet on that. But the fact remains that he'll run UBC into the ground once you're gone. Is that really what you want?"

Instead of answering, her father asked, "Why should you care if he does? You've got IBS."

"And it's doing well, but we've got a long way to go to equal the size of UBC."

"You always were impatient."

She shook her head, rejecting that explanation. "I'm annoyed at having to build something from the ground up, whereas my brother has been handed all sorts of advantages that he doesn't know what to do with."

Her father snipped off the end of his cigar with a little silver tool that looked like a miniature guillotine and reached for a box of wooden matches. Striking one, he went on. "Aren't you overlooking something?"

Alexis watched the flame in unwilling fascination. Despite the trembling of his hand, he did not allow it to touch the tip of the cigar, only held it close enough for the heat to ignite the carefully wrapped leaves. He drew a deep breath and expelled it in a cloud of smoke, tipping his head back as he did so in the characteristic pose of a man enjoying a purely male privilege.

"What's that?" she asked quietly.

"You're a woman."

"You make it sound like a disability."

"It is. No matter how smart or ambitious you are, there are certain things you're never going to be able to do."

"Such as?"

''Control money and power. Not to offend you're delicate ears, but you just don't have the balls for it.''

She repressed her instinctive rejection of his crudity and contented herself with saying simply, ''Balls are something children play with.''

The bark of his laughter resounded against the damask-covered walls. ''Like I said, you've got plenty of me in you. How did you ever stand that fancy finishing school I sent you to?''

''I spent my time cadging cigarettes and plotting revenge.''

''Useful activities.'' Without warning, he asked, ''Is marrying Callahan part of the revenge?''

Surprised, she shook her head. ''No, that appealed to me strictly on its own.''

''So you say, but are you right?''

''Yes... Anyway, if it wasn't in the beginning, it is now. I like being married to him.''

''Better than those society boys you went out with?''

She smiled gently. ''Much.''

Brockton seemed to have forgotten the cigar in his hand. He was looking at her, but his gaze was focused inward. ''I wanted you to be a lady.'' Alexis waited, knowing what was coming, knowing that she had to hear it. ''Like your mother.''

''My mother died.''

His attention flicked back to her. ''So does everyone, sooner or later.''

''It's not the same; you know that.''

He sighed, as close as he would come to an admission. ''She was beautiful like you, the same blond hair and pale skin. Tall and graceful, made to wear lovely clothes and live in elegant rooms. When we went anywhere together, people always stared, men and women. I could hear them thinking, 'How did a rough bastard like him get so lucky?' ''·

"But it wasn't luck, was it?"

"'Course not." He chuckled reminiscingly. "Her father was one of the world's all-time worst businessmen, but he figured he had to know more than a kid from the slums. He was only too happy to invest in a couple of schemes I suggested, with money I loaned him. Ended up owing me more than a million back when that was serious money."

"So you collected through Mother?"

"That was about it." He looked at her challengingly. "Shocked?"

"No, I've heard the story before, and besides, I never had any illusions about the two of you being happy together."

"Happy? She lived in the lap of luxury, was waited on hand and foot. What more could she have wanted?" He spoke irritably, as though demanding the answer to a question he had asked too many times before.

"I think she wanted you to respect and value her as a person rather than as an object. But she had no idea of how to go about achieving that, because to do it, she would have had to respect and value herself *first*."

He made a slight sound of disgust. "What the hell is that supposed to mean?"

"It's one of those things that you either understand or you don't. Anyway, it doesn't really matter now. She wanted something she couldn't have and she paid for it. Her part in all this has been over for a long time."

"You really believe that?"

"I have to; otherwise the past would have so firm a grip on me that I wouldn't be able to do anything about the present, much less the future."

He nodded somberly. "When you get to be my age, you relive the past."

"It's called justice."

He flinched slightly and with a touch of sarcasm said, "Tell me again why you came."

"To see you as you are now. . . . It's rather like being a small child in a very large, dark bedroom, trembling under the covers because you've been told there's a bogeyman under the bed." She smiled faintly. "One night I got out of bed and looked under it. All I found were a few dust kittens. The housekeeping wasn't what it should have been. I guess the servants knew they could get away with a lot so long as they played their parts."

Her father stared at her. Emotions flitted across the ruin of his face: surprise, anger, finally—for the briefest instance—sadness.

Alexis looked away. She had what she had come for, but somehow his repentance did not lighten her own burdens. Instead, it only brought home to her the fleetingness of youth and strength that were the strongest barriers against remorseless self-knowledge.

"There was another reason I came," she said huskily. "You are my father and I didn't want us to part as adversaries."

She thought at first that he didn't intend to respond, but at length he said, "That's a pretty sentiment."

Alexis knew what he thought of such things. She stood up and reached for her coat. "I'll be going now."

At the door she paused, glancing back for an instant. He still sat slumped at the desk, the red glow of the cigar tip wavering slightly. She hesitated. "If you need anything. . ."

It must have been her imagination that she thought she could see his eyes. At that distance and in such dim light, that was impossible. But his voice was clear enough, as though time had briefly turned back to restore the firm, unrelenting timber she knew so well. "You can't have it both ways, Alexis. Either be strong like me or weak like your mother. Don't try to combine both."

Coldness washed over her. She wanted to tell him that there had to be a choice in between, but the words, lacking conviction, would not come.

CONVICTION BECAME a major preoccupation for Alexis as the new decade of the fifties began. She had always thought of herself as an intrinsically decent person, prepared to do the right thing, whatever that might be. But in the early months of 1950, she found herself caught between pragmatism and principle.

The guilty verdict returned by the jury in the second Alger Hiss trial triggered a wave of panic in a nation bewildered by the direction of the postwar world and fearful that everything won in bloody sacrifice would be lost through betrayal.

President Truman responded by ordering construction of the hydrogen bomb. The GOP warned that the issue in the coming election would be liberty versus socialism. Toward the end of February, the junior senator from Wisconsin, Republican Joe McCarthy, stacked dossiers on his desk in the Senate chamber and for six hours turned rumor and innuendo into charges of Communist infiltration into the State Department.

"I never thought I'd see anything like this," James said one late winter morning as they were having breakfast with Matthew. "The whole country is going nuts."

"I thought the America Committee was bad," Alexis mused, "but this is far worse."

"What's a fifth column?" Matthew asked, reaching for the toast.

Alexis and James glanced at each other. He answered. "It means an enemy force that sneaks into a country and pretends to be good citizens while waiting to take over."

"Is that what the Reds are going to do to us?"

"They might want to," James acknowledged, "but we're pretty strong, son, and smarter than we look right now. So I don't think you really have to worry."

Matthew hesitated a moment before he said, "My teacher at school says that Communists are everywhere, including radio and television. She says the Reds have to be rooted out before they take over completely."

"People are very frightened right now," Alexis said quietly. "I don't pretend to understand all the reasons, but I think it's because after the war we discovered that we couldn't retreat back behind our borders as we had before, that we had to face a world becoming increasingly complicated and threatening. But no matter how scared we are, we can't sell our freedom to buy an illusion of safety."

"What's a 'lusion?"

"Illusion. Remember the fun house we went to last summer, where the mirrors made you seem twisted into different shapes?" When he nodded, she smiled gently. "Those were illusions, and so is this."

She was afraid the parallel might go over Matthew's head, but he seemed to draw some comfort from it, perhaps because he understood that what happened inside fun houses wasn't to be taken seriously. Unfortunately, things were a little more complicated in the read world.

Charles Brockton suffered a heart attack and went into the hospital early that spring. Alexis did not go to visit him, though she did send flowers and a book about Ireland's struggle for freedom that she thought he might enjoy. Rather to her surprise, she got back a note that said he had read it through and thought it made some good points. Also, he'd been watching IBS recently and didn't find it as bad as he'd expected. At the bottom of the note was a P.S.: "Graham comes by daily to see if I'm still alive. Masks his disappointment well."

He went home in May and they exchanged letters again; his handwriting was spindlier and the words rambled. He said he was thinking of going to Europe in the summer, then lapsed into memories of a trip taken more than twenty years before. "Your mother liked Venice especially. I remember the kick she got out of boat rides on the canals. Maybe we should have done more things like that."

Alexis put both letters away in the bottom of one of her lingerie drawers, down among the lavender sachets. She tried not to think about what he'd said too often. Distracting herself proved easier than might have been expected since her pregnancy was now certain.

James did not hide his exhilaration. He had been delighted when she stopped using birth control, but had carefully controlled his anticipation for fear of scaring her off. Their lovemaking had taken on a new degree of tenderness that moved her intensely, even as it scared her a bit. He wanted another child so much, while she could only muster mild pleasure at the thought.

In the early months of her pregnancy, even that was denied her. It was hard to have warm thoughts about motherhood while standing with her head over the bathroom sink.

"Why didn't anyone warn me about this part?" she asked Maggie one Saturday afternoon at the end of June, when both women were sitting in the backyard of the Garganos' Long Island home. They were dressed in Bermuda shorts and cotton blouses in an effort to ease the ninety-degree heat. Anthony and James had taken the kids off to an air-conditioned theater to see *Treasure Island*, leaving the women to enjoy a rare moment of privacy.

"I would have told you if you'd asked," Maggie said cheerfully, "but maybe it's better you didn't." She paused to take a sip of her lemonade and brush a strand of chestnut hair from her forehead. Her lightly tanned legs glistened with baby oil, as did her arms. At thirty-one, she still had the slender grace of a young girl, but her light blue eyes shone with gentle wisdom acquired sometimes painfully over the years.

"I suppose your doctor offered to give you something."

Alexis grimaced. "He hands out pills as though they were pieces of candy. Maybe I should just take them and be glad, but somehow I think I'm better off without."

"So do I, though it's not a popular viewpoint. Anyway, you'll feel better once the first few months are passed."

"The worst part is not being able to work as much as I'm used to," Alexis said. She shifted slightly to loosen her waistband. Before too much longer, she was going to have to buy some maternity clothes. "I keep falling asleep in the middle of the day."

"From what I hear, you're lucky. The craziness is definitely getting worse. Do you know teachers here are now being required to take loyalty oaths?"

Alexis shook her head in sorrow rather than disbelief. "Has Anthony showed you that booklet we got?"

"You mean 'Red Channels'?" Maggie wrinkled her nose in distaste. "I couldn't believe some of the people that thing labeled as Communists: Leonard Bernstein, Lee J. Cobb,

Ruth Gordon, Dashiell Hammett, Lena Horne. We're really supposed to buy the idea that they're threats to the country?''

''I'm afraid plenty of people will do just that. It seems as though the public is ready to believe anything so long as it's shouted loudly enough.''

''That's McCarthy's tactic; shout, wave arms and claim to have evidence. Only he never lets anyone see it.''

Alexis laid her head back and closed her eyes. She was tired, as usual, but at least the chicken soup Maggie had fixed her for lunch was staying down. ''I think I'll just nap for a bit,'' she murmured.

It was dark when she awoke. Instead of being in the backyard, she was lying in bed in Maggie and Anthony's guest room. Her sandals were on the floor beside her; a thin cover had been pulled up to her chin. The windows were open and a slight breeze ruffled the dotted Swiss curtains. From downstairs, she could hear muted voices.

Maggie, Anthony and James were sitting around the card table playing gin. They glanced up as she appeared at the foot of the stairs. ''Welcome back to the land of the living,'' James said. ''We saved you some dinner.''

''Great; I'm starved. What time is it?''

''Just after nine. Sit down and I'll get you a plate.''

''I'll do it,'' Maggie offered. ''Are you feeling better?''

''Sure am, as though I'd slept for days.'' She did full justice to the thick turkey sandwich and glass of milk that Maggie set before her, then joined the game. Anthony was about to deal the cards again when the phone rang. He got up to answer it as the others chatted about nothing in particular.

When he came back, he was frowning. ''That was the office. Something's come over the wire service about trouble in Korea.''

Chapter Nine

THE IBS NEWSCASTER smoothed down his hair, straightened his tie and waited for the signal that he was on the air. When it came, he smiled decorously and began.

"Good evening. United Nations invasion forces landed today at Inchon, the port of Seoul, Korea, some one hundred and fifty miles behind enemy lines. Elements of the First Marine Division stormed ashore on the island of Wolmi, took control of it within forty minutes, and crossed the causeway to the capital. General Douglas MacArthur, Commander of the UN forces, applauded the successful landing. North Korean soldiers were reported to be throwing down their arms in large numbers and surrendering without opposition. More after this word from our sponsor."

A commercial for Maybelline eye makeup came on. Alexis shifted in an effort to find a more comfortable position on the couch.

"How are you feeling?" Matthew asked. He was stretched out on the floor nearby, ostensibly doing his homework, though he found the reports from the war zone far more interesting.

Alexis gave him a wan smile. "All right. At least it isn't as hot as it has been." Mid-September had brought a break in the heat wave that had plagued much of the country throughout the summer. The apartment windows were opened wide, letting in the sounds of rush-hour traffic. Lights were flicking on as dusk settled over the city.

"Dad should be home soon."

"Yes..." James was working later than usual, partly because of pressure to get as much war news on the air as possible, partly because Alexis was able to spend only a few hours a day at the office and sometimes not even that. In her sixth month of pregnancy, she had already gained twenty-five pounds despite rigorous efforts to avoid overeating. She tired easily and sometimes found herself crying for no apparent reason.

"Maybe I can get him to tell me more about when he knew MacArthur," Matthew was saying.

He spoke so eagerly that Alexis couldn't help but laugh. Gently, she said, "Your father didn't really say he knew MacArthur, only that he was in his command for a while. And he was none too thrilled about that." Which was putting it mildly; as ex-Marines, both James and Anthony had very mixed feelings about the general.

"Yeah, but he saw him lots and talked to him. They even fought together."

"Generals don't actually go into battle, at least not very often. It was men like your father and your uncle Anthony who fought." Quietly, she added, "Many of them died."

Matthew hesitated a moment before he asked, "You don't think that could happen to Uncle Paulo, do you?" He was referring to one of Anthony's brothers, a quiet young man who had been finishing his masters degree in American Literature at Columbia University when his reserve unit was called up. He was now at sea with the Navy somewhere off Korea. His wife, pregnant with their first child, was staying in Brooklyn with Maria and Joseph Gargano.

"I don't think so," Alexis said softly. "From the sound of things, the war may be over soon."

"I hope you're right." Eyes as blue as James's hardened slightly as Matthew added, "I told a kid at school about Uncle Paulo and he said he was a two-time loser 'cause he'd had to fight in both wars."

"That wasn't nice."

"It's okay; he won't say it again."

Alexis raised an eyebrow. "Oh? Why not?"

"Uh. . .I just told him not to."

"You didn't get into a fight, did you?" It was rare for Matthew to be in trouble, but every once in a while his strong sense of moral purpose caused him to spring to someone else's defense. Fortunately, he was large and strong enough at ten to protect himself as well as others.

"Not a fight exactly. He took a swing at me, so I grabbed hold of his arm like Dad showed me and threw him."

"You didn't hurt him?"

"Nah. We were in the gym and I made sure he landed on a mat." Gravely, he said, "Dad told me it's wrong to use strength to hurt people."

"Good; I'm glad you remember that. Now, since you're feeling so strong, how about helping me up?"

Matthew was instantly at her side, supporting her as she gingerly stood up and smoothed the skirt of her maternity dress with a grimace. Her feet were invisible, as was a large portion of the carpet immediately beneath her. "I feel like an elephant."

"You look great," he insisted reassuringly.

Alexis cast him a skeptical glance. "I hope you won't mind having a linebacker for a baby brother. . .or sister."

Despite himself, Matthew giggled. "I can hardly wait till it gets here, whatever it is."

Alexis felt the same way, though for different reasons. Her unwieldy size had become more than simply an irritant. She was growing more concerned with each passing day. Her doctor, however was not. He continued to assure her that everything was fine and to suggest indulgently that she simply relax and leave herself in his more than capable hands.

"Easy for him to say," she groused to Maggie a few days later as they were wandering through the baby department at Saks. "It's not his body that feels as though it's about to explode."

"Maybe you should consider seeing someone else," her friend suggested gently, "if only to ease your mind."

"Aren't all obstetricians alike basically? All-knowing males in white coats benevolently dispensing wisdom to poor benighted females?"

Maggie fingered a tiny dress and smiled dryly. "There are a few exceptions. For instance, I went to a woman who's very good. She listened to everything I said and took me seriously."

"That would make a nice change."

"Give it a try." For added emphasis, she pressed Alexis's hand gently.

Dr. Spencer turned out to be thin, gray-haired woman with a ready smile an a no-nonsense manner. She took one look at Alexis and frowned. "You're due to deliver when?"

"In three months."

"We'll see about that. Just lie back and relax."

At least the examination was less uncomfortable than the others that had preceded it. When the doctor had finished, she looked thoughtful. "Go ahead and get dressed, then we'll talk in my office."

It seemed to take Alexis forever to get back into her lingerie and the soft apricot wool suit she had had specially made after becoming disgusted with maternity clothes that made pregnant women look like misshapen little girls. Joining the doctor in her sun-filled office, she asked nervously, "Is everything all right?"

"Sure is, so long as you don't mind having twins."

"T-twins...?"

"Yep...two of the little things. One slightly larger than the other, but both good sized. My guess is you'll deliver early, possibly as much as a month, and a Caesarian may be needed, but otherwise you should do all right."

"Why didn't the other doctor tell me?"

"He may have decided it was better to keep it from you for a while so you wouldn't worry."

"That wasn't his decision to make," Alexis protested.

"I agree, but it's still common practice. Now, am I to understand that you want me to take over your care?"

"Yes, if you will."

"Certainly, provided we get the ground rules straight. I have no objection to your working; I did it myself while I was pregnant, but I was sensible about it and you have to be, too. Do as much at home as you can; don't let yourself get overly tired and don't try to stand for long stretches."

"Is that all?" Alexis asked with uncharacteristic meekness. She was ready to agree to just about anything, now that she felt she was really with someone she could trust.

"Not by a long shot," the doctor assured her good-naturedly. "There's a whole list of dos and don'ts, but I'll let you read them over for yourself. Call me with questions. Usually at this stage of a pregnancy, I'd want to see you every month, but since you're carrying a double load, let's make it every two weeks. All right?"

Alexis nodded numbly, accepted the list, made another appointment on her way out and eventually found herself standing in the late-summer sunshine on Park Avenue. She waved down a cab, got in, gave her address and settled back in the seat, all without any awareness of what she was doing. Only a single thought stood out in her mind: There were two babies.

James would be in absolute heaven, whereas she... Better not to think about that right now, or perhaps ever. There was, after all, absolutely nothing she could do about it. As her father had said, you throw the dice and you take your chances on how they'll add up.

Despite Dr. Spencer's warning, Alexis did not deliver a month early, though she had reached the point where she would have welcomed anything that made her stop feeling like a grossly distorted blimp. No position was even remotely comfortable. James did his best, sitting up with her, rubbing her back, trying to help her cope with the multitude of problems weighing down on them.

In addition to concern about her own condition, Alexis worried about her father, who had suffered another heart attack and been returned to the hospital. She was also well aware, despite James's attempts to keep it from her, that IBS was under increasing pressure from sponsors to conform to the demands of groups such as the America Committee and Counterattack, the group that had published the inflammatory "Red Channels" booklet. So far he was resisting, but at the loss of vitally needed advertising dollars.

Meanwhile, events in the world beyond tumbled madly one after the other. By October, fears were mounting that the Communist Chinese intended to enter the war. They were realized in early November, when more than a hundred thousand troops streamed over the border into Korea.

American and other U.N. soldiers quickly discovered that they were fighting a new kind of enemy who attacked out of nowhere, vanished as swiftly, then reappeared in lethal strength where least expected. Again and again, allied forces fell in great numbers as a disaster of historic proportions threatened to develop.

"If this country can't defeat an enemy that's still in the Middle Ages," James said one evening shortly after Thanksgiving, "then we're in even worse trouble than I thought." He sneezed and reached for the box of tissues, silently cursing the head cold that he privately believed was the result of frustration.

For the last month, intercourse had been off-limits, which might have been just as well, since Alexis had lost all interest in sex. She seemed to think James had, too, at least with her. He couldn't bring himself to admit that he found her more desirable than ever.

That compounded feelings of guilt stemming from the belief that she had become pregnant at his urging. Though he continued to look forward eagerly to the children who would soon enter their lives, his happiness was tempered by concern for Alexis. Frequently he would wake in the middle of the night, worrying about how she would come through the delivery and whether she would feel the suffering had been worthwhile.

Alexis wondered the same thing herself, though they did not speak of it directly. Instead they both concentrated on making a happy Christmas for Matthew. James bought most of the gifts for him, since Alexis had such a hard time getting out. He found the stores crowded with shoppers who, like him, seemed to be doing little more than going through the motions. On the other side of the world, Americans continued to die in record numbers in a war everyone had thought would be over months before. Yet at home they felt the need to pretend that everything was normal.

On Christmas Day they were up early to unwrap presents. Matthew seemed to really like his trains and chemistry set. James was pleased by the leather-bound books and gold cuff links. Alexis held up a silk negligee ruefully and wondered out loud if she would every be able to fit into it.

The afternoon passed quietly. They enjoyed a turkey dinner prepared by James, who followed careful directions left by the housekeeper before she went off to visit her family. Maggie and Anthony came to visit later in the day, bringing the children. In deference to Alexis's condition, they didn't stay long.

Matthew went to bed after thanking them again for his presents. James and Alexis stayed up a while longer, watching the glowing colored lights on the Christmas tree and talking quietly. By midnight they, too, were in bed. Alexis slept better than she had in a while, though she woke several times, aware of a dull pain in her lower back. Having been uncomfortable for so long, she thought little of it. Until the following morning.

"James...?"

"Yes, what is it honey?"

"I...think something's happened."

He turned around from the bathroom basin where he had been shaving, brush still in hand and foam spread over his jaw and face. His chest was bare, the hair still damp from the shower he had just taken. A towel was wrapped around his waist.

Alexis stood in the bathroom door. The lower part of her nightgown clung to her. For a moment he wondered how she had gotten wet; then he realized her water must have broken.

Dropping the brush, he reached for a towel and wiped the soap from his face with single motion. Before he had finished, he had crossed the room to her. "Come on, honey. You're going to lie down while I call the doctor; then we'll get you dressed and head for the hospital.''

She nodded silently, making no comment as he lifted her carefully and carried her back to the bed. That more than anything told him how startled she was.

''What's going on, Dad?'' Matthew asked when he found his father partially dressed and rummaging through the hall closet for the bag Alexis had packed several days before.

James straightened and put a hand on his son's shoulder. He contained his own mounting nervousness enough to smile reassuringly. ''The babies are on their way, so we're headed for the hospital. I've called Maggie. She'll be over right away to pick you up.''

''Okay, Dad.'' He hesitated a moment, then added, ''I hope Alexis will be all right.''

James bent down and gave him a quick hug. Love for his son filled him even as he silently echoed the little boy's hope.

''SHE'S DOING FINE,'' Dr. Spencer assured him a short time after their arrival at the hospital. Alexis had been whisked away somewhere, while he was relegated to the waiting room. His last sight of her had been overly large gray eyes set in a pale face.

''May I see her?''

The doctor hesitated. ''If it was up to me, you could. But it's against hospital policy.'' She smiled ruefully. ''You're supposed to stay here, drink the terrible coffee from the vending machine and pace a hole in the carpet.''

''Great,'' he muttered under his breath. ''I feel like a fifth wheel.''

''Don't worry; you'll get your chance to shine once the babies are here. Got enough nickels for phone calls?''

"I think so." With a faint smile, he added, "Do me a favor, Doc, and fix it so I can make them soon."

"I'll do my best," she assured him before hurrying off again. Left alone, James slumped into a chair near the door and surveyed his surroundings. The hospital was one of the best in the city, but the decor left much to be desired.

The wall immediately opposite him was painted a dreary institutional green. Worn linoleum of an indiscernible color covered the floor. To his left, a wooden venetian blind hung crookedly over a window that looked out on an air shaft. Beneath it was a sagging couch, mate to another on the other side of the room. Half a dozen more chairs were scattered around, along with several small tables holding frayed magazines. The vending machine the doctor had mentioned dominated the far corner.

He had the place to himself for a little more than half an hour, during which he must have glanced at his watch a dozen times. The minute hand moved with the speed of half-frozen molasses. He shook his head in irritation and stood up, walking over to the window and back again before discovering that the activity did him no good at all. Nothing seemed likely to ease the tightness in his belly and the disjointed thoughts running through his mind. Nothing except news of Alexis and the babies.

That was a long while coming. The waiting room filled up gradually. There were three other expectant fathers, one not more than eighteen, the other two in their twenties. They made a strained effort at nonchalance, laughing and talking among themselves. Other vigilants arrived: a plump, stern-faced grandmother-to-be, who shot a single disdainful glance at the men before settling down to knit; somebody's younger sisters, who giggled between themselves interminably; a young man

with a blankly incredulous look, who took pains to tell everyone he was "just a friend."

The pale winter light came and went; lamps were turned on.
James tried to read, could make no sense of the words, gave up.
He paced, slumped, then paced some more. Slowly the ab-
surdity of his situation began to eat away at him.

He was being shunted aside as though he had nothing to do
with what was going on, when in fact he was intimately involved. Moreover, Alexis was being left alone with no one to
protect her except the doctor, a well-intentioned woman certainly, but hardly the same as a husband.

With a gesture of disgust, he tossed aside the cardboard
container of coffee and stood up. The other people in the room
glanced at him in surprise as he stomped out.

In the corridor, he corralled a nurse. "My wife's Alexis
Callahan. I want to know what's going on with her."

"You'll be informed in due time, sir."

"That's not good enough. I want to know now."

The nurse hesitated. She was young enough to be impressed by James's dark good looks and aura of authority, but
experienced enough to know the rules. "I'm afraid you'll have
to wait, sir, until..."

"Forget it. I'll find her myself."

As he strode down the corridor in the general direction of the
delivery room, the nurse gasped and ran after him. "You can't
go that way!"

The long hours of waiting had taken a toll on his patience.
Visions of Alexis in pain, perhaps even in danger, tormented
him. Without stopping to think, he demanded, "Who the hell's
going to stop me?"

The nurse stared at him blankly. She hadn't been trained to
handle such a contingency. Expectant fathers simply did not

go barging into delivery rooms; they stayed where they were put and were humbly appreciative of any attention given to them. But not this big, hard man with the unruly black hair and glittering blue eyes. He looked ready to march through anyone who got in his way.

"Uh...sir...if you would just wait one more moment, I'll find your wife's doctor and get a report on her condition."

James hesitated, then nodded grudgingly. "Double-time it."

The military parlance, lapsed into unconsciously, did the trick. The nurse hurried down the corridor propelled by a sense of purpose.

Alexis was only dimly aware that someone had come into the curtained alcove where she lay. Convulsed with pain, she moaned raggedly. Her hair was damp with sweat; deep grooves scored her palms where her nails had dug into them; her lower lip had been badly bitten.

"We can give you something for this," Dr. Spencer was saying gently, "but I have to tell you it will slow things down."

"It's all right," Alexis gasped. "I'm okay."

The doctor had her doubts. Labor was proceeding very slowly. After almost ten hours of unremitting agony, there was very little to show for it. Bending closer, she put a cool hand on Alexis's brow. "You don't have to prove anything. I can intervene if necesssary."

"Intervene...?"

"A Caesarian, before the last of your strength goes."

Alexis's head moved back and forth against the pillow in rejection. The doctor sighed and withdrew her hand. The young nurse hurried to her side.

James was pacing back and forth in the corridor like an angry bull. He glared at an orderly who approached him, sending the man scurrying away. Pushing an impatient hand through his hair, he turned toward the labor room door just as the doctor emerged.

"Threatening to bust up the joint?" she demanded briskly.

Abashed, he dropped his hand. "I'm worried about Alexis. Why is it taking so long?"

"That's just the way it is sometimes. She has a very narrow pelvis and she's carrying two good-sized babies. But she's also strong and has plenty of guts. I'm still hoping for a normal delivery."

"Normal? As opposed to what?"

"Nothing terrible. Calm down or I won't let you in there."

James opened his mouth, about to argue further, then shut it abruptly. When the doctor was satisfied he could behave himself, she opened the door for him. "Come in, then. But if you start feeling faint, I want you out immediately."

Faint? Surely she was kidding? He was an ex-Marine who had gone through more battles than he cared to remember. Men had been blown to bits in front of him; others had died in his arms. He'd seen everything there was to see....

At least he thought he had. Never had he seen anything like what he encountered when he walked into the room divided into a dozen curtained alcoves. A few stood open, enabling him to see the narrow, steel-framed beds that were their sole furnishings. Women, their bodies twisted into unnatural shapes by acute pain, lay in them, moaning fitfully. A few cried out loudly or cursed. All looked like denizens of a private hell in which suffering was the only reality.

He glanced at the doctor in angry disbelief. "Is it always like this?"

Gently, she explained, "If we don't medicate a woman in labor, she's liable to scream from the pain. If we do, the drugs break through her inhibitions and she's liable to tell us what she really thinks of her condition." A slight smile lit her eyes. "That's part of the reason husbands aren't generally allowed in here."

"There has to be a better way," James insisted.

"Not until women are trained to help themselves during childbirth, with proper breathing and other techniques. My patients get at least some grounding in that and it does help."

He nodded slowly, remembering the strange exercises he had seen Alexis practicing. "But then they're left pretty much on their own."

"Yes, which is why you're here." She gestured for him to wait and stepped behind the curtain shielding an alcove at the far end of the room. He heard her say, "Alexis, your ornery husband wants to come in."

"J-James...?" a weak voice whispered. "What's he doing here?"

"It was either that or have him tear up the waiting room. Since he doesn't look like the type who will make a mess on the floor, I thought we'd give him a try. Okay with you?"

"Yes...I guess so..."

He didn't wait to hear any more. Sweeping aside the curtain, he stepped into the alcove. Alexis had propped herself up on her elbows. She looked at him bemusedly. "Are you sure you want to do this?"

"Positive," he informed her briskly, ignoring the sudden lurch of his heart as he took in her condition. She looked so damned helpless, and so tired. Clad in a white hospital gown, with a sheet pulled up over her, her body looked absurdly small in comparison to the immense swell of her belly. He sat down beside her swiftly on a stool provided by the doctor and took her hand in his.

"It's going to be okay, honey. Try to relax." The words were meaningless, as he discovered an instant later when yet another contraction hit her. Though Alexis clenched her teeth and managed not to utter a sound, he could see that she was in agony. "Dammit, there's got to be something you can do!"

"There is," the doctor said calmly, "and I will, soon, unless the labor proceeds much more quickly."

"You said the drugs would slow it down," Alexis protested, gasping.

"You know the other alternative."

"I don't want to be knocked out. I want to see my babies born."

"Why?" James blurted. "What the hell difference does it make? You'll see them when you wake up." He didn't mean to sound so angry at her, but dammit, he was getting mad. Why was she arguing when there were drugs that could spare her the pain?

"It's important to me," Alexis protested, fighting against the tears that burned her eyes. "After coming this far, I don't want to miss it."

"Most women are given ether right at the end anyway," the doctor pointed out quietly.

"No! I want to be awake." Why that had become so vital to her, she couldn't say. All she knew for sure was that she didn't want to be made incidental to the birth of her own children, not after conceiving and carrying them for nine months.

"All right," the doctor said soothingly. "Don't get upset. Concentrate on helping them and I'll do my best to help you."

That seemed fair enough. Alexis relaxed slightly, though her hold on James's hand did not lessen. Another contraction overwhelmed her and she was once more swept into a realm where pain was the only reality.

Time passed; they both lost track of how much. Between the contractions, James held her, murmuring words of reassurance and love. When the pain hit, he endured it with her, wishing he could take it on himself and desperate for it to end.

At length the doctor returned. James waited outside the curtain while she examined Alexis again. She emerged with good news. ''We can go upstairs now to delivery.''

''Thank God,'' he murmured fervently.

''I'll come and get you when it's over.''

''Wait a minute. You've let me go this far, why not all the way?''

The doctor frowned, considering that. ''You'd have to scrub. . .''

''Fine; show me where.''

''It's. . .not pretty.''

''Somehow, I had already picked up on that.''

His sarcasm wrung a reluctant smile. ''All right, but no one will blame you if you decide to leave.''

Fat chance, James thought as he followed her to the scrub room. Nothing would get him away from Alexis now. Clad in surgeon's greens, with a mask over his mouth and nose, he emerged into the delivery room to find Alexis stretched out on a table, her feet in stirrups. Struck by how exposed and vulnerable she was, James hurried to her side.

An anesthesiologist stood behind her, apparently dismayed to find her still in command of her faculties. ''You should be out by now,'' he complained.

''Put a lid on it,'' James growled as he stepped between Alexis and the man.

''Who the hell are you?''

''The husband.'' His voice dropped to a threatening growl. ''Want to make something of it?''

"N-no...it's just highly irregular."

"Don't worry," Dr. Spencer said as she took her place at the foot of the table. She glanced down and nodded. "We'll be done here soon."

"About time," James muttered, grasping Alexis's hand. His stomach was twisted in knots and he had broken out in a cold sweat, but he was determined to ignore both.

Purposeful silence settled over the people clustered under the spotlights. "Push," the doctor instructed. "Good... again...once more..."

Soft mewing sounds broke from Alexis, but her concentration did not waiver. She gripped James's hand with both of hers and, at the doctor's direction, pushed again.

A scream broke from her even as the doctor exclaimed, "There's the crown.... Push.... Stop.... Good.... Let's see what we've got here...."

James stared at the small bundle the doctor held aloft. It was streaked with blood and mucus and an umbilical cord dangled from it. "You have a son," Dr. Spencer announced, her eyes above the mask crinkling. As she spoke, she laid the baby on a small table and cleaned out his mouth. His tiny chest rose once, then fell with an exhalation of pure outrage.

"Son..." James repeated bemusedly. The baby looked nothing at all like pictures he had seen on soap boxes and the like, nor did he bear any resemblance to Anthony and Maggie's children who, by the time they had been available for viewing, were pink and smooth. "Is he all right?"

"As rain. Now, back to business..." Returning to Alexis, the doctor said gently, "Almost done. How are you feeling?"

"Tired..."

"It'll be over soon. Let's have another push."

With a weary moan, she obeyed. The first spurt of joy at the sight of her son had faded. In its place was only exhaustion and the dazed feeling that the whole agonizing business would never end.

Yet fifteen minutes later, when the second baby, this one slightly smaller, was ushered into the world, she was still conscious enough to be aware of what was happening. "Another boy...?" she asked weakly.

"A girl," the doctor corrected, repeating the procedure of clipping and cleaning.

James discovered he had forgotten to breathe and inhaled sharply. His daughter wasn't as red as the boy and seemed less wrinkled. Her tiny head was covered with a sleek down of blond hair. As he watched, her eyes opened and looked directly at him.

He stared enraptured for a long moment before becoming aware of the wetness on his cheeks.

Chapter Ten

"THEY DON'T DO MUCH, do they, Dad?" Matthew asked. He was hanging over James, Jr.'s crib in the sun-filled nursery at the back of the apartment. The walls were decorated with stenciled characters from fairy tales; mobiles dangled from the ceiling; shelves were filled with stuffed animals and other toys.

"It's a little early yet," James said, ruffling his son's hair. "Give them a while."

Matthew ducked out from beneath his hand and frowned. "Was I like that?"

"Sure you were. So was Tessa. Remember?"

"I guess.... I promised to call and tell her about them. Okay if I do that now?"

James nodded, mildly disappointed that his son did not want to linger in the nursery but unwilling to press him. Matthew was being very good about the two-week-old twins, showing no jealousy and apparently content to cede the limelight. Which was just as well, since the new arrivals seemed to suck in all available energy and attention.

Glancing back down at the occupants of the two cribs placed side by side, James smiled. His daughter slept on her stomach, with her tiny, diapered rump in the air and her thumb firmly in her mouth. Except for a few brief wails when she was wet or hungry, she was the picture of contentment. Not so her brother.

James, Jr.—already nicknamed Jamie—lay on his back, having screamed so loudly when placed on his stomach that he had to be turned over. The new position didn't seem to please him, either. Even in sleep, his face was screwed up into an incipient bellow. The night nurse had walked the floor with him for hours before dawn and at last he had dropped off, but his rest, if it could be called that, was clearly uneasy.

His father felt for him, but he was also puzzled and a little annoyed, since the doctor had assured them there was nothing wrong with the baby. He simply had a cranky disposition. "Some infants are just like that," she had said. "He'll get over it."

Soon, James hoped. Even with the help of nurses, neither he nor Alexis was getting much sleep. For himself he didn't mind, but without proper rest her recovery would be that much more difficult.

Before he left to take Matthew to school and go on to the office, he went into the bedroom to check on her. The blinds were closed and the lights off. Alexis lay curled on one side, her hair spread out over the pillow, her knees drawn up and her hands folded childlike beneath her chin. She was breathing slowly and deeply.

Bending over the bed, James touched the back of his hand to her cheek, relieved to feel that her skin was cool and dry. For several days after returning from the hospital, she had run a slight fever and endured a lingering soreness severe enough to sometimes bring tears to her eyes. The doctor had prescribed medication, but the pills made her feel lethargic and confused. The bottle was still mostly filled when she flushed its contents down the toilet.

For all that she had been through, James couldn't help but think that she had never looked lovelier. His desire for her was both a pleasure and a torment. Dr. Spencer had let him know that since the births had been rather difficult, it would be at least a month yet before Alexis would be completely healed. That, added to her exhaustion and the general strain of motherhood, made him feel like a heel for even thinking about making love to her. He smothered a sigh and dropped a light kiss on her forehead before leaving.

After dropping Matthew off at school, he headed on downtown and parked the car in a lot near the office. On his way through the lobby, he paused to buy a paper. As usual these days, headlines blared the latest news from Korea. Allied forces were still reeling from the massive Communist attack the day after Christmas. Seoul had fallen again. Victory was further away than ever. Public opinion was divided between those who said America had no business being there and those who advised using nuclear weapons against the Chinese. MacArthur was believed to be among the latter.

James's face was grim as he folded the paper and tucked it under his arm. He had enough on his mind without worrying about the struggle going on thousands of miles away. It had nothing to do with him. Or so he thought.

The morning passed quickly in a flurry of meetings and phone calls. Much that Alexis would normally have been handling fell to James instead, giving him a new appreciation of how important her role had been to IBS. Yet he was still concerned about her insistence that she would return to work part-time when the twins were a few months old. So far he had refrained from arguing with her about it, but that couldn't last forever.

He was thinking about how to broach the subject diplomatically when lunchtime rolled around. He and Anthony sent out for sandwiches, which they ate in the conference room while going over the day's business.

"We've got to get back to Carlson about buying his station," Anthony said as he opened two bottles of beer. "The figures look good."

James nodded and reached for a pickle. Both men were taking advantage of the relative privacy to relax. They had shucked their jackets and rolled up their shirt sleeves. Anthony had his feet up on the table and James had loosened his tie. For all that, they were sharp-eyed and intent.

"How's our credit with the banks these days?" James asked. Normally he was up on such things, but the twins' births had left him somewhat out of touch.

"A few problems, nothing serious."

"Are we getting much more pressure to go along with the blacklist?"

"Some, though no one comes right out and says it." Anthony grimaced slightly. "They talk a lot about protecting the country, but they don't seem to understand much about what it stands for."

James shook his head sadly. "They're running scared, every last one of them, afraid they'll be the next ones dragged in front of some godawful committee and accused of getting into bed with Stalin."

"Hell, I'd be the last guy to turn soft on Communism," Anthony said, "but I'm damned if I don't think we're doing ourselves more harm than good."

James agreed; he had the niggling sense that his fellow citizens were in flight from reality rather than toward it. And who could truly blame them when reality, as represented by the brutal struggle in Korea, was too terrible to contemplate.

"Are you sure you still want to make that trip?" he asked as they packed up the remnants of their lunches and tossed them in the trash can.

Anthony shrugged. "I don't see any alternative. You know we're having a lot of trouble lining up reliable stringers to cover the war for us. I've got a couple of leads in Japan, ex-servicemen who know how to take care of themselves, but I need to check them out for myself. Once we're set, I figure to get them established in Korea and then head home."

"Sounds simple," James admitted. "I just hope it will work out that way."

"You worry too much," Anthony told him good-naturedly. "Just concentrate on that gorgeous wife of yours and the kids."

"Yeah. . .the kids. . .they're a handful."

"How's Matthew doing?"

"Fine, I guess. He's quiet as usual, agreeable, never causes any problems."

"You're complaining?" Anthony asked with a grin.

"No, of course not. It's just that I wonder what's going through his mind sometimes."

"Tessa thinks he walks on water."

James laughed softly. "They're a pair. He's been nuts about her since she was born."

"It's mutual, so I don't think he'll have any trouble with the twins."

James hoped he was right, but as the days passed, he began to wonder. Matthew showed no resentment at the upheaval in his life; he was as pleasant and conscientious as ever. But he also made no effort to have any contact with the babies, steering clear of the nursery and turning down opportunities to hold them.

Instead, he asked for permission the following weekend to stay at Maggie and Anthony's. Like James and Alexis, they were becoming a little concerned about his avoidance of the twins, but they were also happy to have him, if only for Tessa's sake.

James dropped him off Saturday morning, then returned to the apartment. He was glad to get back inside. The weather had turned cold and gray, with a hint of snow in the air. On this last weekend of January, winter seemed determined to stretch out forever.

After helping Alexis feed the twins, he retired to his den to get through the paperwork he had brought home from the office. By mid-afternoon, the light had faded sufficiently for him to turn on the lamps and draw the curtains. With his feet propped up on the desk, he was reading the proposed contract for the purchase of a new station when the phone rang.

"Dad..." a small voice said hesitantly.

James sat up straighter in the deep leather chair. He couldn't identify the note he heard in his son's voice, but he knew it was nothing good. "What is it, Matthew?" he asked gently.

There was a moment's silence before, "Uncle Anthony got a call from Mr. Gargano.... When he hung up, his face was gray and he looked really sick. He said something to Aunt Maggie about Uncle Paulo being...d-dead...."

"My God," James murmured under his breath. The last he had heard, Paulo was on a destroyer off the coast of Korea, generally one of the safer places to be in a war fought almost entirely on land and in the air. Yet his own experiences in the previous war had taught him how shallow the illusion of security could be. All it took was a single bullet or shell fragment to rip it to shreds.

"They went into the bedroom together," Matthew was saying, "but I think they're going to come out soon and call you 'cause they have to go to Brooklyn and somebody has to watch us kids." The last part came in a quick rush interrupted by a sniffle. For Matthew, who kept his emotions to himself to an almost worrisome degree, it was the equivalent of a cry for help.

James's hand tightened on the phone. Quietly, he said, ''Tell them you've already called me and I'm on my way.''

As soon as he hung up, he hurried to find Alexis. She was in the nursery with the twins. Wrapped in a red velvet robe, with her silver hair tumbling around her shoulders, she looked particularly lovely. But he couldn't stop to enjoy that. As gently as possible, he told her what had happened.

As he spoke, the color fled from her cheeks. When he was done, she swallowed hastily. In a shocked whisper, she said, ''Call me when you can. If there's anything Maggie needs...''

''I'll bring the children back with me. They're too young to be exposed to this.''

Alexis nodded and reached up to kiss him swiftly. It was meant as no more than a gesture of comfort, but quickly turned to far more. Long weeks of abstinence coupled with the grim reminder of how death could make a mockery of life shattered their restraint.

A low groan broke from James as his arms locked around her. Heedless for the moment of her fragility, he half lifted her off the ground as his mouth locked on hers. Like a starving man, he plumbed the sweetness of her lips and tongue as though there were no other reality in the world except Alexis and his rampant need for her.

He was not alone in his hunger. Desire she had thought still dampened down by the birth of the twins flared within her. She met him fully, holding nothing back. Only when the slowly dawning awareness of where they were headed penetrated the mist of their passion did they reluctantly draw apart.

"I have to go," James murmured huskily, his eyes lingering on her flushed cheeks and the gleaming disarray of her hair.

She nodded again, shakily. At the door, her hand touched his in silent appeal. "I'll be back as soon as possible," he promised before striding down the hallway to the elevator.

Traffic was better than he'd hoped; he made it to the Island in under an hour. Maggie opened the door for him. Her face was white and he could see that she had been crying.

"C-come in.... Anthony will be out in a minute. We have to leave soon." She spoke distractedly, her mind blanketed by shock.

James touched her arm gently. "I'll get the kids ready."

"Thanks.... I'm afraid I'm not thinking too clearly."

"That's okay." He hesitated a moment. "Is it definite, then?"

Her mouth compressed tightly as she nodded.

James's eyes lowered in sorrow. He had met Paulo Gargano only a handful of times but had been impressed by the young man's intelligence and sensitivity. Having survived World War II, including the D-day landings, he had seemed headed for a brilliant academic career. Now he was dead, and his family, including his pregnant wife, were left to cope as well as they could.

Before leaving, Anthony and Maggie helped to get the children into the car. They said little, grateful that there was no need to do so. "Be good," Maggie murmured as she kissed Tessa and Joe, Jr.

The little girl pouted mutinously. A few months short of her fifth birthday, she was old enough to sense that something was very wrong and to want to stay near her parents. "Go with you," she said determinedly.

As the adults glanced at each other, momentarily at a loss as to how to deal with the situation, Matthew stepped forward. Taking her hand, he said gently, ''If you come home with me, I'll let you play with my trains.''

Despite her fears, Tessa allowed herself to be cajoled. She settled into the back seat of the car, next to Matthew. Joe, Jr., going on four, automatically followed his big sister's lead and slid in next to them.

''This may be for a couple of days,'' Anthony murmured as James got behind the wheel.

''Don't worry about it. Just look after yourselves.''

Maggie slipped an arm through her husband's. Softly, she said, ''Thank Alexis for me.''

He did, shortly after he got home and was settling the children in for the night. They were all to share Matthew's room, since the nursery was too crowded and they were liable to feel scared anywhere else. Joe, Jr., was ensconced on a roll-away bed, while Tessa was being tucked into the lower of the bunk beds.

''If you need anything during the night,'' Alexis said gently, ''all you have to do is call.''

''We'll be okay,'' Matthew said matter-of-factly. His long legs clad in pajamas hung over the top bunk as he smiled reassuringly at the little girl. ''Right, Tessa?''

''Right,'' she agreed in perfect conviction.

''Want glass of water,'' Joe, Jr., declared.

''You just had one,'' Matthew pointed out.

''Want 'nother.''

''I'll get it,'' Alexis said with a faint smile. She marveled at the resiliency of children even as she realized that they had little conception of what had happened. Except for Matthew. It worried her sometimes how much he understood.

When she returned with the water, Joe, Jr., took a few sips before indicating he'd had enough. She covered everyone more securely, then switched off the light and left, checking on her way out to be sure the door was partially open.

"Everything under control?" James asked as she joined him in their bedroom. He was emptying his suit pockets, preparatory to getting ready for bed.

"I wouldn't go that far, but they seem to be settled down."

"Matthew's great with them."

Unbuttoning her robe, she nodded. "I suppose...but it's just beginning to dawn on me that he doesn't really behave like other children his age."

"From what I've seen," James said wryly, "we ought to be grateful for that."

"I'm serious. He acts so grown-up."

"That isn't so surprising, considering what the first five years or so of his life were like."

Alexis did not make the mistake of thinking that her concerns were being brushed aside. She heard the underlying note of regret in her husband's voice. Tossing her robe on the foot of the bed, she said, "You're a good father, James. Matthew couldn't ask for better."

He glanced at her ruefully, trying not to notice how lovely she looked even in the ankle-length flannel nightgown chosen for its warmth and practicality. "He never seems to ask for anything. I'm still surprised that he called today."

"You see, when he was frightened, he knew where to turn."

"I don't want him to have to be scared to need me."

"Of course not. But we can't get around the fact that Matthew learned to be self-reliant at an extremely early age, before you came back from the war. It isn't surprising that he's never shown any inclination to give that up."

"If I'd been able to get him away from Charlotte—" He broke off, embarrassed by the ease with which he was tempted to unburden himself to her. She had more than enough to cope with as it was.

"James...don't shut me out."

"I'm not. It's late and we're both tired." He hung his jacket over the back of the valet and began to remove his belt without looking at her.

Alexis's mouth tightened. Part of her agreed that this was not the time or place for such a discussion. On the other hand, when she was more herself, she might be less willing to confront the issue.

"You always do this," she said quietly. "And I'm just as guilty. We bury things instead of airing them."

"Like what?" he demanded, his hands on the buttons of his shirt.

"My job, the twins, Matthew. How often since we got married have we really talked?"

James took a deep breath, willing himself to be patient. "Look, I realize this is a very hard time for you. The doctor warned me that..."

Alexis's head snapped up. Her hands tightened at her sides. "Warned you of what?"

"Nothing. Forget it. Let's go to bed."

"James, it may have escaped your notice, but having children did not turn me into one."

Prompted by his own frustration, he asked, "Are you sure of that?"

"That's unfair."

He took a step toward her, regretting his hasty words. More gently, he said, "I'm sorry, Alexis. The last thing I want to do is hurt you. All the doctor said was that you had been through a difficult time and that I shouldn't expect you to bounce back too quickly.''

''That's common sense. But it *has* been five weeks.''

''And two days.'' The words were out before he could stop them. Their eyes met, his dark with chagrin, hers filling with the light of comprehension.

''Is *that* why you've hardly touched me?'' she asked softly.

He looked away, aware of the urgency coiling within him. ''I should think it would be obvious.''

At her soft laugh, his eyes jerked back to her. ''I'm sorry,'' she murmured with a gentle smile, ''but it wasn't to me. I had all sorts of other thoughts.''

''What do you mean?'' he asked, genuinely perplexed.

She shrugged self-consciously. ''That I wasn't attractive to you anymore.''

He shook his head in astonishment. ''That's crazy.''

''Maybe, but until this afternoon you hadn't done anything to show otherwise.'' Softly, she added, ''In fact, we've hardly touched at all for the past several months.''

''Because I didn't want to hurt you.''

Despite herself, his righteous indignation made her laugh. ''I'm sorry,'' she gasped at his fierce scowl. ''It's just that I'm getting the feeling that we've been at cross-purposes over nothing.''

''You call your health nothing?'' he demanded angrily. ''Remember, I was there when the twins were born. I saw what you went through.''

''You're making it sound far worse than it was. I'm fine now.''

''The doctor said...''

''Hang the doctor! It's my body and I say I'm fine.''

Seeing her with her head thrown back, her cheeks flushed and her eyes shooting daggers, he wanted desperately to believe her. The rapid rise and fall of her full breasts beneath the nightgown were a sweet torment. He wondered dimly if she realized that by moving in front of the light, she had caused the fabric to become all but transparent. He could clearly make out the dark areolas of her nipples, the indentation of her navel, the shadowed triangle between her thighs.

Startled by her own vehemence, Alexis did not at first notice his preoccupation. She was too caught up in wondering why she seemed bound and determined to insist that she was fully recovered. For too many months her life had been dominated by pregnancy. It had encroached on every aspect of her existence, to her increasing resentment, and had finally plunged her into a torment of suffering.

Knowing that she wasn't supposed to feel anything but pleasure at her motherhood, she was nonetheless driven to regain control of her life for herself.

"James. . .this afternoon I got the definite impression that you wanted to make love to me." Gathering her courage, she added softly, "Was I wrong?"

He stared at her for what seemed like a very long time. Alexis flushed under his scrutiny but refused to back down. As the seconds passed, she became acutely aware of the clock ticking on the bedside table. It sounded very loud, much like the hammering of her pulse.

At length, just when she thought she couldn't bear it a moment longer, he murmured, "No, you were right. But. . ."

Whatever else he had meant to say, he didn't get the chance. Alexis had crossed the small remaining distance between them and was in his arms before he could draw another breath.

"You are the most infuriating man," she murmured, her fingers making short work of the few buttons still fastened on his shirt.

"M-me?" The warm curves of her body settling against his made him gasp deep in his throat.

"You don't see anyone else in here, do you?" Her nose wrinkled. "What did you wear an undershirt for?"

"It was cold today."

"Take it off." Before he could obey, she busily slipped his shirt from him and tugged the offending garment over his head. A soft sound halfway between a purr and a growl rippled from her as she laid her palms flat on his bare chest. "That's much better."

Whatever second thoughts she might have had about behaving so aggressively vanished as James pressed her closer to him. His arousal had never been more evident. It excited her almost unbearably.

Her head fell back, drawing his gaze to the vulnerable line of her throat. His mouth was hot against the silken skin, his teeth raking gently. Big hands slid down her back to clench the rounded firmness of her buttocks.

"Last chance," he rasped. "Are you sure you want this?"

"More than anything," she told him honestly, her lower body undulating against his. "I've been thinking about it for ages."

The confession wrung a grin from him. "You and me both."

"Then shall we...?" Her head slanted toward the bed.

His answer was to bend slightly and lift her into his arms. Alexis laughed delightedly. "I feel just like Scarlett O'Hara."

"Too bad there's no staircase."

"That's all right." Wickedly, she added, "I wouldn't want you to get worn out before we even got started."

James had quite a different fear. He was acutely conscious of his arousal and concerned that he might not take enough time with her. That worry increased when he set Alexis gently on her feet and stepped back, watching as she began to undo the half-dozen buttons at the neckline of her nightgown.

She stopped almost instantly and glanced at the lamp beside the bed. "Uh...would you mind turning that off?"

Surprised, since she had always enjoyed making love in full light, he nonetheless nodded. As his fingers fumbled with the switch, Alexis unfastened the remaining buttons and lifted the gown over her head. For a moment she held it clasped in front of her, then took a deep breath and let it drop.

The heat of James's gaze threatened to scorch her. She felt it even in the darkness and trembled slightly. Instantly, he reached for her. "Cold?"

"No...not exactly." Far from it; she had never felt warmer. The gentle stroking of his hands along her back combined with the rough friction of his chest hair against her nipples sent darts of exquisite pleasure through her.

His breath was warm against her cheek as he murmured, "Alexis...you're not frightened, are you?" It seemed impossible, yet he was hard-pressed to find another explanation for the sudden change in her behavior. From being the aggressor, she had become distinctly shy and halting.

"Not afraid exactly," she murmured into his shoulder.

"Then what?" Putting her away from him slightly, he gazed down at her. His eyes had adjusted to the dimness enough for him to see her fairly well. It was suddenly very important for him to understand what was going through her mind. "Talk to me, Alexis," he urged. "Tell me what's wrong."

"Nothing," she insisted too quickly. "Besides, I don't want to talk."

"You said we should."

"That was before. This is...now...."

He laughed huskily as a surge of tenderness rose within him. She was usually so strong and self-contained that to see her in a fit of sheer feminine illogic was a delight.

The laughter was a mistake. Alexis stiffened and pulled away from him. "I'm glad you're amused. As it happens, I'm rather tired after all." She yanked the covers back and got into bed, moving jerkily toward the opposite side, as far from him as she could get.

James stared at her back for a moment before realizing that she was serious. In silence he removed the rest of his clothes, then propped a knee on the bed and leaned over her.

"Alexis," he said with dangerous softness, "if you think for one moment that I'm going to let you do this to me, you are out of your ever-loving mind."

Her reply was muffled by the bed clothes. "Go away; I'm tired."

His sigh was a long-suffering plea for patience. "Tessa wouldn't behave this immaturely."

"Humph."

"What was that?"

"You laughed at me."

"Not the way you mean. I laughed because I was happy."

"Oh..." She turned over slowly, holding the covers up around her chin, and regarded him warily. "I want you to be happy."

He smiled gravely. "Thank you. I feel the same way about you." As he spoke, he tugged gently on the blanket. It gave, slowly. Easing it out of the way, he moved closer to her.

"Your feet are cold," she complained breathlessly.

''So are yours. Not only that, but you've got goose bumps.'' His hands, stroking her arm, confirmed that. Along with other things. He sat up slightly in order to see her face more clearly. ''Alexis...surely you don't think that I expect your body to be exactly the same as it was before the twins?''

''I.... No, of course I don't think that. But...''

''Changes were bound to happen.''

''I used to be so slender,'' she murmured wistfully.

His hand searched further. ''You still are.''

''No...my stomach sticks out a little.''

He chuckled softly. ''So it does. Very tempting.''

''Don't tease.''

''I'm not. It makes a lovely little pillow.''

Even in the darkness, he thought he could see her blush. Assured now that he was on the right track, he went further. ''What else has changed? No, don't tell me. Let me find out for myself.''

About to protest, she was stopped by the gentle questing of his hands drifting up to cup her breasts. Once they would have only just filled his palms; now they overflowed noticeably. ''Do you mind my touching your breasts?'' he asked huskily. ''They must be tender from the nursing.''

''No...I mean, yes, they are...but it doesn't matter.'' In fact, she wanted him to keep on touching her there but was concerned about how he would react when he discovered the inevitable response. As he laved gently at her nipples, his shoulders stiffened in surprise. Beneath his tender ministrations, her milk had begun to flow. It was sweet and warm on his tongue. The sensation was unlike anything he had ever known, prompting both extreme enjoyment and contrition. Not enough of the latter, however, to make him stop.

"My God, Alexis," he murmured when he at last raised his head, "you're exquisite."

Somehow, her hands had tangled in his thick black hair. Somehow, the covers had been pushed away from them both. Somehow, her doubts had vanished.

"I was afraid you might not like it," she admitted huskily.

He laughed deep in his throat. "*Like* is too mild a word." In the darkness, he reached for her. "Let me show you how I really feel."

Chapter Eleven

JAMES LAY ON HIS BACK, staring up at the ceiling. One arm was folded under his head; the other lay loosely at his side. The covers had been pulled up to his waist, leaving his chest bare. In the darkness, the red glow of his cigarette shone through the film of ashes. It was very quiet. The only sounds he could hear were the ticking of the bedside clock and Alexis's breathing.

She was not asleep.

He hadn't expected her to be, considering what had happened. But her silence gave him the opportunity to pretend she slept. He chose not to take it. They needed to talk; there was no getting around that. If only he knew how to start.

"Alexis...?"

"Yes." Her voice was low and husky, the voice of someone determined not to cry.

"I'm sorry."

"Don't say that. It wasn't your fault."

"I should have realized sooner that something was wrong."

"You did. You stopped."

"Not in time." He moved slightly, stubbing out the cigarette in the ashtray beside the bed, then turning toward her. "It was too soon, wasn't it?"

"I suppose." Her head was turned to one side, away from him. "Anyway, it's over and done with; so let's forget it."

Exasperation stirred in him, undercutting his guilt. He resented being brushed aside, as though what had happened was of no importance when they both must know that was not the case. Worse yet, he resented her reluctance to accept comfort.

He raised a hand to touch her shoulder, thought better of it, and let the hand drop onto the covers near her. "I hurt you."

"I hurt myself," she corrected quietly. "By wanting to be back to normal before I was ready."

"Why?" he asked quietly. "There were other things we could do. It didn't have to be like this."

Tired, in pain, at odds with herself, Alexis lacked the strength for polite deception. "You know that would have been very one-sided, which I don't like."

He did, though they had never spoken of it. Over the years he had taught her to enjoy receiving pleasure from him in a variety of ways, but had never encouraged her to reciprocate as fully. If on occasion he was tempted by memories of the skills he had sampled before his marriage, he reminded himself that his wife was a lady, not a whore, and that she had no need of such tricks.

Alexis, however, felt differently. She had badly needed sexual release that night, but had been unwilling to accept it without giving James the same pleasure. The alternative made her feel too much the supplicant. That, more than anything else, was responsible for their lack of intimacy toward the end of her pregnancy when intercourse became awkward for her. Now it seemed she was trapped in the same bind for several more weeks, until her body could heal completely.

James lit another cigarette and lay back against the pillows. Alexis wished he would say something, even if it was critical of her. But the silence drew out between them.

It was with a feeling of relief that she heard James, Jr., begin to whimper and went to tend to him.

A WEEK AFTER PAULO'S DEATH, the subject of the Korea trip came up again. "There's no way I can go now," Anthony said as he sat in his office, his elbows on his desk and his head resting wearily in his hands. Deep lines were etched into his face and his broad shoulders slumped. "My parents just couldn't stand it, not to mention how Maggie would feel." His voice was drained of all emotion, marked only by extreme weariness. Even his normally clear black eyes were clouded and unfocused.

"Of course you're not going," James agreed. "You've got to stay here and help the family as best you can."

"The sticking point is that it's a chance for us to really step out ahead of the competition." He managed a faint, rueful smile. "Just between you and me, buddy, that's what we need right now if we're going to keep the banks in our corner."

Looking at his friend and partner, James nodded thoughtfully. He had been over the figures himself and knew Anthony was right. Since its creation a little more than five years before, IBS had been growing at an extremely rapid rate. That momentum was the sole reason the banks tolerated their refusal to knuckle under to the blacklist.

"It seems to me there's an obvious alternative," James said quietly.

"What's that?"

"I'll go myself."

"You? What about Alexis and the twins?"

"I didn't say it was the ideal solution, just the only one."

"Yeah, but...it's dangerous. You could get hurt."

"Me? Cat Callahan?"

At Anthony's surprised look, he laughed. "You thought I didn't know what the guys called me during the war? They said

I had nine lives, and considering some of the tough spots I got out of, I have to figure they were right.''

"Maybe," Anthony conceded slowly, "but why push your luck?''

James glanced away. He knew his friend too well to believe he could put anything over on him. Quietly, he said, "I just think it might be a good idea for me to be away from home for a while.''

Anthony hesitated a moment before he asked, "Something wrong?''

James shrugged, embarrassed by his friend's perceptiveness yet glad not to have to spell everything out. "You know how it is.''

"I think so.... Having kids is more complicated than most people figure.''

"That's about the size of it.''

"If it's any consolation, things do get back on track eventually.''

"I hope so," James said quietly, "but in the meantime we could do with a breather.'' He stared out the window at the lunchtime crowds hurrying along, bodies bent into the wind and heads down. Piles of gray slush littered the sidewalks and more snow was forecast for that night. February was a graceless time in New York. "I figured I'd get a flight out to Los Angeles, lay over for the night, then go on to Tokyo. How long do you think I'll need there?''

"Not more than a few days," Anthony assured him, "and maybe a couple of weeks in Korea.''

"That's fine, then. I'll be home by the end of the month.'' By which time Alexis would be well again and they could concentrate on getting their relationship back to normal.

When he told her his plans, she showed no surprise. They discussed the reason for his going and she agreed that it was a good idea. But beneath that matter-of-fact acceptance another reaction lingered. Though she would not admit it, Alexis was privately glad that they would have some time apart. She needed a chance to think things over for herself without being influenced by James. Though he might not mean to do so, his presence alone was enough to steer her in certain directions, sometimes away from where she really wanted to go.

The night before he left, Alexis packed for him. Together they laughed over the World War II-vintage clothes he was taking with him: sturdy khaki shirts and slacks from his days as a Marine, boots that looked impervious to anything man or nature could throw at them, a disreputable poncho still stained with dried mud.

"What about this?" she asked, emerging from the back of the closet with a battered helmet in her hand.

He regarded it nostalgically. "Does this ever bring back memories. You see these two holes here, one on either side?" She nodded. "That happened on the outskirts of Manila. We'd been fighting for days, and though we didn't know it at the time, we had weeks to go yet before the Japs caved in. Anthony and I were holed up in a ditch, trying to get some rest. For some reason, possibly having to do with the home brew we'd liberated, I had a miserable headache, so I took the helmet off and stuck it on top of my bayonet."

He grinned as he remembered. "Next thing I knew, it was the middle of the night and all hell was breaking loose. Seems our ditch was right on the dividing line between Jap territory and ours. Anyway, we got out of there as best we could and it wasn't till the next day that I noticed the holes. 'Course, good old Anthony had to tell everyone I'd been wearing it at the time and thank God I'd been shot in the head or I might have gotten hurt.''

Alexis laughed at the story, but her eyes were somber. Try though she might, she couldn't evade the knowledge that James might be in danger in Korea.

His smile faded as he caught her expression. Gently, he asked, ''What's wrong, honey?''

''Nothing...just...you will be careful, won't you?''

Pleased that she worried about him, James grinned. ''Of course I will, and I'll be back before you know it.''

Alexis believed him; it was inconceivable to her that this man who always seemed to get what he wanted no matter how difficult would let a little matter like a war interfere with his plans. In three weeks he would be home. By then she hoped to have worked out for herself how she felt about becoming a mother and how to resolve that with the other aspects of her life— namely, her career and her marriage.

James left early the next morning. He called Alexis from Los Angeles to say everything was going well and he was looking forward to reaching Tokyo. She had a letter a few days later from the Japanese capital, in which he commented on the rapid pace of rebuilding in the aftermath of the war's devastation. In particular, he was struck by the courage and determination of the Japanese businessmen.

''I know everyone thinks 'Made in Japan' equals junk,'' James wrote, ''but those gimcracks they're turning out these days are only the beginning. They're breaking ground for much more serious industry, especially steel, electronics and, believe it or not, cars. Seems they've got some idea they can compete with Detroit. What impresses me the most is how willing they are to learn from us. It's as though the whole country has very logically decided that since we beat them, we must have something good behind us and they want to know what it is.'' He concluded on a semi-serious note: ''Once they find out, we just might find ourselves with some real competition.''

By the time Alexis received the letter, he was on his way to Korea with the team of correspondents and cameramen he'd lined up in Tokyo. He'd gotten word that an old war buddy of his and Anthony's, an Australian named Jake Dylan, was attached to the U.N. forces there and was hoping to meet up with him.

''Jake will give him the straight dope,'' Anthony said when he heard what James intended. ''Not that pabulum the press office tries to serve up.''

''It's hard even for them to put a good face on what's happening,'' Alexis said quietly. Seoul remained in enemy hands and there were no immediate plans to try to recapture it. The Eighth Army was on the march, but stiff Communist resistance made progress agonizingly slow. The war many had believed would be over in a matter of days was stretching into the new year with no sign of victory. On the contrary, more and more people were talking of a stalemate as though that were the best that could be hoped for.

Sensing the direction of her thoughts, Anthony smiled reassuringly. ''James will be fine. He knows how to look out for himself.''

Alexis nodded, though she had begun to wonder. His absence was proving harder on her than she could have expected. They had been separated before by business trips without her experiencing any particular loneliness or concern.

This time was very different. The days weren't too bad, since she was busy with Matthew and the twins, but at night, lying awake in the big bed, she found herself longing for the warmth of James's body and the comfort of his touch. Not even the memory of their unsatisfactory lovemaking could change her hunger for him.

To distract herself, she tackled a problem that had been on her mind since the children's births. However tenuous her relationship might be with her father, she could not deny him at least some contact with his grandchildren. Writing him a brief note to tell him about them, she enclosed a photo of the twins taken shortly after their birth and sent both off to him.

Within a week she had received back an enormous box from F.A.O. Schwartz, the exclusive Fifth Avenue toy store, containing not one but two immense teddy bears. A card, written in a spidery hand, said only, "For my grandchildren."

Two days later a letter arrived on the heavy vellum stationery favored by the law firm Charles Brockton had dealt with for several decades. The attorney wrote to inform Alexis that substantial trust funds were being established for Amanda and James, Jr. The amounts involved staggered her, even though she knew her father could well afford them. They seemed to contradict his often-stated determination to keep the family fortune intact for Graham.

Alexis had little time to think of that before the papers were filled with reports that a new offensive was about to be launched in Korea. General MacArthur had seen fit to make a statement to that effect despite concerns that such a breach of security would mean increased U.N. casualties. Nonetheless, the drive went off as planned, with two divisions of the Eighth Army attacking across the Han River.

IT WAS AN IDEAL OPPORTUNITY for dramatic, up-to-the-moment news broadcasts, which James did not hesitate to make the most of. Within days he had an efficient system set up to

develop film on board planes rushing it to New York. At Idlewild Airport it was picked up by motorcycle couriers who
transported it to IBS headquarters where it was immediately
put on the air. Within a week of the launching of Operation
Killer, as the new offensive was called, viewers were watching
reports fresh from the battlefield.

It was a spectacular coup for IBS and sent ratings spiraling
upward, just as the 1948 election-night coverage had done. But
this time the stakes were far higher. Watching the reports, Alexis could not help but be struck by the ferocity of the fighting.
The knowledge that James was in the middle of it, repeatedly
exposing himself to danger, tormented her. Worse yet, he had
decided to extend his trip to assure that coverage of the offensive would continue. No longer able to count on exactly when
he would return, the long nights became even more endless as
she struggled with her fears for him.

On the night of Wednesday, February 28, toward 2:00 A.M.
she had finally managed to drift into an uneasy sleep when
those fears were suddenly crystallized into stark reality.

People came and went at the apartment on Central Park
South the next day. Anthony and Maggie were there, of course,
as were several IBS staff members. They coped with the influx
of calls and reporters demanding a statement of some kind. A
man from the State Department was there, and another from
the Pentagon. There was little they could say except to offer
assurances that everything possible was being done.

Alexis listened to them through a wall of numbness that had
descended on her the instant she learned that James had been
reported missing in action. He had been with his old division,
the First Marines, near Hoengsong, when a firefight broke out.
It was believed that he had left his camera crew and gone to as-

sist a beleaguered platoon in need of reinforcements. In the aftermath of the fighting, no trace of him could be found.

"That doesn't mean he's dead," Anthony insisted as he and Maggie sat in the living room with Alexis. "There are plenty of other possibilities." When she did not respond, he and Maggie exchanged a compassionate glance.

Alexis had voiced no disbelief about what had happened or shed so much as a single tear. Instead, she sat upright in the chair, her hands resting in her lap, her features perfectly composed and every silver-blond hair in place. To those who didn't know her, she might have been discussing the weather or some equally unemotional topic.

But neither Anthony nor Maggie was fooled. They knew her well enough to see beneath the deceptively calm exterior. Leaning forward, Anthony said urgently, "Battles are complete chaos; no one's ever sure of exactly what's going on. Maybe he simply got lost. I won't be surprised if he turns up any minute."

Alexis smiled very faintly. Fatigue had shadowed her eyes and washed the color from her face, but it had not robbed her of her common sense. "Thank you for trying to reassure me," she murmured, "but we all know that James hasn't simply wandered off. Something far more serious has happened to him."

No one had to spell out the alternatives. James might be dead, his body blown to bits or unidentifiable. Or he might have been captured. Alexis couldn't decide which would be worse, death in its terrible finality or captivity with the continual potential for terrible suffering. The coward in her prayed that he was beyond hurt even as she clung to the hope that he yet lived.

Hope sustained Alexis through the days and weeks that followed. She nurtured and protected it as a shield against despair. When the initial excitement about James's disappearance died away, the reporters withdrew to pursue other, hotter stories and the merely curious eventually lost interest. The man from the Pentagon called occasionally to assure her they were still making every effort, but as winter yielded to spring and the twins turned three months old, even his attention faded.

Maggie and Anthony were constant in their support, but not even they could ease the burden of worry and grief weighing down on her. Only some substantial distraction could make life even marginally endurable. When, early in April, Alexis announced her intention of returning to work, Anthony was not surprised. James would have wanted her to stay home with the children, but in his absence she had to make her own decisions.

Alexis slipped back into the routine at IBS as though she had never left it, the only difference being that she did not venture near James's office. It remained untouched, awaiting his return. In May, there was a brief flurry of hope when the State Department reported that it was investigating the possibility that he might be being held prisoner. Nothing came of that, although diplomatic feelers continued to be put out.

In June, Alexis received a note from Delia Follett. The television star wrote to say that she was praying for James and was sure he was alive. In passing, she mentioned having seen him on his way through Los Angeles and how happy he had been about the twins.

Alexis read the note several times, struggling with contradictory feelings. On the one hand, she wanted to believe only the best about James, especially under the circumstances. But on the other, she could not shake the fear that he might have turned to Delia for the satisfaction his wife could not provide.

As the first wave of summer heat settled over the city, she struggled to cope with the demands of her job and the responsibilities of being a sole parent. Far from dying down, the Communist panic was growing ever more fervid as the situation in Korea remained unresolved. High ratings and meticulous standards gave IBS a measure of protection, but they also made the company an ever more tempting target for self-declared superpatriots.

In July, as fear of an outbreak of polio spread across the country, Matthew became ill with a high fever and stiff neck. Alexis rushed him to the hospital in the middle of the night. He turned out to have nothing more than a bad summer cold, but in the days before that diagnosis could be confirmed, she got almost no sleep.

Returning to the office, she discovered the rumors of a pending investigation of IBS had prompted the leading member of the news staff to quit along with several reporters.

"We'll have to get a replacement anchorman quick," Anthony said tiredly. During her absence, the brunt of the work had fallen on him. For the first time, he was beginning to look older than his age. "If we don't," he went on, "this could be just the start of a general hemorrhage."

Alexis heard him out, then nodded. "I'll take care of it," she promised. "You go home and get some rest."

He looked doubtful but willing enough to let her solve the problem. He had others to cope with.

When he had left, Alexis stared at the phone for several minutes, weighing her alternatives. She was almost relieved that there weren't many. Without allowing herself to dwell on the wisdom of what she was doing, she took the receiver off the hook and dialed Winston Harcourt's number.

Part Two: 1952-1963

Chapter Twelve

"WE NEED SOMETHING NEW on Tuesdays between 8:00 and 9:00 P.M.," Alexis was saying. "Everything we've tried so far seems to have as much appeal as the proverbial wet noddle."

Anthony leaned back in his chair and stretched slightly to relieve the kink between his shoulder blades. It was late in the afternoon and he was tired. Glancing out the window, he noticed that traffic heading out of town was already heavy. Looked like he'd be late getting home yet again. Resignedly, he turned his attention back to business. "It's tough going up against Milton Berle. He's a big draw."

"True, but I can't believe IBS has nothing better to offer than 'Guess This Tune' and 'Sports Round-up.'"

"You aren't thinking of dropping those, are you? They're both popular shows." As he asked, he was silently calculating the cost of coming up with a new show or shows to fill an hour of airtime. The numbers made his stomach tighten.

"I know they're good," Alexis agreed, "but they'd have a better chance in different time periods."

He could see that, unfortunately. "All right...suppose we did decide on something new. What do you have in mind?"

She smiled sympathetically as she met his wary gaze. He had a right to be concerned. For the first time since its inception, IBS's revenues were heading downward. Several sponsors had bowed to pressure over the blacklist and pulled out. Until they could be replaced—if they could be—risks had to be kept to a minimum. "Don't look so worried. It won't be terribly expensive. What I'd like to try is a half-hour news show.''

Anthony straightened up in his chair and stared at her. ''A what?''

''You heard me. It's about time that side of programming got more attention.''

''Alexis...that's fine in theory, but we're talking audience pull. You want to put a guy reading headlines on against Uncle Miltie?''

The headache that had begun to develop behind her eyes was getting worse. She restrained a sigh. ''No, that's not at all what I have in mind. We need something vigorous, exciting, a show that involves people intensely rather than merely amusing them.''

''And you say it won't be expensive?'' He laughed doubtfully. ''That kind of miracle we could use.''

Alexis shot him a fond look. Anthony really was the soul of patience; he had more than proven that over the past year as they struggled to keep the business going without James. Together they were keeping things afloat, but not without difficulty. Each week seemed to bring new problems and longer hours. In a way, she almost welcomed the exhausting work load because it kept her from thinking too much. But for Anthony it was different. He had a life away from the office.

''I've worked up a description of what I have in mind,'' she told him. ''Why don't you take it home and give it some thought over the weekend? Then we can talk again.''

''We could do that now,'' he suggested tentatively. ''I'm sure you're eager to get started.''

''It will keep until Monday,'' Alexis assured him. ''Besides, you look done in.'' There were shadows under his dark eyes and lines around his mouth that had not been there the

year before. She knew they were due only in part to the difficulties at work. The burden of knowing that James had gone
to Korea in his place weighed heavily on him, despite her best
efforts to convince him he was in no way responsible for what
had happened.

He grinned wanly. "I feel it. It's hard to believe there was
a time when I could go nonstop for days and barely notice."

"We all change." She had, certainly. The past year had left
its mark. She was more slender now than she had been before
the twins' birth, and there was a somberness about her that
never quite faded despite her best efforts. For the sake of the
children, especially Matthew, she tried hard to hide her sorrow and loneliness, but the passage of time, far from making
that easier, seemed only to accentuate the difficulty.

She missed James terribly. That was the single, ruling fact
of her life. From first waking to uneasy sleep, he dominated
her thoughts. Perhaps if she had been able to mourn him
properly, she would have been better off. But as it was, she
could only go from day to day wondering if he was still alive
and, if so, what was happening to him.

That last part she could hardly bear to think about. The
men from the Pentagon and State Department were kind and
reassuring. Initially they had held out considerable hope,
knowing as they did that James was an ex-Marine very experienced in combat situations. But with the passing months
not even they could hide their growing conviction that he was
dead. "He's an important man, Mrs. Callahan," one of them
had said about six months after he was reported missing. "If
the Communists had him, it's likely they would be trying to
make the most of it."

"How could they?" Alexis had asked, not at all certain that
she wanted to hear the answer.

The man had glanced at his partner before he said, "Several ways; they might offer to trade him for prisoners being held on our side or they could try to convince him to appear in a propaganda broadcast on their behalf."

"James would never do that!"

"He wouldn't want to, of course, but. . ."

There had been no need to spell it out. She had heard the whispers of brainwashing that left men little more than zombies willing to do whatever their captors ordered. Visions of James in that condition tormented her, yet she still could not relinquish the hope that he was alive.

After Anthony had left, she packed up her briefcase, then walked slowly down the shadowed hallway to the elevators. It was quiet; most everyone else had gone home. Only a few technicians remained in the studios several floors below, overseeing the taped programs going out on the air.

She was very tired; the back of her neck hurt and she couldn't remember when she had eaten last. Breakfast? Probably; she had a faded memory of corn flakes and orange juice gotten down in between helping the housekeeper feed the twins and asking Matthew how school was going. Fine, he had said, but then he always did.

Alexis shook her head wearily, wishing she could get closer to her stepson. In his father's absence, she had hoped he would turn more to her, but instead he seemed further away than ever. Only with Maggie and Anthony did he unbend at all, and then only slightly.

Thank God, the twins were still too young to have any awareness of what was going on. Amanda seemed perfectly content to burble and babble at anyone who happened to glance her way. Jamie, on the other hand, was impartially difficult with everyone.

The Checker cab she had requested was waiting for her in front of the building. She got in, gave her address, then settled back and closed her eyes. Thoughts of a hot bath kept her pleasantly occupied during the ride uptown to her apartment.

Letting herself in, she took off her coat and hat, then tiptoed in to check on the children. The twins were both fast asleep. She tucked their covers in more securely, dropped a kiss on each forehead, then stood for a few moments gazing down at them. In the dim glow of the night-light, they looked irresistibly angelic. Her throat tightened as she wished James was there to share them with her. She longed to be able to lean her head against his broad shoulder, feel his strong arm around her waist, know that she was not alone.

Instead, there was only an empty bed and another lonely night. Avoiding both for as long as she could, she stopped by Matthew's room. His door was closed. A neatly lettered sign taped to it read: Top Secret Installation. Keep Out! Alexis smiled at that; in some ways, he was very much a little boy. Opening the door silently, she looked at the sprawled figure on the bed.

Matthew slept with an abandon he never showed when awake. His arms and legs were askew, one bare foot stuck out from beneath the rumpled sheet and blanket. He was tall for his age, and rather gangly, but with the promise of broad shoulders and a powerful torso. Yet, in sleep, his features still had the round softness of a child. Careful not to wake him, Alexis straightened the covers. As she did so, her gaze drifted, as it always did, to the picture beside his bed.

Maggie had given him the photo of James taken in Manila shortly before the end of the war. He was dressed in Marine utilities and was leaning up against a tree. His head was bare, his black hair tousled by some invisible breeze. The camera had caught his devil-may-care grin and the gleam in his eyes that suggested anything was possible. He looked strong, capable, vibrantly alive.

Alexis's hands shook slightly as she forced her gaze from the photo and finished covering Matthew. He murmured faintly in his sleep but did not wake. She did not linger over him as she had the twins. The older Matthew got, the more he resembled his father, and the more difficult it was for her to be with him.

He seemed to sense that, for he managed to be out of the apartment much of the time she was there. That weekend he had arranged to get together with a school friend who lived nearby to work on a social studies project. Maggie's brother Tad, a lawyer in Virginia, was running for Congress on the Democratic ticket in November. He had agreed to be "interviewed" while on a recent visit to New York and had patiently answered all of Matthew's questions, afterward commenting good-naturedly that he had seldom received such a thorough going-over.

Left alone except for the twins and the housekeeper, Alexis found that the hours dragged by. She knew she could have spent them with Maggie and Anthony, who had made it clear she was welcome any time, but they had already done so much that she was reluctant to impose further. Instead, she played with Amanda and Jamie, helped to bathe them, then changed into dry clothes and got busy with paperwork she had brought home.

James's office at work remained undisturbed, but Alexis had finally begun to use his den a few months before. Nothing in it had been touched; the books and papers were just as he had left them. An ashtray and a pack of open cigarettes sat on one corner of the leather-topped desk. Nearby, in a double silver frame, were photos of the twins and Matthew. A separate frame held a picture of Alexis taken at the beach. She was wearing shorts and a halter top, her hair tumbling around her shoulders and her eyes bright with laughter—far removed from the pale, withdrawn woman she had become.

Something was going to have to give, and soon. She simply could not go on existing from day to day, jumping every time the phone rang, her eyes drawn irresistibly to every tall, black-haired man she glimpsed. In a few months she would be thirty years old; that birthday loomed ahead of her, an inexorable reminder that time was passing. She could not live out her life longing for James. Eventually she would have to give him up and go on.

Her heart insisted that he was still alive, and probably always would so long as there was no definitive news to the contrary. But her mind was slowly, painfully coming to terms with the alternative.

"You look a little tired," Winston said when he picked her up for dinner a few evenings later. Shortly after he had joined IBS the year before as anchor of the nightly news, they had drifted back into the routine of seeing each other. There was nothing romantic about it, at least from Alexis's perspective. Winston was simply a friend, someone she felt comfortable with, and one of the very few able to penetrate her emotional isolation.

"It's been a long week," she explained as they sat over plates of lasagna in a small Italian restaurant on the West Side. "We're under constant pressure now from HUAC, not to mention Gunner Joe."

The House Un-American Activities Committee had, in Alexis's estimation, been virulent enough without the added assistance of the junior senator from Wisconsin who was proving a master at exploiting his fellow citizens' fears. Alexis was baffled by his appeal; he struck her as so careless with other people's reputations and lives as to be contemptuous of them. Moreover, she had glimpsed him from a safe distance at several political affairs and was convinced that the rumors about his heavy drinking were true. He had the unblinking stare and reflexive tremor found at the bottom of a whiskey bottle.

Yet this was the man many looked to for a solution to what was surely one of the most complex and challenging problems facing the country, preserving liberty without at the same time undermining it.

"There's a basic moral principle involved here," Winston said as he refilled their wineglasses. On the red-and-white checkered tablecloth between them sat an empty bottle in a straw container. Generations of candles had dripped down it so that the straw was almost invisible beneath layers of white and red. The flickering light of the flame half shadowed, half revealed the facial features so familiar to millions of viewers.

His square face with its strong jaw and chin inspired confidence, as did his gray-green eyes set beneath arching brows. The straight line of his well-shaped nose was balanced by a firm, narrow-lipped mouth. Hair that had once been dark brown had turned silver prematurely. He took the teasing about that good-naturedly, knowing that it was the combination of youth and wisdom that contributed so much to his success. At thirty-five, he was confident without being arrogant, a man who had clearly defined his goals and was well on the way to achieving them.

"Do people in this country have a right to due process under the law or do they not?" he asked quietly, his voice low and resonant, compelling attention. "Is the state the ruler of the people or its servant? Do simple human decency and fair play have any place in a world where man has acquired the dubious ability to blow himself to bits within minutes?''

"We seem to be caught between what we wish we were and what we're afraid of becoming," Alexis murmured. "On the one hand, I think most of us truly believe in democracy, but we're also afraid it will make us an easy target for a more ruthless system.''

"By giving in to that fear, we automatically defeat ourselves.''

She smiled slightly and took a sip of the Chianti. It was crisp and slightly tart, sliding pleasantly down her throat. "Things aren't quite that bad yet. If a few strong people would stand up against the hysteria, it could still be overcome.''

"Isn't that what you've been trying to do at IBS?''

"Yes...but not vigorously enough. Which is what we need to discuss." Intent on what she was about to say, Alexis only absently noticed that his attention was focused less on her words than on the delicate curve of the lips shaping them.

"I think the problem is that we've been too reticent about saying what we really believe—namely, that the country needs to pull itself up short and take a hard look at what we're doing to each other before it's too late.''

Winston blinked, shook his head slightly to clear it and gave her a long look. "I take it you have something in mind?''

She nodded. "A longer-length news show that would simply and clearly deal with the key issues of the day. No polemics, no editorializing; just concise words and pictures.''

"We do that already in the nightly news.''

"You've said all along that fifteen minutes aren't anywhere near enough. I'm talking about half an hour once a week to explore important stories in greater depth."

Reaching for a slice of bread, Winston paused. "Wait a minute. I thought you were planning to replace an entire hour on Tuesdays?"

"I am...but we've got to be realistic about this. It won't work unless we can draw a strong audience—against Uncle Miltie, no less. So what I thought we'd do is revamp 'Sports Round-up' into a half-hour show, then follow it with thirty minutes of news."

"Great; equal time for hydrogen bombs and spit balls."

Alexis laughed gently at his chagrin. "No one said it would be easy. Besides, the only other newsman on the air with a really serious half-hour program is Edward R. Murrow, so you won't exactly be in shabby company."

The mere name of the fabled CBS reporter was enough to make him sit up a bit straighter. He made no secret of modeling himself after him. "Well, since you put it that way, maybe having a jock for a lead-in won't be so bad after all. Got anyone in mind?"

She nodded. "I haven't discussed it with Anthony yet, but I think his brother Dom would be perfect for the job."

"Has he had any experience?"

"No," she said cheerfully, "but everyone has to learn sometime."

Winston grimaced slightly, not taken with the idea of a novice sportscaster setting the tone for what he already envisioned as his award-winning news show. But he never let himself forget that television was part of show business, where anything could happen and usually did.

Over tortoni and coffee, the talk turned to other topics: Truman's announcement the day before that he would definitely not run for another term; the likelihood that Adlai Stevenson would therefore get the nod from the Democrats, despite the handicap of his divorce and his alleged support for Alger Hiss; how much that would hurt him in a race where his opponent seemed certain to be former General Eisenhower.

Neither mentioned the brutal, seemingly endless war going on thousands of miles away: Alexis, because she could not bear to think of it; Winston, because he did not want to say anything that would remind her of James. He was, for all his ambition, a patient man, and he believed that time could only work in his favor.

MARCH PASSED INTO APRIL, and the twins turned sixteen months old. They were both toddling about fairly well, though Amanda was steadier on her feet than Jamie. With their growing interest in the world around them, they demanded more personal attention, something Alexis tried to give despite her hectic schedule and frequent doubts about her maternal abilities. Maggie seemed so much more adept at handling small children, but claimed that simply came with experience. Alexis wondered if she wasn't wrong; although she loved the twins, she never felt really comfortable with them. They were too vulnerable, too unpredictable, too frighteningly dependent.

Still, she did her best, determined that they would not be shortchanged by the lack of a father. The news from Korea continued to be discouraging; negotiations were stalemated, with the prisoners of war on both sides the major stumbling block. The Communists insisted on all of theirs being repatriated, while the U.N. side refused to force anyone to go back who preferred to stay. No solution seemed in sight.

James remained officially listed as missing. Alexis went to Washington and listened yet again to the same assurances that everything possible was being done to determine his true status. They rang more hollow with each repeating. The growing conviction that nothing of any consequence would happen until after the presidential elections made her decide to take matters into her own hands. She used a well-connected law firm to make discreet inquiries for her to representatives of the North Koreans and Chinese. So far no response had been forthcoming, but she remained hopeful.

In the middle of April came the stunning news that Douglas MacArthur had been relieved of his post as supreme commander in the Pacific by Harry Truman. The two men had wrangled over the correct approach to the conflict for years, the general wanting to pursue the fight into China and the president determined not to do so. Their struggle had often appeared that of a bantam cock challenging an eagle. Only now there was some question about which was which.

May arrived, and on increasingly sturdy legs, the twins chased after drifting dogwood blossoms in Central Park. Matthew led his school's basketball team to a state championship and brought home a report card with straight A's.

The two new shows, "Sports Arcade" and "Spotlight On..." premiered to surprisingly good ratings. Dominick Gargano proved to be that rarest of all show-biz phenomena, a true natural. He was relaxed and unaffected in front of the camera, knew his subject inside and out, and quickly gathered a loyal following willing even to forsake Uncle Miltie. Winston caught on a little more slowly, but still did well enough for "Spotlight" to be considered a success. One of his first shows featured coverage of a New England town meeting after which participants spoke with quiet dignity about what democracy meant to them. No reference was made to HUAC or McCarthy; viewers were left to draw their own conclusions.

The warmer, sunnier weather was a balm to Alexis. She made a dent in the pile of work on her desk and thought about taking a few days off. The beach house had stood empty since James's disappearance, and she was not anxious to visit it on her own, even with the kids. But there were alternatives.

She was trying to decide on one when she returned from a stroll with the twins. The phone was ringing and she hurried to answer it as the housekeeper bundled them out of their jackets and listened to their chatter.

A lawyer from the firm that looked after her father's affairs was on the other end. His calm, somber voice rolled over her. Alexis heard little beyond the first few sentences; the required expressions of sympathy meant nothing to her. She sat down without being aware of doing so and stared unseeingly at the wall until he stopped talking and she realized he had asked a question.

"What? No...there's nothing I need. Where—" She broke off, clearing her throat. "Have the arrangements been made?"

Graham had already seen to them. She noted the details without comment. When she hung up, it took her a moment to realize that Matthew was staring at her. He had come out of his bedroom, where he had been doing his homework, in time to hear at least part of the conversation.

"Is something wrong?" he asked quietly.

She swallowed hard and managed to answer, though her voice was little more than a whisper. "My father...has died."

His eyes widened slightly and he ducked his head a little awkwardly. "I'm sorry."

Alexis took a deep breath and stood up. Her legs felt weak, but they held her well enough. She saw how taken aback Matthew was, and that made it easier to deal with her own shock. Going to him, she put an arm around his shoulders. For once, he didn't try to squirm away. "He'd been sick for a long time, so this really wasn't unexpected." Except that she had never let herself truly think about it and was therefore unprepared.

"I never heard you mention him."

"We didn't have much to do with each other, just a few letters and some presents he sent the twins." So terribly little for a lifetime.

"Why? I mean...I guess it isn't any of my business, but didn't you like each other...?"

She closed her eyes for an instant and cast around for some explanation that would make sense to a twelve-year-old boy who had reason to be concerned about his relationship with his own father. At length, she said, "We'd never been very close, and after I left UBC, it was hard for us to keep in touch."

She prayed he wouldn't ask why, knowing she would never be able to explain how she and her father could have worked in the same city, even the same industry, yet found so little opportunity for contact. If she said that what small amount they did manage had been an unlooked-for gift, surely his bewilderment would only deepen.

Sensitivity and reticence beyond his years combined to keep Matthew silent, for which she was unashamedly grateful. She knew she would need all her strength for what lay ahead.

The funeral was held the following Saturday, a dreary, rainswept day that belied the promise of spring. There was an impressive turnout. Charles Brockton had been a powerful man who, if he could count few friends, at least had loyal enemies. Alexis noted many among the somber crowd who had opposed him in life but were willing to honor him in death. Either that or they wanted to make sure he was really gone.

Graham held center stage. His face carefully expressionless, he stood at the top of the church steps to greet the lesser mourners. As each one passed before him, murmuring a few words, he inclined his head graciously. Until he caught sight of Alexis. Then the smooth sequence of nod, smile sadly, nod again broke down, and he went rigid, glaring at her.

The young man who stood directly behind him glanced in her direction and instantly left his post. He moved effortlessly through the crowd to reach her side. In a low, hushed tone, he asked, "May I help you, Mrs. Callahan?"

Alexis glanced at him coldly. The simple black dress she wore emphasized the pallor of her alabaster skin. Her hair was swept back from her face to reveal the stark purity of her features. She might have been a figure carved of marble, so little emotion did she show. "Just tell my brother to stay out of my way."

The young man started, stared at her for an instant, then hurried off. A moment later he was speaking quietly in Graham's ear. Alexis watched as her brother stiffened, but made no further move toward her. Satisfied that he had gotten the hint, she went on into the church.

Beside her, Winston murmured, "Bravo, my dear. You handled that perfectly."

She smiled wanly but did not comment. Her attention was focused on the ornate mahogany and silver casket on a bier before the altar. Banks of flowers surrounded it; baskets of chrysanthemums and gladiolus, crosses of lilies and roses, wreaths of carnations and baby's breath. The too-sweet smell clawed at Alexis. Beneath its onslaught, her senses reeled. She swayed slightly and had to grip Winston's arm more tightly.

"Are you all right?" he asked as he steered her into a front pew.

"The flowers...they're a bit much." She fumbled in her purse for a handkerchief, and when she found it, put it in front of her nose. The crisp, fresh linen filtered the smell somewhat, but not enough. After a moment she realized the futility of what she was trying to do and let the scrap of cloth drop into her lap.

The back of the pew was hard against her spine. She shifted slightly and kept her eyes focused straight ahead. Behind her and to the side, the church was filling up. She heard a few whispered comments as people caught sight of her, but ignored them. When Graham took his seat in the pew across from her, she did not glance in his direction. Yet she was glad of Winston's tall, agile body interposed between them.

The service was long and elaborate. There were several eulogies. The priest gave a homily about the transience of life and how the wise man used it to prepare for the world beyond. He managed, without coming right out and saying it, to suggest that Charles Brockton had done just that. Communion was offered: Graham went to the altar; Alexis did not.

At length it was over and the coffin was carried from the church. When most of the mourners had filed out, Alexis indicated to Winston that she was ready to leave. "Are you sure you want to go to the cemetery?" he asked as they walked down the stone steps to the street. Several people looked inclined to come up to her, but thought better of it when she avoided eye contact.

"I'm sure. Graham would like nothing better than for me to stay away. Besides, having come this far, I may as well see it through."

She spoke more confidently than she felt. The drive to the burial ground seemed interminable. Seated in the back of the limousine with Winston, she stared out in silence. Rain splattered against the windows, obscuring her vision. She could see only the distorted shapes of buildings and her own blurred reflection. The smell of the flowers clung to her.

At the cemetery, the soil was so soft that her heels sunk into it. Winston held an umbrella over both of them as the graveside prayers were read and the coffin was lowered into the ground. Stripped of its floral finery, it looked smaller and less imposing. Dangerous feelings welled up in Alexis: compassion for her father as he had been at the moment of death, when none of life's brash pretenses amounted to anything; pity for the fear that was surely inevitable at such a time; remorse for all she herself had left undone.

Down that path lay the erosion of her courage, already sorely tested. To avoid that, she focused on the simple marble headstone marking the grave next to her father's. The inscription stood out clearly: *In memory of Olivia Georgetta Brockton, loving wife and mother, 1900–1930.*

Strange, how little had changed since the day twenty-two years before when she had stood on the same spot to watch her mother being buried. Then it had also been spring, and raining. Remembered fear and bewilderment had somehow gotten twisted up in her mind with the smell of funeral flowers. She felt eight again, and alone.

Winston came up with her to the apartment. The children were staying with Maggie and Anthony. The housekeeper had the day off. There was a pot of soup on the stove.

"Are you hungry?" he asked when he followed her into the kitchen were she had gone to make coffee. "I could warm that up."

Alexis shook her head. "No, thanks," She glanced down at the percolator she was about to fill with water. "In fact, I think I'd rather have a brandy. Would you mind getting it?"

"Not if I can join you." He smiled gently as he took the coffeepot out of her hands and set it back on the counter. "Does that fireplace in the living room work?"

"It's electric."

"Perfect. Come and sit down."

With the fire lit and the first few sips of brandy warming her stomach, Alexis had to admit that she felt better. Winston had drawn the curtains to shut out the rain before joining her on the couch. She glanced at him from the corner of her eye. The elegant gray suit he wore was the perfect foil for his tall, slender body. His silvery hair was thick and well-groomed. A recent vacation in Florida had left him with a tan, yet his aquiline features still looked somewhat drawn.

"Thank you for coming with me," she said softly. "I know it wasn't pleasant."

He turned to her, surprised. "I couldn't have let you go alone. That would have been awful."

She laughed a little shakily. "Too true. Funerals aren't my forte."

Several moments passed as they both stared into the fire. At length, he said, "I don't want to pry, but I couldn't help but notice...your mother was very young when she died."

Alexis took another sip before she nodded. "She was my age."

"Was that...why you had so little contact with your father?"

She looked up, meeting his eyes. "Yes, you could say that. I was eight when it happened, and I guess I blamed him." She broke off for a moment, to take another sip. "I kept on doing that for a long time."

"But not now?"

"No...somewhere along the line I realized that people are responsible for their own lives. That sounds so simple, but it really isn't."

"No one likes to feel completely alone in this world."

"Of course not, but we all are, in the final analysis." She thought again of the grave under the leaden sky and shivered. "At best, we can only offer each other a little warmth along the way."

"Is that what you want?" he asked softly. "To be kept warm?"

She looked at him, seeing the gray-green eyes half-lidded, the firm mouth, the tightness of his skin over strong bones. He smelled of slightly damp wool, soap and after-shave. The hand that held his brandy snifter was large and well-shaped. She guessed that his palms and the tips of his fingers would be smooth, without calluses.

He was very different from James, which was all to the good. "What I want," she said quietly, "is to feel alive again."

Chapter Thirteen

"YOU COULD HAVE KNOCKED ME OVER with a feather when I heard," Anthony was saying. "If anybody had told me what your father—God rest his soul—had up his sleeve, I'd have said he was crazy."

"I'm afraid Graham couldn't agree with you more," Alexis said cheerfully. "But there's nothing he can do about it. The will is ironclad." Charles Brockton had never been one to leave anything to chance. He had disposed of his wealth with meticulous care, leaving—as expected—the controlling interest in UBC to his only son, Graham. But also leaving—as most definitely not expected—cash and securites valued in excess of five million dollars to his only daughter, Alexis.

"I wish I'd been a bug on the wall when the lawyer dropped that little bombshell," Maggie said as she set a platter of veal on the table. "It must have been quite a scene."

"It was," Alexis assured her with a smile. Thoughtfully, she added, "I really don't think I'd ever seen anyone turn quite the shade of purple that Graham did."

"Such an unbecoming color, purple." The two women laughed as Anthony grinned tolerantly. He could afford to, since the elder Brockton's legacy meant the end of IBS's financial problems, at least for the foreseeable future. Alexis had insisted on investing all of it in the company, knowing that was what her father had intended and pleased to be able at last to carry out his wishes.

"How come your brother didn't want you to have any of the money?" Matthew asked as he dutifully helped himself to a spoonful of string beans. Tessa, at his side, sighed as he did so, but followed suit.

"I guess he wanted it all for himself," Alexis said carefully. "Some people are like that."

"Selfish," Tessa murmured, her small nose wrinkling. She cast a telling glance across the table at Joey. "Like certain people I could mention."

He shrugged unapologetically. "Don't want you to play with my toys."

"That isn't nice," Maggie pointed out quietly. "Tessa shares with you."

The little boy shook his head firmly. "She has dumb stuff. Dolls." He screwed up his mouth to show what he thought of that.

"I like dolls," Tessa protested, "but I like blocks and trains and other stuff, too. So why can't I..." her voice began to rise, prompting her father to interrupt.

"That's enough," Anthony said firmly. "Settle down and eat your dinner."

The little girl pouted mutinously but did as he said, as did Joey. Both knew better than to disobey, unless they wanted to go the rest of the week without television or suffer some equally effective punishment. The rules were very clear in the Gargano household, and discipline was both swift and fair.

After dinner, Alexis helped Maggie clear up while Anthony settled the children down in the family room. George Burns and Gracie Allen were on. Their show was a favorite, even if it didn't run on IBS. Anthony claimed to watch it only to keep up with the competition, but he laughed as hard as everyone else.

Listening to them, Maggie smiled. "I'm glad you could come over tonight. It's been a while."

"I know," Alexis said apologetically as she scraped plates into the garbage. "We've been so busy at work and all. . . ."

"Tell me about it." Maggie laughed. "But at least Anthony doesn't drag home exhausted anymore. Things are really better now. . .aren't they?"

Alexis nodded quickly, hastening to assure her. "Definitely. You know what they say about banks? That they only want to lend money to people who don't need it. Something like that is happening to us. Once word got around that IBS was no longer in trouble, everybody wanted to be friends again."

"Hypocrites," Maggie murmured without much rancor. She knew better than to waste her anger on people who would never change. "At least the pressure's off, for a while."

"I'm hopeful that once we get past this election, the whole situation will improve. Neither Stevenson nor Eisenhower strikes me as the sort to tolerate witch-hunts."

"Who do you think will win?" Maggie asked as she set the last of the dishes in the sink. The maid would do them in the morning. She took off her apron and smoothed the skirt of her sundress. Days working in the garden surrounding the large house she and Anthony had moved into the year before had given her a golden tan. Lately she had been playing golf at the local country club, where she also swam daily.

"I don't know," Alexis admitted. "Stevenson is a far more effective speaker and comes across much better on television. But it remains to be seen how much of a difference that will make."

The sound of laughter reached them again from the family room. George and Gracie were going into their windup. Alexis planned to head for home in about half an hour. She had several meetings scheduled for the next day and wanted to be well rested.

"Would you like some coffee?" Maggie asked.

"That sounds good. Let me help you."

They sat at the breakfast table, in a cheerful, plant-filled alcove overlooking the garden. "This is my favorite spot in the whole house," Maggie said. "Sometimes I think I could sit here for hours."

"But I'll bet you don't. You're always busy."

"Because I work at it." At Alexis's surprised look, she explained, "Now that the kids are both in school and I have help in the house, there isn't that much to do." She hesitated a moment, then added quietly, "I've been thinking about going back to work."

Alexis's eyes widened. She had sensed for several years that her friend was not completely satisfied in her role as wife and mother, but she hadn't really expected her to do anything about it. "How does Anthony feel about that?" she asked carefully.

Maggie shrugged. She reached for a spoon and twirled it absently between her fingers. "He wants me to have another baby."

Alexis put her cup down. She really had no idea what to say, but some response was clearly necessary. "Well...I can see how he might feel that way. You are a wonderful mother and Anthony loves children."

"I know he does," Maggie said quietly. "So do I. But I remember when there was more to life than wiping noses and picking up socks." She grimaced apologetically. "Strike that. I sound like I'm wallowing in self-pity, when in fact I know perfectly well that I've got a great life. Maybe that's the problem...."

"I don't follow..."

"Maybe it's too good, too easy. Back during the war everything was tough. I mean *everything*. Anthony and I stole moments together, never knowing for sure that we'd both be alive the next day. We were always vividly aware of how precious life is. Somehow, that made it better." She sighed softly, glancing out at the garden obscured by darkness. "I was a good nurse, a *damn* good one. I saved lives. I made a difference. I want to do that again."

Alexis heard her out in silence. What Maggie said struck a sympathetic chord. She herself had experienced the conflict between career and family, only for her the choice had been easier. She had always known that she couldn't give up her work. If James had not gone to Korea, they would in all likelihood have ended up fighting about it.

"It's funny," she said softly, "I'd give anything to be able to have a good rousing blowup with James about my working. Chances are, he'd take the same attitude as Anthony. But at least the two of you can discuss it."

Maggie grimaced and shook her head. "Somehow our 'discussions' always end one way."

Alexis didn't have to ask what that was. If Anthony wanted his wife to have another baby, he knew perfectly well how to bring it about. "Would you really mind getting pregnant again?" she asked gently.

"I don't know," Maggie admitted. "It would take the decision out of my hands, but I suspect I'd just have to deal with the same problem a few years from now anyway." She shook her head ruefully. "Somehow, I don't think my mother ever worried about such things."

"The world is changing," Alexis said quietly.

There was a spurt of noise from the television: "Amos'n' Andy" had come on with another rollicking look at life in Harlem. *"We's all got to stick together in dis heah thing,"* Kingfish was saying.

"I'm not sure people are ready for change," Maggie murmured. "They seem comfortable with the way things are."

"Sometimes I wonder if they know how things are."

"What do you mean?"

Alexis shrugged. "It's hard to explain, but every once in a while I get this sense of something stirring—" she gestured vaguely toward the window "—out there."

Maggie shot her a wry look. "The only thing stirring out there is the spoon in the martini pitcher. This is the suburbs, remember? Little League and kaffeklatsches, barbecues and car washes. The American dream."

"We is all brothers," Kingfish proclaimed amid much laughter.

Alexis picked up her cup and saucer and carried them to the sink. "I suppose. At any rate, I wish I could help you in some way. You've done so much for me."

"Not really; besides, it helps just to talk about it." She stood up and smiled. "Anthony and I will work things out, one way or another."

Alexis hoped she was right, but she had her doubts. There were some problems that seemed to defy solution. For Maggie, it was the question of whether or not to have another baby. For her, the choice was whether to try in some way, however tenuous, to keep faith with the past or to accept fully that it was over and go on.

Winston was encouraging her to do the latter. "I know this is very hard for you to talk about," he said one evening when they had returned to her apartment after having dinner out. It was midsummer and the windows were wide open to admit as much breeze as possible. Alexis was giving serious thought to installing air conditioners. She reached over to turn on the fan as he said, "It's been months since either the Pentagon or the State Department held out any hope. The Chinese boast about how many American prisoners they have and even parade them in front of the cameras. If they had James, we'd know by now."

"Perhaps," she said softly, not looking at him. "But there could still be another explanation."

"Such as?"

"He might be hiding out somewhere."

"For eighteen months? Come on, Alexis. You know you don't believe that."

"All right, then; he may have been taken prisoner and given a false identification."

"For what reason?"

"So that they couldn't make use of him."

"You're not thinking about what you're saying. James was wearing civilian clothes when he disappeared. Without military insignia in a war zone, he might be considered a spy. It would be in his own best interest to identify himself as a newsman immediately. At least that way he'd have a chance of staying alive."

"He might not have been able to tell them who he was," she insisted stubbornly. "Suppose he was wounded and unconscious for a time?" She didn't want to think about that possibility, but it was better than what Winston was suggesting.

He sighed and put his arm around her gently. "The last thing I want to do is cause you any pain. I know you cared for him a great deal."

"I still do," she pointed out quietly.

Winston grimaced but went on determinedly. "You have to think about yourself. Do you want to spend the rest of your life waiting for James to come home?"

Alexis glanced at him from beneath her thick lashes. "I'm not doing that."

"No," he admitted softly, "you're not. But you haven't come completely to terms with the truth, either."

His arm felt heavy on her shoulders. She stirred restively. "I'm doing the best that I can. Please don't ask more than that of me."

Winston sighed deeply. He heard the implicit warning beneath her words and knew he would be wise to heed it. If he pushed too hard, he would lose her. "All right," he murmured, "I won't. Just please remember how I feel about you. This...relationship or whatever it is we have now is only a stopgap. I want much more."

Alexis already knew that, but she wasn't ready to confront it. Especially not in light of the letter she had received that morning. Jake Dylan, the Australian Marine both James and Anthony had known during World War II, had written to say he understood there was still no news but that he was keeping his money on James.

"Nobody ever got the better of Cat Callahan," he wrote. "In a pinch, he was worth any ten men I know. When I saw him in Inchon before the push north, he looked tough as ever, maybe even tougher. He probably just got caught up in some long-running poker game and will end up owning the whole damn country."

Anthony laughed when Alexis showed him the letter next day at the office. "Good old Jake; he hasn't changed. We had some real times together. Especially when we were all on New Britain." His smile faded slightly. "The Green Hell they called that place, and it fit the bill."

"Was it very bad?" she asked softly. Like most men who had seen a great deal of combat, Anthony rarely spoke of his experiences in the war. She wouldn't press him to do so, but she longed for every tiny scrap of information about James.

He lifted an eyebrow quizzically. "Bad? Yeah, I guess you could say that. A lot of men died there."

"But not you...or James."

"That's right. Part of it was luck, I admit that. But we were also tougher, faster and meaner than most anyone else." His smile returned, sardonically. "Now we both know that I am a completely reformed character, a real pussycat. But old James...he hasn't changed much at all. I still wouldn't want to tangle with him, even it he had both hands tied behind his back and was standing in concrete."

Alexis smiled gently. She appreciated what he was trying to do, but she was also growing weary of living on nothing but hope. Winston was right; she had to come to terms in her own mind with what had happened and go on from there.

She was making a genuine effort to do that, or at least so she believed, when the situation suddenly changed radically.

It began simply enough, with a call from Washington to alert her to the fact that her discreet contacts had at last paid off. An unnamed Chinese was claiming to have information about the fate of James Callahan.

"We have no way of evaluating this man's bona fides," the lawyer warned. "All we can tell you is that he has been identified as someone fairly high up in the military structure, at the level of colonel. He is fluent in English and seems willing to cooperate.''

''Why?''Alexis asked quietly. She and Anthony were sitting in the law firm's conference room a few blocks from Pennsylvania Avenue. They had flown down within hours of receiving the news. ''Why should he want to help us?'' she asked. ''Is it a question of money?''

Charles Blair, senior partner of Wincomb, Stuveyscent and Blair, shook his head. He was a smooth-faced man of about fifty, one of the many well-educated, well-connected expeditors who flourished in the capital. ''It doesn't seem to be. We're in the process of trying to ascertain exactly what he does want; but it's difficult.... The Chinese are very cagey.''

''Is he in this for himself,'' Anthony asked, ''or is he acting officially?''

''Again, it's impossible to say. At least right now. If you will authorize us to proceed, we hope to have answers to at least some of your questions very quickly.''

But in fact a week passed without further word, then another. The political conventions were over and the campaign would not get up to full speed until after Labor Day. In the summer hiatus there was little to do and even less to think about, except what might or might not be happening thousands of miles away.

Alexis spent long hours at her desk but accomplished little. No matter how hard she tried to concentrate, her thoughts kept returning to James and what it would mean if he was still alive. Part of her rejoiced at the mere possibility, but another part wondered what chance they would have of resuming their life together.

She said nothing to Matthew of what was going on, not wanting to raise his hopes unfairly. But he must have sensed something, because he began to stay around the house more and tended to appear whenever the phone rang.

At length, just when she thought she could not possibly bear the suspense any longer, Charles Blair called again. "I'm afraid the situation is more complicated than we thought initially," he said. "You and Mr. Gargano had better come down here again."

Despite her best efforts, he would not tell her anything more, refraining on the grounds that it was best to discuss such delicate matters in person. Again she and Anthony caught the next available flight. They were in Washington by 6:00 P.M. The law offices were all but empty. Only Blair and a man they did not know were present.

The stranger—who was about forty with a short, powerful build and a face that had been in more than a few fights—was identified as Vincent O'Donnell, an associate of the firm. He had made the actual contact with the Chinese informant. To Alexis, he looked like one of the numerous men who lived by their wits, generally relying on methods best not examined too carefully.

"Colonel Chou and I met in a hamlet near the 38th parallel four days ago," O'Donnell related. "We spent about an hour together. As we had been told, he is fluent in English and seemed willing to cooperate, up to a point."

"What do you mean?" Anthony asked. He sat beside Alexis on the couch, his hand gently holding hers. Beneath his fingers, her skin was very cold.

"I explained that we would need proof that he actually had access to Mr. Callahan and that his information was current. He agreed to all that and then he explained what he wanted." O'Donnell glanced at the lawyer who nodded for him to go on.

"Apparently Colonel Chou is acting in at least a semiofficial capacity. He and his superiors are aware of Mr. Callahan's position at the Independent Broadcasting System. They want to make use of that."

"What the hell are you talking about?" Anthony demanded harshly. He was rapidly running out of patience with the little ritual going on before them and didn't care who knew it. "This guy wants something; you know what it is. So quit beating around the bush and spit it out."

O'Donnell frowned slightly, then shrugged. It didn't matter to him; he was, after all, only a go-between and a well-paid one at that. "They want IBS's coverage of the Korean conflict slanted in their favor," he said mildly. "In return they guarantee to keep Mr. Callahan alive and in good health until a truce can be signed and prisoners released."

Alexis opened her mouth to speak and found that she could not. Her throat was so tight that no sound escaped it. Her hand closed convulsively around Anthony's.

"I'm sure you have many questions," the lawyer was saying soothingly. "We'll do our best…"

"Damn right, you will," Anthony interjected. "To begin with, what proof do we have that James is still alive and why have they waited this long to let us know?"

"On the matter of proof," the lawyer said ponderously, "they have offered to relay any question you wish to Mr. Callahan and to report his answer. It is suggested that the question should be something of a private, family nature, the sort of information no one else would have, so that you can be sure the response could come only from him. As to the rest, we don't know why they waited, but we can speculate…" He hesitated.

"Go on," Anthony ordered.

"This plan requires a certain amount of cooperation from Mr. Callahan, as I have just described. Perhaps he hasn't been willing until recently…"

"Oh, God," Alexis murmured brokenly. She buried her head in her hands as tremors shook her.

Anthony put an arm around her and drew her close. "Easy now," he murmured, "It'll be okay. Just hold on." Turning his attention back to the lawyer, he said coldly, "We get the point. First thing that has to be done is to confirm that this is on the level. We'll come up with a question and get back to you…"

"No," Alexis said, lifting her head. Her eyes were red and her mouth trembled, but she refused to lose control. "I know what to ask. Tell that…tell Colonel Chou to find out the wrong name of the people who gave the party where James and I met."

The men glanced at one another puzzled. "The *wrong* name?" the lawyer repeated.

"That's right." Alexis's voice cracked slightly, but she went on. "James was confused about who they were. I want to know what he thought their name was." To Anthony, she explained, "It's remotely possible that the Chinese might be able to find out the real name of the people who gave that party, but I can't believe anyone except James and me knows who he thought they were."

He stared at her for a moment with admiration in his eyes before nodding decisively. "That's it, then. The wrong name." Grimly, he added, "And tell Chou we want it fast; otherwise we go to the Pentagon and blow this wide open."

"I wouldn't advise that," O'Donnell said hastily. "These guys play tough."

They rose together and faced the men. Alexis's features were once again expressionless, her eyes shuttered. Anthony looked much the same. Only the jagged pulse beating in his square jaw revealed his true feelings. Quietly but with unmistakable determination, he said, "So do we."

The answer came back three days later, a single word written on a piece of paper handed to them by the lawyer.

Dunleavey.

Alexis nodded quickly and looked away. She was perilously close to breaking down and knew that would do no one any good. Least of all, James.

James. The knowledge that he was alive overwhelmed her. She was at once radiant with joy and cold with fear. For him, for herself, for both of them together.

Rather than think of all that, she concentrated on what had to be done immediately. "Are the Chinese still insisting that IBS become a conduit for their propaganda?"

"They don't phrase it exactly that way," O'Donnell said dryly. "Chou has given me a three-point program for what he calls 'political correction,' which he wants to see incorporated into future news broadcasts."

Alexis's hand shook slightly as she took the list and scanned it quickly. After a moment, she said, "This is outrageous. He can't seriously expect us to tell the American people that 'the U.N. police action is illegal and an act of aggression against the sovereign peoples of Korea and China,' that 'it is part of the overall Western strategy of world dominance' and that 'the United States government is a lackey of the capitalist elite.' We'd be laughed off the air in two minutes flat."

"I don't believe Colonel Chou expects you to use those exact phrases," the lawyer murmured. "They are simply the underlying themes he would like you to express."

"He's out of his mind," Anthony snarled. "Even if I agreed with him—which I sure as hell don't—nobody can put garbage like that on television. Doesn't he understand that the airwaves are government-regulated? We'd have our licenses yanked in no time, and quite rightly."

"Nonetheless, that's what they want," O'Donnell said. "If I were you, I'd deliver."

"Oh you would, would you?" Anthony rasped. "What a surprise. Seems to me like you've got a pretty good little deal for yourself, carrying messages back and forth between here and Korea. Doesn't really matter who wins, does it? You make out either way."

The man shrugged unapologetically. "I do my job. All I'm saying is that if it was up to me, I'd give them what they want." He paused a moment before adding, "Unless, of course, the two of you have other priorities besides keeping Callahan alive."

"*Why, you...*" Anthony leaped to his feet, only be be pulled back by Alexis.

"Forget it," she said firmly. "Let's get out of here and go someplace where we can talk." As he reluctantly agreed, still glaring at O'Donnell, she told the lawyer they would get back to him shortly.

Outside, they both paused to take deep breaths and try to get a grip on themselves before setting off in the general direction of the park around the Washington Monument.

"This is really incredible," Anthony muttered. "In one breath I find out that my best friend is still alive and in the next I'm told I have to betray my country to keep him that way."

"That is what it amounts to, isn't it?" Alexis murmured. She was still partially in shock from the realization that James was alive, but her mind was nonetheless working clearly.

"Actually, what they're asking could be done. It would simply be a matter of shifting emphasis, selecting certain stories over others, stressing particular elements."

Anthony stopped walking and turned to look at her. "You're not…thinking of going along?"

"I don't see what choice we have? Do you?"

He continued to stare at her for a moment before finally shaking his head. "No," he murmured despairingly, "not if James is going to come home."

"We have to convince the Chinese that we're ready to cooperate fully but that we're in the best position to decide how their plan can be implemented without arousing suspicion. After all, what they want to do is subvert public opinion, and that can only be achieved subtly."

"I suppose…"

"Once we persuade them of our good intentions, we'll explain that we need some time to get set up. Most particularly, we have to convince the commentator who will do the actual broadcasts to go along with us."

"Winston…" He cast her a quick, worried look.

"Exactly." She continued briskly. "I'll handle that part. He'll have to believe that we genuinely intend to cooperate."

Anthony frowned. She had lost him. "What do you mean?"

"I wouldn't put anything past the people who set this up. It's not impossible that they have a contact inside IBS who will be keeping an eye on things for them. Winston has to seem upset, out of sorts, worried. The best way to assure that is to make him believe we really intend going along with them."

"Don't we?"

She turned to face him. A few stray wisps of silver-blond hair clung to her forehead. Her eyes were shuttered, her mouth set. "Sure we do, up to a point."

"I'm not usually dense," Anthony said, "but I get the feeling I'm missing something. What are you talking about?"

She hesitated a moment, then very quietly said, "For eighteen months the Pentagon and State Department have assured us that they're doing everything possible to determine if James is a prisoner. They've had absolutely no luck. Then, suddenly, this guy O'Donnell delivers proof that James is alive and tells us he can stay that way if we turn traitor."

"That's the size of it."

"So why is it happening now? Why didn't they admit to having him months ago?"

"You know what Blair said. It's because James wouldn't...cooperate."

"They could still have offered us the same deal. In the first few days, even weeks after he was captured, we would have accepted photos of him as proof that he was still alive. His cooperation wouldn't have been needed. But they didn't do that. Why not?"

"I don't know. Christ, none of this makes sense to me."

"I'm fumbling in the dark, too," Alexis admitted. "But I'm beginning to see a few glimmers of light." She took a deep breath and said grimly, "I think James's status has been known by our people for a long time, probably since shortly after he was captured. I think they made their own deal with the Chinese to keep him under wraps."

"What the hell for?" Anthony demanded. He was stunned by what she was suggesting and for a moment seriously considered the possibility that the strain of it all had proven too much for her.

"Right now I can't say for sure," Alexis went on calmly. "But one possibility does occur to me. James is president of IBS; if he comes home after however many months in captivity and he's in reasonably good shape, there's going to be suspicion that he made some sort of accommodation. If in the meantime we've been broadcasting programs slanted toward the Chinese, it won't be hard at all to accuse him—all of us, in fact—of being pro-Communist."

Anthony whistled softly. "Gunner Joe would have a field day with that. He's been claiming all along that people high up in the media are working for the Reds. Finally he'd be right."

"Exactly, and he wouldn't hesitate to exploit that to the fullest. Our licenses would be revoked so quickly we wouldn't know what hit us."

"And with our licenses gone, IBS would have to go on the block."

She nodded firmly. "Which network is most likely to be in the market for additional affiliates? Who needs them the most to make up for his own poor judgment and incompetency?"

"UBC…" Anthony stared at her with a sick expression in his eyes. He understood now what she was saying, even though he wished he did not. "Graham…?"

"He used to work at the Pentagon, during the war," she went on remorselessly. "He still has a lot of friends there, and in the State Department. Special friends, if you get what I mean. Friends who hang together because if they don't, they know damn well they'll all hang separately."

"You really believe they'd take advantage of a situation like this to help him?"

"Why not? What have they got to lose? It isn't their lives or futures on the line, only ours—and James's."

"I don't know…how could they convince the Chinese to go along?"

She shrugged dismissively. "That's simple. The Chinese have always known that eventually a peace treaty would have to be worked out. They're negotiating right now with…" She paused, letting him fill in the blanks.

"With representatives of the Pentagon and the State Department," Anthony finished for her, his face gray.

"You got it," Alexis said quietly.

"My God," he murmured, "it's so simple, really. They give the Chinese something they want, and in return, James is discredited and Graham gets IBS."

"The best plans are always simple," Alexis said quietly. "I learned that from my father."

"It seems Graham learned his lessons, too," Anthony muttered, unable to hide his bitterness. He felt only sympathy for Alexis, but her brother he would cheerfully see in hell.

Sadly, she nodded. "Yes, it seems he did." She stared out toward the pale swathe of the river. The heat and humidity pressed down on her, reminding her of another summer day six years before, when she had come to Washington for the FCC hearings and met James. That was when they had ceased to be adversaries and begun to take the first steps toward becoming lovers.

She had chosen him over her family, and had never regretted that decision. Until now. It was because of that choice that he had become a target.

The magnitude of her father's legacy no longer puzzled her. Charles Brockton had anticipated that his two heirs would one day clash violently. He had done what he could to assure they would be equally matched.

What was it he had said to her the last time they had met? That she had to make a choice between being strong like him or weak like her mother.

Now the choice was upon her and she could feel no fear or regret. Only the cold, implacable knowledge that whatever the cost, she had to win.

Chapter Fourteen

"IT WAS A LITTLE COCKER SPANIEL DOG in a crate," Richard Nixon was saying over the television set in a corner of Alexis's office. "Our little girl, Tricia, the six-year-old, named it Checkers. And you know, the kids, like all kids, love that dog, and I just want to say this, right now, that regardless of what they say about it, we're going to keep it."

Alexis barely heard him. She knew the speech was important; it would determine whether or not he remained the Republican vice-presidential candidate on the ticket headed by Eisenhower, despite allegations of a secret slush fund set up to funnel money to him from wealthy contributors. But she couldn't really find it in herself to care. Far more personal issues dominated her thoughts.

For eight weeks they had managed to string along Blair, O'Donnell and—through them—Colonel Chou, promising that IBS was fully prepared to cooperate but that they simply needed time to get properly set up.

Patience was wearing thin, she and Anthony had been given to understand during their most recent trip to Washington. The Chinese would have to see action soon or James would be in serious jeopardy.

Sighing, she rose and clicked off the TV. Nixon's fight for political survival would have to go on without her. It was time to go home. She was gathering up her purse and briefcase when there was a light knock at the partially opened door. Glancing up, she found Winston standing in it.

"You're leaving..." he began tentatively.

"Yes, I thought I would. Was there something you wanted?" She winced inwardly at her poor choice of words, but he let it pass without comment.

"I've been thinking over what we talked about. There are some things we need to discuss."

Alexis put her purse and briefcase down and gestured to the couch. "All right, let's do that."

"It could wait..."

"No, we'd better clear the air now. There's not much time left."

"I see...you're getting pressure to begin the broadcasts."

"A great deal of pressure," she confirmed quietly, sitting down beside him and turning slightly so that they were facing each other. Winston looked tired; his features were drawn and there was slight pouches under his eyes. Alexis doubted she looked much better. In the mirror that morning she had noticed the beginnings of tiny crow's-feet. They might have more graciously been called laugh lines, but she knew that wasn't the case. She hadn't laughed in a long time.

"It's so incredible," he murmured. "The Chinese trying to influence the American public through the news media. That makes it seem as though the witch-hunters may have been right all along."

Alexis wanted to tell him that it did not, if only because the plot would not succeed. But he had to believe the opposite. Quietly, she said, "I know how hard it is for you to even consider cooperating."

"Of course it's hard." His jaw moved convulsively. "I don't go around waving a flag, but the fact remains that I love my country. Moreover, I despise the very thought of the news media serving any cause other than the truth."

Alexis reached out gently and put her hand on his. He stiffened but did not pull away. "Winston, please believe me, if there were any other way, I would never have asked this of you." Her voice was low and slightly husky, touched by a restrained note of pleading, irresistible to him.

He exhaled shakily and met her eyes. "I wonder if you understand how much you're asking."

"I realize how you feel about your responsibilities to this country and to your profession."

A small, disparaging smile lifted the corners of his mouth. "Yes, that's all very laudatory, isn't it? But we both know there's far more involved."

Alexis looked away. She didn't think she could stand too much honesty just then, but Winston seemed bent on it. "You're a very strong woman," he went on. "I believe you could survive the death of your husband, but I don't believe I could survive your blaming me for it."

She stiffened slightly, wishing he had not put it in such stark terms; she already felt guilty enough about what she was doing to him. Because of her, he was trapped in a situation where no matter which way he turned, he would lose. If he put honor first and refused to help, she would blame him for whatever happened to James. If he put his principles aside and did as she asked, he ran the risk that she would choose her husband over him.

"I really thought he was dead," Winston murmured, almost to himself. The funny thing was that he had actually liked and respected James Callahan. Because of that, he had been able to accept Alexis's marriage to him, even though it meant profound personal disappointment. But when James had disappeared, all his hopes had revived.

"I was beginning to believe it myself," she said softly.

"Will he understand that, when he comes back?"

"I don't know. All I'm thinking about is how to get him out of there. I'll cope with whatever happens afterward as best I can." She saw no reason to explain that she did not feel the same impulse to honesty that Winston did. To him, the means by which anything was achieved mattered at least as much as the ends. To her, it was just the opposite; she cared only for results. In that, she was truly her father's daughter.

Her deliberate evasion was intended to leave him a remnant of hope. That was essential; she knew him to be a good man, but still a man. Besides, she wasn't really sure herself what would happen once James came home.

"I see..." he said tentatively. "Well, then, there isn't much else to say, is there? It has to be done, so we may as well get on with it."

Alexis hesitated a moment. She did not overlook the enormity of what he was agreeing to. All considerations of honor and decency aside, he was placing himself at enormous risk should what he believed to be the plan become known. Her throat was tight as she said, "Thank you, Winston. No one else has ever done more for me."

That, at least, was the truth. What the rest of it—the evasions and outright lies, the deliberate use of another person who cared deeply for her—would ultimately mean did not at that moment matter. She would cope with the cost later.

It was, at best, a Faustian bargain, but it was the only one available to her.

"THE MAIN PROBLEM we see with Colonel Chou's plan," Anthony said a few days later, when they were once again meeting with Blair and O'Donnell, "is that it doesn't go far enough. Hardly surprising, since we have no reason to think that the colonel has any experience with television.''

''I don't think I'm following you,'' the lawyer hedged. ''When you say the plan doesn't go far enough, it sounds as though you're offering to do more than you're being asked for.'' His tone left no doubt of how likely he considered that to be.

Alexis moved swiftly to ease his doubts. ''We're simply interested in doing this right, in order to best protect James,'' she explained. ''Television is a visual medium; its effectiveness rests on pictures, not words. That's what many people in our industry are still struggling to come to terms with.''

Blair nodded slowly, ''Pictures, not words...''

''We need film,'' Anthony said succinctly, ''that reflects the North Korean and Chinese view of the conflict.''

''Burning hamlets,'' Alexis offered, ''homeless children, that sort of thing.''

''To get it, we'll need access above the 38th parallel,'' Anthony pointed out mildly, as though that were no more than routine.

''For a film crew,'' Alexis explained before any objections could be made.

''Which I will lead,'' Anthony said, putting the final touch on the proposal.

Both Blair and O'Donnell looked genuinely taken aback. Clearly, they had expected an attempt at further delays rather than a seemingly wholehearted effort at cooperation. Yet, in a way, the proposal made sense. It could result in vastly more effective propaganda.

''The Chinese may suggest producing their own film,'' O'Donnell suggested cautiously.

Anthony shrugged as though he really didn't care one way or another. He was simply a professional trying to do his job as best he knew how. "Not if they want it to have the greatest possible impact on an American audience. We know what they will respond to; the Chinese don't."

"In addition," Alexis pointed out, "the quality of our film will be far superior. After all, we are the ones with the experience. American audiences have come to expect the best. They won't put up with grainy pictures, jagged cutting, anything like that."

"You do have a point," Blair murmured, rubbing his chin thoughtfully. He looked at Anthony. "Do I understand that you would be willing to supervise the film crew yourself?"

"That's right."

"And the Chinese could review the film before it's taken out of the country?" O'Donnell asked.

"Of course." Anthony smiled slightly, as though their concerns were rather amusing. "It is, after all, their show."

"DO YOU THINK THEY bought it?" Alexis asked a short time later as she and Anthony took a cab to the airport and the flight back to New York.

"My guess is that they did," he confirmed, "so we'd better finalize our plans."

"I suppose…" She shook her head tiredly. "I just wish there was some other way that didn't involve endangering you and the other men."

Gently, he said, "We've been over this a dozen times and we all agree our only chance of getting James out unharmed is to go in there after him."

"But we have no idea exactly where he's being held," she pointed out, hardly for the first time. "The Chinese aren't going to let you wander around wherever you like. You'll be guarded every moment.''

''Which is why, once we're over there, I'm going to tell them that unless I meet with James, the deal is off.''

That was the part of the plan that worried Alexis the most. What was to stop the Chinese from simply refusing and perhaps even killing or imprisoning the entire film crew, including Anthony?

It was pointless to raise that question again, since he had already answered it as best he could. There were no guarantees; the Chinese might do exactly as she feared. On the other hand, they might not.

Anthony and the other men who would form the rescue team had talked it over among themselves and decided the risk was well worth taking. Which was hardly surprising, since, by apparent coincidence, IBS had recently hired half a dozen cameramen and sound technicians who were all ex-Marines with combat experience in the South Pacific, Anthony and James's old stomping ground. The sight of Jake Dylan trying to pretend that he knew which end of a camera was which might be amusing, but there was no doubt of his, and the other men's, very special abilities.

Alexis reminded herself of that over and over during the next few days as they waited for word of the Chinese response to their plan. When it came, she did not know whether to be relieved or regretful.

''It's a go,'' Anthony declared as he stuck his head in her office early Monday morning. ''Blair just called. Chou went for it hook, line and sinker.''

''Great,'' she murmured weakly. There was an energy about him, a vitality that took her aback, almost like that of a war-horse pawing the ground in its eagerness to be once again in the midst of battle. "You're actually looking forward to this," she said, surprised.

He shrugged unabashedly. "I was a Marine. Hell—inside, I guess I still am. Same goes for the rest of the guys. It'll be good to see action again."

She could not comprehend that. Her battlefield was the executive suite where even the greatest victory—or defeat—was neat and sanitized. He was talking about something which she could barely envision but which nonetheless filled her with horror.

"I just hope you'll. . .be careful." Such inadequate words, yet there was nothing else she could say. How did one thank a man for being willing to risk his life to save another?

"Tad's gone all out to assure coooperation from our side," Anthony said later that day when he and the four other members of the team were gathered together in the living room of his home for a final rundown of the plan.

Maggie's brother accepted the praise with a slight nod. He had interrupted his campaign for Congress to lend his support. As a former Army Air Corps pilot with many friends flying in Korea, he had known whom to go to for help and—just as importantly—whom to avoid.

"The anti-Communist underground will be standing by to move you south as soon as the mission is completed," the tall, blond young man with the keen-eyed gaze and firm chin said. He unfolded his six-foot-plus frame and walked over to the easel that held a large map. "You'll be flown by helicopter to Seoul and from there directly to Tokyo. Once you're out of Korea, American authorities will be brought into the picture." He smiled slightly. "And so, of course, will the news media. Should be quite a circus."

Indeed, Alexis thought as she sat off to one side, listening. If the mission succeeded, James and the other men would return home heroes, the Chinese effort to control American public opinion exposed, and Graham foiled in his effort to take over IBS.

The way the men talked, the success of the mission was a foregone conclusion. But it was very far from that. So much could go wrong so easily, with such devastating results for all concerned.

Looking around at the faces of the rescue team—all as hard and eager as Anthony's—she wondered if perhaps her father hadn't been just the tiniest bit right about there being some fundamental difference between men and women. She would gladly have gone on the mission if she could have contributed to its success, but she would not, for the world, have enjoyed it. As it was, she could only stay behind and pretend that business was being carried on as usual.

Anthony and the other men left the following day on the first leg of their journey, flying from New York to Los Angeles and then on to Tokyo. They were following the same route James had taken more than eighteen months before, but with one crucial difference. From Japan they would be smuggled into North Korea; after that they would be on their own until they could link up with the underground.

Alexis had arranged to stay with Maggie. There was plenty of room in the big house for her and the twins, and Matthew was used to bunking with Joey on his many visits. They had barely arrived when Tessa dragged him off to watch television. At seven, she had little awareness of what was going on. Her father had told her he had to take a business trip and would be back soon. That was enough, at least as long as she had Matthew nearby.

"I'm worried about him," Alexis admitted to Maggie later that day as they were clearing the table. "Matthew has always been very reticent, but it's gone way beyond that now. I have no idea how to handle him."

"Maybe it's better not to try," Maggie suggested gently. She was sleeping badly, as was Alexis, and looked tired, but she still had a firm grip on her emotions. "Matthew has always been very mature for his age; he might resent interference, no matter how well meant."

"I suppose...but I keep feeling I should be doing something more. It's so much easier with the twins. Now that they're beginning to be self-reliant and can talk more, I seem to get along with them better." She smiled a little apologetically.

"You're too hard on yourself," Maggie said gently. "Not everybody enjoys changing diapers and wiping up spills. In fact, I can't really think of anyone who does. Besides, it takes time to learn to love a child."

"I always thought it was supposed to happen instantly," Alexis admitted, "the first moment you saw a baby that was your own. When that didn't happen with me, I was scared to death."

Maggie laughed softly. "When I first saw Tessa, do you know what I thought? That somebody had made a terrible mistake. I couldn't possibly have given birth to that ugly, red, wrinkled thing with the iron lungs. Of course, I changed my mind after a while."

"I should hope so," Alexis teased. "Tessa is wonderful."

"She can be borrowed, you know, for extended periods of time. Provided Joey goes along, too. It's a package deal."

Alexis didn't take her seriously for a moment. She knew Maggie was devoted to her children, but that didn't mean she didn't also have longings of her own. Quietly, she asked, "Have you given any more thought to what we talked about before?"

"You mean about having another baby? No, I wouldn't say I've thought about it. But what with one thing and another..." She shrugged a little self-consciously. "I don't know if I'm pregnant or not yet, but I hope I am."

Alexis wasn't particularly surprised. Though she and Maggie were very different in some ways, she suspected that in her position—with a husband going off to an uncertain fate—she, too, might have been tempted to keep something of him within herself. Gently, she asked, "Does Anthony know about the possibility?"

Maggie shook her head. "I didn't tell him. Oh, I was tempted, thinking that maybe if he got in a really tight spot, it could make him fight just a little harder, maybe make the difference between whether or not he got out. But things don't work like that. He'd worry about me, and that would just get in the way of what he has to do."

She spoke matter-of-factly, but the significance of her words did not escape Alexis. Maggie had courageously refrained from burdening her husband with reminders of his responsibility to his family. She had left him free to do his job as best he could.

Gratefully, Alexis said, "If it's true, he'll be so happy."

Maggie smiled, though her eyes were overly bright. "He'll be on cloud nine. I can't wait to see it."

Neither could Alexis. To see Anthony and the other men home safe, with James, would be the fulfillment of her greatest dream. But before that could happen, so much had to be overcome.

"I'm not used to waiting," Alexis said a few days later as she was helping Maggie in the garden. It was a Saturday in early October. The last of what had been a bumper crop of tomatoes and basil needed to be gathered. Daffodil and tulip bulbs had to go in the ground before the first frost. The lawn needed mowing. All of which was just as well, since time was weighing heavily on both women. Pushing a strand of hair out of her eyes, Alexis smiled wanly. "I don't think I'm much good at it."

"It takes practice," Maggie said, wiping her hands on her coveralls. Matthew had taken Tessa and Joey to the movies to see Gary Cooper and Grace Kelly in *High Noon*. He'd already seen it six times and claimed it was the best movie ever made. In the absence of their preferred playmates, the twins were grudgingly taking a nap.

"I've done my nails three times in the past two days," Maggie went on, "baked six dozen cookies, cleaned out the refrigerator, and washed every bit of crystal and china in the house. The maid thinks I'm crazy, and I'm not sure she isn't right."

Alexis laughed gently. "You seem pretty sane to me, thank God. I don't know what I'd do if I had to go through this alone."

"You'd manage," Maggie assured her. "Women always do. We may not be as strong as the men, but when it comes to sheer endurance, we can't be beat."

Alexis remembered that as day passed day and no word came. For herself and Maggie, the situation was tough enough, but now even the children were being affected, especially Matthew. She wondered sometimes how much he knew about what was happening. He had seen Anthony off with a somber nod and the quietly voiced wish that he was going with him. Since then, he had said little. Alexis drove him into the city each morning and picked him up each afternoon for the trip back to the Island. In between, she went to the office to tend to the absolutely essential matters that would not wait. Anything else would have to.

During their drives, Matthew answered her questions about school but volunteered no information on his own. When she ran out of questions, he stared out the window silently. As soon as they reached the house, he went off to do his homework, with Tessa at his side.

After a week of that, Alexis decided she couldn't stand it any longer. As he started to get out of the car, she said, "Come into the house with me, Matthew. I want to talk with you."

He hesitated, but obeyed. She took him into Anthony's den and shut the door. His shoulders were hunched and his eyes averted. Alexis smothered a sigh and smiled gently. "I didn't mean to speak so sharply just now, but I'm very worried about you."

"I don't see why," he muttered, still not looking at her. "I'm fine."

"Are you?" She turned away for a moment, struggling to get her thoughts in order. This confrontation with Matthew had happened on the spur of the moment, and she felt unprepared for it. Nonetheless, it would not do to turn back.

Very quietly, she said, "Matthew, don't you think we've known each other long enough now to be honest with each other?"

Whatever he had expected, it clearly wasn't that. Warily, he said, "Yes, I think so." There was a moment's silence before he added, "But you seem to think I'm still some little kid."

Alexis started to respond, to assure him that wasn't at all the case, only to stop herself. He had a point; she did still think of him as a child, when, in fact, he was rapidly approaching manhood and all that entailed.

For the first time, she really allowed herself to notice how like his father he was. Though still some four months short of his thirteenth birthday, he was almost her height. His shoulders were broad and promised to become even more so. There was a natural grace in all his movements and his long legs seemed ready to span great distances. The thick golden brown chestnut hair that tended to fall in his eyes came from his mother, but the direct blue gaze was purely James's, as was the firm set of his mouth and the stubborn angle of his chin.

"All right," she said quietly, "come and sit down and let's talk...honestly."

Though he remained cautious, to her relief he did as she asked. When they were both seated on the couch, Alexis cast around for some way to begin. At length, she said, "It's been very rough ever since your father went to Korea. I miss him terribly."

Matthew shot her a quick glance. "I wondered how you felt sometimes. You didn't say anything and that guy Winston kept coming around."

Despite her best efforts, Alexis flushed. Hoping he wouldn't notice, she said, "Mr. Harcourt and I work together. We're also friends."

"That's okay," he said gently. "Everyone needs friends. The thing is...I kind of wondered if you were trying to forget my father."

Alexis inhaled sharply and reminded herself that this conversation was her idea and that it could serve no purpose unless she was honest. "No...not forget him. I was just very lonely."

He thought about that for a moment, then nodded. "That makes sense. When I get lonely, I come over here to see Tessa and the others. I guess you have to be able to do something, too."

His generosity took her aback, until she remembered that he had always been that way. Possessions, time, understanding, had always been freely given. No wonder Tessa adored him so.

Smiling slightly, she said, "I'm beginning to wish we'd talked sooner, Matthew. You're pretty special."

It was his turn to flush and look away. "I'm okay. I try to do what I'm supposed to and stay out of trouble. But you..." He paused and she watched with fascination as his cheeks turned a deeper red. "You're the one who's special. You're beautiful and nice and smart." He took a deep breath, then blurted, "You remind me a lot of Grace Kelly."

"Grace Kelly...?" There were certainly far worse things to be compared to than the beautiful, glamorous movie star. "Thank you. That's a very nice thing to say."

"It's dumb. I shouldn't have said it. Now you'll think I'm a kid again."

In his obvious distress, she couldn't help but reach out to him. Taking his hand, she said, "Matthew, honestly, it was a nice thing. A compliment. Thank you."

He cast her a doubtful look. "You really think so?"

"I wouldn't say it otherwise. We're being honest, remember?"

"Yeah...I guess." He ducked his head self-consciously. "Anyway, I kind of always wanted to tell you that I was glad you and Dad got married. You've been really good for him."

"I'm glad you feel that way," she told him a little huskily. "He's been very good for me."

There was a moment's pause before Matthew asked quietly, "Do you think Anthony and the others will be able to bring him home?"

Alexis wasn't really surprised to discover that he knew at least the bare bones of what was going on. He was too intelligent to have missed the clues. "I don't know," she admitted. "It's a very difficult and dangerous situation. All we can do is pray."

He sighed deeply. "That's what I figured. Uncle Anthony is very brave, isn't he?" When she nodded, he went on, "I wish I could've gone with them."

Alexis smiled at him gently. "You're a little young yet for that." Thank God. Soon enough he would have his own battles to fight.

He accepted that, though she suspected he did so only for her sake. They sat a while longer on the couch in shared silence. Then the twins began to holler; she could hear Maggie trying to settle an argument between Tessa and Joey; the phone was ringing, and there was someone at the door.

"Guess we'd better get out there," Matthew said with a shy grin.

She gave him a quick hug and smiled back. "I guess so."

I THE MIDDLE OF THE NIGHT a week later and Maggie was shaking her awake. "Alexis," she whispered urgently, "you've got to get up. They're coming out."

"W-what...?" Groggily she reached for the bedside lamp and turned it on. Maggie stood next to her, wrapped in a robe she had tossed on hastily, her chestnut hair falling loosely around her shoulders and her face flushed.

"Tad just called. They're out of North Korea and on the way to Seoul."

"Th-they...?" Alexis stumbled over the word. Her chest was tight and it was suddenly very hard to breath.

Maggie nodded. She was shaking with the effort to contain her emotion. "Including James."

"Sweet Lord..." Her voice broke. She couldn't speak, couldn't think, couldn't do anything, except feel. A wave of heat washed over her, making her tremble. She struggled, almost afraid to believe, until at last the words sank in. Only seconds had passed, but she felt as though she had run a great race. Her heart was pounding and there was a fine sheen of perspiration on her skin. She trembled as she got out of the bed and reached for her own robe. "Tad's sure...?"

Maggie nodded quickly. "He doesn't have any details, but James is definitely with them. They'll be in Tokyo by noon our time today, then on to Los Angeles and the flight to New York. Tad's best guess is that they'll be home in forty-eight hours."

"Forty-eight...? That's no time at all and there's so much to do!"

Maggie laughed, ignoring the tears dampening her cheeks. Alexis stared at them for a moment before she realized that she, too, was crying. They hugged each other quickly, stealing a moment to share their joy, knowing there would be little opportunity later.

In sharp contrast to the months of James's captivity and the days of waiting for news of the rescue mission, the hours before his return flew by. Afterward, Alexis was to remember very little about them. She had only a blurred sense of constant activity—phones ringing, people coming and going, decisions having to be made, instructions needing to be given—with herself at the hub of it all. Several times Maggie set food in front of her and she ate. She slept for perhaps two hours but was not tired. Riding a long, rippling wave of energy, she felt incredibly alert and strong.

There were only a few isolated scenes that stuck in her mind: the look of unbridled joy on Matthew's face when he learned that his father was coming home, the moment in the midst of the controlled chaos at IBS when she caught sight of Winston gazing at her with such regret that she had been forced to look away, the glimpse she caught of herself in a mirror of a woman whose usually cool gray eyes glowed with vindication. She had taken a terrible risk and she had won. At that moment, nothing else mattered.

Sooner than she would have thought possible it was time to go to the airport. To avoid both entanglements with U.S. officials and premature leaks to the media, the rescue team had stayed on the move and out of touch until arrival back in New York. It had fallen to Alexis to cope with the disgruntled government men who wanted to know why they hadn't been informed and who muttered about the inadvisability of civilians taking such matters into their own hands. She ignored them and concentrated instead on stoking the fire of excitement building among the reporters informed of what had happened.

Klieg lights had been set up on the runway at Idlewild where the plane would land. Police barricades were in place. Trucks carrying mobile cameras from all the networks were in position. Care had been taken to give no special preference to the IBS people. For the last stage of the plan to work properly, all the members of the media had to see James equally as one of their own.

It was well after midnight when word came from the control tower that the plane was in its final approach. The temperature had been dropping for several hours and it had been raining off and on. The wives of the returning men were huddled in a small lounge, drinking coffee, staring out the window and saying little. With nothing more to be done, even Alexis felt suspended between one moment and the next, helpless to do anything but wait.

She paced back and forth, took her turns at the window, exchanged reassuring smiles with Maggie. Years before, in boarding school, she had bitten her nails. The habit had long since been broken, but she felt a definite temptation in that direction now. Instead, she bummed a cigarette and smoked it down to the butt.

It had been arranged that the men would leave the plane and come directly to the lounge to be reunited with their families. Then they would go into the larger room next door to answer questions and pose for pictures. Through the thin wall separating the two areas, Alexis could hear the drone of a hundred and more voices edged with impatience and anticipation. It was a big story, perhaps one of the biggest of the war, coming at a time when people were desperate for something that would make them feel proud again. Virtually everyone who learned of it would respond that way. Except, of course, for Graham. She smiled faintly as she thought of him.

There was a sound from the window. Alexis turned toward it. Several women were there, pointing. She got up and went to join them as Maggie did the same. Off in the distance, near the end of the runway, they could see the lights of an aircraft coming in for a landing. It came closer and they could make out the blunt shape of the nose and the flare of wings, the bright yellow circles of windows on either side. The wall of sound hit them from the engines, a dull roar punctuating their own breathless silence. The plane loomed larger, close enough now to see that the door was already being pulled open. Airport workers were racing a stairway into place.

Maggie reached for her hand and squeezed it. Together they watched as five men appeared one by one at the door and walked down the steps.

Chapter Fifteen

IT WAS VERY QUIET in the beach house. The only sounds were the muted pounding of waves and the distant cry of gulls. No trace remained of the storm two nights before. Late-afternoon sunlight shone on foam-specked waters and the sky was a deep autumnal blue. Down on the sand, some little distance from the house, small birds darted back and forth at the tide line.

Alexis turned away from studying the tranquil scene and glanced toward the bed. James was still deeply asleep. His square jaw was shadowed by a thick growth of beard. There were several deep bruises and cuts on his face, some of them fresh. The upper half of his body was partially uncovered, revealing a multitude of injuries to his shoulders, arms and chest. She had helped him remove his clothes and knew the rest of him was the same. He had lost about a quarter of his normal body weight, some fifty pounds, with the result that his face was gaunt, his stomach deeply concave and his ribs sharply protruding.

Sorrow might have been the natural response to his suffering, and she did feel that to some extent. But anger dominated her thoughts, a red slash across her soul.

It was the day after his return, a day spent trying to answer a seemingly endless stream of questions. How had he been treated during his captivity? What was his reaction when he realized his friends had come to rescue him? How had they managed to pull it off? How did he feel about Jake Dylan's death?

He had stumbled over the last one, his speech slurred with exhaustion, as he murmured that Jake had been his friend, a good and trustworthy man, and that there was no way he could adequately express his thoughts about the sacrifice he had made.

"We all understood the risks before we went in," Anthony had pointed out quietly as he stood beside James on the dais in front of the reporters, his left arm hanging uselessly at his side and his clothes stained with blood. "We accepted them. Jake would have been the first to tell you that."

Remembering the scene, Alexis sighed softly and shook her head, trying to clear it. Since the moment she had realized that there were five men instead of the expected six, she had been filled with dread. Something had gone wrong. They hadn't gotten James out after all or one of the team hadn't made it back.

The possibility that it might be Anthony had made her stomach tighten, until she heard Maggie's gasp of relief. Only then did she scan the faces of the other men to discover that it was the gruff, gentle Australian who was missing. He had been killed in the breakout from the encampment where Anthony and the others had been taken to meet with James after they insisted they would not begin filming until assured of his continued well-being. The Chinese and North Koreans had certainly been suspicious, but they had not expected the lightning-fast, savage assault that left several dozen of them dead before it was over. Of the bodies strewn around the destroyed compound, Jake's was not one of them. His friends had carried him out on their backs rather than leave him behind.

There had been no reaction from the Communists so far, and there might well never be, since they would certainly prefer to have the entire debacle forgotten as quickly as possible. The State Department and Pentagon were being equally careful, well aware that any condemnation of such heroic action would rebound on them tenfold.

"TV Executive Rescued from North Korea," announced the staid *New York Times* on its front page. The slightly less restrained *Herald Tribune* declared: "Surprise Rescue Mission Succeeds," while a banner headline in the *Journal American* read: "Pals Snatch Exec From Reds." It was left to the ebullient *Daily News* to sum up public response best with a single line: "WELL DONE!"

On the television and radio news the consensus was the same. Anthony, James and the others were manna to a nation starved for heroes. They made it possible to believe that America had truly not become a helpless giant. Already there was talk of why the government wasn't able to act with equal effectiveness, why it had been left to civilians to take matters into their own hands. The enormous difficulties of trying to rescue thousands of men, as opposed to one, were blithely overlooked.

Alexis stepped closer to the bed, watching the rise and fall of his chest. In the aftermath of all the drama and excitement, the energy had drained out of her. She felt sore all over and badly shaken, as though she had barely survived some great upheaval. Her brief rest had done little good. Unable to lie quietly beside James without constantly waking to be sure he was really there, she had at last gone out to the living room for a few hours and napped on the couch. Her sleep had not lasted long before she was drawn back to his side, tormented by fears she could deny.

How did one react to a husband who had been away for eighteen months under such terrible circumstances? What could she say and do? What should she expect in return? Above all, how could they rebuild a relationship that had been showing signs of strain even before he left? And if they could not, then what were the alternatives?

She sighed again, thinking of how tired she was of questions, doubts, worries, decisions to be made, people depending on her, looking to her to know what was right and how to do it. She was worn down by being who and what she was with no real certainty that she wasn't simply playing a role she didn't fully understand and wasn't sure she wanted anyway. It was the kind of bone-tired that throbs all the way through and makes the body feel as fragile as an eggshell.

She wished that James would wake up and talk to her. She yearned for him to hold her and tell her that everything was going to be all right. The very urge for that sort of comfort was an embarrassment. He was the one who had suffered so terribly, not she. It was unfair to expect him to be strong for both of them.

Reminding herself of that, she started to turn away. It was in her mind to get dressed and do something about dinner. But before she could act on that, fingers closed around her wrist and she was pulled gently down onto the bed.

Still holding her, James smiled hesitantly. "I thought I might be dreaming you."

She shook her head, unable for a moment to speak. The slightly crooked grin and the light in his eyes were just as she remembered. They made it possible for a moment to forget all the rest. His thumb moved in a slow, circular motion over the inside of her wrist, where her pulse began to beat more quickly. She breathed in sharply.

James stared at her for an instant before he said huskily, "I could do with a shower. Want to give me a hand?"

It started out simply enough. After making sure that the water was warm, she helped him under it, then stood by to give whatever assistance was necessary. The shower curtain was open and the tile floor in front of it was getting damp, but she ignored that. Her attention was riveted on James. He stood with his head back, his face turned to the rush of water. A rapturous smile curved his mouth.

"Lord, that feels good," he groaned. "When I think of the things I used to take for granted."

Alexis didn't answer. She had all she could do to keep from crying out against the damage done to him. What she had briefly glimpsed the night before was now starkly revealed. He had suffered greatly, perhaps more than anyone could ever know without going through a similar experience. But he was still very much a man, and she hungered for him.

Turning to her, his black hair plastered to his head and his beard glinting wetly, he caught the expression in her eyes and groaned again. "Alexis...it's been so long...."

She nodded and blinked hard against the tears that threatened. "I was so afraid you wouldn't come back."

He grinned again, a little uncertainly. "You, afraid? I can't imagine that."

"I was, terribly. But I couldn't show it to anyone. I had to pretend to be strong so people would listen to me and not give up on you." She broke off and glanced away, wishing she could retract the words. Hadn't she just been thinking that he was burdened enough without weighing him down with her fears?

James muttered something under his breath. Heedless of the water, he reached for her. His hands on her upper arms were very gentle, yet through the thin fabric of her robe she could feel their strength. Something hard and cold inside her began to give way. Without thinking about what she was doing, she took hold of the belt around her waist and untied it, letting the robe fall open.

"You know," she murmured, "I could do with a shower, too."

There was barely room for both of them in the narrow stall, but they managed. Amid much laughter, shared smiles and slow, tentative touches, they began to rediscover each other. His hands trembled as they moved over her, tracing the contours of her waist and hips, cupping her breasts gently in his palms as he lightly brushed each nipple with his tongue.

"I kept thinking about this," he rasped. "Not the last time we were together, but before. All the good times. I replayed them over and over in my mind, remembering everything about you."

She groaned softly, far back in her throat, straining to get closer to him. The hard shaft of his manhood pressed into her belly, branding her with its heat and power.

"Did I ever tell you," he asked as his teeth raked the delicate line of her throat, "how I love the sounds you make? The soft cries and little whimpers, especially right at the end when you come."

"J-James..." Heedless of the bruises on his shoulders, she dug her fingers into them. The world was swaying dizzily around her. There was nothing to hold on to except him. She was wet inside and throbbing with need so intense as to shock her.

"Talk to me, Alexis," he pleaded softly. "Tell me how much you missed me."

She took a deep breath, trembling all over, and did as he asked. It was strangely easier than she would ever have thought possible. The miracle of their being together overcame her natural restraint. "I lay awake at night thinking about you," she whispered against the wet smoothness of his shoulder. "Remembering how you used to touch me..."

"Where? Where did you like it best?"

"Here..." She moved his hands back to her breasts, then slid them down over her rib cage and belly to the nest of curls between her legs. "And here..."

He wrapped an arm around her low down on her hips, cupping her buttocks. With the other hand, he gently parted her thighs and began to tantalize her with light, feathery touches. "Like this?"

"Y-yes...don't stop...I love that. And I love..."

"What?" he demanded urgently, increasing the tempo.

She leaned forward and whispered in his ear. James's eyes widened and a dark flush suffused his face. Grasping her waist between both hands, he lifted her bodily out of the shower. Not even pausing long enough to turn off the water, he carried her into the bedroom and lowered her swiftly onto the bed.

"James," she protested, a bit taken aback, "I'm not sure this is a good idea. You're supposed to be rest—"

"Later," he said, looming over her, big and hard in the golden light. The dark growth of beard gave him a dangerous look, as did the very determined gleam in his crystalline eyes. "I believe you made a rather specific request."

True, and she had put it rather bluntly, but still... *"Aaah... James..."* Without further preliminaries, he had thrust deep inside her, filling her completely, driving out the throbbing emptiness and replacing it with something far different. She cried out softly, her hips arching upward to take more of him.

Far in the back of her mind she wondered at the force driving them both. It was nothing at all like the tenderness she had thought would shape their first lovemaking after his return. In fact, what was happening between them now had little to do with lovemaking at all. It was far more primitive than that.

Their coming together was a repudiation of death, a reaffirmation of life in all its most fundamental power and urgency. But it was also an intensely personal declaration of how things were between them. Both strong and proud, both fiercely independent yet vulnerable, both striving to gain the upper hand.

Afterward, when they had recovered enough to realize what had happened, they were both embarrassed. Alexis could not quite meet his eyes and James could think of nothing to say. He went to turn off the shower and came back wearing a robe. She had also donned one before stripping the wet sheets off the bed and beginning to remake it. He helped her, and at length it was done. The sheets weren't tucked in quite right and the blanket was askew, but at least it was dry.

Sliding into the bed from opposite sides, they eyed each other warily. James cleared his throat. ''Uh...I didn't really mean for that to.... Things got a little out of control.''

She wanted to look away from him but found she could not. He had revealed a side of himself to her that, while previously suspected, was still a surprise. Even more, she had discovered something about herself that would take a while to come to terms with, if she ever did.

''Yes...well...'' she murmured, ''we've both been under a considerable strain.''

He stared at her for a moment before a slow smile eased the tension from his eyes. ''You could say that.''

''I'm sure we'll...calm down.''

''You think so?'' He lay back and stretched out an arm, inviting her to scoot over to him. She hesitated, then did so.

Held close to him, the warmth of their bodies mingling, Alexis at last let herself feel the aftereffects of their passion. The deadening fatigue that had plagued her was gone; in its place was healthy exhaustion. Later on she would try to come to terms with this unsettling renewal of their relationship. Just then it was enough to know that she was no longer alone.

JAMES'S RECOVERY from his ordeal was far faster than anyone could have expected. He was determined to put it behind him as swiftly as possible, believing that to do otherwise would be, in effect, to continue his captivity. He chafed at what he perceived as the slow healing of his body, denied that he suffered from nightmares even when he woke in a cold sweat, and threw himself back into the ordinary pattern of life with a vengeance.

During the last weeks of 1952 and into 1953, he steadily regained the weight he had lost. To assure that it would return as muscle rather than flab, he took to working out at a gym on the West Side, spending hours lifting weights and going one-on-one in the ring with tough young boxers who gave no quarter. His controlled ferocity surprised them and gained their respect.

In particular, he wasted no time reasserting himself at IBS. Within a week of his return, he was going into the office daily. Within two weeks, he was fully up-to-date on all current matters and ready once again to take the helm.

Alexis's reaction to all this was complex and, to some extent, contradictory. She rejoiced in his returning strength and understood why it was necessary for him to put the past behind him as quickly as possible. But she also realized that much of what he regained would be at her expense.

During his absence, she had become accustomed to making decisions and formulating plans more or less on her own. While she and Anthony had kept in close touch about their respective areas of responsibility, they had rarely, if ever, interfered with each other. With James, it was all suddenly quite different. He not only assumed that she would clear everything with him, but he went further and suggested that now that he was back, there was no reason for her to continue working at IBS at all.

"I understand why you had to help out while I was gone," he said as they were sitting in his office one winter afternoon early in the new year. Eisenhower had been inaugurated after soundly trouncing Stevenson and the Democrats. Despite that, Tad had won his seat in Congress handily. The country seemed to be turning inward, away from the turbulence of the baffling, frightening world. There was no great interest in taking risks. Maggie, who was pregnant again and having a hard time, had said that the pressure to conform was stronger than ever in the suburbs. Alexis believed her. She could see the same thing happening in her own world.

"As much as you've done during my absence," James went on firmly, "there's no reason for you to continue to make such sacrifices. The children deserve a full-time mother."

Alexis stared at him, aghast. She had been half expecting a showdown over this issue but had hoped it might at least be delayed until they both had a chance to become more accustomed to each other. Instead, it seemed that James was determined to settle it without further ado.

"Now, just a minute," she began, leaning forward in her chair. James sat behind his desk, the wide expanse of mahogany and leather effectively separating them. "I don't think you understand the seriousness of what you're saying. I didn't come back to work here just because you were gone. It was always my intention to do so."

James frowned. His fingers drummed lightly on the desktop. "We never discussed that. Naturally, I presumed you intended to be a full-time mother."

"That was quite a presumption," Alexis said tautly. "I thought I always made it clear that my career was equally important to me."

He raised an eyebrow. "Equally? I'm getting a very different impression."

Alexis's hands tightened on the arms of the chair. She had the uncomfortable sensation of being called to account for herself. Taking a deep breath, she summoned patience. "Look, I know we can't expect to see eye to eye on everything, especially after having been apart for so long. But do you really think you're being fair, coming back here and taking over as though nothing had changed? Pretending that everything is going to be just as you want?"

"That isn't what I'm doing," he insisted. "All I'm saying is that there's no need for you to shortchange either yourself or the children any longer. You've done a fabulous job; I realize that. But now it's over, and we can all get back to normal."

"Normal?" Alexis repeated. "What's that? A house in the suburbs and a baby every year?" She shook her head firmly. "No, thanks. In case it's escaped your notice, I happen to be one of the controlling partners of this business and I am not about to be put out to pasture."

James paled slightly and his eyes narrowed. "I wondered how long it would be before you brought that up," he said with dangerous softness.

She clucked her tongue impatiently. Not for a moment was she going to apologize for putting her father's legacy into IBS. Had she done otherwise, it might well have gone bankrupt. "All I'm saying is that I've made a big investment, not just in terms of money, but also of time and effort. What happens here matters a great deal to me. I want to be part of it, not an observer off on the sidelines."

"You're being unrealistic," he insisted. "If you weren't married and didn't have children, then maybe, just maybe, it would make sense for you to continue in your present role. But you *are* married and you *do* have children. I'll be damned if I'll let you pretend otherwise."

"Let me? Pretend? Why you—" She broke off, catching the glimmer of satisfaction in his eyes. He wanted to provoke her into a display of temper; it would confirm his contention that she was not really suited to deal with the pressures of the situation she had taken on. Determined not to fall into that trap, she took a deep breath and said as steadily as she could manage, "I thought my father and brother were about as pompous as two individuals could be, but you take the cake. Who appointed you judge and jury? Who gave you the right to tell me what I should or shouldn't be doing?"

James did not answer at once. Instead, he rose and walked from behind the desk, closing the distance between them. Standing over her in his shirt sleeves, with his tie loosened and the top button of his crisp white shirt undone, he looked irreproachably male and in command. Very softly, he said, "I'm your husband."

She waited, staring at him, thinking he surely intended to say more than that. When he did not, she gave in to her exasperation. "Is that supposed to be the be-all and end-all of everything? Husband doesn't happen to be the same thing as lord and master, in case you hadn't noticed."

Her asperity seemed to amuse him. He smiled as he reached out a hand and lightly stroked her cheek. "Come on, now," he murmured soothingly. "You're not really trying to tell me that you want me to give in to you on this."

Alexis gazed up at him blankly. Her mind seemed to be distancing itself from her body, enabling her to stand apart and watch what was happening with growing irritation. The enormity of the gap between them astounded her. Did he truly believe she would be content to meekly obey his dictates?

Pulling away from his hand, she said, "What I want is for you to respect my right to make fundamental decisions about my own life. Instead, you seem to think that all you have to do is snap your fingers and I'll bow to your wishes."

James muttered something under his breath and walked away. He stood at the window, with his back to her, staring out at the winter-gray street. What on earth was wrong with her? She should be glad he wanted to take over again and free her of the responsibilities she'd been carrying. Instead, she acted as if he was trying to steal something from her.

Alexis stared at his broad back, trying to come up with some way of getting through to him. She was baffled by the turn their lives were taking. At night, in bed together, they made love with passionate honesty. Then there were no restraints between them, no misunderstandings. It was only during the day, when they faced each other across a desk, that differences arose.

Sometimes she felt as though she were two women trying to exist in one body. Part of her wanted to give James everything he desired, to be his helpmate, mother of his children and guardian of his home. But another, far stronger part knew she could never be content with such a life.

"You know," she said, almost to herself, "my father expected me to find my satisfaction in being the wife of a powerful man. He thought women were best when they were purely ornamental. I didn't agree with that when I was a child and I most certainly do not now."

James turned back to her slowly. His eyes were hooded so that she could not read the expression in them, but the cold implacability of his voice left no doubt of his feelings. "Don't ever compare me to your father. If you haven't figured out yet the differences between us, then I really feel sorry for you."

Stung by his harshness, Alexis struck back. She stood up, elegant and remote in a soft navy suit that accentuated the delicate curves of her body, and faced him squarely. "Differences? I can't see many. He needed to prove that he was better than everyone else, and you're the same. You can't stand the idea that people might think you weak. That's why you're so determined to forget what happened in Korea and why you want to make me completely dependent on you."

She thought for a moment that she might have gone too far. James's hands were clenched at his sides. His light blue eyes glinted dangerously. As she watched, oddly fascinated, he took a step toward her.

"You..." He broke off, struck by the enormity of his own rage. She had touched some deep chord of animosity within him, a primal source of conflict that was all but irresistible. That, more than anything else, forced him to consider that there might be some justice in what she said.

Alexis watched the struggle going on within him and knew it had its counterpart within herself. She no longer felt as though she stood apart from what was happening; instead, she was vitally involved and fighting for her life.

"James…" she said softly, daring to hold out a hand to him. "Why are we doing this to each other? We've both been through so much. Can't we take it more slowly, work things out between ourselves without destructiveness?"

He did not respond at once, and she wondered for a moment if he had heard her. At length, a long sigh escaped him. "You're right. We're approaching this all wrong. I shouldn't have expected you to change your life completely just because I came home."

The admission that he might have been wrong made her instantly conciliatory. Deep down inside she loathed the idea of being in conflict with him. All she really wanted was for them to be happy together. Going to his side, she said, "We'll work everything out; you'll see. There are bound to be some problems readjusting, but they'll be over before we know it."

His gaze captured hers as he sought to determine the extent of her sincerity. "Do you understand? I just want things to be normal."

Alexis still wasn't sure what that word was supposed to mean, but she sensed he was using it as a synonym for *safe*. Under those circumstances, she could hardly disagree. "Of course I do, and they will be. But it takes time. You understand that, don't you?"

He nodded and drew her into his arms. She went gladly, knowing that there at least she faced no disagreements. Only much later did she allow herself to think about the price she would have to pay for letting him believe she could even consider doing as he wished.

FROM BEING WILLING to leave IBS, Alexis was determined to expand her role within the company. She had two reasons for doing so: It was essential to that side of her nature inherited from her father, and of equal importance, it would enable her to take her revenge against her brother. Never did it occur to her that Graham should be allowed to get away with what he had done. Because of him, James had suffered. And for that, he would pay. The only question was how.

She thought about it very carefully, going over everything that she knew about her brother, trying to determine exactly what was most important to him and therefore where he was most vulnerable. His private life was a tempting target, but she decided it was beneath her to attack him there. Instead, she would take from him the prize that should never have been his to start with—UBC.

At night, in the tranquil moments between consciousness and sleep, she thought over how it could best be done. Strategies came together in her mind, were examined and inevitably found to contain some weakness that made them unacceptable. Still she persisted, even though she knew the man lying beside her would strongly disapprove if he knew what she was doing.

Shortly after his return, she had told him what she believed about Graham's role in keeping him prisoner. He had listened to her in silence, then whistled softly. "That's the most incredible story I've ever heard. You actually believed it?"

Taken aback, she had said, "Of course I did. I still do. Graham had an enormous amount to gain from discrediting you."

James had laughed gently, actually *laughed*, and shaken his head. "Honey, there is absolutely no proof of what you're suggesting. The whole time I was a prisoner, I was given to understand that I was being held until an optimum moment arose for the Communists to try to make use of me. They're smart enough to know that IBS wouldn't have been able to slant the news in their favor for long before running into trouble. So they waited, until the treaty negotiations were reaching a critical phase, the country was going into a presidential election, and pressure for a solution to the conflict was becoming enormous. That's when the propaganda broadcasts would have been most valuable to them, so that's when they made their move.''

"None of which explains why the State Department and Pentagon were never able to confirm whether you were dead or alive,'' she had shot back. "How do you explain that?''

He had shrugged, as though it were of no importance. ''There could be any number of explanations. The Reds kept me under pretty tight wraps, and let's face it, I wasn't the only thing our people had to worry about. So they didn't do their jobs exactly as they should have. Under the circumstances, I don't think they can really be blamed.''

"I don't believe I'm hearing this. How can you be so forgiving? So blind?''

"What I'm being is reasonable. You're the one who's convinced there was some crazy conspiracy involved. There wasn't. It was just the luck of the draw.''

Remembering that conversation months later, Alexis was still astounded by it. How so intelligent and clear-headed a man could persist in believing that he had merely been a victim of fate astounded her. Yet James did so, and she had finally given up her efforts to convince him otherwise. Even Anthony, who had initially accepted her view, had changed his mind.

"What does it really matter?" he had asked. "We got James out; that's all that counts."

And there the matter ended, at least for the men. Not so for her. Her feelings about her brother were entangled with her conviction that UBC should have been hers. She could not give up one without the other.

Chapter Sixteen

"WHAT A BEAUTIFUL TREE," Maggie said as she sat down on the couch with baby Tonio in her lap and smiled at her daughter standing nearby. "Don't you think so, Tessa?"

The little girl nodded, her gaze riveted on the fifteen-foot Christmas tree that dominated the living room of the town house Alexis and James had moved into some six months before, at about the same time that the war in Korea was finally ending. Situated on the East Side off Fifth Avenue, barely half a block from Central Park, it represented not only a new home for them but also a new start.

"It's the most beautiful tree I've ever seen," Tessa said reverently. At seven, she was a slender, delicately made child, dressed in a red velvet dress that highlighted her warm olive complexion. Ebony hair tied with a matching bow hung halfway down her back. Her large, thickly lashed hazel eyes were turned on Matthew to see his reaction.

He smiled and handed her a small cup of fruit punch. "You said the same thing about your own tree, and the one at Gramma and Grampa Gargano's. They can't all be the most beautiful."

Under his gentle teasing, Tessa flushed. At thirteen, he was her hero, the focus of her unbridled admiration and wholehearted love. But then, he always had been. Fortunately, Matthew was not the sort to let her down. Looking very mature in his tailored suit and white shirt, he added, "Well, maybe they can be, if you say so. Want to see the chemistry set I got?'' She nodded eagerly and went with him as Joey trailed at their heels, determined not to be left out.

Maggie laughed and glanced at Alexis ruefully. ''I wish I could get her to be so agreeable. Do you have any idea how he does it?''

''Magic,'' Alexis suggested as she sat down beside her. In a deceptively simple gown of pleated white chiffon with a fitted bodice, tapered skirt and soft, flowing sleeves, she looked ethereally beautiful. Yet it was an earthly woman who smiled and chucked the baby under his chin. He chortled and grasped hold of her finger. ''That's quite a grip you've got,'' she informed him gently. To his mother, she said, ''He's getting bigger every day.''

''Thank God,'' Maggie murmured under her breath. With a wry grin, she said, ''When I think of how eager I was to get out from under diapers and all the rest.'' She sighed ruefully. ''Oh, well, the time goes so fast, this one will be in school before I know it.'' Her tone made it clear that much as she was looking forward to that great day, she would also be a little sad to see it come.

The baby hiccuped softly and settled back against her, his downy head resting on her breast, as she stroked his hair gently. Maggie kept a soft towel prudently nearby in case an accident seemed imminent; she would just as soon he didn't spit up on her ivory lace blouse or black velvet skirt. But for once little Tony seemed on his best behavior.

The moment of serenity was interrupted by a sudden outraged shriek which Alexis recognized all too easily. She turned slightly, and without raising her voice, said, ''Amanda, that's enough. Give Jamie a chance to play, too.'' Seated near the tree in a dress of sky-blue velvet that perfectly matched her eyes, her daughter turned to her and smiled prettily. "He doesn't want to."

"Do too," Jamie insisted, taking the opportunity to snatch the pull toy away from his sister. He began to toddle around the room, the wooden duck clacking behind him. Amanda watched for a moment, then shrugged and turned her attention elsewhere.

"They're so much alike in some ways," Alexis said as she watched the twins. Shaking her head, she added, "But *soooo* different." Even after three years, she was still hard-pressed to figure out how she had managed to give birth to two such disparate beings. Both had their mother's silver-blond hair and their father's light blue eyes. Their features more closely followed Alexis's, though James's strong chin was evident in both. But there the similarities ended. Jamie was by far the fussier, more inclined to cry over trivialities but also more easily satisfied with small victories. Amanda was another matter altogether. She might look like a little angel, but inside she was pure devil. From early morning to past bedtime, she exuberantly explored and challenged her world. As a result, she was invariably the leader, with her brother following a safe distance behind.

"They are a handful," Maggie acknowledged. "But you manage very well with them."

Alexis shot her a grateful look. "Thanks. I do try, some days with more success than others." She didn't have to explain what she meant. In the slightly more than a year since James's return, they had come nowhere near to resolving the question of her working. He still insisted it wasn't necessary; she still refused to give it up.

The closest they had come to a solution was, in effect, no solution at all. Alexis worked full-time at IBS while also having primary responsibility for the children. Remembering her own childhood, she refused to depend on a nurse for more than the bare essentials. So when a trip to the pediatrician or dentist was called for, she went. When one or both of the children were sick, she stayed home. When they wanted a story read, a drawing admired, a broken toy fixed, more often than not they came to her.

Whenever possible, James spent the evening with them, unless a meeting ran late or paperwork piled up, and he made a special effort to be available most weekends. But he did not take anywhere near as active a role as Alexis. It wasn't that he didn't love his children; quite the contrary. It was simply that he was the man, and no matter how much his wife might contribute to the family income, he considered himself to be the breadwinner. Therefore, his work came first.

A case in point was what was happening right at that moment. While Maggie and Alexis kept an eye on the children, Anthony and James were deep in conversation about events at IBS. Seated in wing chairs near the fireplace, each with a crystal tumbler of Scotch and a fresh cigar, they looked very much at ease after the superb New Year's Day dinner of roast goose with all the trimmings. Still, the topic on their minds did not seem likely to improve their digestion.

"We knew there would be problems with Delia," Anthony was saying. "We've been preparing for months to cope with them. But even so, her latest demands are much greater than we'd anticipated."

"She can afford to make demands," James pointed out. "'Our Gal, Sal' is IBS's top-rated show, and consistently one of the top six nationwide. Who else can go head to head with Lucy and Desi?"

"That's all very well and good, but there have to be limits. Not only does she want her salary doubled, now she's asking for a piece of the advertising revenues and profit participation should we eventually sell the show for syndication."

Alexis listened to them surreptitously. She was not eager to get involved in the situation concerning Delia Follett, but she was curious about how they planned to resolve it. The beautiful comedienne was far too important to IBS to be handled with anything other than kid gloves. Still, there were limits to what any performer could be paid, and Delia was clearly brushing up against them.

"The syndication demand seems fair," James said thoughtfully. "That's an area where a lot of performers are going to get hurt because they didn't think to protect themselves. Not surprisingly, Delia's too smart to get caught in that trap."

"Too smart by half," Anthony agreed. He took another sip of his Scotch and sighed. "It doesn't seem fair, somehow, that a woman should be that gorgeous, that talented, and intelligent to boot."

"An embarrassment of riches," James said with a chuckle, blissfully unaware that his wife was frowning at his words. She had not forgotten his affair with Delia during World War II any more than the ambiguous note the star had sent her while he was being held prisoner in Korea had slipped her mind.

"It's just business," Maggie murmured gently.

Alexis shrugged doubtfully. "I suppose...anyway, they're welcome to her. That's one problem I don't want to have to try to solve." She had her hands full as it was, coping with Winston. The enormously popular newscaster's contract with IBS was almost up. Everyone wanted him to sign another, but he was wavering. If something didn't change soon, they ran the risk of losing him.

''Everything will work out,'' Maggie said soothingly. ''Somehow, it always seems to.''

Alexis envied her equanimity. Hers was in very short supply. Between the pressure at work and the demands at home, she felt constantly on the run, with barely a moment to herself. The long-ago days when she had been free to lunch with friends, spend an afternoon at the beauty parlor or while away a day shopping might have been memories from someone else's life. Never mind that she considered such pastimes the last refuge of bored society matrons and had rarely, if ever, indulged in them. From the other side of the fence, they had a decidedly rosy glow.

She hoped the new year would bring some improvement, but in its early months there was little reason for such optimism. To begin with, Winston showed no inclination to sign the new contract.

''You have to understand my position,'' he said one February afternoon as he and Alexis were having lunch at a small French restaurant near the office. ''Much as I've benefited professionally from being at IBS, I'm not sure I wouldn't be better off elsewhere.''

Alexis took a sip of her Dubonnet and smiled. She had deliberately chosen the restaurant because it was popular with people from television and she wanted Winston to be seen in apparently amicable discussion with her. NBC's star newsman, John Cameron Swayze, was seated at a nearby table, not far from CBS's immensely popular Douglas Edwards, who was lunching with a young correspondent named Walter Cronkite. Alexis had first noticed the latter during the '52 presidential conventions, when his outstanding on-the-air coverage gave IBS stiff competition. Now she made a mental note to keep him in mind if things reached an impasse with Winston.

In the meantime, she set herself to soothe him. "Of course you're bound to have doubts. After all, you're a very talented and intelligent man. But do you really think that any of the other networks or independents could do more for you than IBS?"

"No..." he admitted, stirring the swizzel stick in his highball thoughtfully. "But I wasn't really speaking professionally. The problem is...personal." As he spoke, he looked at her directly, leaving no doubt of his meaning.

Alexis stifled a sigh. It wasn't that she felt no sympathy for Winston, only that she was running out of patience with him. For the life of her, she could not understand how so intelligent and otherwise sensible a man could keep moping over something he was simply not going to get. Still, it wouldn't do to tell him that. Gently, she said, "I know James's return was...unsettling for you. But surely there are larger concerns involved here. After all, at IBS you have complete freedom within the news division. No one interferes with your judgments or attempts to control your broadcasts in any way. You won't find that level of autonomy anywhere else."

He could not dispute that. Not even the dean of television newsmen, Edward R. Murrow, had such freedom. "I know I've been allowed to exercise my own discretion to a great degree, but..."

"As a result," she went on firmly, "'Spotlight' is completely your show—thirty minutes every week to put your views before the public. Why, it isn't an exaggeration to say that you have more impact on what America thinks than almost anyone else in the country." She didn't add, because there was no reason to, that it was thanks to such access that Winston was courted by leading politicians, businessmen, entertainers, anyone and everyone who had reason to care about what people thought. Those thirty minutes per week gave him enormous power which he gave every evidence of enjoying.

"You've had no reason to regret giving me that forum," he pointed out quietly. "In fact, there was a time when you were more than willing to make use of my influence."

Alexis had the grace to flush, but only slightly. She took another sip of her drink and smiled again. "We've been over this before, Winston. I've explained that there was never any intention of giving in to the Chinese demands."

"Yet you still got me to agree to do so."

She ignored the undertone of resentment in his words and let him feel the full force of her cool, gray gaze. In her throaty, slightly husky voice, she said, "I told you at the time that no one had ever done more for me. I still mean that."

Winston stared at her for a moment before reaching for his glass. His hand shook slightly. He took a long swallow, the muscles in his throat working, before he said cordially, "You're a remarkable woman, Alexis. Do you know there have been times when I swear I could have cheerfully strangled you?"

She sat back in her chair with a small smile. "Really? Should I consider myself in some sort of danger?"

He shot her an assessing look that gave way slowly to a wry smile. "Unfortunately, no. If I ever do find myself in a position to wreak mayhem on you, I'll be far more tempted to..." He broke off, abashed by his own frankness. But then, she had always had that effect on him. With her, all decorum and restraint went by the board. Undoubtedly that was part of her appeal. "Never mind. Let's get the waiter and order. Unless this is intended to be a purely liquid lunch..."

"Not at all," she assured him quickly, relieved to have the subject dropped. Innuendo always disturbed her, particularly when it was so out of character.

Nothing was decided that day, but Alexis came away confident that Winston really wanted to stay with IBS. He was simply unwilling to be too easy on her, which, all things considered, seemed fair. She had put him through a difficult time; naturally, he wanted to get something of his own back.

Another, far more serious form of retaliation was on her mind a few days later as she studied the confidential report from the firm of lawyers and accountants she had hired to investigate Graham and his activities at UBC. Without James's knowledge, since he had left no doubt that he would disapprove, she was continuing to make her own plans for revenge.

Graham was not having an easy time of it, according to the report. He was heavily in debt, with UBC's headquarters building and other real estate holdings carrying second—and in some cases, even third—mortgages. Alexis read on, curious to see how the millions of dollars in cash he had raised that way were being spent. Had it been up to her, she would have used the money to launch new shows, update equipment, expand the news bureau and so on—in short, to strengthen the network that was the cornerstone of the Brockton communications empire.

But Graham apparently had different views. He was in the process of making heavy investments in several magazines and newspapers as well as buying a controlling interest in a publishing firm. Which suggested he was still betting that television would turn out to be a passing fad despite all the overwhelming evidence to the contrary.

She put the report down and sat back in her chair, staring unseeingly at the wall opposite her desk. The door to her office was closed; her secretary sat on guard outside. She had asked for all phone calls to be held and had cleared her calendar of all meetings. For a few hours at least, she would be able to consider carefully what she had just learned.

Among Charles Brockton's bequests to his daughter had been a block of shares in UBC, not anywhere near as large as Graham's controlling interest, but still sufficient to give her a continued link to the business. While she had cashed in the rest of her legacy and used it to prop up IBS, she had held on to the stock. It was still in her name and she retained the sole right to dispose of it.

Were she to sell those shares now, she would get a fairly decent price and in the process amass a substantial nest egg for herself. If, as she expected, Graham's policies slowly undermined UBC, the value of the stock would fall as it became less attractive to investors. She would then be able to buy back her shares and many more at bargain rates. Eventually, if all went well, she would amass a large enough percentage of the company to challenge her brother for control.

A great deal could go wrong with that plan: The stock price might stabilize or even go back up, leaving her unable to recover her original holdings, much less add to them. Graham might get wind of what she was up to and move to stop her by buying up the stock himself. Or her actions might come to James's attention.

It was the last possibility that caused her the most concern. So far as James knew, she had accepted his belief that Graham had had nothing to do with his captivity. But in fact, Alexis had never said she agreed with him. It was a source of some amusement to her that he simply assumed she did. Still, she doubted she would find anything to laugh at were he to discover what she was up to.

He had enough difficulty accepting her role at IBS; the chances of him understanding what drove her to strike back at her brother in so ruthless a fashion—and in the face of his own clearly stated disapproval—were extremely remote. Eventually, if she succeeded, he would have to know the truth, but she could deal with that when she came to it. In the meantime, she would have to be very careful not to reveal herself.

That made her plan all the more difficult to carry out. Nonetheless, as winter blossomed into spring, she took the first vital step and sold her UBC stock, then waited to see what would develop.

Meanwhile, there was more than enough to keep her busy. In April, both the twins came down with measles. Jamie got it first, with Amanda succumbing a few days later. Alexis spent hours at their bedside, reading them stories, giving them sponge baths and coaxing them to eat. They recovered after a week or so, but the experience left her exhausted.

In between caring for the twins, she watched the Army/McCarthy hearings on television and was both fascinated and repelled by what she saw. Before the camera's unblinking eye, McCarthy threatened, bullied and made increasingly reckless charges that could not be even remotely substantiated. In effect, he hanged himself on a rope of lies and innuendos, just as in the past he had hanged so many others. When it was over, she could only breathe a sigh of relief that the long reign of the witch-hunters was finally ended.

Back at work, she had no chance to catch her breath before the swift pace of unfolding events swept her up. Winston agreed at last to sign a new contract, provided that in addition to his regular nightly news broadcasts and once-a-week

"Spotlight," he also be allowed periodic one-hour slots to explore major stories in great depth.

Alexis disliked the idea at first, thinking that few subjects could merit such attention. But two events in May of 1954 made her change her mind. In quick succession, the Supreme Court voted to ban school desegregation, and on the other side of the earth, the French suffered a devastating defeat on a small scrap of ground called Dienbienphu.

"If I do agree to the one-hour shows," she told Winston as they sat in her office, hashing out the final details of his new contract, "I'd like you to give some thought to special coverage of those two stories. They both strike me as having long-term importance."

"I can see doing a program on desegregation," he allowed, "but why should viewers care about what goes on in Vietnam? I'd be surprised if one out of a thousand of them has ever even heard of the place."

"Eisenhower has heard of it," she pointed out quietly. "He says Vietnam is of vital strategic importance to the United States and can never be allowed to fall into Communist hands."

He sat back in his chair, one long leg draped over the other, and frowned slightly. "Interesting...but what does all that mean in practical terms?"

"I don't know. Perhaps that's what you should look into."

They discussed it a while longer and at length he agreed to consider doing a story on United States foreign policy in Indochina. Though he made no secret of his lack of enthusiasm, at least he didn't claim it was "the most boring idea I've heard of in quite a while," which was what James said when she told him about it.

"For God's sake, Alexis, what are you trying to do, wreck the ratings? People are sick to death of hearing about Communists and they've had it up to here with war."

She bit back the first heated response that sprang to mind and instead said quietly, "That's no excuse. We have a responsibility to inform the public about major events."

He grimaced disparagingly. "What major events? A bunch of judges sitting in a courtroom in Washington say Negro kids have to go to school with whites. What difference is that going to make in Alabama or Kentucky, or for that matter, right here in New York? And as for that Vietnam business, who cares how those people choose to kill each other? It's got nothing to do with us. If we learned anything in Korea, it's to stay the hell away from that part of the world." Shaking his head, he concluded, "You're just doing this to play up to Harcourt, and Lord knows, his ego's big enough already."

That was hitting below the belt, and Alexis wasn't about to let him get away with it. Angrily, she said, "Winston has nothing to do with it. I'm simply concerned about the quality of what we put on the air. If you can suggest something better, go right ahead."

"*Anything* would be better," he insisted as he unbuttoned his shirt. They were getting ready for bed at the end of what had been a hectic day for both of them. Usually they made a genuine effort not to bring the office home, but just then it wasn't working out that way. "People are only interested in what affects them directly. They don't care about anything else."

"They used to," she pointed out as she removed her dress and hung it neatly away. "People once cared a great deal about what went on in the rest of the world."

"Only because they had no choice," he insisted. "When you or somebody you're close to is getting shot at, it has a remarkable way of concentrating your attention. But as soon as that's over, people forget about everything except their own immediate interests."

"Until the shooting starts again."

"That's about the size of it. I'm not saying it's the way things should be, but we've got to deal with reality. If Winston has to have those hour-long shows to stay with us, then let him have them. But do yourself a favor and leave the content up to him. He's got a good instinct for what people will pay attention to."

"He liked the idea of a show on the Supreme Court ruling," she pointed out from the bathroom, where she had gone to remove her makeup.

"So maybe there's something to that," he allowed. "But I'll bet he didn't go for that Vietnam business."

Since Alexis could hardly claim otherwise, she kept silent. It galled her to realize that Winston's opinion counted for more with James than her own. Hadn't she proven by now that she had at least as good an instinct for programming as anyone else in the business? Apparently not, because James was still more willing to accept the judgment of another man over hers.

The injustice of that hurt, but she said nothing of it. Slowly she was coming to terms with the fact that in the male-dominated world any admission of vulnerability was seized on as proof of weakness. She fell asleep that night wondering why men so consistently confused a thick skin with a strong will, and what one man in particular would do when he discovered his mistake.

WINSTON SIGNED HIS NEW CONTRACT with IBS and started work on the first of his hour-long programs. He had decided it would be on the new generation of leadership, a topic that hardly thrilled Alexis, even though she was willing to concede that it might attract viewers. At least a couple of researchers from the news department were looking into the issue of desegregation for a possible future show. Of Vietnam, nothing more was said.

"New Generation" was broadcast shortly after Labor Day and drew more than respectable ratings. Winston had crafted a sharp-eyed look at the inherent conflicts of ambition and idealism and neatly wrapped it in a very photogenic package. Tad Lawrence, congressman from Virginia, came across very well, as did the junior senator from Massachusetts, John F. Kennedy.

If on the news side everything was going smoothly, the same could not be said of the entertainment division. New problems had arisen with Delia Follett. A compromise had been reached earlier in the year; it gave her a piece of future syndication profits but not of advertising revenues. She had seemed satisfied at the time, but now, less than halfway through filming episodes for the new season, Delia let it be known that she was in fact not happy.

"She's tired of the character," her agent explained after being invited to New York to discuss the problem. "She's done everything she can with it."

Anthony and James exchanged an exasperated glance. They had heard this before and were running out of patience. "Not to put too fine a point on it, Max," Anthony said to the agent, "but Delia is paid extremely well to be Our Gal, Sal. Maybe she should remember that and not be in such a hurry to say she's bored."

"Who said she's bored?" Max protested. "All I'm telling you is what you should already know. Delia is a creative artist, a genius in her own field. She's not about to lower her standards in order to portray a character that's stale and used up."

"Millions of people love Sal," Alexis protested quietly. "They watch her faithfully every week and think of her as part of the family."

"Which is fine," Max agreed. "But how much longer will that be the case?" His voice dropped righteously. "Delia can't stand the idea of disappointing anyone."

"Does that include us?" James inquired dryly. He didn't really expect an answer, so he wasn't surprised not to get one. After a moment, he went on. "There's got to be a purpose to all this, Max. Care to tell us what it is?"

The agent stared at him for a moment, then sighed and got down to business. "She means what she says about wanting this to be Sal's last season. The writers are running out of ideas for story lines. They're starting to repeat themselves. You can coast along like that for only so long." Glancing at each of the three people gathered with him around the conference table, he added, "Let's face it, how many more good years can Delia expect to have? She's past thirty now, though, God knows, she doesn't look it. Her stock in trade is the gorgeous sexpot with the heart of gold. The heart I trust to hold up; the sexpot's another story."

When that failed to get a smile, much less a laugh, he shrugged resignedly and continued. "Anyway, to get to the point, she wants a new kind of show, something that will put the emphasis on her singing and acting rather than on her looks."

"She sings in the show now," James said. "At least one number per episode; that's in the contract."

"And the rest of the time she smiles and plays straight woman to the other characters' jokes. It's not good enough anymore. She's got to think of her future."

Despite herself, Alexis felt a small twinge of sympathy for the star. Delia was an intelligent woman, with no illusions about the business in which she made her living. As things stood now, she probably would have trouble continuing her career for more than a few additional years. Still, it was in IBS's best interest to keep Sal on the air as long as possible.

"Aren't you overlooking something?" she asked Max. "People are always comparing Delia to Lucille Ball; they're even supposed to be rivals of a sort. Do you really think anyone will ever tell Lucy she's too old to perform?"

"Of course not, but Delia's in a different ball game, no matter what people say. Whether you want to admit it or not, a big part of her show's success is sex, pure and simple. And in this country, a sexy woman is a young woman. That's all there is to it."

"That's nonsense," Alexis muttered even as she grudgingly admitted he had a point. With very few exceptions, all the major female stars were girl-women whose baby-smooth complexions and cheerleader figures epitomized an ideal of eternal youth. When reality began to catch up with them, they invariably disappeared from view.

Touching a finger unconsciously to the corner of her eye, she said, "Has Delia considered the contribution she could make by proving to America that its concept of female beauty is wrong? Maybe the answer is to let Sal grow up. Stop portraying her as a giggly little ingenue and let her be a real woman."

Max's large, round eyes blinked slowly. "Uh...that's very interesting...but I...uh...don't think Delia will go for that. She's not really out to lead any kind of revolution. All she wants is a chance to make the most of herself."

"With a new show," James broke in before Alexis could respond. He thought they had gone far enough down that particular road. "The bottom line is that she wants out of Sal and into a new show, right?"

Max nodded firmly. "That's it."

"And a new show means a new deal," Anthony added.

The agent spread his hands ingenuously. "Of course. You certainly couldn't expect otherwise."

"Of course," James parodied, rubbing the back of his neck. "So suppose you tell us what you'd like it to be."

He did, at some length. Delia proposed to set up her own production company to film episodes of a new hour-long variety show starring herself. Not only would she reap all the usual benefits of a star's salary, paid expenses and so on, but by controlling production, she would also receive a far larger share of the profits. In one brilliant move she would transform herself from a sexpot comedienne into a television executive.

Even James was stirred to reluctant admiration. "That's one of the smartest things I've heard in a long time. Trust Delia to come up with it."

Max beamed expansively. "I'd love to be able to say it was my idea, but it just ain't so. The lady has a brain."

"I'll say," Anthony agreed. "She's really outdone herself."

"There are some potential problems," Alexis cautioned. "IBS has never been involved in an arrangement of this kind; we would have to consider it very carefully."

She meant to go on in that vein, but James broke in. "Let's not get so bogged down in the details that we lose sight of the larger picture. This is a very exciting idea."

"We think so," Max said modestly. "Delia is eager to discuss it with you."

"When she's finished filming this season's episodes," Alexis began, "we can—"

"Oh, no," James broke in. "We don't want to wait until then. I'll fly out to the coast tomorrow and meet with her."

"Good idea," Anthony agreed. "Best to strike while the iron is hot."

Alexis had her own ideas about what was hot, but she refrained from mentioning them. Instead, she sat silent through the rest of the meeting while Max graciously provided more insights into what Delia might want in exchange for her services.

"I think you'll find she's eager to do the deal," the agent assured James. "She just needs to be sure she's really appreciated."

"She won't have any doubts about that by the time I get through," James told him with a deep, purely masculine chuckle. His arm was around Max's shoulders as he escorted him to the elevator.

Anthony and Alexis headed back for their offices. As they did so, he glanced at her cautiously. Her cheeks were slightly flushed and there was an uncharacteristic stiffness to her movements, as though she was holding herself in rigid control. Mentally rebuking James for his insensitivity, Anthony said, "Well. . .that was certainly interesting."

The look she shot him from the corner of her eye was nothing short of frigid. "Wasn't it."

He sighed, realizing belatedly that James wasn't the only one capable of an unfortunate turn of phrase. "What I meant was, it could make it possible for us to develop more new shows faster because we won't have to carry all the production risks.''

''How nice for us.'' At his sheepish look, she relented slightly. ''Don't mind me. I just found a little green imp sitting on my shoulder.''

Anthony grinned sympathetically. ''Did I ever tell you about the first time I met Maggie's brother Tad? I thought he was trying to double-time me and almost punched him out. Felt like a damn fool afterward.''

She laughed ruefully. ''I get the point. Anyway, no matter how I feel, James is still the logical person to negotiate with Delia. After all, they...go way back.''

''That's all in the past,'' Anthony said firmly. ''What went on during the war might as well have happened in a different world.''

Alexis hoped he was right, but she had her doubts. She knew James well enough to understand that like her, he tended to keep the various aspects of his life separate. That had certain advantages; for example, it made it possible to rationalize different codes of behavior for different situations.

He was forty-two now, and while he remained the most attractive and desirable man she had ever encountered, there were nonetheless changes in him. The lingering aftereffects of his experiences in Korea, which he still refused to acknowledge, sometimes sapped his strength and made him prone to mild depressions. It would hardly be surprising if during such periods he didn't sometimes chafe at the restrictions of his life and fantasize about being free of them.

What went on in the privacy of his mind was strictly his business; she would never dream of attempting to intrude there. But she understood all too well how easily thoughts could be transformed into actions, and that worried her.

Chapter Seventeen

THE DANK, HUMID HEAT HIT James as soon as he stepped off the plane in L.A. When he had left New York, it had been a properly cold, gray winter day. Here the sun was shining, birds were singing, and people were walking around in Bermuda shorts and sunglasses. No matter how many trips he made to the West Coast, he would never get used to it.

Sighing, he loosened his tie and went in search of a taxi. His suit jacket was slung over his shoulder and he carried his only luggage, an overnight bag with a fresh shirt, a change of underwear, his shaving gear and the file on Delia Productions. With luck, he hoped the problems with the new show would be straightened out quickly and he could be on the way back to New York by the following day. Getting into the cab, he gave the driver Delia's address in the Bel Air hills high above the city, then settled back and let his thoughts drift.

This was his third trip to the Coast in as many months. The first had resulted in the signing of an agreement between Delia Follett and IBS to set up Delia Productions. The second, in January, had finalized the plan for her new show and gotten it rolling. Now it was March and the honeymoon was clearly over. All he'd been hearing from Max lately was a litany of complaints: The budget wasn't big enough; Delia didn't like the studio; IBS wasn't cooperating; how could they expect her to get anything done when they were separated by thousands of miles and everything was being handled through intermediaries?

"She could come to New York," James had suggested at one point, only to have Max look at him as though he had taken leave of his senses.

"Delia come here? Impossible. She's strictly a California girl."

"I seem to remember she was originally from Kansas."

The agent had shrugged laconically. "So she's been a few places; so what? Now she's a star and she doesn't come knocking on anybody's door. Not even yours. You want to see her, catch a plane."

He had, without caring to examine his motives too closely. Certainly the new show was important to IBS and the problems had to be straightened out. But he could have sent a subordinate or simply dug in his heels and insisted that Delia make the trip. Instead, he had come himself and already he was wondering why.

"This is the place, mac," the driver said as he pulled up in front of a low ranch-style house at the end of a steep gravel driveway. Screened by large bushes and trees, the house was all but invisible from the road, but James was able to catch a glimpse of a kidney-shaped pool off to one side. The bright blue water glinted in the sunlight.

After he had paid the tab and the taxi had left, he stood for a moment to get his bearings. It was very quiet this high in the hills. He could hear little except the low, haunting cry of mourning doves and the whisper of the wind in the chaparral. Off in the distance, he could see the rolling surf of the Pacific. A drowsing mist obscured the horizon, but he thought he could make out the tiny black dots of seals cavorting near the shore.

Almost despite himself, a sense of pleasure at being there crept over him. He was tempted to put aside the concerns that had brought him and simply enjoy the setting. Until the door of the ranch house opened and he saw the woman standing there.

"I thought I heard a car drive up," Delia said in the soft, breathless voice millions of viewers knew so well. A slow smile curved her full mouth. "Planning on staying out here all day?"

James shook his head and picked up his overnight bag. "No, just enjoying the view. I haven't been up here before."

"I know; that's why I thought it would be so much nicer to meet here rather than in that stuffy old office." As she spoke, she came toward him, a delectable figure in snug slacks and a sweater that hugged her curves lovingly. Her titian hair tumbled around her shoulders, her perfect features were free of makeup, and her upward-tilted green eyes glinted with amusement.

"I see you're traveling light," she said as she glanced at the bag, "as usual." Thus prodded, a memory rose to the surface of his mind of Delia watching him pack. That had been a dozen years ago and he had been on his way back to the war he had no real expectation of surviving. She had been a USO entertainer whose chief talent could not be advertised and whose future was, to say the least, uncertain. They had come together in Australia while he was on R&R, and for a time shared the comfort of a warm body in the night and the forgetfulness of sexual release. They had also, though he didn't like to dwell on it, become friends.

"You're looking good," he said as they walked into the house together. "As usual."

She laughed and took his arm in a spontaneous gesture that was so much like her. "Thanks. I was tempted to put on the war paint, but then I thought, what's the sense? You're too smart to be fooled by that stuff.''

He raised an eyebrow quizzically. ''Fooled? You mean because it makes you look younger?''

At her rueful nod, he laughed. ''If I didn't know better, I'd swear you were still twenty-three. Except now you're...'' He broke off, abruptly aware that he was walking out onto thin ice. He would be far wiser to keep their discussions strictly impersonal.

Delia, however, had other ideas. Softly, she prompted, ''I'm what...? Go on, tell me. Don't leave a girl in suspense.''

Her wide-eyed gaze, exaggeratedly eager, made him laugh. Grinning wryly, he said, ''You're better-looking now than you were then.'' Somewhat abashedly, he added, ''The French have a saying about women getting better, not older. I guess, in your case, that's true.''

''Why, James, how sweet of you to say so. You know, you were always the most charming man. Back in Australia, there were still a few rough edges, but they seem to have worn away most delightfully.''

He shot her a quick glance, wondering if she was teasing him, but the look in her eyes was completely sincere, even innocent. There was no sign of flirtation, no indication that she meant more than what she had said. Only a relaxed, openhearted desire for his understanding and friendship.

He would hardly have been a man if he failed to respond to that. His wariness dropped away as innate confidence reasserted itself. Of course he could handle the situation. How could he have thought otherwise? Delia was, after all, only an old friend with whom he happened to share a business interest. To think there might be anything else between them was plain foolishness.

"Shall we get started?" she asked as she folded herself down gracefully onto the plush wall-to-wall carpeting, behind a low-slung coffee table. The living room was large and filled with light. Two walls of floor-to-ceiling windows gave way to a wraparound terrace with wrought-iron railings that commanded a breathtaking view of the adjacent canyon and beyond, to the ocean. Inside, the color scheme was purely feminine, lavender and mauve with delicate touches of beige. In contrast to the stark Danish Modern style that was so popular elsewhere, Delia had selected pieces with gently rounded lines. Opposite the arrangement of seating units was a field-stone fireplace that looked well-used. He supposed that on cooler nights she enjoyed a fire there and caught himself wondering whom she shared it with.

That would not do. Lowering himself to the couch, he said, "It looks as though you've been busy." Papers were spread out on the table in front of them: The budget for the new show, a list of performers, sheet music and so on.

"I'm trying to keep all this organized," she said, glancing up at him with a wry smile. "But it isn't easy."

"You'll get used to it. The trick is to take care of problems as soon as they arise instead of waiting until they get out of hand." As he spoke, his gaze drifted downward along the neckline of her sweater to the shadowed cleft between her breasts. From where he sat, above and to the side of her, the view was enticing. In the back of his mind, he wondered if she had arranged herself deliberately, then pushed that thought aside. It made no difference whether she had or not. He was there strictly to talk business.

Reminding himself of that, he cleared his throat and said, "Max indicated there were problems with the show's budget. Suppose we begin by going over that?"

Delia sighed in mock resignation. ''All right, if you insist. But I'd better warn you, I'm a better comedienne than I am an executive.''

James shrugged, confident that she was a good deal more astute than she cared to admit. Three hours and two pots of coffee later he was sure of it. Delia had points to raise about every item. The allocation for music and choreography had to be increased: ''This is a variety show, after all,'' she said. ''Good people don't come cheap.'' Likewise the budget for writers: ''They won't work for peanuts, you know. You get what you pay for.'' The office staff was inadequate: ''We need more personnel to help round up the talent and get it on the air.'' Not incidentally, her wardrobe would have to be far more expensive than originally estimated: ''I need a new, more glamorous look. The clothes I wore as Sal were fine because I was supposed to be a little nightclub singer. This is very different.''

James laid down the glasses he wore now for reading and sighed. Nothing that she said was unreasonable; on the contrary, it was all carefully thought out and basically irrefutable. He only wished she had come up with the numbers sooner.

''You know,'' he said gently, ''the original budget was based on your estimates.''

She shrugged apologetically. ''That was before I had any production experience. Now I do and I can see that I was being unreasonable about what I thought things would cost.''

''I see...'' He glanced again at the new figures. ''Well, I suppose we'll just have to work with things as they really are. The show is important to us, so the money has to come from somewhere. But,'' he added a bit sternly, ''remember, we have to be able to realize a certain profit or it isn't worth doing.''

"Oh, I understand that," she assured him hurriedly. "But there's no problem. I can see ways to save money, too."

At his urging, she went on to describe them. Listening to her soft, melodious voice, James lost track of the time. He was surprised at length to notice that the sun was setting beyond the ceiling-high windows. Bands of cerise and gold streaked the sky, giving way slowly to the deeper hues of mauve and violet in which the first stars glimmered. The water was tinted a deep red, as though blood had spilled across the sea. He looked away. "It's late."

"Oh, I'm sorry," Delia said, breaking off and getting to her feet. She smiled down at him apologetically. "I had no idea we'd been at it so long. You must be starving." Before he could reply, she said, "I'll get dinner started. It'll be ready in a jiff."

He stood up slowly, his body stiff and his mind somehow disoriented. "Dinner? There's no reason for you to bother."

"No bother," she assured him over her shoulder as she headed toward the kitchen. "Steak and french fries all right?"

"Yes, of course, but I could just grab a bite at the hotel." As he spoke, he glanced at his watch. He really ought to be going soon. His room was guaranteed for a late check-in, so that was no problem, but he had told Alexis he would call.

Following her into the kitchen, he paused at the door as a sudden thought flashed through his mind. Despite himself, he smiled.

"What's funny?" she asked, opening the refrigerator and rummaging around in it.

His gaze drifted to the beautifully rounded posterior nicely displayed as she bent over. More steadily than he felt, he said, "I was just wondering if your fans ever think of you like this, bustling around the kitchen to fix some guy a meal."

She laughed and met his eyes. "If they don't, they don't really know me. I've got a strong domestic streak."

"From Kansas?" he teased gently.

"I suppose, though I haven't thought about that much lately." Laying the steaks out on the drainboard, she said, "You know what else I haven't thought about in a while? Australia. Remember the good times in Brisbane, that little room I had and how we used to cook on the hot plate with all the windows open so no one would know?"

He nodded, remembering. "Didn't we burn the beans one time and bring the landlady down on us?"

"We sure did," Delia confirmed. "But you told her you'd been wounded and had to have a special diet. I don't think she bought it, but who could argue with such a great-looking guy?"

"Was that what I was?" he asked, not hiding his amusement.

She nodded very seriously. "Take my word for it. You were a terrific catch. All the other girls in the USO were horribly jealous of me."

"I think they had a few other reasons for that," he reminded her. "You did kind of put the rest of them to shame."

"Do you really think so?" she asked, pleased. "It seems so long ago, sometimes I wonder if it really happened."

But it had, and try as he did, James had not been able to forget it. Now, standing near her in the quiet intimacy of the kitchen, memories of those long-ago days flooded over him. He had been so much younger then, or at least it seemed that way, and life had been much simpler. Instead of a multitude of possibilities, there had been only two alternatives: Either he would die in the war, a literally unimaginable event he could think of only in the most impersonal terms, or he would live and the future would be his, given the slightest opportunity.

In retrospect, that confidence seemed on the far side of naiveté, yet it had made perfect sense back then. And to a large extent, it had turned out to be justified. He had achieved great success, far beyond most other men's dreams. The business he had helped to create endowed him with wealth and power. His wife was the most beautiful and passionate of women. His children were a source of deep pleasure and satisfaction.

Why, then, this niggling sense of something missed, something speeding away from him with terrifying swiftness? What was slipping from his grasp? Youth? Optimism? He had lost something in Korea, a belief in his own immortality, which was the most precious possession of the young. With maturity had come the realization that his time, however long it might turn out to be, was limited. Eventually it would run out and then what would there be? The void into which no man could truly see, though many claimed otherwise?

A great thirst was growing in him, to drain life of everything it offered, to leave not a single drop unsavored at the end of the long day when the light flickered out.

Delia turned to him. There was a tentativeness about her that he found oddly touching. She did not presume anything about him, only about herself. "James," she said softly, "you know I want you to stay?"

He looked at her for a long moment. She was very beautiful with her red hair and deep green eyes, the damask smoothness of her lightly flushed skin and the tempting curve of her full mouth. But more than that, she was a vivid reminder of what he had once been. Within her memory, the young man of boundless possibilities and endless confidence still lived. Through her, might he not be recaptured for at least some little time?

She met his eyes, hers infinitely soft and full of appeal. Slowly, she held out a hand. "Will you?"

He hesitated through the space of a heartbeat before he nodded.

WHEN JAMES RETURNED TO NEW YORK a week later, Alexis did not ask him why a trip that had been expected to take only a day had gone on so much longer. The question was very much on her mind, but she preferred not to know the answer, at least for the moment. Her reluctance to confront the issue might be taken for cowardice, but at least it wore the gloss of prudence.

The night after he got back, they lay in bed talking about what had happened during his absence. "Matthew has discovered some strange, new kind of music," Alexis said wryly. "He's been playing the same record all week."

James laughed softly. "Is it that bad?"

"The lyrics seem to consist solely of 'Everybody, rock, rock, rock. Everybody, roll, roll, roll.' Whatever that means. Anyway, it apparently has to be played at very high volume in order to be properly appreciated."

"I'll have a word with him."

"No, don't. He's normally so well behaved I'm glad to see him loosen up a bit."

"Hmmm...all right, so long as he understands there are limits to that. How have the twins been?"

"As usual. Amanda leads and Jamie follows. If I hear one more rendition of 'Davy Crockett, King of the Wild Frontier,' I may choke."

"Can't Matthew drown them out?"

"There's an idea. They've informed me that if they don't both get coonskin caps, they will be unable to show their faces at the playground."

He sighed resignedly. "I'll pick up a couple tomorrow. In the meantime…" Propping himself up on an elbow, he smiled down at her. "I missed you."

She resisted the impulse to ask if he really had and instead said, "I missed you. Care to do something about it?"

His smile deepened as he moved over her. "I thought you'd never ask."

Perhaps it was her imagination, but his lovemaking that night and in the nights that followed seemed at once more passionate and more tender. She caught herself wondering what prompted it, frustration or guilt. While she might hope it was the former, either was a bad bargain.

Work, as always, proved a great distraction. Winston's second hour-long show ran in April. "America's Shame" was a biting indictment of racial policies in the South. Most regular sponsors had refused to have anything to do with it, with the result that the program was shown almost without interruption. It was still on the air when several IBS affiliates received bomb threats and a deluge of enraged callers jammed the switchboard at headquarters.

In its aftermath, Alexis was pleased that both James and Anthony supported her decision to air the program. "I have to admit I'm surprised by the virulent reaction it got," Anthony said when they gathered to discuss the matter. "But I guess that just proves it hit a nerve."

"The funny thing is," James pointed out, "that for all the threats about getting back at us, our ratings are up across the board. It's almost as though people are tuning in to see what we'll do next."

"Then let's not disappoint them," Alexis suggested. "Winston wants to follow up with a show about racial discrimination in the North. I'd like to give him the go-ahead."

James frowned slightly. "In the North? Is there that much of it up here?"

"He says so. Besides, as some of our callers pointed out, the problem isn't confined to the South. It's nationwide."

Approval was given for the second show, but with the condition that it would not run until at least six months after the first. Anything sooner was considered to be pushing their luck.

In the meantime, Alexis had other matters on her mind. UBC's stock had begun to fall significantly. Just as she had expected, Graham's policy of diversification was slowly undermining the company. Less than four years after their father's death, the empire Charles Brockton had built was starting to flounder. That saddened her even as she moved determinedly to take advantage of the situation. Quietly, she began to buy back her shares, doing so in very small blocks that would neither attract attention nor stop the downward slide of the price.

That summer of 1955, James had to make several more trips to the Coast to confer with Delia. Her new show was due to premier in September, but there were still some problems that required his attention. In his absence, Alexis had lunch occasionally with Winston, but otherwise she restricted her social activities. She wanted to spend as much time as possible with Matthew and the twins.

At fifteen, her stepson was a handsome, well-built young man with a gentle manner and a keen mind. Not surprisingly, he was extremely popular with the young ladies at his school. He had started dating recently and seemed to enjoy it, though he confessed to a certain nervousness. "I don't always know what to say," he told Alexis, "and sometimes I can't figure out what to do with my hands."

"You will," she told him, hiding a smile. "It just takes time."

"Maybe, but the girls seem better able to handle it. Do you know, some of them are already talking about getting engaged their first year in college and getting married as soon as they graduate? Heck, I've heard a few describing how they're going to decorate their houses and what their kids will be like."

"That is a bit precocious," she agreed cautiously. Teenagers, as they were now called, were a mystery to her. They seemed to have evolved into a distinct species with their own status symbols, fads and even language. Matthew was better by far than most, but even he scorned what was "square" and aspired to be "cool."

He spent most of his allowance on records, favoring Bill Haley and the Comets, and Ray Charles. Alexis had finally found out what "rock and roll" meant; she was even learning to like it. Matthew's deep admiration for Grace Kelly continued, but he was also becoming a Marlon Brando fan, having gone to see him twice in *On the Waterfront*. He liked to read and had all but memorized J.D. Salinger's *Catcher in the Rye*. His favorite TV programs were on IBS, but he took time out to enjoy "Alfred Hitchcock Presents" and the "Red Skelton Show," both on CBS.

The week after Labor Day, "Delia Follett Presents!" premiered to runaway ratings and rave reviews. Alexis grudgingly admitted that whatever else she might be, the beautiful star was a superb performer. She came across on camera as warm, friendly, intelligent, funny and downright lovable. Alexis had the sinking feeling that she was the same way in person.

The need to know more about the woman who might or might not be her rival began to consume her, yet she could still not bring herself to broach the subject with James. As a compromise, she turned to the only person she knew who would tell her the truth.

Maggie was glad to see her, as always, when she drove out to the house on an early autumn day. Tessa and Joey were at school and little Tony was having his nap. "Of course, he'll probably wake up the moment we get comfortable," Maggie said with a smile, "but let's give it a try." She fixed coffee for them both and they sat in the newly built sun room overlooking the garden and pool. "I hate to see the summer end," she said after they had quickly caught up on each other's news. "With the kids back in school, it's too quiet around here."

"I thought you'd love that," Alexis said teasingly, considering her own relief that the twins had started to kindergarten. "Besides, doesn't little Tony keep you busy?"

"No...not really. Maybe because he's the third, I don't feel I have to do all the things I did with the others. I'm more relaxed about it, which seems to be to his benefit."

"But not necessarily yours," Alexis said softly. "Do I detect a note of boredom?"

Maggie smiled ruefully. "That's about the size of it. Anthony says I should join a woman's club or something like that."

"What do you say?"

She hesitated a moment, then shrugged. "I say I'm going back to school, to sharpen up my skills and renew my nurse's license."

Alexis's eyes widened. Though she knew Maggie had longed to return to nursing for years, she hadn't expected her to do anything about it until Tony was in school like the others. "Uh...how does Anthony feel about that?"

"He's furious," she said calmly. "We've had three fights about it in the past month and there's no end in sight."

The idea of Maggie and Anthony seriously fighting was all but incomprehensible. She had always considered their marriage to be as close to perfect as any could get. Taken aback, she said, "I'm sorry to hear that. If there's anything we can do, anything at all, don't hesitate to ask."

Maggie looked at her curiously for a moment before she began to laugh. "Thank you," she said gravely after she had caught her breath, "but Anthony and I are just having a little difference of opinion. This is hardly the first time. We'll work it out."

"Are you sure? I mean, it sounds as though neither of you is going to give in."

"We aren't. Sometimes compromise just isn't possible. He's going to have to live with my going back to school and I'm going to have to live with his disapproval."

"Can you do that...really?"

"What's the alternative? Anthony and I have been together for almost fourteen years. And in that time I've come to love him more, not less. I know he feels the same way about me. That isn't wishful thinking or bragging; it's just a fact. We belong together, but that doesn't mean we always see eye to eye."

"But when you don't...you work it out?"

"One way or another." She smiled wryly. "The toughest part of marriage, in my opinion, is saying what you think even when you know the other person is going to disagree, or even be hurt. There's such a temptation to fudge the truth a little or to evade it altogether. But sooner or later, that catches up with you.''

''You sound as though you speak from experience.''

''I do. Remember after Korea, when Anthony had to have physical therapy for his arm?''

Alexis nodded. ''I remember.''

''Well, he had this absolutely gorgeous physical therapist. She was Swedish—just my luck—tall, blue-eyed, with honey-blond hair and curves in all the right places. Anyway, she and Anthony really hit it off. He'd been reluctant to go for the therapy, but once he met good ol' Ingrid, all that changed. Then it was 'Ingrid this' and 'Ingrid that' night and day, or so it seemed. Anyway, I finally got sick of it, and one night in bed, I just asked him flat out, 'What's going on with you two?' At first, he pretended he had no idea what I was talking about. She was just his therapist; he was just trying to get well—all that stuff. But finally he admitted that there was more to it.''

''There was?'' Alexis repeated, frankly astonished. She could not imagine Anthony being unfaithful. If he was capable, then no man on earth could be trusted.

Maggie smiled gently. ''He felt a need to prove to himself that despite his injury, he was still strong and intact as a man. At that time, I was being very solicitous of him, taking care of him almost as I would one of the children. Ingrid, on the other hand, kept challenging him, insisting that he could do more. For a while it seemed as though with her he could be a man, while with me he was a child.''

''And because she made him feel like a man, he was tempted to prove it with her?''

''Exactly, but he didn't want to give in to that temptation. His constant references to her were a roundabout way of trying to tell me that I needed to treat him differently.''

"I take it you got the message?"

"In spades! And in time. Anthony felt guilty enough about just being attracted to her; if it had gone any further, I think he would have been eaten up inside."

"So, because you were honest with each other, everything worked out all right?"

Maggie nodded, looking at her closely. "Of course, you have to realize it was my behavior that to a large extent caused his. So, by changing what I was doing, I could affect what happened with him. That isn't always the case. Sometimes even people who love each other do things for reasons that have nothing to do with the other person."

"The reasons might not," Alexis agreed, "but the consequences certainly do. If you love someone, you can be hurt by their every word or deed, however careless or impersonal."

"And there you have the problem. Do you try not to care so you won't be hurt, or do you leave yourself open to pain in order to love completely?"

Alexis smiled faintly. "I know how you'd answer: Love no matter what the risk."

"That's true, but I trust Anthony, as he trusts me. Without that, such love isn't possible."

"Trust can be lost."

Maggie's eyes met hers, full of gentle understanding. Quietly, she said, "Yes, it can be, and that's always very sad. But sadder still is when trust is arbitrarily thrown away, without being given a chance. If you lose something, you may get lucky and find it again. If you throw something away, it's usually gone forever."

ALEXIS REMEMBERED THAT in the days and weeks that followed as she struggled to come to terms with her fears and confront James directly. It was not so much what he would say that frightened her, since she was rapidly reaching the point where anything was better than doubt. What she shied away from was the possibility that once she questioned his behavior, he would feel free to do the same with hers. That was a Pandora's box she was not eager to have opened.

She therefore did not make any true effort to bring up the subject, indulging instead in uncharacteristic procrastination, and allowed herself to be carried along on the stream of events that seemed to be moving at an ever accelerating rate.

few weeks after her conversation with Maggie, the Dodgers at last avenged themselves against the Yankess by beating them in the World Series. Dom took the occasion of that long-awaited victory to announce his retirement from baseball. He joined IBS full-time and in December was made director of the newly created sports division.

Early in 1956, IBS went through a period of rapid expansion as some ten new affiliates were signed on. The additions were made possible by steadily improving ratings and the increased advertising revenues that resulted. With the five stations now owned directly, the maximum allowed by the FCC, plus the dozen affiliates signed up over the years, what had begun as a small independent operation had emerged as a full-scale network. While still not of the size of the Big Four—NBC, ABC, CBS and UBC—it was large enough to give them all competition.

Two foreign bureaus were opened, one in London and the other in Moscow, where Nikita Kruschev was emerging as the man in charge. He and Eisenhower clashed regularly, and there were some who thought a showdown was inevitable.

Alexis did not ignore the shifting currents of power and intrigue in the world at large, but her personal situation absorbed her much more. As the eighth anniversary of her marriage approached, she found herself no longer able to live with doubt. Whatever the consequences, she and James had to talk.

Her choice as the place to do so was the beach house, where they went for a long weekend early in May to celebrate their anniversary. Matthew, now going on seventeen, was left in charge of the six-year-old twins, who seemed to think it very amusing that he should be trusted with such responsibility.

James, commenting rather ruefully, said it was hard for him to grasp, too. He had a difficult time coming to terms with the fact that his eldest son would soon be going off to college. At Matthew's age, he had been only a few years away from marriage, fatherhood and war. When he looked at his son, now as tall as himself, he often felt a deep sense of helplessness because he could no longer protect him. He had to be allowed to make his own mistakes, and to suffer the consequences.

When Alexis had first broached the possibility of their spending some time alone together, James had swiftly agreed. He had felt the growing tension in her and suspected its cause. His own failure to address the matter directly rankled. They were overdue for a clearing of the air.

It came their first night at the beach house as they sat in front of the fireplace sipping brandy. Dinner had been largely taken up with chitchat about the children and work. Only toward its end had the talk been punctuated by stretches of silence. They had both risen with relief from the table and James had helped Alexis clear away the dishes. While she finished straightening up, he got the fire going. It was cool for May. Somewhere far out over the ocean a storm must have been brewing, for the waves pounded with unusual vigor against the nearby beach. He checked to make sure the windows were securely latched before settling down on the couch.

Alexis joined him there. The fire cast a half-circle of light into the room. Shadows moved beyond its boundaries, but within, there was warmth and safety. Seated beside him, with his arm around her shoulders and the first sip of brandy heating her from within, she put aside her fears of what was to be and resolved to cope moment by moment.

Her gaze on the dancing flames, she murmured, "Do you remember the first time we were here together?"

He shifted slightly so that he could look at her. "That was the first time we made love. Of course, I remember."

A soft laugh broke from her. "You know, every time we come out here with the kids, I think of that and get a little embarrassed."

"Wondering what they'd say if they knew what we'd been up to?"

"I suppose. It's the old conflict between trying to be a mother, deserving of all that implies, and still being a woman."

He drew her closer, his chest warm beneath her cheek. "You manage very well."

"Do you really mean that?"

"Of course; why would I say it otherwise?"

"I don't know...but there was a time when you seemed to feel I was taking something away from the children by working."

"Yes," he admitted, "I did feel that way. But let's face it, a lot of my concern was for myself, not the kids. You'd handled everything so well while I was in Korea that I wasn't sure you still needed me."

"Was *that* why you wanted me to quit?"

"Mostly, though I still think there's a lot to be said for a woman being home with the kids."

"That just isn't possible for me," she said quietly. "I need something more."

"Let's not get into that again," he suggested, dropping a gentle kiss on her forehead. "Neither of us is going to convince the other, so what's the point?"

"We'll just agree to disagree?"

"Why not? It's worked so far."

Alexis took a deep breath and sat up, disentangling herself from his arms. Her silver-blond hair, freed from the chignon she wore during the day, glinted in the firelight. Before dinner, she had put on a pair of sapphire silk lounging pajamas, the top of which was cut low enough to reveal the curve of her breasts. Her skin, scented with Arpège, had a smooth and creamy texture, warm to the touch and infinitely inviting. James was gazing at her appreciatively, the light in his eyes telling her how easily he could be persuaded to forego any further discussion. Though she was tempted, she refused to do so. Instead, she said quietly, "That just isn't good enough anymore. I think we need to be more open with each other."

He looked at her, puzzled. "You really want to pursue the issue of whether or not you should be working?"

"No," she said impatiently, "not that. As you said, there's no point. But there is something else...."

James waited, his eyes hooded and his expression unreadable. It was very important to him that she broach the subject; anything else would put him at a disadvantage.

Alexis moved away from him a little more, so that they were not touching. Only then did she say softly, "It's occurred to me that you may be having an affair with Delia."

He did not respond immediately, at least not verbally. Inside, his reaction was instant and complex. He was at once saddened that they had come to such a point and proud of her for having the courage to bring it about. Now it remained to be seen if he could match her strength.

Slowly, he asked, "You really believe that's a possibility?"

"If I didn't, I would hardly have brought it up. You spend a good deal of time with her, she's an extremely attractive woman, and you did have a past relationship."

"Very past," he said dryly. "The last time Delia and I shared a bed was back in October, '43, right before I left for New Guinea."

Alexis stared at him, unsure she had heard right. "The last time...?"

"That's right." He smiled gently. "I know I should have said something about this to you sooner. It didn't completely escape my notice that you might be coming to the wrong conclusion about Delia and me. As to why I didn't speak up, I guess I was a little embarrassed."

"Embarrassed? I don't understand...."

"It's hard to explain exactly...this is something that has to do with being a man...and with the pressures men live under. Even when you're married and in love with your wife, there's still a feeling that if a very beautiful and desirable woman is available and it looks as though no one would really be hurt, you should make the most of it. Otherwise, you're not quite a man."

A rueful smile flickered across his face. "I was very tempted by Delia; I don't deny that. Things came to a head during that trip last March when I was alone with her at her house. We...talked a lot, had dinner together. You have to remember she'd never met you in person; in a way, you weren't quite real to her. What was real was our being together again.''

''What happened?'' Alexis murmured, her voice choked.

James touched a gentle hand to her cheek, stroking her lightly. ''I said you weren't real to Delia. You certainly were— and are—to me. I wanted to be able to come home to you with a clear conscience.'' He smiled ruefully. ''I ended up drinking too much and falling asleep on the couch.''

''That must have annoyed her,'' Alexis ventured tremulously. Relief was flowing through her like a hot, liquid balm. But it passed quickly, leaving a bitter residue of shame.

James shrugged lightly. ''There are plenty of women who wouldn't have forgiven me, but she did. She told me the next morning she'd always suspected that when I finally fell in love, it would be forever.''

Better and better, worse and worse. James loved her; he had not been unfaithful. He was guiltless. Only she had sinned.

''James…there's something…I don't want to tell you, but I think I really have to.''

He nodded slowly, his hand cupping her chin, compelling her to meet his gaze. ''About Harcourt?''

Stunned, she could only stare at him. ''Y-you know…?''

''I've suspected…. I should have said something, but I guess I've been afraid of what the answer would be.''

That feeling, so like her own, reminded her of the intimate bond between them stretching back over the years and encompassing so much shared experience. Holding on to that, she drew a deep breath and said, ''The night of my father's funeral I went to bed with him. I was so afraid and alone. You were in Korea, and I was beginning to believe you might truly be dead.'' Her voice dropped slightly. ''I was beginning to feel that way myself. Winston was there and he cared about me. It was a moment of weakness I've regretted ever since.''

James absorbed her words in silence. The knowledge that she had been with another man stabbed through him, but only briefly. Beyond it was the larger awareness of what her admission seemed to suggest.

''There was only that once...?''

She laughed thickly. ''That was more than enough. Winston is a friend and I value him as such. He's stuck with me when I haven't really deserved it. But I don't want him to be anything more.'' Quietly, she added, ''The only man I've ever really wanted in that way is you.''

James became aware suddenly that he had been holding his breath and exhaled shakily. Something was breaking loose inside him, a hard band of arrogance and self-righteousness. In its place was humility...and gratitude. He had not lost her as he had begun to fear. On the contrary, she deeply regretted that one misstep, so understandable in light of the circumstances under which it had occurred.

The sweet warmth of forgiveness flowed through him as he reached for her. She was a little stiff in his arms, as though still unsure of his reaction. It gave him deep pleasure to reassure her. ''Sweetheart, for all you knew, I was dead. And if I had been, I'd have wanted you to go on living. I like and respect Harcourt. If there had to be another man in your life, I'd just as soon it was him.''

She looked up hesitantly, hardly daring to believe him. ''You really mean that?''

He nodded firmly. ''I do. Put it out of your mind. From now on, nothing matters except the two of us.''

Alexis was more than willing to do so. The burden of guilt being lifted from her shoulders filled her with an ebullience she had not known in years. If a small voice whispered far in the back of her mind that the race was not done and that the highest hurdle still lay ahead of her, she tuned it out resolutely and concentrated instead on the man who was all things to her—lover, husband, and most precious, friend.

Chapter Eighteen

THE VISIT TO THE BEACH HOUSE and the events that transpired there marked a turning point in Alexis and James's lives. Afterward, there was a quiet happiness about them, almost as though they shared some great secret known only to them. That wasn't true, of course. Other people knew the same depth of love and inner contentment, but it was an experience so intensely private that each time it occurred, it seemed like it was theirs alone.

Beyond the golden shores of that exclusive realm only the most fortunate ever glimpsed, the world went on, a relentlessly grinding march in which individuals could so easily and so often did become lost.

James and Alexis did not. Whether from some greater strength of will or some extra quality of character, they reached together and separately toward a high place where the air grew very thin and the light was very bright. There was danger there in the clash of dream and reality, a giving up of at least some of the safety so laboriously won in the years since the war. But that seemed a price worth paying.

It was the time of a slowly rising tide. The land was awash with murmurs not yet fully articulated but still unmistakable. A new generation was preparing to assume at last the mantle of power worn so long by its fathers.

Beginning early in 1957, Alexis stepped up her buying of UBC stock. She worried that the company might actually be in danger of being destroyed by Graham's ineptitude. There was evidence to support that in the spring, when IBS overtook UBC in the ratings and moved into position to directly challenge the remaining three networks. Success proved to be a two-edged sword, as it resulted in a takeover bid by a large communications consortium. James and Anthony spent long hours fighting it off, while Alexis was left in charge of day-to-day operations.

By summer, the threat was over, but it had taken a heavy toll on them all. Alexis was relieved to get away for a while with James and the children. They toured England and France before spending a week in Ireland, visiting the harshly beautiful west country where James's parents had both been born. Amanda and Jamie went riding every day, while Matthew and Tessa roamed over the countryside, content with each other's company. Alexis had asked Maggie to let Tessa come along because she knew how much the eleven-year-old girl loved Matthew and how she dreaded his going away to college the following year. She suspected her stepson would miss Tessa, too, since there had always been a very special friendship between them.

Returning to New York right before Labor Day, Alexis and James were kept busy both at work and at home. Several new shows were launched, some with better results than others, but overall the trend was good. The twins started second grade at the private school near their home. They were in separate classes, which was probably just as well, since Amanda continued to grasp new ideas much more quickly than Jamie. He had to plod along, often with far less satisfactory results. Alexis admired his diligence even as she worried about what might happen if and when his patience finally ran out.

Matthew started his senior year at prep school and began making serious plans for college. On the recommendation of his advisor, he applied to Harvard, Yale and Princeton, with the intention of studying history and literature. He had decided to be a writer and spent hours in his room trying to learn how it was done. His usual habit was to excuse himself after dinner, but on an evening late in September he made an exception and stayed downstairs with the rest of the family.

Alexis and James sat on the couch in the big, comfortable family room at the back of the town house overlooking the small garden. Matthew was in a chair nearby and the twins were stretched out on the floor. The television was tuned to IBS's evening news.

"The president of the United States announced today that Federal troops will be sent to Little Rock immediately to end resistance to the enrollment of the nine Negro children at Central High School," Winston said.

The scene shifted to a mob of angry whites. Close-ups of faces distorted by rage were interspersed with shots of the nine children, their expressions carefully closed as they were turned away from the school.

"This move follows the placing of the Arkansas National Guard under direct presidential control," Winston said when the camera cut back to him, "and has been done, according to President Eisenhower, in order to avoid anarchy. And now this word from our sponsor."

"Upset stomach? Try Alka-Seltzer! It dissolves stomach gas ten times faster than..."

"What on earth is going on?" Alexis asked softly, casting a quick glance at the twins, who were ignoring the commercial. They had their heads close together and were whispering about something. "I can't believe this could happen in this country. Aren't we better than that?"

"Apparently not," James said. His face was grim and his eyes bleak. He reached for the snifter of brandy on the table beside him and took a sip. The scene had upset him more than he wanted to admit. After all the brutality he had witnessed in his life, he had thought himself pretty much inured to it. But the sight of those children being threatened had been almost more than he could take.

"It's an obscenity," Matthew said suddenly. He stood up with his hands jammed into his pockets and glared at them. "It makes me ashamed to be an American."

"Don't say that," James ordered. "This is still the greatest country on earth. If we've got problems, we'll deal with them."

"*If?*" Matthew shot back. He gestured to the television, where a pretty young woman was demonstrating the easy-cleaning feature of a built-in oven. "Didn't you see what was going on there? Little kids being threatened by a bunch of hate-filled yahoos. That's America?"

James started to answer, but Alexis put her hand on his arm and gently stilled him. "No, of course it isn't," she said quietly. "It's an aberration, a sickness. You have to feel sorry for those people."

"You make it sound as though they're the exception," Matthew said, "but they aren't. This is a deeply racist country."

"Where the hell did you get that from?" James demanded. Horrified though he was by what he had just seen, he did not take kindly to hearing the country he had fought for run down.

"James Baldwin. I read his *Notes of a Native Son*. You ought to give it a try. Maybe you'd learn something."

"Matthew..." Alexis began warningly, only to be cut off by James as he got to his feet.

"That's enough. I'll be damned if I'll listen to that kind of garbage. We're the best; we always have been and we always will be." Looking Matthew up and down disdainfully, he added, "Maybe once you dry out behind the ears, you'll realize that."

A dull flush spread over his son's features, so like his own. "I'm not some kid anymore," Matthew muttered. "You can't treat me like one."

"*Can't?*" James repeated with dangerous softness. "Do I have to remind you whose house this is?"

Alexis jumped up, putting herself between them. "James, Matthew—that's enough. You're both saying things you don't mean. Please, just stop it."

They both started to speak at once, thought better of it and broke off. In the sudden silence, they became aware that the twins were staring at them curiously.

"What are you fighting about?" Amanda asked in her clear, high voice.

"Nothing," Alexis assured her hastily. "It was just a misunderstanding."

The little girl looked unconvinced, as did Jamie. After a moment, he said more softly, "Is it about those kids on TV?"

"Something like that," James said wearily. The anger had gone out of him, leaving him to wonder where it had come from in the first place. It wasn't like him to fly off the handle, but Matthew's condemnation had stung him deeply. Much as he agreed with him about the situation in Little Rock, he felt his son had turned on him personally and denounced everything he had fought for and lived by.

"Forget about it," he said at length, sitting down again on the couch and reaching for his drink. After a moment, Matthew also resumed his seat, though he did not look at his father.

Alexis smiled reassuringly at the twins, hiding her lingering concern. The argument had broken out so abruptly and had been so fierce, then was over—almost like the mighty clashing of two stags coming upon each other in the woods. "It's time for you two to have your baths," she said as she held out a hand to Amanda and Jamie. At least they were still at a comprehensible age.

Even so, that did not mean they were always compliant. Far from it. Amanda instantly got that look in her eyes that meant her heels were firmly anchored to the carpet. "It's too early yet," she declared. "Besides, there's something I want to know."

"What's that?" Alexis asked with a sigh. She knew better than to try to avoid her daughter's questions. Amanda would only keep asking until her curiosity was finally satisfied.

"About those kids. How come people don't want them to go to that school?"

Alexis glanced at James and then at Matthew. Neither looked as though he had any idea of what to say. At length, she ventured, "Because they have the idea that Negro children shouldn't go to school with white children."

"Oh. . .is that why we don't?"

"What do you mean?"

"There are no Negro kids in our school," Jamie piped up helpfully. "I know; I looked."

"Why did you do that?" James asked. He was leaning forward now, with his attention all on his younger son.

James wasn't used to that. He looked taken aback for a moment before he said, "'Cause I heard people talking about in'gration. So I wanted to see if we had any." A small frown furrowed his forehead. "It doesn't look like we do."

"It's not the same thing at all, Jamie," Alexis assured him earnestly, bending down so that she was facing him directly. "You go to a private school."

"So?" Amanda queried. "How come we don't have in-te-gration?" She shot her brother a quick look to stress her greater mastery of that new and rather puzzling word.

"Why...because you..."

Alexis cast James a pleading glance; she definitely needed some help. Gently, he said, "Most Negro people aren't as well off as most white people. That's happened for a lot of complicated reasons that we'd all like to change. If we work together, someday things will be better."

The twins looked at each other, clearly doubtful. "When's someday?" Amanda asked.

"Soon," James told her as he stood up again and briskly hoisted her onto his shoulder. She squealed delightedly. "Right now, it's time for your baths." Alexis took Jamie's hand and together they managed to get both children upstairs without another barrage of questions.

But later, when they were lying in bed together, the subject came up again. "I didn't know what to say to them," James admitted. "How do you explain to children that in parts of this country we're still fighting the Civil War?"

"I don't know," Alexis said softly. "How do you convince a seventeen-year-old boy that his country is still a good place?"

"That really bugged me, what he said about America. Doesn't he understand how much better things are here?"

"He understands what he sees: angry mobs and men with guns. It's bound to be frightening."

In the darkness, they moved closer, drawing warmth from each other. Alexis's head rested on his shoulder as James stroked her hair gently. After a while, he said, "Sometimes lately I get the feeling that we may be heading toward tough times."

"Why do you say that?" Alexis asked softly. "I know there are problems, but on balance we aren't doing too badly."

"Maybe not, but just what is it we're doing? Basically keeping the lid on, like with a pressure cooker. You can only do that so long. Eventually something gives."

"Do you remember that party at Anthony and Maggie's right before we left for Europe?"

James nodded. "What about it?"

"I was talking with Tad and he said something similar. Since he moved up to the Senate, he seems to be taking a rather more pessimistic view of everything."

"Maybe he wants to appear properly solemn to his constituents."

"I don't think that's all there is to it. He pointed out that we aren't really solving any problems, not with Russia or the bomb or the troubles here at home. It's as though we're simply marking time."

"For what?"

"I don't know...something new, maybe. Or some*one* new. Someone with answers."

"The last man I heard with answers to everything was Joe McCarthy. The only trouble was, he didn't have the right questions."

"I don't mean answers to everything, but enough to point us in the right direction."

James drew her closer, his hand lying lightly on her bare arm. Amusement threaded his voice as he said, "I know who you're talking about now: Jack Kennedy. You think he's cute."

"*Wellll*, you have to admit he has got great hair, and that Boston accent is...delicious."

"I'll give you delicious," he growled warningly, pressing her down into the mattress.

"IT'S CALLED A SPUTNIK," Joey said one evening a few weeks later as they all sat around the dinner table at Maggie and Anthony's. "That means 'fellow traveler' in Russian."

"Of course in Russian," Amanda interjected. "What else would it be in?" Without waiting for an answer, she went on, "It weighs almost two hundred pounds and it has four antennas. It can see what we're doing."

"Cannot, dummy," Jamie said.

"Can so."

"Not."

"It can't see us," Tessa insisted firmly, "but we can see it if we go outside at the right time and look."

They did that evening and for quite a few evenings afterward, peering up through the twilight for a glimpse of the shimmering little dot hurling across the heavens. There was much discussion among the children, with Matthew joining in occasionally, about what it all meant. Joey, a science-fiction fan, contended that it would be only a few short years before men were living in space. The others accepted that matter-of-factly. Science projects were suddenly very popular. A meeting was called at the school Amanda and Jamie attended to discuss the need for better science education. Parents and teachers alike agreed it was imperative to catch up.

Not surprisingly, that Christmas there was a preponder-
ance of chemistry sets and other scientific "toys" under the
tree. But for Matthew there was a very special gift. He had
been accepted to all three Ivy League universities, and after
careful thought, he had chosen Princeton. James went around
the house for days with a quiet smile that hid his immense
pride. Their argument over Little Rock was forgotton. On
Christmas Day, Matthew opened the front door of the town
house to find a shiny red MG parked in front, his father's gift
to him. The two of them spent a good part of the holiday season tooling around town in it.

Alexis had privately thought that the car was a little too ex-
travagant, but she said nothing. Instinctively she understood
that it was important to James to be able to give his son such
a generous present. It symbolized how very far he had come
since he had been Matthew's age.

That drive to achieve the wealth and security he had not
known as a young man reached new heights as the decade
waned. Under James's astute guidance, several of UBC's
most important affiliates were persuaded to move over to IBS.
As a result, the price of UBC's stock declined even further,
which enabled Alexis to increase her purchases. By the middle of 1958, she held, through various shell companies, some
ten percent of the total number of common shares. The time
was very quickly approaching when she would have to drop
the shroud of secrecy and confront the matter directly. Yet she
still had not decided how to make James accept what she had
done.

The enormity of that task threatened to overwhelm her. At
its inception, the plan had seemed a perfectly reasonable response to an outrageous situation. Graham had done her a
deep personal injury by conspiring to harm James; she could

not let him go unpunished. But before time ran out, she wanted to make one last attempt to convince James that she was right about her brother and persuade him to join her in her quest for revenge.

The addition of the former UBC affiliates to the IBS fold seemed to give her the opportunity to do so. It was well after midnight at the end of a week late in the year when she and James returned from the celebration held at the Plaza Hotel. Outside the tinted windows of the limousine, the city was quiet. Rain-washed pavement glinted in the yellow light of the street lamps. Only a few tired revelers like themselves were still abroad.

The party had been a great success, with the media turning out in force both to cover the event and to participate in it. Graham's friends, however many he still had, either forgot about him long enough to attend or stayed away and were not missed.

"I had a good time," Alexis murmured as she laid her head back against the plush leather seat. Her eyes were closed, the thick lashes dusting her cheeks. Over her evening gown, she wore a magnificent ankle-length lynx coat, the latest addition to her fur collection. Diamonds glinted at her ears, wrists and throat. The seductive scent of Arpège, warmed by her skin, floated around her.

James smiled appreciatively. After all these years, she was still the loveliest and most desirable of women. Throughout the evening, as they circulated among the guests, his eyes had continually sought her out. In the strapless gown of tissue-thin silver lamé, she had looked like a glittering idol carved of marble draped in precious gems. Yet the glow of her smile, the husky ripple of her laughter, the sheer vibrancy that radiated from her, had all been pure woman. He was proud to be the

man going home with her and he would have fought anyone
for the privilege.

"So did I," he said softly. "We'll have to do it again
sometime."

"Add another ten stations to the network and we will."

"It's a tempting thought." He stretched out his long legs
and let the deep feeling of satisfaction that had been at the edge
of his mind all evening at last creep over him. Pensively, he
added, "Tonight has been a long time coming."

She opened her eyes and turned her head so that she was
looking at him directly. The plain black tuxedo was particularly well suited to his long, hard body. It accentuated the
sweep of his broad shoulders and chest. The veneer of elegance heightened by contrast her awareness of the tensile
strength never far below the surface. A crisp white shirt,
without frills, made his weathered skin look darker than usual
and emphasized the firm set of his jaw. He had shaved before
they left for the party and she could still smell the faint aroma
of bay rum, the same after-shave he had always worn, dis-
daining anything more exotic. His thick hair was freshly
washed and worn just a shade longer than was fashionable. He
excused that with the claim that he didn't have time for regular visits to the barber. Glancing down, her gaze focused on
his hands with their long, blunt-tipped fingers resting lightly
on his knees. The gold of his wedding band stood out clearly.

She smiled as she said, "You have every reason to be feeling good tonight. To accomplish so much in such a short time
is quite a feat."

He laughed softly. "It hasn't seemed short."

"Barely twelve years since you and Anthony founded IBS
in those terrible little trailers out in the potato field. That's al-

most no time at all.'' Almost to herself, she added, ''My father worked twenty-five years to get as many stations.''

Distracted by his memories, James didn't hear that last part. ''God, it was hot in those things! We spent most of that first summer trying to keep the equipment cool.''

''Nowadays, you'd have air-conditioning.''

''Not on the same kind of budget. We had trouble filling the grocery cart. Somebody gave Maggie a book about fifty-seven ways to serve hamburger and I swear she went through all of them several times over.''

''Those were still good days, weren't they?''

''Certainly, but I'm satisfied just to look back on them; I'd never want to go through all that again.''

''No...it's impossible to ever go back.'' Fatigue, the champagne she had drunk, and the thoughts that weighed heavily on her mind combined to make her sound sadder and more wistful than she would have wished.

That did not escape James. He cast her a swift glance. ''Is something wrong?''

''Wrong?'' Recovering herself, she flashed a brilliant smile. ''Of course not. Although I do admit to being a wee bit fuzzy.''

''Oh, really?'' He grinned warmly. ''That's a rarity for you.''

''Mmmm...I know, but I thought with the occasion and all, what the heck?''

''By all means, what the heck.''

''Do I detect the beginnings of a smirk?''

''Let's call it a little smile.''

''You think it's funny that I say 'heck' instead of 'hell'?''

''No,'' he murmured, his eyes very tender, ''you're a lady and that's fine with me.''

"Even though I insisted on working?" She really must be tired to raise such an issue now. It had slipped out unawares and she had no idea how to cope with whatever he might say in response.

But James merely shrugged. "I'm reconciled to it. However..." His eyes caressed her explicitly. "Tonight, I'd prefer a wife to a business partner."

Despite herself, Alexis blushed, which brought a warm chuckle from James. In the darkness of the back seat, he did not hesitate to reach out to her, his hands moving beneath the fur to find the satin smoothness of her skin. Their lips met in a long kiss that melted from tenderness to sensuality.

When they at last drew some little way apart, Alexis caught her breath and murmured, "Can I tell you something rather shocking?" Unable to take his eyes off her, he nodded. Her tongue darted out to moisten her lips before she said, "Tonight, I don't think I want to be a wife. I'd rather be a...courtesan."

It took James a moment to realize he had actually heard what he thought he had. When it finally sunk in, his reaction was swift and to the point. Leaning forward, he said, "Driver, step on it."

The limousine sped through the darkened streets, carrying them home to the town house, where the children were all asleep. They crept inside, carefully closing the door behind them as they shared muffled laughter.

Alexis slipped off her coat, letting it fall away slowly, first from one shoulder and then the next, before drifting down the length of her body to be caught just before it touched the floor. With a smile, she handed it to James and started up the stairs. He followed her quickly, his gaze on the gentle sway of her backside. Halfway up, he laid a hand on her possessively and she laughed.

They left the lights off in their bedroom. The glow of the street lamps reflected in raindrops revealed familiar, if shadowy, shapes. James loosened his tie and pulled it off, then undid the top button of his shirt. All the while his gaze was on Alexis as she walked away from him to the center of the room, then turned to face him. Her eyes were half closed, her expression slumberous as she raised slender, bare arms and undid the diamond clip holding her hair in place.

She shook it free, letting the silken mane tumble over her shoulders. It shimmered against the darkness, almost as if each strand was lit by an inner iridescence. With deliberate care, she set the clip on top of a marble-inlaid table before slowly removing the rest of her jewelry. Only then did she reach around to unfasten her dress, first crossing an arm over her breasts to prevent the gown from falling.

James watched unblinkingly. Alexis in so seductive a mood was a relatively rare experience for him. He wasn't quite sure why it was happening, but he intended to enjoy it fully.

She turned and he caught his breath at the graceful line of her alabaster back bared to the curve of her buttocks. Hardly aware of what he was doing, he pulled off his jacket and cummerbund, and tossed both onto a nearby chair, then finished unbuttoning his shirt. As he did so, Alexis bent over to remove her delicate high-heeled sandals. When that was done, she straightened and, still smiling, let the dress fall from her.

Beneath it her breasts were bare, the nipples dark and erect. Her rib cage bent inward at the waist before yielding to the gentle flare of her hips. She wore a lacy garter belt over a scrap of panties. The gap between the tops of her pale silk stockings and the other garments drew his gaze. Her upper thighs were slim and taut.

"You know," he murmured huskily, "you're a hell of a beautiful woman."

She laughed softly. "Thanks. I remember when I thought anything over thirty was downhill. It's amazing how your perspective can change."

"My perspective right now is just fine, thanks. I wouldn't change it for the world."

She laughed again, genuinely pleased. It was nice to know that he still thought her so desirable. The temptation to hurry things along surfaced in her, only to be firmly ignored. She wanted him to remember this night for a very long time.

Carefully balancing a slender foot on the edge of a chair, she unclipped, then peeled down, her stocking. Following the process with the other leg, she cast him a glance over her shoulder. "How am I doing?"

"Pretty good," he muttered, his voice unnaturally thick and hoarse. "But then, you've never been any slouch in this department."

"Mmmm..." Straightening, she let her head fall back so that her breasts thrust forward. As he took a quick step toward her, she unclipped the garter belt and tossed it away. "Do I detect a gleam of impatience?"

His large hands settled on her waist, holding her firmly. Slowly he drew her to him until her belly was pressing against his loins. "I think you probably detect more than that."

She did, and the sensation made her catch her breath. With deliberate provocation, she rotated her hips against him. His grip on her tightened as his fingers moved downward beneath the rim of her panties. "You know," he murmured, "a girl could get in trouble doing that."

Her eyes opened wide. "Is *that* how it happens?"

He chuckled softly. "It's certainly a step in the right direction."

As he spoke, she was busy removing his shirt, sliding it from his broad shoulders and down his arms where it caught at the wrists. He hadn't removed the gold cluff links. With a small chiding glance, she did so and gathered the shirt to her, covering her breasts.

A small tug-of-war ensued, which she let James swiftly win. When she was once again exposed to his gaze, she took advantage of his distraction to adroitly undo his trousers and ease her hand inside. The soft gasp that broke from him pleased her immensely, but she had little chance to enjoy it before James pulled her to him.

His kiss was infinitely passionate and possessive, staking his claim on her in the most unmistakable terms. They fell together across the bed, with an abandon not present in their lovemaking for a very long time. The tender habits of an old married couple could be very pleasant, but there was something to be said for recapturing the full fury of desire that took nothing for granted and allowed nothing to be withheld.

Sweet, hot pleasure shimmered through Alexis, making her forget everything except the demands of her body. They came together fiecely, taking each other completely and in the process giving of themselves without restraint. Afterward, when they lay in a tangle of arms and legs, their sweat-streaked skin pressing close together, they were both shaken by what had happened.

"That was incredible," James murmured drowsily against her hair.

Alexis heard him as though from a great distance. Utterly satisfied, she was rapidly slipping into sleep. But before consciousness fled entirely, she remembered that in the back of her mind there had been some vague idea of getting him into a receptive mood before trying one last time to convince him that her brother deserved what he was shortly to get.

She felt a vague sense of astonishment that she had even thought of doing such a thing. To make such use of what they had just shared would be to diminish it, and herself. That she could not do. A soft sigh escaped her as she yielded to her better nature and sank gladly into her dreams.

At breakfast the next morning, Matthew looked at them, grinned, and said, "Must have been some party last night." As they exchanged a wary glance, he added, "I heard you come in pretty late."

"Since when do you wait up for us?" James asked quietly, spearing another slice of melon.

"Since never. I just happened to be a little restless."

Amanda looked up from her oatmeal and said, "Mommy and Daddy are allowed to stay out as late as they want."

"That's right, honey," James said, with a quick grin for Alexis. "Now finish your breakfast."

She stared down into the bowl and wrinkled her nose. "I like Cheerios better."

"They aren't good for you," Alexis said patiently.

"I don't care. I like them better."

"Me, too," Jamie added. "They give you muscles."

Alexis gave a long-suffering sigh and said, "I'll tell you what, if you eat your oatmeal now, you can have Cheerios on the weekend. All right?"

"I guess," Amanda murmured grudgingly. She brightened, though, as she remembered something she had meant to mention. "We're having a Hula-Hoop contest at school next week. I can do three at once now. Want to see?"

"Uh…not right now, honey. Just be careful with those things. I'm still not convinced you might not hurt your back."

Amanda gave her a tolerant look. "It's okay, Mommy. Everybody's doing it. Do you know Tessa can keep five Hula-Hoops going at once?"

"Now *that's* talent," Matthew drawled.

"Oh, to be young again," Alexis murmured a while later as she and James were leaving for work, "and have the world revolve around a circle of plastic tubing."

"Don't knock it," he advised with a grin, "if we'd thought up those damn things, we could retire to Tahiti and never even look at another television. Doesn't that sound great?"

"Depends," she informed him as they got into the limousine. "What would we do in Tahiti?"

He whispered the answer in her ear, bringing both a blush and a quick, delighted laugh. Glancing up at him through her lashes, she said, "But we can do that right here at home. We proved that last night."

"You've got a point. Forget Tahiti."

They settled down then for the ride to work, reluctantly turning their thoughts to more businesslike matters. At the entrance to IBS's executive floor, they parted, heading for their separate offices, but not without a quick, shared smile redolent of the previous night.

Alexis had barely had time to have a cup of coffee and begin wading through her paperwork when her stockbroker called. "I thought you'd want to know," he said briskly, "it looks as though someone is trying to acquire UBC."

She sat up straighter and glanced toward her office door to make sure it was closed. "I've been afraid this would happen once the stock price fell far enough. Who are they?"

He wasn't absolutely sure but named several possibilities, all large companies which might conceivably be interested in taking over a television network. One was the same organization that had tried earlier in the year to acquire IBS.

"Them again. I can understand why they wanted us, but they have to be crazy to want to clean up Graham's mess." Or did they? After all, wasn't that exactly what she was looking to do?

"Whether they're crazy or not," the broker said, "it looks as though they're serious. So I suggest you move quickly."

Alexis hesitated. Now that the moment she had so long dreaded was upon her, she hoped some alternative would suddenly reveal itself. When none did, she said briskly, "I'll get back to you by this afternoon."

After she had hung up, she sat for a time staring off into space, doing some quick mental calculations. She figured that given the current price of the stock, she needed above five million dollars to secure control. While her personal accounts did not hold that kind of money, IBS's certainly did. The partnership agreement she had signed when she and James were married specified that any partner had the right to make major capital disbursements provided the other partners agreed they were in the best interest of the firm. Surely the acquisition of UBC had to be considered as such?

Her mind made up, she reached for the phone. James's secretary put her through without delay. "Something has just come up," she told him, "I have to see you immediately."

"All right. . ." he said slowly, surprised by the hard edge of her voice.

"And Anthony as well. He'll have to be in on this."

"The conference room, then? Five minutes?"

She agreed and hung up, then took a deep breath. Five minutes to come to terms with what she was about to do and think of some way to convince James it was for the best. It was not long enough. Her face was pale and her hands shook slightly when she entered the conference room and took her place on one side of the large mahogany table.

James and Anthony were both already there, looking perplexed. "What's up?" Anthony asked. "A tower collapse or something?" He smiled as he spoke, knowing full well that if such a disaster ever occurred, she would not be the one called first.

Alexis did not return his smile. Instead, she said quietly, "I'm sorry to have to spring this on you both so suddenly, but there's no time now for anything else. We have a chance to take over UBC if we move quickly enough."

The two men exchanged bewildered glances. After a moment, James said gently, "Honey, that just doesn't make any sense. We'd need at least fifteen percent of the common stock to take control, or about fifteen million dollars. Even if the shares were available, we can't afford that."

"No, but we can afford five million for five percent which will be enough."

"How?" Anthony asked, frowning. "According to the last financial statement, Graham's got ten percent and..."

"And so do I."

"That's impossible," James said. He was leaning forward now in his chair, staring at her. "You sold your shares years ago to support IBS."

She met his eyes cautiously as she said, "No, I sold other securities my father left me for that. The money from the UBC shares went into a private account which I've used over the years to buy back the stock. Since the price has been falling steadily, it worked out quite well."

"I'm not following this," Anthony said slowly. "You're saying that you've been buying up shares for several years?" When Alexis nodded, he went on, "But why hasn't it shown up on the financial statements?"

"Because I've used shell companies," she explained quietly, not looking at James. She could only imagine what he was thinking and did not want to see it confirmed in his eyes. "The stock price is now less than half of what it was when I sold my original shares. Since the bulk of my purchases have been recent, I've been able to double my interest until it now matches Graham's without his being aware of what was happening. The only problem is that he can count on another two or three percent from stockholders who are personal friends of his. So, to be absolutely sure of beating him, we need more than that, say five percent."

Both men were silent, waiting for her to continue. She finally dared a glance at James and found his expression unreadable. Quietly, she said, "I've just been informed by my broker that another company is interested in a possible takeover. So we have to act now."

"For five million we can have the whole ball of wax?" Anthony asked as though he could scarcely believe it.

"That's right," she said firmly. "Think of what we could do with it."

He was, obviously, because he was becoming more excited by the moment. "We'd be in a position to really go head-to-head against the other networks," he exclaimed. "Challenge them for every sponsor dollar nationwide."

"The problems at UBC are really the result of incompetency at the executive level," she pointed out. "It's still got a solid foundation of talent, equipment and so on. All that's needed is decent management.''

''What makes you think the Federal Trade Commission would let us do this?'' James asked softly. ''It could be interpreted as a restraint of trade.''

Encouraged by his willingness even to consider the matter that far, she said, ''They might, but I don't think it's likely, not considering how conservative and pro-business this administration is. Besides, we have an excellent record for serving the public interest at a time when that's becoming increasingly important. If we were turned down, I think it's fair to say there would be quite a hue and cry.''

She didn't add that James and Anthony were still something of folk heroes to a large segment of the public—taxpayers and voters all—who remembered how they had brought a glimmer of hope into what had seemed an unredeemable situation. They would not take kindly to the government causing problems for them.

''She's right,'' Anthony said eagerly. ''All those news programs and other service-oriented stuff could really pay off for us now. People are getting sick of the crap that's dished out just to make a buck. They know they can depend on us for something better.''

''You've thought all of this out very carefully,'' James said thoughtfully, holding her gaze. ''Going back years. The programs...the money...the shell companies...it took an enormous amount of planning.

Anthony glanced from one to the other of them cautiously. ''I'm amazed myself at how you did it,'' he admitted, ''but from what you've said, this isn't the time to discuss that. We have to make a decision.''

She nodded quickly. "I told my broker I'd call back by this afternoon." Meeting James's eyes, she went on gently, "I know it's a shock, but please try to judge it objectively. To take over UBC now would be a brilliant coup for us."

He held her gaze for a moment before he asked tonelessly, "Is that why you want to do it?"

She hesitated. The temptation to lie was very great. If she could excuse what she had done on the basis of it being good for the business, maybe, just maybe, there was a chance he would accept it. But that failure of honesty would gnaw away at her forever. If there was anyone in the world who deserved truth from her, it was James. She took a deep breath and said, "No, that wasn't the reason."

Anthony looked genuinely puzzled. "Then, why? What else could have prompted this?"

Still looking at James, she said, "I wanted revenge against Graham for his part in what happened in Korea."

Anthony shook his head in bewilderment. "But I thought you'd agreed there was no real evidence of that."

"It doesn't matter," James broke in before she could answer. "The lack of evidence is unimportant. Alexis needed an excuse to go after her brother and she used me to get it."

The color drained from her face as a wave of coldness washed over her. "W-what are you talking about?"

"Do I really have to spell it out for you?" When she didn't respond but simply continued to stare at him, his mouth tightened grimly. "You're an intelligent woman; there's no way on earth you could have nurtured a grudge for so long when it was founded on so little. That whole Korea theory of yours was shot full of holes from the beginning, and you know it. But that doesn't matter; you're still willing to use it rather than admit that I've got nothing to do with your hatred of

Graham. You want revenge against him for one reason and one reason only: Because your father gave him what you have always believed should have been yours.''

Anthony looked acutely uncomfortable; he did not want to be party to such a discussion, but neither could he think of a graceful way to remove himself. Instead, he did his best to vanish into his chair and hoped it would be over soon.

''That's ridiculous,'' Alexis shot back. ''My father and I made our peace before he died. If we hadn't, he wouldn't have left me the stock.''

''It never occurred to you that he knew you and Graham would eventually clash?'' James demanded.

It had, but she wasn't about to tell him so. Or at least she tried not to. Her expression gave her away.

He laughed harshly and shook his head. ''You know, somewhere in hell that old man is laughing. This is working out exactly as he planned.''

''You're wrong,'' she choked. ''It has nothing to do with him, or even with Graham. It was for you.''

''Bullshit.'' The harsh expletive made her recoil. James ignored that and pressed on unrelentingly. ''I should have known these past few years that something was going on. You were too content with the status quo, too satisfied to be one of the team with Anthony and me. All that ambition I had once sensed beneath the surface—to be up there at the top strictly on your own—seemed to have died away.'' He laughed again, coldly. ''You know I was stupid enough to think it might be because our marriage had given you a new set of priorities, made you realize that power wasn't the ultimate goal in life.''

''I did realize it,'' Alexis said quietly. Her throat was tight and she was having difficulty breathing, but she still had to try to make him understand. "It's true that I've always wanted power, but not at any price."

"No?" he demanded harshly. "Then why have you been willing to lie and deceive to get it?"

"*I haven't. . .*"

"You lied to yourself about Korea and you deceived me by not being open about what you were doing. How else would you characterize it?"

She shook her head dazedly, struggling against the relentless fury of his accusations. Her vision blurred as hot tears burned her eyes. Pride stiffened her resistance; she would not cry in front of him.

"I did what I had to," she said tightly. "If I had told you my plans, you would have tried to stop them."

"And just why would I have done that?" He demanded mockingly. "If this is such a brilliant coup for us, wouldn't I jump at at?"

Their eyes met, his full of derision, hers bleak with the unraveling of the defenses that had protected her even from herself. Her voice was low and husky as she at last gave voice to what she truly wanted. "No, you won't jump, because you realize that while IBS will hold five percent of the stock, I'll hold the other ten. And that means I'll run UBC on my own."

He stared at her for a long moment before he said, "You've tried to have it all, haven't you? To be a wife and mother, yet still your father's daughter. But you must have known that sooner or later it would come down to this. What did you think would happen then?"

"I thought. . .I hoped. . .you would understand, and accept."

Silence stretched out between them, drawing tauter than a bowstring. Their gazes remained locked, filled with mute entreaty to which neither could respond. At length, James drew a shaky breath. His face was very pale as he said, ''I understand only too well. As for accepting...there really isn't any question of that, is there? You'll do what you have to no matter how I feel.''

Alexis stared at him silently for long moments, wishing there was some other answer. Then, slowly, she nodded.

Chapter Nineteen

"I DON'T SEE WHAT DIFFERENCE it makes that Kennedy is a Catholic," Tessa said one spring afternoon when they were all gathered at Anthony and Maggie's house. Matthew was home on Easter break from his freshman year at Princeton. The months away had matured him. Already in his manner there was a new confidence born of self-awareness and accomplishment.

He smiled as he said, "It shouldn't matter, but a lot of people seem to think it does."

"Why?" she persisted, not about to relinquish his attention. "We're Catholic, but that doesn't mean we'd do what the Pope told us if it would hurt the country."

"Of course not, and I don't think many people are really afraid of that. They're just ignorant, and in some cases, bigoted."

Tessa pushed a strand of ebony hair out of her eyes and shifted to a more comfortable position. She was sitting on the floor of the sun room, with Matthew on the couch nearby. It was a warm day and she was wishing they could go out, but dinner was almost ready.

"Do you like it at school?" she asked suddenly, peering up at him through her long lashes. Matthew's thick chestnut hair was a little longer than usual; she was glad he didn't keep it cut short like most other boys or smear that greasy stuff on it. Then she remembered that he wasn't a boy at all, and flushed.

"It's fine," he said. "My classes are great and I'm thinking about going out for football."

"There aren't any girls there, are there?"

He smiled again, gently. "No, Princeton doesn't admit women. None of the Ivy League schools do."

"We have to go to the Seven Sisters?"

"That's right. You should start learning about them and decide which you'd like to attend."

Tessa wrinkled her nose. "I'm not sure I want to do that. The girls I hear talking about them at school sound snobby."

"There is some of that," he admitted, "but they're still good schools."

She shrugged her slender shoulders and looked away. "Maybe I'll be a nurse, like Mom."

Matthew frowned. He had nothing against women working, but he had seen the problems it could cause with his father and Alexis. Carefully, he said, "You have to do what's right for yourself, but a lot of people think that the most important job a woman can do is raising her children."

Tessa cast him a quick, wary glance. Her fingers worried the wool of the rug beneath her plaid skirt. With it she wore knee socks and an argyle sweater, the latter chosen because it showed off her bosom, which she thought was coming along nicely. "Is that what you think?"

He hesitated, wanting to live up to what he knew to be her image of him as a wise older brother of sorts. But on the other hand, he couldn't bring himself to pretend an assurance he didn't feel.

"I don't know," he said at length. "I agree that children need a lot of attention and care, but I can see how some women might want to do other things. It's a tough situation."

"I think Mom is happier since she took that job at the hospital."

"Maybe, but is your Dad?"

She thought about that for a moment, then shrugged. "He loves her, so his happiness depends a lot on hers, and vice versa. Isn't that the way it's supposed to be?"

"Yes...I guess it is." He left it at that, not wanting to disillusion her. There would be time enough for her to learn that nothing was ever quite so simple.

Maggie stuck her head in the sun-room door to remind them that dinner would be ready in fifteen minutes. Then she returned to the kitchen, where Alexis was giving her a hand. It was the cook's night off, so they were having a simple meal of lasagna, salad and Italian bread.

"It smells delicious," Alexis said as she set out plates. "But now that you're working, I don't know when you get time to do things like this."

"I wonder myself," Maggie admitted. "We have at least a dozen major cases a day—accidents, appendicitis, ulcer attacks, that sort of thing. I don't know where the time goes when I'm there."

"Do you regret not starting out with something less hectic?"

"No, I can't say I do. Emergency-room nursing is ideally suited to me, given what I learned during the war. Besides, I wanted to get some on-the-job experience before I tackle surgery again."

Alexis nodded, glad that her friend was satisfied with her choice. She wished she could have said the same for herself. In the eighteen months since the takeover of UBC, she had worked hard to rebuild the network. Her efforts were beginning to pay off, yet somehow that didn't seem to mean as much as she had expected. The dream that had once been so important was proving to be an arid reality. There was a growing sense of emptiness at the center of her being, as though something essential had deserted her. She had known a similar feeling only once before in her life, when her mother had died.

"Is something wrong?" Maggie asked gently.

Alexis managed a wan smile as she shook her head. "There's just a lot going on at work." That wouldn't fool Maggie, but she was too understanding to probe further. Although they had never spoken of it, Alexis was sure she knew about the scene Anthony had inadvertently witnessed between her and James on the day the decision was made to acquire UBC.

"I won't try to stop this," he had said when it became clear that she was determined to go through with the merger, "but don't expect me to have anything to do with it. You wanted your own network and now you've got it."

And so she did. The only question was whether or not it was worth the price.

As they were taking their places at the table, Alexis stole a glance at her husband. He looked tired, but there was nothing unusual about that. They were both feeling the strain of the past months. In retrospect, the years when they had worked together, albeit with frequent disagreements, appeared halcyon. Then they had shared both victories and failures. Now they were separated by far more than the half-dozen or so blocks between the UBC and IBS buildings.

There was a wall of suspicion and mistrust between them; he couldn't understand why she wouldn't be satisfied with what he could give her, and she couldn't give up the need for something of her own. Those opposing positions placed them firmly at odds with each other. And yet, even given that, there was still a bond that ran deep and true between them. It made them come together silently in the shelter of the night to find for at least some little time a release from pain and bewilderment.

That strengthened her resolve not to simply accept the problem between herself and James but to do something about it. No matter how risky that might turn out to be.

"THE GOOD NEWS is that we're pulling ahead in the ratings," Alexis told her staff at the next Monday morning meeting. "The bad news is that we're still fifth behind CBS, NBS, IBS and ABC."

Assorted groans and grimaces met this statement. It was hardly unexpected, but still the knowledge that they remained in last place was hard to take. The dozen or so men and the one lone woman listening to her knew their jobs were riding on the survival of the network. If it went, so did they.

"I don't see what more we can do," a balding middle-aged man said wearily. "We broke our backs almost completely revamping the schedule. Not that I'm complaining," he added quickly, "it had to be done. And we did a good job; those numbers you just read prove it. But so many people got out of the habit of watching UBC that now they aren't even giving us a chance."

The others nodded as he spoke. It was the ultimate frustration of their business that a show, no matter how good, could die on the vine unless people switched from what they would ordinarily have been watching to take a look at it.

"That's the problem in a nutshell," Alexis agreed. "We've got the programs but not the viewers, or at least not enough of them to satisfy the advertisers." She glanced around the conference table encouragingly. "So are there any suggestions as to what we might do?"

"More promotion?" a young, blond-haired man suggested. "More publicity? I know it eats up revenues, but I don't see how else to get people's attention."

Alexis frowned slightly. "We've spent a considerable amount to advertise the new schedule. I don't see that it's done us much good. Frankly, we're way past the point where we can afford to throw good money after bad."

Several more ideas were kicked around, but nothing useful surfaced. Alexis returned to her office more convinced than ever that something radically different had to be done. But what?

That question absorbed her for the next several days during which she spent long hours in the office that had once been her father's. For reasons of his own, Graham had chosen to occupy an office on the opposite side of the executive floor. That did not suit Alexis. She wanted there to be no mistake about what the merger signified, a return of the leadership that had made the network so successful and an end to the incompetency that had almost destroyed it.

But while she meant to keep faith with her father, she did not care to recast herself in his image. Her first directive, therefore, had been to have half the furniture removed from his office, along with the heavy velvet drapes haunted by the smell of violet pastilles and cigar smoke. Still, something of UBC's founder lingered in the spacious room. She found that reassuring as she struggled to find a solution to her problems, both personal and professional.

Twice a month Alexis met with Anthony and James to discuss matters of mutual interest. The meetings took place in the IBS conference room and were held at lunchtime over a meal prepared in the executive kitchens. Occasionally other members of the UBC and IBS staffs were invited to attend, but at the meeting which took place at the end of May, only the three partners were present.

"I'm beginning to think that I've done as much as possible with conventional programming techniques," Alexis said. "We're not gaining in audience share rapidly enough to satisfy the advertisers, and in fact, there's reason to believe we may have reached a plateau of sorts."

"What do you propose to do about it?" James asked as he cut into his steak. His face was expressionless and his tone flat, as though the matter were of no real interest to him and he were merely going through the motions of being polite.

Alexis willed herself to be patient. It would do no good to attack his detached pose by pointing out that the two networks' fortunes were now closely linked. If James wanted to pursue the fiction that what went on down the street was of no concern, then she would let him.

But that wouldn't stop her from laying out her plan and seeing what kind of reaction it would get. "What we need to do," she said quietly, "is to offer people a greater alternative to the shows they're already getting. For example, everyone broadcasts evening news from 7:00 to 7:15 P.M. But a lot of people are eating dinner then, so why doesn't one of the networks do a news show at eight o'clock? Or earlier, say at five? The same holds true for comedies, variety shows, Westerns and so on. They tend to get bunched together so that people really don't have all that much choice about what they watch."

"Which helps to keep down the arguments in a family," Anthony pointed out dryly.

"Not really. What's happened in the past is that someone in the family picks what to watch and the rest make do. But that's changing now. We're reaching the point where a lot of families have more than one TV, yet when it comes to programming, we still pretend this is ten years ago when everyone gathered around the set together and watched the same programs. It just doesn't work that way anymore."

James put down his fork. Despite himself, he was interested. "What you seem to be saying is that instead of trying to design programs for the whole family, we should be designing them for separate portions of it."

She nodded quickly. "That's it exactly. When you come right down to it, most programs today are designed for children or teenagers. It's programming by the lowest common denominator, the theory being that the parents will go along with anything that's tolerable so as not to feel that they're depriving the little darlings. I'm not saying we should dump those programs; let the kids have them. But let's also do something for grown-ups."

"We?" James repeated cautiously. "You mean UBC and IBS?"

Alexis nodded. What came next was the most delicate part of her plan and she approached it with appropriate care. "What I'm suggesting," she said quietly, "is that our two networks should coordinate our programming so that between us we offer shows for both children and adults in each time slot."

James and Anthony glanced at each other. Neither spoke for a moment; then James said slowly. "You realize that means we'd have to work together to at least some degree?"

"Yes," she acknowledged carefully, not wanting to make too much of that. While the plan was genuinely intended to strengthen both networks, it also held out a chance of healing the breach with James. If he could learn to accept her as a true equal in the business world, perhaps he could also do the same in their personal life. "I have no objection to working with you," she continued in the same guarded tone, "so long as it's understood that in the final analysis we are each responsible for programming at our respective networks."

James thought about that for a moment, trying to anticipate what problems might be involved. If the plan worked, they would still be in direct competition, since only one network could come out on top. But they would also be cooperating. He had a hard time envisioning how they could manage both, yet he felt an overwhelming need to try.

Alexis was as tentative about the new arrangement as James. Each approached it warily. Throughout that summer, as the political conventions were held and the presidential campaign prepared to begin in earnest, they met regularly to plan the fall schedule. Since both had so much other work to do and neither was eager to meet on the other's territory, it seemed inevitable that their discussions took place at home where there was little to distract them.

Matthew was working that summer as an intern in UBC's news division. He put in long hours, but he also found time to squire a young lady from Bryn Mawr around town. Alexis and James rarely saw him.

The twins were away at summer camp. Amanda wrote excitedly of her riding and swimming lessons. Jamie was less enthusiastic. His letters were short, offered little information and came with many misspellings and smudges. "He just doesn't apply himself," James said one evening after they had finished work for the day and he had read the latest dutiful note from his younger son. "I keep hoping that will change, but it doesn't."

"He's overshadowed by Amanda," Alexis said. "Almost anyone would have a hard time competing with her."

Their gazes met over the dinner table, hers watchful, his rueful. "Men hate having to compete with women. It puts us in a quandary."

"How so?"

His broad shoulders rose and fell. "There aren't any rules to go by." Her silence prompted him to continue. "When two men compete against each other, it's simple; they both go all out to win. But with a woman, it's much more complicated. There's always the temptation to give her a break, be chivalrous, all that stuff."

"I don't recall ever asking for a break," Alexis said quietly.

"You don't have to ask; that's the point." He studied her for a moment across the dinner table, watching the play of light from the chandelier on her silver-blond hair, before he said, "Take Jackie Kennedy, for example. What man in his right mind would ever want to compete with her?"

Alexis held the stem of her wineglass lightly between her thumb and forefinger. Her attention seemed concentrated on the pale gold liquid within. "You think she's beautiful?"

"In a unique sort of way." He smiled faintly. "If Kennedy wins, every woman in America will be trying to look like her."

"Pillbox hats and chic little suits?"

"Exactly."

"Sounds tiresome to me."

"Well, of course it does. You have your own particular style."

"Ah...and what, I wonder, is that?"

He regarded her steadily for a long moment before he said softly, "Beautiful...intelligent...strong." His smile deepened, becoming wry. "With more facets than I can count."

That last part made her feel oddly hurt, perhaps because he seemed to be saying that she was a mystery to him. Some women might have been flattered to be thought so intriguing, but she was not. After twelve years of marriage, she wanted to believe that her husband understood her. Instead, it seemed as though they might in the end both have to settle for a wary coexistence.

THE DOWN-TO-THE-WIRE presidential campaign offered a welcome distraction from more personal concerns. Played out against the background of a cold war gone into the deep freeze, it carried the implicit suggestion that far more was being decided than simply the fate of one man. Nixon remained ahead in the polls, but never by very much. Kennedy campaigned with all-out aggressiveness, seeming to miss no opportunity to drive his points home.

"I get the impression that Nixon wants very badly to be president," Alexis said one afternoon in late September as she was chatting on the phone with Winston a few hours before the first televised presidential debate, "but Kennedy seems to have actually projected himself ahead into that role, almost as though he'd already won. And he's done it without appearing arrogant or complaisent."

"That could turn out to be the crucial difference. The image that comes across on the television set tonight is going to be at least as important as what's actually said."

"Which makes me a little nervous. We need to elect a man, not an image."

Winston laughed gently. "Don't knock it. It's our ability to create the image that gives us our clout."

"Hmmm. . .I suppose. Are you enjoying covering the campaign?" Winston had taken a break from his other duties to travel with the candidates.

"It's certainly a change of pace," he said wryly. "I get the feeling that the winner will be the one who's left standing at the end."

"There are rumors that Kennedy has health problems."

"There are also rumors that he's quite a ladies' man," Winston pointed out with a chuckle. "If you believe everything you hear about him, you have to wonder when he had time to decide to run for president, let alone actually do it."

They talked a while longer before Alexis hung up. As always, a few minutes with Winston had brightened her day. Apparently reconciled to the fact that they were never going to be more than friends, he made no demands on her. Which certainly couldn't be said of James.

He was stubborn, infuriating, exasperating—in short, very much a man. *I don't agree with that, Alexis. I don't think we should do it that way. I suggest we consider this instead.* How many times had she heard those and similar phrases as they plowed their way through the schedules for the two networks, trying to come to an accord. Of course, she had to admit that as often as he disagreed with her, she did the same with him. And somehow, between the two of them, they usually managed to come up with a third alternative that worked.

But all the while there was the sense that they were tiptoeing around each other, being oh-so-polite and cautious. Where was the passion that had once characterized their relationship? Where was the vulnerability that had taken such courage and brought such reward? Even their lovemaking had become courteous.

The feeling of something lost continued to haunt her. She began to think more and more of her mother. It struck her as almost incomprehensible that she was now eight years older than Olivia Brockton had been at the time of her death. Yet she was not at all ready to face her own mortality. How had her mother done so?

Once she had thought she knew the answer to that, back when she had been willing to blame her father for everything. But now that she had lived through the years her mother had never known, and seen for herself what could be done with them, she was more bewildered than ever.

On the thirtieth anniversary of her mother's death—a raw, cold autumn day more suited to winter—Alexis went out to the cemetery. It was the first time she had observed the occasion and she tried not to think about why she was doing so. Very little had changed since her last visit to the grave site at the time of her father's funeral, only now there were two marble headstones instead of one. The grass was kept neatly clipped and the two small vases held bedraggled chrysanthemums. She threw them away and put in their place the fresh asters she had brought. Then she stepped back a few paces and brushed the dirt from her knees before looking at the stones.

The cold words incised into them seemed to tell the whole story: Olivia Georgetta Brockton, 1900–1930; Charles Philip Brockton, 1890–1951. Neither could have been said to have lived a long life, but at least her father had known a more generous measure of years. Whereas her mother...

Alexis blinked hard against the sudden dimness of her vision. Her sense of time and place was fading, giving way to a long-buried memory. The house in Connecticut, an autumn day ablaze with color, the crisp smell of wood smoke, her own eight-year-old's excitement over a new pony. She relived the exaltation of at last jumping the fence down near the river and galloping all the way back to tell her mother she had done it.

Olivia Brockton had very much wanted her daughter to ride, just as she had since her own girlhood in the pristine hunt country of Virginia. She had made one of her increasingly rare excursions away from the house and its surrounding property to select the new pony for Alexis. Surely she would be thrilled to learn how good he was. Perhaps she would even come out to see them take the jump again.

Alexis ran up the marble steps two at a time, up to the second floor where her mother had her spacious apartment. Her father's was at the other end of the house, an arrangement she took for granted at the time. She raced down the carpeted hall, breathing hard and aglow with pleasure. The sitting room was empty, as was the bedroom. But the bathroom door was open.

Even now, so many years later, she could remember her surprise at that. Olivia Brockton had been an intensely private woman. She had never appeared before her children less than perfectly groomed, yet she had chosen to die on a cold tile floor, with her robe soaked in blood from her lacerated wrists and her gray eyes staring sightlessly as though a careless tenant had departed in haste and left the doors of the house standing open.

A chill wind blew across the graves. Alexis shivered and drew her coat more tightly around her. It had been a mistake to come. There were no answers for her in the mute earth or the silent stone. If they existed anywhere, it was within herself.

Years before, when she was struggling to puzzle out the reason for her mother's suicide, she had decided that Olivia had killed herself because all her life she had been a victim, a pawn in the hands of uncaring men, first her father and then her husband. That lack of control over her own destiny had finally become unendurable.

Deciding that had made Alexis feel very mature, even profound. Only very gradually, as she herself had gained more experience in life, had she come to realize that such an explanation was in fact no explanation at all. No one was handed that precious sense of freedom; it had to be won, often at great cost.

James had accused her of wanting to be everything—wife, mother, yet still her father's daughter. He could not have been more wrong. All she had really wanted to be was herself.

Staring down at the grave, she realized with a small sense of shock that when all was said and done, she had no regrets. If she had had her life to live over again, she would have made exactly the same decisions. Even now that she understood their price.

In stark contrast to her mother who had found no way to take control of her own life except in an act of self-destruction, she was truly the architect of her own destiny. If she failed to achieve all that she wanted, there would be no one to blame except herself. That was both a blessing and a curse.

It was also frightening. Alone in the graveyard with not another soul in sight and no company except the crows circling over the drooping willow trees, she began to tremble. She desperately needed warmth, comfort, understanding. She needed James. She even had the courage to admit it.

He was already home when she got there, in his den going through some papers. Alexis stood at the door for a moment, looking at him. His long legs were stretched out in front of him, his body relaxed, his expression thoughtful, just as she had seen so many times before.

She must have made some little noise, because he looked up suddenly and saw her. "I was wondering where you'd got to," he started to say, only to break off as he took in her appearance.

The damp wind had loosened her hair and caused tendrils of it to stick to her forehead. Her face was pale, her eyes unnaturally bright. She stood with her arms wrapped around herself as though overcome by cold.

Quickly he got to his feet and crossed the room to her side. "Honey...what's wrong?"

She shook her head numbly, fighting an absurd desire to cry from the sheer gladness of being away from that empty place and back with him again. "Nothing...I just..."

His arms went around her, drawing her to him. Fear welled up in him as he tried to come to terms with the possibility that she might be hurt. "What happened?" he demanded huskily. "Where have you been?"

"The cemetery..." She felt him stiffen with shock and went on quickly. "It's the anniversary of my mother's death. I went out there...I don't know why exactly...just something I had to do."

"Why didn't you tell me? I would have gone with you."

She shook her head as it rested against his shoulder. "No, I had to do it alone. I've always been afraid before....a weakness..."

His shock faded, replaced by anger he could not deny. His hands tightened on her arms as he pushed her back and glared down at her. Fear too long dammed up, for her, for himself, for both of them, made him harsh. "Weakness? That's what you call it? What the hell is wrong with you? You're always so damn afraid of not being strong enough. When are you going to figure out that you don't have to be that way with me?"

Stung by the sudden change in his manner, she shot back, "Maybe when you figure out the same thing about me."

"I don't understand what you mean..." he claimed in a halfhearted attempt at denial.

"Yes, you do," she insisted fiercely. The long-buried memory she had finally confronted in the graveyard gave her the courage to speak bluntly. "You want me to be dependent on you, but you don't want to be the same way with me. You want the upper hand in our relationship because you're afraid of what will happen otherwise. That's always been the problem between us from the time you returned from Korea and even before. You're not willing to believe that it's enough for us to love each other. You can't feel safe unless you're in control."

"And you can?" he demanded harshly.

"It's taken me a long time," she acknowledged. "I was suspicious of what it meant to love someone, afraid that it would make me betray myself. But I've realized that isn't true." She paused for a moment before she said, "My mother committed suicide because she didn't have the courage to love anyone, not even herself."

"Suicide...?"

"I could never bring myself to say it out loud before, but it's true and it's what I've been afraid of all my life. She depended on other people for everything, even her own sense of who and what she was. In the end, she turned out to be nothing. I refuse to let that happen to me."

Slowly, James struggled to come to terms with what she was saying. The experience was humbling. It brought him face-to-face with a part of himself he didn't want to admit existed. Her single lapse with Winston had reassured him that he was really the better, stronger person and therefore deserved to be the one in control of their relationship. In a very real sense, he had expected her to do penance for her transgression by surrendering her own hopes and dreams and being content instead to live through his. But unlike her mother, Alexis would not conspire in her own destruction.

To deserve her love, he had to step beyond his own limitations and meet her on truly equal ground. James would have given anything at that moment to be able to say with assurance that he could do it, but that was by no means guaranteed. All he really knew was that he had to try, even if it took the rest of his life.

Chapter Twenty

ON A FRIGID, WIND-WHIPPED DAY in January, 1961, Alexis and James stood under a cloudless blue sky and heard John Kennedy proclaim that the torch had been passed to a new generation. They knew whom he meant. The long apprenticeship of their youth was over; they had at last come into their own.

For James in particular, the charismatic young president was a symbol of everything their generation had lived through and triumphed over. He identified closely with the new administration's successes and failures. Perhaps not surprisingly, given his status as both a powerful media executive and a certified hero, he was rapidly welcomed into its inner circles.

To Alexis, that was a mixed blessing. While she enjoyed the glittering soirées where witty conversation flowed as freely as French champagne, she was troubled by subtle undercurrents she could not quite identify. Beneath all the elegance and grace, there lurked a certain impatience to prove that what had been won was deserved. Not only had they achieved power but they knew how to use it.

At a White House ball late in the year, after the worst shock of the Bay of Pigs debacle had worn off and confidence had been somewhat restored, she at last voiced her concerns to the only person she knew who shared them. Unlike many of his fellow journalists, Winston took a somewhat jaundiced view of the New Frontier. Alexis suspected him of being deliberately provocative when he called it "a band of knights in shining armor off to find the Holy Grail, never doubting for a moment that it's out there waiting for them.''

"That sounds so cynical," she protested gently.

He shrugged unabashedly. ''I just keep thinking the world is more complicated than they want to admit.''

Alexis cast a glance in the direction of the well-built, chestnut-haired man at the center table. He was laughing at something the beautiful woman beside him had said. There was a look about him of utter confidence and boundless possibilities.

"Surely you don't think he's naive?" she asked.

"No," Winston agreed, "I certainly wouldn't use that word. But there's something else…an absolute conviction that we can shape our own destinies. If we do the right things, it will all come out right in the end."

"Don't you believe that?"

He met her puzzled gaze steadily. "No; sometimes, no matter how hard we try, we can't have what we want."

She averted his gaze and after a moment he changed the subject. Later on they danced together until James cut in and whirled her away for a waltz.

UBC'S RATINGS CONTINUED TO RISE, as did IBS's, thanks in large measure to Alexis's strategy of alternate programming. With practice, she and James began to work more smoothly together, though by no means all the time. There were still flare-ups when she would accuse him of trying to take over her stations and he would say someone had better, since she didn't know what to do with them. After one such brief explosion, they stared at each other for a moment and then grinned.

"That beats tiptoeing around you," James admitted good-humoredly.

"Same here. Now do you think we can get back to business?"

"I suppose, though that idea of yours really stinks."

She wrinkled her nose. "You wouldn't know a good idea if it fell on you."

"Try me and see."

Some meetings were longer than others, and some got sidetracked, but she could live with that. What counted was that James was genuinely trying to overcome his own insecurities and accept her for who and what she was, a strong and capable woman.

Not unexpectedly, that had a softening effect on Alexis. As he became more open and trusting, she became more willing to overlook small lapses and brief backslides. One such occurred in October, 1962, when vague rumors began to circulate that there might be fresh trouble in Cuba.

"Something is going on down there," Alexis said one evening after dinner when the twins were in bed. "I can feel it."

James smiled tolerantly. "It's your imagination."

"No...I don't think so. A UBC stringer in Miami has sent a report that the Russians are stepping up their activity in Cuba."

"Oh...really...which stringer is that?"

She told him the man's name and thought nothing more of it, until several days later when the head of her news department reported that their contact seemed to have disappeared. "I can't raise him, which is strange because he's very reliable."

"Give it a bit longer and try again," she advised.

He did, with no further success. Curiosity piqued, Alexis decided to pursue the matter. She sent a UBC staffer to Miami to find the missing reporter. He returned with a very strange story. It seemed that witnesses had seen the man plucked off a downtown street by several tall, muscular young men driving a nondescript black car.

"One of them said the guys looked like Feds," the staffer said.

"How on earth could they know that?"

He shrugged offhandedly. "There's a certain look to them —crew cuts, skinny ties, white shirts, spit-and-polish shoes— you know what I mean?"

"Hmmm. . .I suppose, but why would the Feds want Manuel?"

"It's just a guess, but maybe it's got something to do with that report he sent in."

Maybe, but that would have to mean that someone had tipped off the government. She ran down a mental list of people who had known about the report, only to come to a dead stop when she remembered that she had told James. It was absurd to think he had anything to do with it, but still. . .

That evening Kennedy went on television to announce that the Russians were trying to put nuclear missles into Cuba and that the island would be quarantined until the threat was removed. For several days the world seemed on the brink of war. Amanda complained about the extra air-raid drills at school, in which the children were taught to "duck and dive" under their desks, as though those could protect them from nuclear destruction.

"It's silly, Mommy," she protested, her mouth trembling. "If the bombs go off, we're all going to die."

"They won't, honey," Alexis promised, though the words were hollow. She was frightened herself and trying hard not to show it.

Not until the crisis had passed did she confront James. "You knew," she said, "what was going on when I told you about Manuel."

"I had some idea," he admitted, "enough to know that the lid had to be kept on tightly. There were very delicate negotiations in progress. A leak could have wrecked them."

"Why didn't you tell me?"

He had the grace to look slightly embarrassed. "There was no need for you to know."

"No need? I had to decide whether or not to put Manuel's story on the air."

"And you made the right decision when you didn't."

"Only because we couldn't get a follow-up. Are you aware that he's missing?"

"He'll be returned now, unharmed. Believe me, Alexis, it was for the best."

She thought about that and came to the conclusion that she couldn't really blame him for what he had done. Even if their major loyalties were to each other—as she certainly hoped—they both had to be allowed other allegiances. James needed to keep faith with the president he admired so much. She couldn't dispute his right to take a different path from hers when he felt he truly had to, so long as they met up again a little farther down the road.

At least there was no disagreement between them about how to handle the events in Washington the following summer. Both agreed that the Freedom March would have saturation coverage. "This may be one of the most important nonviolent events in history," Alexis told her news team. "I want as complete a record of it as it is humanly possible to get."

"Let's hope it's nonviolent," one of the camermen muttered. "Otherwise, things could get a little hairy."

Alexis prayed they wouldn't, not simply because any outbreak of violence would diminish what the march was all about, but also because Matthew would be there along with Tessa. Both sets of parents had tried to talk them out of going, but they had remained quietly insistent.

"It's important," Tessa had said. "What happens in Washington will help to determine our future."

Alexis had looked at the seventeen-year-old girl and not known what to say. For so long the future had seemed to belong to her own generation, not the next. But now she realized that was changing. Time was a deep and strong flowing river that swept them all along inexorably.

Sometimes when she looked in the mirror, she wondered who she was seeing. The woman who looked back had just past her fortieth birthday. There were lines at the corners of her eyes and mouth. Her hair was now more silver than blond. She still wore the same dress size and a lifetime of slenderness had kept her body firm. Certainly James gave every evidence of finding it as enticing as ever. But she was aware of changes within herself, for the most part welcome. Youthful anxiety had given way to mature steadiness. She knew her strengths and weaknesses, and understood what to do about both.

Alexis had also decided to go down to Washington. She felt a need to witness whatever was to happen, be it good or bad. For the first few hours she stayed in UBC's communications trailer. But eventually the images on the screens drew her outside, into the humid heat of the Washington summer and the crowd of people moving slowly with quiet dignity. Young and old, black and white, all were coming together in the vast sweep of verdant ground that linked the Washington Monument and Lincoln Memorial. There, between the symbols of freedom's beginning and testing, they gathered, thousands upon thousands, until the ground was hidden beneath a human sea surging to the currents of a sacred dream.

She craned her neck to see the man on the speaker's platform, but he was beyond her sight, if not her vision. His voice floated over them all, gathering up the heat of that summer day and radiating it out in calm, measured words. "We hold these truths to be self-evident," the voice said, "that all men are created equal." And the crowd swayed and nodded, joining their multitude of voices into a single response: "Amen."

"I have a dream that one day on the red hills of Georgia sons of former slaves and the sons of former slaveowners will be able to sit down together at the table of brotherhood."

"Amen."

It was a song now more than word, a chant of hope and affirmation. Under the blue sky, in the still air, the song grew. "Dream some more," they cried, and he did, of a day when injustice would be gone from the land and children would blossom in freedom.

Alexis felt the tears on her face and made no attempt to wipe them away. She didn't think about whom she was crying for or why. She simply opened herself to the emotion and let it flow through her, leaving behind a golden memory that was to strengthen her in the darkest days ahead.

The sun shone on the capital when the best of the nation—all its hope and faith and courage—came together to declare that old wounds could be healed, old sins redeemed. But there were new wounds and new sins to come, and on them also the sun shone in merciless intensity.

ALEXIS'S FIRST AWARENESS that something had happened that Friday afternoon came at about 1:30 P.M. as she was walking down a corridor at UBC headquarters on her way to a meeting. The sudden ringing of the three bells on the teletype machine—signaling a bulletin—made her stick her head inside the newsroom to see what had happened.

A young man hurried over to the teletype and peered through the transparent cover to see the words as they appeared. The half-dozen or so other people present looked up from what they had been doing as he began to read out loud.

"Dallas, November 22 (UPI)—Three shots were fired at President Kennedy's—" his voice broke for a moment, then picked up more slowly "—motorcade in downtown Dallas."

Coldness washed over Alexis. The icy blast of denial. She seemed to be turning numb, all emotion switched off in an instinctive move at self-preservation. Automatically, she took control.

"Dave, get on the phone to our Texas bureau; get whatever details they've got and keep the line open. Pat, warn the control booth that we'll be breaking for a bulletin within five minutes, no longer. Jack, stay by the wires. Let us know the minute anything new comes through."

"Dallas bureau says he may be seriously wounded," the man on the phone yelled. "He's been taken to Parkland Memorial Hospital."

"Make sure we've got someone there."

"Flash—Kennedy seriously wounded...perhaps fatally by assassin's bullet."

Without allowing herself to think, Alexis straightened and turned to the people now thronging the newsroom from other parts of the building where word of what had happened had quickly spread. "We're going on the air immediately and staying on. Get the entire news crew in; tell them to be ready to go round the clock, possibly for several days.''

The young man at the teletype shook his head in dazed rejection of what must surely be a mistake. ''He'll be all right. He has to be...''

Alexis had no time to answer him before someone else shouted, ''Mrs. Callahan, your husband is on the phone.''

''We're about to go on the air with it,'' James said without preamble. ''How about you?''

''The same.'' She hesitated a moment. ''Do you think he'll make it?''

''I don't know...there's a report...unconfirmed...that he's been given the last rites.'' His voice broke.

''Oh, God...''

Alexis was to remember forever after the hours and days that followed, as though they had been imprinted on her mind in excruciatingly slow motion. As further details of the shooting flowed into the newsroom, she supervised the on-the-air coverage, striving always for a tone of reasoned calm. The temptation to panic was enormous. Rumors were circulating that an all-out attempt was under way to overthrow the government of the United States. All high-ranking officials might be in extreme danger. The children were sent home from school abruptly. Alerted to this by her housekeeper, Alexis gave instructions for them to be kept inside and away from the windows. She did not feel foolish doing so; it was a time to think of the unthinkable.

At 2:34 P.M. yet another bulletin rattled out over the teletype machine. ''Flash—President Kennedy dead.''

She stared at the stark words for a long moment, only gradually becoming aware that people gathered around her were sobbing, and that she was doing the same. Her news director had his face in his hands. She went over to him and put her arm around his shoulders.

It rained the next day, a cold, dreary drizzle. Alexis went home briefly to see the children. There was little she could say to them. They were almost thirteen, old enough to know that something terrible had happened but not to understand how or why. But then no one understood that.

All regular television and radio broadcasting was suspended nationwide. IBS provided twenty-four-hour-a-day news coverage, as did all the other networks. Cots were set up in the hallways; food was brought in. There was a certain comfort in the discipline of work. It allowed the anguish to be held at bay for at least a little while longer.

On Saturday, the president's flag-draped coffin lay in the East Room of the White House as row on row of somber dignitaries filed past. Pictures of that scene were interspersed with scenes from around the world: Londoners attending a requiem mass in Westminster Abbey; Berliners marching in the dark with torches; Moscovites weeping as they lined up to sign a book of condolence at the American embassy; Tokyo shoppers bowing their heads in prayer. From Paris, Nairobi, Berne, Seoul, the images flickered across the screen. A world gathered in grief.

On Sunday, Alexis and James went to Washington. They held hands in the limousine on the way to the airport and again on the plane, but said little. There really was nothing to say. The rain of the previous day had ended and the city was filled with a cold brightness.

They had been invited to join the crowd of dignitaries at the capital rotunda, where the president would lie in state until the next day. Approaching the glittering white dome, Alexis was struck by the absolute silence of the crowd waiting to see the cortege pass. It was as though all their voices had died.

Beneath the dome, bathed in rays of golden light from the clerestory windows, the coffin lay. Three eulogies were given. Throughout them, Alexis's gaze was drawn again and again to Jacqueline Kennedy. The woman she had always privately thought of as too ethereal to be real stood with quiet dignity, her lovely face a classic mask of tragedy. When the last speech was done, she approached the coffin with her little daughter and they knelt together for a final good-bye.

Later, back at the hotel, Alexis watched the scene again on television and wondered at the source of such regal strength.

The news that Lee Harvey Oswald had bled to death from a gunshot wound while the service at the rotunda was in progress was only one more horror in a season of horror.

Throughout the rest of that day and far into the night, television cameras recorded the river of mourners passing the coffin. Almost all were ordinary men and women who had waited as long as eight hours to pay their respects. By the time it was over, a quarter of a million would have made the small, personal gesture of mourning for a man few of them had ever met but all felt they knew.

Lying in bed that night, Alexis thought about what Winston had said: "Sometimes, no matter how hard we try, we can't have what we want."

Kennedy had tried, and died for the effort. As had so many others. But she had not. All her life she had wanted to be only one thing: herself. And she had succeeded well enough to be able to share that self with James. Perhaps not completely and not always, because in real life there were no tidy solutions. But she could still be there for him in the darkness, as he was for her.

Gently she drew him into her arms and held him as he wept.

AT NOON ON MONDAY the bells of churches throughout the capital began to toll. The iron wheels of the caisson creaked. The muffled tread of drums began. The hoofbeats of a riderless horse rang out in the cold air.

"O God, who alone art ever merciful. . ." the prayer began at the funeral mass. Alexis bowed her head. Her hand was in James's. She could feel the slight trembling of his fingers. His eyes were dry now, though his face was pale. He met her gaze for an instant and his hand tightened on hers.

Outside in the cold autumn light a little boy saluted. He was three years old that day and his father was dead. Not all the dignitaries or all the eulogies or all the flags flying and drums beating could change that. But there could still be pride and dignity even in this most ultimate of defeats.

The long funeral procession wound past the Lincoln Memorial before crossing the bridge toward Arlington National Cemetery. As they passed the graceful Greco-style temple to freedom, Alexis glanced up. It must have been a trick of the light but for an instant she thought the statue was crying.

On the green slopes that were the final resting place for so many of the nation's honored dead, the last prayers were offered. The national anthem was played. There was a roar of jets as fifty planes representing the union flew overhead, followed by Air Force One flying alone. In the aftermath of that wall of sound, the pure, sweet notes of taps rose to the sky.

Then it was over. The season of hope had come and gone, almost as though it had never been. As she left the cemetary on James's arm, Alezis could not help but think that it would not come again for her generation. What hope remained lay with the rest.

Epilogue

THE THANKSGIVING AFTER DALLAS was a somber affair. Alexis and James had debated skipping it entirely but then decided to go ahead for the sake of the children. Amanda and Jamie had been frightened enough by the grief of the adults and the sudden presence of death in their young lives. They needed to feel there was still some sense of order and continuity.

Matthew was home from Princeton. He said little about what had happened; Alexis suspected he was deeply in shock. Her heart went out to him even as she knew there was little she could do. He was beyond the age where he could be protected from the knowledge that life could sometimes be savagely unfair. But at least he did not have to bear his anguish alone.

Tessa sat beside him at the table, straight and slim in a simple white wool dress. She had called Alexis several days before at her own initiative and asked if she might be allowed to share Thanksgiving with them. Maggie and Anthony had approved, understanding that it was important for her to be with Matthew.

After the turkey had been brought to the table, James stood up. He glanced around at each of them before he said quietly, "There's no point pretending that this is an ordinary Thanksgiving and I'm not going to try. It's very easy right now to think that the world is a terrible place. Sometimes that's true, but not always. There is something good in this world, something that can save it."

His eyes met Alexis's. "Love makes you very vulnerable, but in the end it's also the only thing that gives you any real safety. Everything else can be taken from you, including life itself. But love remains."

He looked at the children as he concluded gently, "I don't expect you to really understand that now, but I hope you'll remember it. Because time is passing very quickly and soon this world, with all its pain and all its beauty, will be yours."

In the silence that followed, he and Alexis gazed at each other. In their eyes was everything that was in their hearts. Love had come to them not in an instant but in a slow, gentle conquest. And it had come to stay. For them, that was the ultimate victory over danger and death.

But there were other battles still to be fought.

Across the table, unnoticed by the others, Tessa put her hand in Matthew's.

EYE OF THE STORM

MAURA SEGER

A powerful
portrayal of
the events of
World War II in the
Pacific, *Eye of the Storm* is a riveting story of how love
triumphs over hatred. In this, the first of a three-book
chronicle, Army nurse Maggie Lawrence meets Marine
Sgt. Anthony Gargano. Despite military regulations
against fraternization, they resolve to face together
whatever lies ahead.... Author Maura Seger, also known
to her fans as Laurel Winslow, Sara Jennings, Anne
MacNeil and Jenny Bates, was named 1984's
Most Versatile Romance Author by *The Romantic Times*.

The final book in the trilogy by

MAURA SEGER

EDGE OF DAWN

The story of the Callahans and Garganos concludes as Matthew and Tessa must stand together against the forces that threaten to destroy everything their families have built.

From the unrest and upheaval of the sixties and seventies to the present, *Edge of Dawn* explores a generation's coming of age through the eyes of a man and a woman determined to love no matter what the cost.

COMING IN FEBRUARY 1986

EDG-H-1

WORLDWIDE LIBRARY IS YOUR TICKET TO ROMANCE, ADVENTURE AND EXCITEMENT

Experience it all in these big, bold Bestsellers— Yours exclusively from WORLDWIDE LIBRARY WHILE QUANTITIES LAST

To receive these Bestsellers, complete the order form, detach and send together with your check or money order (include 75¢ postage and handling), payable to WORLDWIDE LIBRARY, to:

Quant.	Title	Price
_____	**ANTIGUA KISS**, Anne Weale	$2.95
_____	**WILD CONCERTO**, Anne Mather	$2.95
_____	**STORMSPELL**, Anne Mather	$2.95
_____	**A VIOLATION**, Charlotte Lamb	$3.50
_____	**LEGACY OF PASSION**, Catherine Kay	$3.50
_____	**SECRETS**, Sheila Holland	$3.50
_____	**SWEET MEMORIES**, LaVyrle Spencer	$3.50
_____	**FLORA**, Anne Weale	$3.50
_____	**SUMMER'S AWAKENING**, Anne Weale	$3.50
_____	**FINGER PRINTS**, Barbara Delinsky	$3.50
_____	**DREAMWEAVER**, Felicia Gallant/Rebecca Flanders	$3.50
_____	**EYE OF THE STORM**, Maura Seger	$3.50
_____	**HIDDEN IN THE FLAME**, Anne Mather	$3.50
	YOUR ORDER TOTAL	$_____
	New York and Arizona residents add appropriate sales tax	$_____
	Postage and Handling	$___.75
	I enclose	$_____

NAME _____

ADDRESS _____ APT.# _____

CITY _____

STATE/PROV. _____ ZIP/POSTAL CODE _____
WW2